CHARLES BEAUMONT

A SPY ALONE

First published in the United Kingdom in 2023 by

Canelo
Unit 9, 5th Floor
Cargo Works, 1-2 Hatfields
London SE1 9PG
United Kingdom

A CIP catalogue record for this book is available from the British Library.

Print ISBN 978 1 80436 478 9
Ebook ISBN 978 1 80436 479 6

Cover design by Tom Sanderson

Cover images © Arcangel, Shutterstock

Look for more great books at www.canelo.co

Printed and bound in Great Britain by Clays Ltd, Elcograf S.p.A.

1

Praise for *A Spy Alone*

'Beaumont was a bona fide British intelligence officer and it shows. This is a marvellously confident debut, sharply observed and exceptionally well-written'
Charles Cumming, author of *Box 88*

'Charles Beaumont's debut novel has such a ring of authenticity about it that it reads like an inside job. But there's much more to *A Spy Alone* than being well-informed and highly credible: the plot is clever and tight, the story is gripping and the characters are all well drawn. A highly recommended espionage thriller'
Alex Gerlis, author of *Agent in the Shadows*

'*A Spy Alone* is as intricate as it is absorbing, as fantastically entertaining as it is disturbingly plausible, and is delivered with the confidence of a writer who knows how to handle the highest stakes'
Tim Glister, author of *Red Corona*

'Underneath Oxford's dreaming spires lies a dark web of Russian power. *A Spy Alone* is a cracking debut novel by a former MI6 operative. If you read it, the Kremlin won't like it'
John Sweeney, author of *Killer in the Kremlin*

'This book is timely. It's a well-written and atmospheric tale of espionage. But it hits hard at some of the real issues facing Britain and the world today. As a first novel, I am tremendously impressed'
Dan Kaszeta, author of *Toxic: A History of Nerve Agents*

A Spy Alone

Charles Beaumont worked undercover as an MI6 operative in war zones, on diplomatic missions and in international business. His work spanned two decades and four continents. This is his first novel.

To the people of Ukraine,

as they continue their fight for freedom

In memoriam

John Costello

1943–1995

Prologue

It is their shoes that give them away. As a lifelong fieldman, Simon Sharman hasn't forgotten the lesson: walkers might change their jackets, pull on a pair of glasses, even a wig. But nobody changes their shoes on a job. *Look at their shoes.*

Staring at shoes is only necessary when you have reason to believe you've got a tail. When old spies meet in shabby pubs to lament the state of the modern world, one of the things they say is that nobody learns the old skills. Anti-surveillance, counter-surveillance, it's all been forgotten. These days, it's all done by tracking your phone, those little beacons we all carry with us, shining out to any of the world's intelligence agencies. But Simon is old enough to remember the traditional ways. Look at their shoes.

Earlier that day, Simon had deliberately left his phone on a train at Reading, switched on and broadcasting a false trail as it headed into the West Country. He had crossed the platform onto an Oxford train. On reaching that city's famously underwhelming station, he climbed onto a bus that crossed the city. At the Cowley Road, he got out and started looking at shoes.

Simon spots Reg first, possibly on the bus, but definitely later on the pavement. *Give them a name.* That was another mantra they drilled into you in the spy school at Cardross before they dropped you off in Glasgow to see if you could fend for yourself in hostile territory. *Give each one a name.* Makes it easier to remember them when there are half a dozen. Reg, late middle-aged, square shoulders, clean shaven, moustache, broken nose. Rugby player, boxer maybe. On the Cowley Road, with few people around, he clocks Reg following at a safe distance, too far away to get a good look. Simon dives into a newsagent, forcing Reg to come closer if he is to continue to appear to be 'acting naturally', the obsessive priority of surveillance operatives everywhere. Simon comes out of the shop half a minute later with a freshly purchased newspaper under his arm. This gives him the excuse to turn his head both ways and get a good look at Reg and his shoes. Sturdy black leather with a gleam of daily polish: Reg is ex-military; makes him a likely surveillant. A few minutes later, in Radcliffe Square, Simon does a lap of the Camera, the domed centrepiece of the Bodleian Library, pretending to gawp at the building along with all the other tourists. Like a dog on a long lead, Reg follows at a distance, but Simon keeps losing him among the crowds of tourists waving their selfie-sticks.

Another Cardross lesson: *the transition from busy areas to quiet is where you force your surveillant to show their face.* Simon turned into New College Lane, under the Bridge of Sighs, past the cut-through to the Turf, along the backside of All Souls. After the crowds of Radcliffe Square, it is quiet again. Reg is with him all the way, now obvious without the crowds to hide in.

One swallow does not a summer make, and nor does one walker make a proper surveillance job. *I've got Reg*, thinks Simon, *but Reg can still be some old fart strolling through Oxford. There has to be a team and I need to find the box. Get to the High. Crossing a nice wide road gives an excuse to look right round, gawp at Reg, studiously ignoring me. Head back up towards Carfax. Find the box.*

The grizzled instructors at Cardross all had decades in Northern Ireland behind them and the thousand-yard Special Forces stare that goes with it. 'The box, gentlemen.' There were several women on each training course, but the trainers invariably said 'gentlemen'. 'Once you've found your first walker, gentlemen, find the team. They will have you in a box. There'll be two behind you, left and right, one to your side, possibly more. That's the box.'

Simon is in the box, but he can't see its corners yet. *Reg is still at four o'clock. Look for two o'clock, opposite side of the road.*

A possible.

Let's call her Usha.

Asian female, a bit heavy on her ankles. He'd noticed her ten minutes earlier, waiting at the bus stop at The Plain, long dark hair, halfway down her back, grey sweatshirt. Now she had a full headscarf and abaya. But the shoes were the same: white trainers, no brand but a muddy line on the left one.

Then Igor. Six o'clock.

Simon goes into Shepherd and Woodward University Outfitters, feigning an interest in college scarves in order to get a look back through the display windows and eyes on Igor, sauntering past the Old Bank Hotel. Slavic cheekbones, burly arms. Big, curly black hair and a creased black leather jacket. Earlier in the day, with a shiny bald pate and denims, Igor had been in a queue for coffee at Reading station. Converse high tops – navy blue – both times; surprisingly new, therefore memorable.

There are probably more. A big job like this wouldn't be left to just three or four. Probably a few cars, maybe a drone. But once you have repeat sight on more than one follower, you know there's a team.

Simon decides Igor is the one least likely to know his way round Oxford. So it is about timing. He leaves Shepherd and Woodward the proud owner of a Christ Church scarf, ensuring that Igor is his closest walker. He cuts down through Oriel Square and saunters through the back porters' lodge at Christ Church. He doesn't slow his pace, just gives a familiar nod to the porter, who grins back from under his bowler. Simon walks on purposefully towards Canterbury Quad, the pale stone buildings yellow in the feeble spring sun.

Look like you know what you're doing, they told you in Cardross, *and nobody will ask if you do.*

If the box had been the other way round, Reg would have been the one facing the Christ Church porter. Reg, ex-forces, talking to one of his own: like almost all college porters, this one had a previous life as a Redcap and in Thames Valley Police. Reg could have communicated that there was something 'a bit funny' going on with Simon. 'Mind if we take a look?' A subtle hint that this is a bit of MI5 business unfolding, and the porter would be ushering Reg in to look at CCTV displays in his little cubby-hole. Instead, it is Igor on the follow, strolling up to the porter. He slows his pace as he tries to figure the deal: what is this place? Museum? Monastery? Private club? Igor's time in Britain has not been long enough for him to learn that, like every Oxford college, Christ Church is all three.

'Can I help you, sir?' The porter's question is accompanied with a straightened back and squared shoulders. The politest form of 'who the fuck are you?'. The porter's been doing this job long enough to know the difference between an Oxonian and a tourist, or other dangerous species. Igor is no Oxonian, so he decides to be a tourist. He sees a sign promising a picture gallery and asks to visit. He is steered towards a ticket office in a small wooden booth, stuck in a queue behind an elderly couple from Droitwich, fumbling for their pensioners' discount cards. Igor exhales in frustration: he has lost Simon who is out of sight, striding across Peckwater Quad, a square of handsome stone buildings resembling a terrace of grand houses in Bath. At the third doorway, Simon looks up to make sure he's in the right place. A student has hung a Ukrainian flag from a third-floor windowsill. In another time it could be a signal, but it isn't. Just a kid wanting to show they're on the right side of history. Simon pulls a plastic card out of his wallet, maybe it's a library card, and jiggles it purposefully in the doorjamb of the double door. It clicks obligingly, and Simon pushes in. The door swings shut behind him, a full minute before Igor, clutching his compulsory tourist brochure, wanders into the quad, his face a combination of anger and panic. As Igor turns back towards the porters' lodge, Reg and Usha are standing on the far side, trying to look purposeful as they stare at their phones.

Standing in an airy hallway, Simon glances at a polished wooden board mounted on the wall offering room numbers and the names of their distinguished inhabitants. Room four:

Professor Sarah du Cane, MA, DPhil, FBA. Not mentioned on this helpful sign is Du Cane's job as professor of contemporary Slavonic studies at Oxford University. Known only to a very few people, and not written down anywhere, is Du Cane's other job: chief Russia strategist for British intelligence. Simon is in the right place. He is also there at the right time: according to the in–out slider next to her name, she is upstairs.

If there hadn't been a well-equipped surveillance team just a few metres away, he would probably have hesitated, gathered his thoughts. But there is no time to lose. He bounds up the wide oak staircase to the first floor and knocks on the door. It opens quickly.

Too quickly? Has she been expecting him?

Sarah. Aged a little, but aged well, he thinks. The familiar deep brown eyes light up on seeing Simon, a wide smile of welcome.

'Well hello, Si. I wondered when we'd be seeing you.'

Chapter 1

Simon has lost his audience, but he can't bring himself to get it back.

Thanks to the talents of his assistant, Evie, he somehow wangled an invitation to speak at a conference on corporate intelligence for due diligence in financial services, but he has no presentation, no prepared speech... and now he's lost his audience.

Simon's problem, ever since he left his obscure part of the British intelligence community to join the world of corporate gumshoes, was that he thought most of his clients were dickheads, and he didn't feel much of an urge to hide that.

There was a speech that Simon would have *liked* to give. It went something like this:

'Ladies and gentlemen, for twenty years I was privileged to serve on Her Majesty's Secret Service, specifically the bit that none of you have heard of, which we call the Pole and is officially called the Joint Intelligence Directorate. The Pole has its odd nickname because the headquarters used to be the Metropole Hotel on the corner of Whitehall. But I didn't spend much time in there because I was a fieldman: Moscow, Kyiv, Baghdad, Mogadishu and plenty of other places I probably can't mention. On the ground in dusty souqs, helicoptered in to remote valleys in Afghanistan or in the gaudy lobbies of five-star hotels and nice posh restaurants here in London, the trade was the same: it was about human relationships.

'Human intelligence, for that was my trade, is about what one person says to another. An intelligence source is someone who knows something and who is willing to share that knowledge with someone who doesn't know it. But all human relationships are full of lies: we lie to our loved ones to make them feel better, we lie to our enemies to scare them, to our friends to impress them and to our colleagues to get them off our backs. In the intelligence world you persuade someone to tell you things that they shouldn't; so you're asking that person to lie to someone else about what they're doing with you. It's a bit like an extra-marital affair. Sometimes, it *is* an extra-marital affair, but that's another matter.

'The relationship is built on deception, but the purpose of intelligence is to find facts. Intelligence is gathered to allow our bosses to have a better understanding of what's happening, to help them make the right choices. That ambiguity is at the heart of it – it's founded on a tissue of lies and deception, yet we use it to help us make sure of things, to increase certainty.

'At this point, you might reasonably ask, what's the point? Why bother if everyone's a liar anyway? Well, sometimes, even when someone is lying to you, they might be telling you something important.'

That was the speech that Simon *would* have given, had he not been bound by the omerta of his previous government service. Instead, he has found himself talking blandly about 'the best traditions of public service excellence' and 'very strong networks in key emerging markets, essential at this turbulent time'. The audience shift and play on their smartphones, clearly bored and hoping that their 'complimentary buffet lunch' will start soon.

'Any questions?' asks Simon. Normally the absence of any would be embarrassing; in this case it is a relief for all concerned as they race for first dibs on the Pret a Manger sandwiches.

A young man is lingering, bashfully approaching the stage where Simon is making a point of staring at his phone to avoid having to talk to anyone.

'Mr Sharman?'

7

'Mmm?' Simon can't quite bring himself to talk to him.

'Thank you. *Such* a fascinating talk.'

This is so obviously untrue that Simon has to ask who he is talking to.

'Benedict O'Brien. I'm with Grosvenor Advisory. I'd *love* to know more about your work.'

Simon took great pride in his ability to figure someone's biography out in seconds: a life of watching, calculating and the crushing rigidity of the British class system made this easier than many imagined. Benedict O'Brien had an overly posh voice, leather-soled black brogues and wore a signet ring. But his name gave him away as a left-footer. Therefore, he had been to one of the Catholic boarding schools, probably Ampleforth, followed by a Russell Group university. These days it seemed to be Exeter and Bristol that were taking the nice chaps from the private schools. Father had been in the City, probably in the army before that – *Irish Guards or Royal Irish?* Our Benedict hadn't quite made the cut for a serious City job, now that his lot were being replaced by people with maths doctorates and an ability to write algorithms. This was why he was working for one of those bullshit oligarch concierge services that called itself 'Advisory' to make them all feel better about being Oleg's bitch.

Simon climbs down from the stage and shakes hands. Firm grip. Definitely a military family.

'As I said, Grosvenor Advisory. We're a corporate advisory boutique with—'

'It's okay, Benedict. I know Grosvenor.' Grosvenor is led by Marcus Peebles. Like Simon, Marcus has spent time in the intelligence services. Unlike Simon, he's never been a fieldman; to Sharman's knowledge he never left the safety of Whitehall, but that didn't stop Marcus from dropping heavy hints to his clients that he was more or less the real-life James Bond. Also, unlike Simon, Marcus was charming, funny, tall and very successful – his client base stretching from major banks to the London-based oligarchs. A couple of years earlier Marcus had paid Simon not

8

very much to help Oligarch A get dirt on Oligarch B. This was because A believed that B was shagging his estranged wife. A and B, both of whom of course paid no tax in Britain, lived in exquisite houses in beautiful parts of London. Their children attended elite public schools, their wives enjoyed the diverse restaurant scene for their lunches. Their fear of assassination and robbery was minimised by the largely uncorrupted Metropolitan Police keeping the streets safe for them. And most important, Britain's finest lawyers, accountants and former spooks were on call to structure their investments, launder their money, harass the pesky journalists that snooped on their dodgy deals, and ensure that all of this took place under the aegis of Britain's unimpeachable legal system.

'How can we help Grosvenor Advisory?' asks Simon, wearily, wondering why Marcus hadn't rung him directly.

'Well, you know the sorts of things we do,' says Benedict unnecessarily, fiddling with his floppy hair. Simon finds himself wondering bitterly whether Marcus now regards him as a bit of loser, preferring to palm him off on this junior chinless wonder. 'As you might imagine, after the Ukraine *thing*, there's been a few clients wanting to take some back-bearings.'

Simon sighs. The endless euphemisms are so tiring. What O'Brien was avoiding saying was: *for years we have been helping the Russians launder their dirty billions and now we're feeling a bit silly about it. So you have to help us clear up the mess.*

'It's a deep-dive on an oligarch,' continues Benedict confidently. 'Wanting to review the sanctions risk given, ah, recent *events*. What makes it slightly unusual is the client has the resources to do a really proper job. Throw the kitchen sink at it. And it's kind of open-ended. Give us your weekly rate, get started and invoice us each month. Can I grab a card and email you with some more info? Great! Oh, and Marcus Peebles says hello.'

O'Brien is in a rush to get on, and Sharman isn't going to stand in the way of what seems like a dream assignment. But later on, his professional paranoia sets in. The way O'Brien had said 'Marcus Peebles', rather than just 'Marcus'. *Odd way to refer to a colleague in a small company*. He does a LinkedIn search on O'Brien and is gratified to find that his instincts are still solid: not Ampleforth, but Downside. *Close enough.* A direct hit on the university: Exeter. A slightly thin profile otherwise: O'Brien didn't have that many connections. Simon can tell from the metadata that the profile has been set up quite recently, but Benedict is fairly young – so this is plausible. Still unsure, Simon calls Marcus, steeling himself for faux bonhomie and ill-concealed condescension.

Unusually, Peebles answers on the first ring. 'Simon, my dear fellow!' Marcus would ordinarily begin by asking fondly after family, but since Simon had failed to produce anything in that department he falls back on spy-banter. 'How're things in the world of the real secret agents?'

'From what I hear, you're the one to answer that question, Marcus.'

'Very droll, very droll.' Marcus clearly thinks it isn't. 'All well, though? Nice and busy? Business flourishing?'

'As you'd expect, Marcus.' Things were desperate: Simon had been paying Evie out of his savings.

'Well I expect you're too busy for that thing Benedict wants you to do. He did catch you at the session today?' *So he's for real*, thinks Simon, *or at least as real as anything else Marcus talks about.*

'I'm sure I can squeeze it in. Just trying to get a feel for it, seems a bit of an odd one.'

'Well, strictly *entre nous*, as they say, it is a trifle… *unusual*. Not for banks or the 'garchs, you see. It's one of the universities, I'm not saying which, but it's *your* one.' Simon's time at Oxford often felt to him like his last real success. 'You'll get the full pack from Ben, but they want you to look into Sidorov, I'm sure you know him? They agreed to take a huge endowment from him a couple of years ago, hundreds of millions, and now they want to know if they can still get away with having his dosh, what with Ukraine. They're being *super* cagey, so I don't know much more, but they've made very clear we leave no stone unturned. Whole hog. You know what these universities are like: terribly risk averse, but *desperate* for the money. But we know you have the sources, Si. That's always been your thing.' At least Marcus has some regard for Simon's work.

Georgy Sidorov is one of those mid-table oligarchs: not the richest in the deck, but definitely a real billionaire. There are two broad categories of Russian oligarch: the thick-necked gangsters who want gold-leaf slapped on everything and serve caviar out of ice buckets; and the smaller group, educated, *nomenklatura* types. These are often former diplomats and intelligence officers. Sidorov had served in the SVR, the foreign intelligence service. Simon remembered the story. A few dons and newspaper columnists had asked whether someone whose money had been made in the wild west of Russia in the nineties was really a suitable donor to Britain's grandest university. But an appointed board of the Great and Good had decided Sidorov was *very* suitable and Oxford had announced it would take the money.

He won't admit it to Marcus, but Simon really needs this job. Everything else has dried up. 'Well, Marcus, obviously this would be a lot of work. And I'm juggling a few projects at the moment. Plenty of other stuff going on. But I think I can squeeze it in.'

'Yes, yes.' Marcus clearly knew this was bollocks. 'Young Ben will send you the stuff. Usual drill, NDA and all that. Deal with Ben, if you don't mind.' That was odd. Marcus always made sure he handled the important projects directly. Why would he pass up the opportunity to be in touch with the governing body of an Oxford college? Lunch in the Senior Common Room, high-table gossip...

'Marcus?'

'Mmm?' The response does not suggest enormous enthusiasm for the continuation of the discussion, but Simon has to get something off his chest.

'Marcus, we both served in intelligence to defend Britain from external threats. And we both know that this country is awash with dirty Russian money. It's only now he's gone and invaded Ukraine and started killing people that anyone's doing something about it. I mean, why the fuck did anyone take this loot in the first place?' Simon really wasn't sure why he had brought this up.

There is a pause on the line and Simon thought he could hear a sigh. Deep down, beneath the bluster and cynicism, did Marcus feel it too?

'Steady on, old chap! Our job is just to provide the intelligence, not set ourselves up as some sort of ethical oversight board. Anyway, Sidorov isn't a *Kazakh*!'

This was true: the best thing you could say about him was that he was from the better class of oligarch.

Chapter 2

London

1995

Simon is sitting in the file registry at the headquarters of the Pole. He is a newly recruited intelligence officer fresh from Oxford, full of enthusiasm and desperate to prove himself. So he is reading Sidorov's case file. Georgy Sidorov is a third-generation *Chekist*: his grandfather had been a secret policeman for the early Bolsheviks, his father in the NKVD during the Second World War and then the KGB in a series of diplomatic cover jobs across post-war Europe. Young Georgy had attended international schools in Paris and London. His own pathway into the KGB was almost inevitable. A stint at the elite Moscow State Institute of International Relations, and from there into the KGB's First Chief Directorate, its foreign intelligence arm. A talented linguist, Sidorov had picked up English and French during his childhood. The only problem with Sidorov's intelligence career had been his timing: joining in the late 1980s, he was in the service of an empire in decline. His first substantive assignment had been in Poland, trying with little success to infiltrate and sabotage the Solidarity movement.

In 1989, democratic revolutions swept through the Warsaw Pact countries and Sidorov's world was crumbling. As Poland elected the first non-communist prime minister of the Soviet era, Tadeusz Mazowiecki, Sidorov and his colleagues frantically cabled to Moscow for orders. Should they collect *kompromat* on Mazowiecki and the Solidarity leadership? From their bugging of the Polish security services they knew that Lech Walesa had once been an informant of the secret police state he was now trying to bring down. Should they release this information, to discredit his movement? Sidorov was an ambitious, talented young officer, pushing his jaded superiors to keep fighting. But the answer had been devastating: 'Sidorov, we cannot do anything without orders from Moscow. And Moscow is silent.' The empire had given up.

Worse was to come. In 1991 the Soviet Union disintegrated and Sidorov's employer, the KGB, ceased to exist. Sidorov found himself an employee of a new organisation, the SVR. It appeared to have the same employees as previously, the same standards, operational systems and technical resources. Most importantly, it had the agents. The people all over the world who had been recruited by the KGB's First Chief Directorate to pass secrets to the Soviet Union had not disappeared. There were ideologues, mostly ageing communists wondering what had happened to their socialist dream. There were cynics, who had something to sell and had found a willing buyer. There were the blackmail victims, prisoners of their shame. And the biggest group of all: the pragmatists. People who saw a relationship with the KGB as some kind of reinsurance against the other risks in their lives. Those agents, especially the pragmatists, mostly saw no reason to change the arrangement now that the customer was capitalist Russia, not the Union of Soviet Socialist Republics. Even the ideologues found the monthly payments to have a comforting familiarity.

The problem *was* the payments. In 1991, at the end of the Soviet Union and the birth of the Russian Federation, the SVR was running out of money, its roubles worthless and its access to hard currency limited. Soon after, Sidorov had managed to land his dream posting in London, the scene of some of the happiest years of his childhood. But the deal had changed. At the height of the Cold War, Russian diplomats had to show the West that their system was superior. They lived lives of considerable comfort, if not exactly luxury. By 1995, Russian officers abroad were being paid a worthless currency by a failing state.

From the file, Simon comes to know Sidorov's world intimately. The Pole had a long-established bugging operation against the SVR's *rezidentura* in London. It produced hundreds of hours of recordings, laboriously transcribed and translated by a small army of linguists. In his first job as a desk officer, Simon has the task of combing through the transcripts for nuggets of valuable intelligence. This has proved one of the dullest, least consequential jobs imaginable, about as far from James Bond as you could get. In the chaos of the new Russia, the SVR was so struck with inertia that it barely moved at all. Simon is supposed to be looking for operationally important information: evidence that the SVR officers were about to meet one of their sources, for example. Signs of vulnerability were to be noted for potential exploitation: the officer who was particularly hopeless with his drink after lunch; the one that was sleeping with his secretary whilst claiming to his wife that he'd been held up at yet another diplomatic function. The Brits are prissy about blackmail, however, so these leads don't excite much enthusiasm in Simon's superiors.

He is enjoined instead to comb the transcripts for signs of *ideological* disenchantment. Major Robertson, a dusty veteran from the Intelligence Corps and Simon's first boss, says: 'We need to find the ones that have lost faith in the Soviet system. The ones who see that it's falling apart and don't believe any more. The ones that are willing to question their orders, criticise what's coming from Moscow Centre. Find us those, young man, and you will be doing the Pole a significant service.'

With all the enthusiasm of a new recruit, Sharman sits down with piles of transcripts, immersing himself voyeuristically in the quotidian lives of others. The difficulty for Simon's ability to deliver a significant service to the United Kingdom is that *all* of the targets have lost faith in the crumbling Soviet system. None of them believe in it any more. All of them will happily question Moscow's orders, ignoring them or making only cursory attempts to execute. The main preoccupation of the members of London's SVR station is making money. The transcripts are littered with bitter jokes about corrupt officials and endless discussions about possible business ventures.

The *rezident*, Grotkin, is a corpulent veteran of service politics whose greatest skill lies in managing the endless power-games between the SVR's conflicting tribes. He had landed his plumb posting as head of the SVR London station as a reward for years of making sure he was close to the right people. As *rezident*, and therefore the most powerful Russian intelligence officer in London, he had long been assigned a codeword by the Pole (COSSACK – a bit of mischievous irony from Robertson, for Grotkin looked more kulak than anything else).

COSSACK is meticulously followed by an MI5 surveillance unit. In the permanent social hierarchy that governs British intelligence, surveillance is a working-class activity, desk-based targeting largely for grammar-school types and running agents reserved for the public schoolboys. The occasional exceptions to this rule only try to reinforce it, strenuously acquiring the habits and language of their adopted class. Titch, the unimaginatively nicknamed head of the surveillance team, all coiled-spring energy and toothy grin, is called to Robertson's Russia House to brief his social superiors. Doing so, he adopts a policemanlike stiffness that he believes appropriate to his elevated audience. Titch has surmised what Grotkin's colleagues in the embassy all knew already.

'Basically, your COSSACK is not operationally active,' Titch intones in a ponderous voice, little knowing that he will be remorselessly mimicked as soon as he leaves. 'He has rarely, if indeed ever, departed the office location. We have no recorded incidence of his attending an agent or covert human intelligence source meeting-place.' Simon suspects this is because Grotkin doesn't have any sources. Given the value of a diplomatic posting outside Russia in the 1990s, Grotkin wasn't about to take the risk of being caught in the act of espionage activity. That would get him sent straight home by the Foreign Office and he could wave goodbye to the wide opportunities for self-enrichment offered him by his diplomatic status.

'On numerous occasions we have observed COSSACK attending used-car vendor locations,' continues Titch.

COSSACK has given up international espionage to become a second-hand car dealer. He was buying cars and shipping them to Russia as 'diplomatic baggage', free of the heavy tax that other importers paid. COSSACK's business is irregular and a little bit illegal, on the Russian side, at least. And it is enough to let Robertson think it might be worth trying a pitch. A Russian-speaking officer from the Pole contrives a meeting at one of his favoured car dealerships. COSSACK is presented with evidence of his trading activity and asked whether he wants this brought to the attention of bosses in Moscow. An alternative, the officer suggests, is to have a chat with the nice people from the Pole.

As Simon reads in the after-action report, COSSACK's response is unexpected: after a brief pause in which he stared in fury at the Pole officer, he had thrown back his head and released a guttural laugh. 'You can tell anyone you like in Moscow about this operation,' he spluttered. 'Who do you think brings in the shipments? Clears the cars through customs? Sells the vehicles? Do you think I can do any of this without my colleagues in the SVR?' In the wash-up, Robertson admits that he hadn't considered the possibility that the entire organisation was in on the scam.

The COSSACK operation teaches Simon a crucial lesson: your targets need to be playing the same game as you are. British intelligence is obsessed with collecting political information that it could put into reports for carefully vetted readers across White-hall. Once upon a time the KGB had the same objective, relying on Philby, Blake and others to feed detailed reports on British politics that were pored over by KGB analysts. By the time the drunkard Boris Yeltsin is in the Kremlin, the priority is business. Every Russian intelligence officer is on the lookout for a trade. The Pole has little to offer in this department. The British government is particularly neuralgic when intelligence operations propose shady business deals, even when the objective is the recruitment of a senior Russian intelligence officer. So,

COSSACK and his friends continue their trading largely undisturbed.

COSSACK probably knows about the bug in his office, saving the really sensitive information for conversations that take place outside in a noisy street or deep in the embassy where it is believed they have a 'tank' – a secure speech room. The transcripts from the bug tend to feature COSSACK and his most senior lieutenants chatting about trivia. In a large intelligence station, many of the more junior officers are occasional, strangely intangible figures, rarely admitted to the office of their boss. One of Simon's jobs is to try to match the bit-part players in the recordings to real people on the diplomatic list. Rather like the credits of a movie, these minor characters often have no names, just descriptors: 'Young Man 1', 'Angry Older Visitor', 'Sassy Female'. One of these is clearly young, studious and rather serious.

'Ah, Georgy Ivanovitch, what are we reading this week?', COSSACK would call out in a mocking tone. The reply suggests a young man with a liking for classic English literature: Austen, Dickens and Trollope. Simon visualises a skinny, undergraduate-type, prominent cheekbones and bulging Adam's apple, a tatty Penguin Classic tucked under his arm. There are four men potentially answering to 'Georgy Ivanovitch' on the official list of diplomats at the Russian Embassy. Sharman starts out with 'Book Man' and gradually narrows it down to Georgy Ivanovitch Sidorov, whose cover job is third secretary (Cultural Relations) and who has an active user account at Kensington Central Library, just a few metres from the Russian Embassy.

Aside from his literary endeavours, neither Simon nor any of his colleagues have any idea what Sidorov is up to. There is no evidence of his participating in the more lurid business schemes preoccupying many of his colleagues. The inward shipment of Ukrainian 'models' to supply London's increasingly diverse sex trade was run by the GRU boys: they have excellent connections in Kyiv to source the raw materials. There is a rumour doing the rounds on London's diplomatic circuit that the ambassador himself is smuggling premium-quality Afghan heroin in through the diplomatic bag. But Sidorov features in none of these. The only regular activity they can pin on Sidorov is three trips up to Oxford in his first year.

Simon is excited by this: perhaps Sidorov is debriefing a high-level agent in one of the colleges? He checks the recorded dates against the Oxford University calendar and feels he can predict the pattern: it is always the Tuesday of the second week of the full university term. So he persuades Titch & Co. to accompany Sidorov, now codenamed FLIGHTING, on his next visit.

A few weeks later, Simon is excited as Titch begins his debrief of the surveillance run. 'We picked up target FLIGHTING at Paddington station, as per our orders,' Titch intones, after an officious throat-clearing. 'He proceeded to board the 1415 Worcester Shrub Hill train, calling at Reading, Didcot Parkway...'

'Titch,' Robertson interrupts. 'Not sure we need the list of stations. What did he do when he got to Oxford?'

'Right you are, Major. FLIGHTING, having voyaged alone on the aforementioned train, during which he made no contact with other persons and read his book, *The Mystery of Edwin Drood*, alighted at Oxford, where he proceeded on foot in an easterly direction, towards Carfax. He continued down the High Street, turning left into Turl Street, before making a right turn in Broad Street, thereby proceeding in an easterly direction towards –' a pause as Titch checks his notes '– the Wadham College.'

'Wadham?' Simon is trying to recall whether there were any notable or politically connected dons at that particular college.

'Yes, Shar, the Wadham College. FLIGHTING proceeded to enter that location. We did not follow him inside: this being a high-threat environment for surveillance operations,' by which, Titch means that his blokes would stand out like sore thumbs in an Oxford quadrangle. 'In order to be able to control his likely re-emergence from the aforementioned college, we took up strategic locations outside a nearby hostelry.' Simon isn't able to resist a grin at the earnest seriousness with which Titch described his taxpayer-funded boozing session outside the King's Arms.

'After approximately a hundred and twenty-five minutes –' *Three pints? Or just two*, wonders Simon '– FLIGHTING is observed departing the Wadham College and returning to Oxford station via George Street. At no time was he observed undertaking anti-surveillance measures. He boarded the—'

'Thanks Titch: we'll drill down into the train times once you've had a chance to do the write-up.'

Titch then produces a photograph of the signboard that listed current events taking place at Wadham. Simon eagerly scans it and then feels a wave of disappointment wash over him. Under the Mary Eccles Room there is a listing for the 'Oxford – Diplomatic Forum'. This is a talking-shop for bearded lefty academics and their female counterparts. They would invite inconsequential diplomats from 'the Global South' and other victims of Western imperialism for worthy discussions on the challenges of American hyperpower and neocapitalist desublimation. Simon knows that none of the dons in attendance have access to any intelligence of any interest whatsoever. These people are about as far from the seat of power as it is possible to be. FLIGHTING is using the train journeys to catch up on his reading and perhaps enjoys a stroll through the dreaming spires. He is probably there to talent-spot the other diplomats for future attention from the Russian services. He definitely isn't running a top-secret agent in Wadham College.

For good measure, Simon has persuaded Titch's team to follow FLIGHTING on his next visit to Oxford. His routine is the same. Exactly the same. Attendance at the diplomatic forum, no interaction with other people, no lingering or deviation from a journey that took him straight to Wadham College and back again. He even walks the same route. The FLIGHTING case is going nowhere.

–

Simon devotes the rest of his energy in that first job to trying to break up the GRU's human-trafficking operation. The Cold War is over and the intelligence services are desperately trying to justify their existence. For the SVR and GRU, this means business. For the Brits, it means trying to prove your worth in the fight against serious crime. And Sidorov disappears from Simon's field of view for the next thirty years.

London, March 2022

As Simon tells Evie about the new project, he can feel her palpable relief. He has sensed her drifting away in recent months, unsurprising as he had basically no work for her. He is a good enough intelligence officer to know that she's been putting out feelers to rival businesses. There was the long flirty lunch she was spotted having with Marcus Peebles where no doubt she had been given the impression that there might be a role for her with Grosvenor Advisory. But Simon hasn't reached a conclusion: Peebles probably liked to be seen buying a much younger woman an expensive lunch.

The Sidorov piece is a welcome change: open-ended, well-funded and focusing on Evie's favourite subject – Russian oligarchs. Simon likes to cultivate good sources, but he is fundamentally lazy and does little reading around his core subject. Evie, on the other hand, who grew up speaking the language to her Russian mother, has an unquenchable thirst for information about Russia's business elite. She combs through media and think-tank reports, social-media records and caches of leaked documents. She can easily fill in the gaps in Simon's knowledge of Sidorov: the return from the London posting in the early nineties to the chaos of post-Soviet Russia; his departure from the SVR and entry into the world of banking; the rollercoaster ride of takeovers, corporate raiding and leveraged buyouts. Banks that failed, consolidated, rose again. And through all of this, the intriguing figure of Sidorov: seemingly conservative in his tastes, little interest in owning brash houses, flash yachts or rash purchases of indebted football clubs. Politically connected, but not right at the top. Donations to various supposedly academic foundations.

'Thing about Sidorov,' Evie had said to Simon, 'is that he's always kept his head below the parapet, stashed his cash, done the right things. He kept in with Putin, of course, but he's not from Petersburg, so he's never going to be part of the inner circle.'

Simon knows that Evie has enough on Sidorov to file a report immediately. But he hasn't forgotten that his mysterious client wants him to throw everything at it, and he can invoice for his trouble. And there is something odd about the story — a sort of echo. Sidorov making his strangely pointless pilgrimages to Oxford and then his decision to endow an Oxford college. Simon knows that intelligence professionals aren't supposed to jump to conclusions. He also knows that these jumps often take him to where he needs to be.

He asks Evie to see if she can find any long-running connections between Sidorov and Oxford. Between the distant days of his London posting and this big donation. 'Links to colleges, visiting lectures, that kind of thing.'

A few days later Simon and Evie speak via Signal secure video-conference. She looks deflated. 'I can't find Oxford. I mean, I can't find any link to Oxford University. Tried everything. Companies House, offshore leaks, Panama papers, I trawled through there looking for Sidorov or one of his companies. And, to be honest, there's almost nothing interesting or new.'

'Nothing?' This isn't what Simon had been expecting. He can feel a tension rising, annoyance with Evie, which is a proxy for his real annoyance: at himself, for assuming that she would do all the work.

'I said *almost*,' she corrects him, a slight clip of frustration in her voice. 'I found one thing, which might be worth including. Sidorov is a shareholder, probable owner, of a company in the British Virgin Islands. One of those shell companies, meaningless name, no data publicly available on it anywhere.'

'So?' Simon sighs. In his world, British Virgin Island companies — *BVIs* they called them — are dead ends.

'So, I guess we have to include it in the report, even if it doesn't really add anything.'

Simon's mind is wandering, he's losing interest in this underwhelming progress report and he's checking last night's football scores in another tab on his laptop.

'Do we know what it does? This shell company,' he asks, only half listening to the answer.

'I looked everywhere. I went back to that Luxleaks exposé – you know, all the BVI bank transactions.' Evie's fascination for Russian oligarchs is equalled only by her familiarity with the world of OSINT – open-source intelligence. A loose global network of ethical hackers, transparency campaigners and freelance investigators, these anarchic youngsters had shed more light on the murkier corners of international finance than years of effort by state intelligence agencies. 'I could only find one thing that looked relevant: there were some payments from the BVI company, via MMB – you know, the Russian bank – to the International Transparency Committee, which was a British-registered charity.'

'You mean Transparency International, the anti-corruption organisation?' Simon asks.

'No, that's what I thought at first. But this is a different organisation set up with practically the same name, like a sort of fake Rolex. Anyway, it's a bit unusual for a BVI shell company to make donations to a British charity, don't you think?'

Simon has a sensation of near comprehension, like a crossword clue that is both obvious and opaque at the same moment.

'What's the company called? The BVI one?'

'It's called Domimina Holdings. Like I said, it's meaningless. It's not a word, or a place.'

Simon screws his eyes tight shut, straining to drag out a memory. And then it clicks and he splutters with laughter.

'Care to share the joke?' asks Evie, pointedly.

'Domimina. It's an Oxford joke. *Domimina nustio illumea.* You know the thing, with the Oxford crest?' Simon fumbles on his smartphone to get an image of the Oxford University crest, depicting an open book with Latin words in block capitals. He holds this up to the laptop camera, ensuring Evie can see it clearly.

DOMI MINA
NUS TIO
ILLU MEA

'On the Oxford crest you're supposed to read down each side for "dominus illuminatio mea" – the Lord is my light – university motto. But the layout of the text is confusing,' he continues. 'If you misread it across the page instead of down, it comes out as "domimina nustio illumea" – gobbledygook. That's a really "inside Oxford" thing... Sidorov must have loved the place.' In a jolt, Sidorov had gone from dull banker to playful wit. 'That's brilliant!' Simon is genuinely delighted at the conceit.

'So much so that he imbibed the clever-dick culture,' observes Evie, unimpressed.

'I can see what's going on here, Evie,' says Simon, suddenly animated. 'Look up that Transparency thing. Where was it registered?' Evie is tapping away at her keyboard now. 'You have Sidorov's Domimina Holdings,' continues Simon, quicker now. 'They have an account with the Russian bank MMB, which of course he also owns...'

'It's just been sanctioned, actually,' Evie chimes in.

Simon ploughs on, '...and this account made a payment to the International Transparency Committee, a British charity... I'm sure there's something odd about the ITC. Wasn't it closed down by the Charity Commission?'

On his laptop screen Simon can see Evie's eyes – they're green – scanning Wikipedia. She is half murmuring as she summarises. 'It ran for a few years... fairly controversial. Transparency International hated it – like it was a deliberately misleading branding... took very contrarian positions on things like human rights...'

'Okay, fine, Evie, but anything to do with Oxford?'

'Wait. That's interesting...' Evie then stops, tantalising.

'Come on!' Simon is wondering – is she playing with him? Or does it just feel like that?

'The International Transparency Committee had its headquarters in Oxford. At Jesus College. Its chairman was Professor Peter Mackenzie.'

Evie is blinking in delight. She smiles, pleased with their progress. Simon should be enjoying this moment of shared endeavour. But he can't see Evie any more, because it feels as if the floor has disappeared and he is freefalling into the darkest recesses of his memory.

Chapter 3

Oxford

January 1992

Oxford, and the freezing fog is hanging in the narrow streets, floating spectrally around the streetlamps. Simon Sharman pulls his newly acquired, scratchy college scarf tightly around his neck and shivers down Holywell Street. January, the first week of term. Simon is on his way to Jesus College for his first tutorial with Professor Peter Mackenzie, adviser to the prime minister, controversial newspaper columnist, scourge of 'woolly leftist' historians and somehow still with enough time to tutor second-year undergraduates. Simon is desperately excited. This was the point of being at Oxford: to join with the powerful and the influential, to be an insider, part of the system that runs things.

Mackenzie's rooms are in the corner of the front quad, up a freezing cold stone staircase. Simon knocks, responds bravely to a grunt that could have been an invitation to enter or, equally, to fuck off. Inside, the room is pure telly-don: fireplace with roaring logs, mantelpiece above groaning with invitation cards, walls of books two-deep and reaching high above a wheeled stepladder, ancient dark-brown furniture and Flemish oil paintings (from the college collection: everyone knows that Mackenzie is poor and angry about that). On side tables there are three silver-framed photographs, Mackenzie with Thatcher, Mackenzie with Reagan, Mackenzie with Gorbachev. Papers are piled on any flat surface, including most of the chairs. And there, with his back to him, staring out of a corner window onto the street below is a large man, his silver hair unkempt and outlined against the pale yellow from a streetlight outside, gleaming into the late afternoon gloom. He turns round and slouches into one of those bottomless armchairs that are the speciality of Oxford dons and which put the knees up around the ears.

'Which one are you?' The 'r's have a Scots burr, but the rest is deep smoker's gravel.

'Sharman, sir.' Simon hasn't called anyone sir since coming to Oxford, but somehow it seems appropriate.

'Ach, *Scharmann*,' Mackenzie appears to be affecting a *Mitteleuropa* accent. '*Shalom, shalom.*' Before Oxford, it had never occurred to Simon Sharman that his name sounded a bit Jewish. Now he was asked about his 'heritage' about once a week. Sometimes it was a pleasant error, like when Hannah Shapiro seemed to be asking him if he wanted to have dinner with her on Friday night, until Sharman realised it was an invitation to the J-Soc Shabbat. On other, rarer occasions it was painful, such as when a dozen sozzled, baying public schoolboys in matching bowties had hammered on his bedroom door and shouted, 'Rabbi! Pray for us!' This would have all come as a surprise to his parents, Anglican Saxons from a small town in Worcestershire.

Faced with the awful prospect of having to correct Mackenzie within the first minute of their acquaintance, Simon decided in an instant that, for Mackenzie, scholar of central Europe and of world wars, he would be Jewish. Not practising, obviously. His relationship with Mackenzie, three years before Sharman would join the Pole, began with a cover identity.

The unfolding complication is cancelled by knocking on the door. Loud, confident, insistent even. 'All right, ALL RIGHT! Come in then!' A shambles enters. Tight jeans, baggy jumper under a ghastly shiny baseball jacket – white arms and black torso. There's no evidence he's brought anything to write on, or even with. A pinched, slightly aggressive face under a shock of fair hair, almost albino-white.

'Sorry I'm late. If I'm late. Then I'm sorry.' The surprise is the voice: Simon doesn't know much about accents but this one is northern. Not Yorkshire, Liverpool or Geordie, but one of the other ones. Sharman feels elation: in Oxford's complex hierarchies he is sure that he is above a shabby northerner in a knock-off baseball jacket.

But instead the newcomer is greeted as an old friend. 'The late Mister Gough, ha ha ha. Dr Burgess warned me about that. Well, gentlemen, you need places to sit, don't you?' Simon tries a corner of a sofa, carefully squeezing between piles of paper. Gough looks at an inviting armchair, lifts up the pile of books on the seat and drops them to the floor with a thud and a grin.

'That's the spirit, Gough. Find a perch.'

Simon is already resentful and Gough compounds this by leaning across and whispering, 'Hey, mate, gis some paper.' Sharman pulls out some pages from his carefully selected notebook. 'Oi, and a pen. You got one?'

'So, Scharmann and Gough. Sounds like a tailors', don't you think? *Scharmann und Gogh* –' the *Mitteleuropa* voice again '– vonce tailors to ze Imperial Court in Vienna ve are now able to service your needs here in ze City of London. Ha ha ha.'

Simon didn't know what to do at this point. Gough sniggered, more at, than with.

'Well, until the tailoring takes off, you're here to learn about early twentieth-century Europe so we'd better get on with it.' He pauses for effect, and then assumes more of a lecture theatre register. 'These are great and terrible years, that call for big thinkers. I can't take the weeds, you know, the *insipid* ones. You're not a weed, are you, Scharmann?'

Simon shakes his head furiously. It's not clear that Mackenzie is taking any notice.

'Think of this transformation: the capital cities of Europe in 1910, grand, imperial. Even bloody Belgium is the centre of a great empire. Technology, culture, medicine, all these things moving forwards in leaps and bounds. Telegraph wires mean that real-time market information is buzzing around the world. Globalisation. Then go forwards only thirty-five years. The two largest wars ever fought have happened, one after another. Berlin is rubble with zoo animals prowling the streets looking for food. London's not much better. I'm talking about the same period of time between now and 1960. An entire world ruined, millions dead and atomic devastation. How did this happen? What's the theory here?'

Mackenzie has stopped talking. Simon can't bear the silence. He decides to give it his best shot: 'Umm, the *Rise and Fall of the Great Powers*?'

'Ooh. Kennedy. We've got a Kennedy man here. Gough, are you a Kennedy man?'

'What, JFK?'

'No, you utter *weed*, I'm talking about Paul Kennedy, whose book Scharmann here wants you to think he has read. Well, Gough's never heard of it, and frankly, that's just as well because it's utter BOLLOCKS! There is no theory. Theories are for the people who don't know the details. History is all events, stories, contingency. The moment you make up a theory I can tell you where it goes wrong, so don't bother. Save yourself the time.'

'Anyway, I always preferred Nixon.' Gough grins at his own joke.

Mackenzie throws back his head and barks out a wolfish laugh, which descends into a racking, tar-phlegm cough. 'Nixon! Tricky Dicky. The greatest president of the twentieth century? Hounded from office for telling complicated lies about a matter of no importance. Brought down by a hostile liberal media that pushed him into paranoia. Half of them couldn't deal with his anti-communism. I can see why you preferred him to that invalid priapist JFK, too busy fucking Marilyn Monroe to care about the rest of America… You seem to be a good egg, Gough.' With considerable effort, Mackenzie hauls himself out of his armchair and wanders towards a well-stocked drinks table. 'Nixon, that anti-elitist, used to drink Chateau Lafite, but he gave some ghastly table wine to his guests. Now, whatever they might say about me, I won't stoop that low. So, Scotch? Gough? Thirsty? And you, Scharmann? A scotch on the shtetl?'

Two hours later Gough and Simon stagger down the steep stairs, clutching the rope banister to steady themselves. Sharman's mind is fizzing elatedly with ideas, stories, pictures. The cynical victors' justice of Treaty of Versailles; the indignity pressed on Princess Schönburg as she tried to travel by train to England under exchange controls; a detour, for Scharmann's benefit, on Viennese Jews who had committed suicide; the Finns in the Winter War, encircling entire Red Army divisions on their skis; the croaking frogs that masked the advance of the German army over the Aisne; Lenin's train to Russia and minor Austro-Hungarian generals who seemed to have stepped straight off the pages of a comic opera. Simon can barely think through the whisky, but he is sure that, buried under the sozzling imagery, there is a thread. A meaning. The importance of individuals and their decisions, their power to make a difference.

As they part company, Simon wants to say something to Gough about how amazing it is that they have just spent two hours getting drunk with one of the world's greatest historians. But Gough barely grunts a farewell before heading towards the High Street. Simon realises that he doesn't even know what his first name is, or which college he has come from, the most important definition of Oxonian identity. He is left with a lingering suspicion that Gough takes Mackenzie's attention for granted, not a much-desired goal to be fought for. And worse: that for all of Simon's better learning and manners, Mackenzie prefers Gough's rough iconoclasm.

Chapter 4

'Simon Sharman? It's Benedict O'Brien here. How are you getting on with our little *project*? We were thinking it would be good for you chaps to come and give us an update in person. You know, do a bit of a *deep-dive*, so to speak.'

Every two weeks, Evie had put together a summary of their research on Sidorov, which they sent to Benedict O'Brien via an encrypted Wickr message. For the first two reports, they receive nothing more than a bland acknowledgement from O'Brien. Simon keeps any reference to Mackenzie out of these. Partly because he needs to keep this project running for as long as possible. But ever since Evie told him about the payment from Sidorov's shell company to the International Transparency Committee there has been something about that story that Simon doesn't want to share with O'Brien. As if the research into Sidorov would require him to recover memories he's tried to forget.

But now he is worried that they might run out of things to say, and then he can't keep sending in those invoices. So, for their third report, Evie goes all-in, explaining the spider's web of offshore jurisdictions, shell companies and nominee directors that had been dedicated to the simple task of letting Sidorov pay money to a small Oxford-based charity. And this seems to do the trick. O'Brien had called within minutes of Simon sending the report, proposing a meeting.

Simon had let the lease expire on his tatty upstairs office near the Edgware Road a couple of years previously. He doesn't miss the rent payments, but he does miss the simple camaraderie of seeing his one colleague in person. Indeed, working alone from his one-bedroom flat in Kilburn, he rarely sees anyone at all. So it is a welcome contrast to be asked to an actual meeting in an actual office.

'I'm sure those secure messaging platforms are all very safe, but you keep hearing these horror stories, don't you?' says O'Brien as he ushers them into the ground floor of a soulless townhouse in the heart of Russian oligarch country: Mayfair. When O'Brien had suggested the meeting, Simon thought he would be going to Marcus Peebles's ostentatious suite of offices for Grosvenor Advisory. Those are familiar territory, as Marcus likes to host events for ex-spooks, giving him the perfect opportunity to show off to former colleagues whose businesses aren't nearly as successful. But O'Brien has specified a different building altogether, which, he explains to Simon and Evie, is 'the project office for Sidorov's new foundation. It's tremendously exciting what's being planned. Huge ambition. Grosvenor's just handholding as it gets off the ground. But we're very excited to be involved.'

However huge the ambition, the building is obviously empty. Simon notices a pile of junk mail shoved into a bin near the entrance. In the expensively equipped meeting room the boxes for the newly assembled video-conference equipment have been stuffed into a storage cupboard. Either the 'project office' has been opened within the past week, or this is a hastily assembled cover story. O'Brien has a colleague, a sharp young Black woman called Kemi who doesn't offer a surname, but then nobody offers a surname these days. When Simon asks Kemi how long she'd been with Marcus, she seems momentarily confused, as if her employer was an unfamiliar entity.

'Now,' says O'Brien, once everyone has generated their personalised coffee from a machine with more processing power than the lunar module, 'we were *rather* interested in the reference to the payment to the International Transparency Committee in your last. Domimina Holdings, bet you got that straight away, eh, Simon? Little Oxford joke for the punters, it seems. From what we see, it could be important to get to the bottom of that. There could be some, er, *reputational* risks associated with the ITC, don't you think? I'm thinking of Professor Mackenzie.'

Oxford, 1992

Rather like one of Mackenzie's later works, when bitter alcoholism had shifted him from insightful to disjointed, Simon's memories of the man are episodes without a narrative. Some of these are pure pleasure: a night playing bridge and drinking shocking wine in Fergus Lewis's rooms.

Lewis, an Old Etonian whose father had been something big in the Tory Party and wrote well-thought-of articles in the posh papers, doesn't normally notice Simon. But he was walking through the front quad on his way to Hall when he saw two disconnected planets briefly in conjunction: Gough talking to Lewis outside the porters' lodge. This was enough to give Simon a thread of attachment and before long the three of them are in Lewis's room, opening Hungarian wine. To Simon, Lewis, whose family live on an ancestral estate, is impossibly glamourous. Simon hints at a genteel, rural background. Ponies and so on. The reality is a comfortable, well-insulated detached house in a cul-de-sac that his parents had every right to be proud of, but which he found himself feeling embarrassed about.

The evening keeps getting better: to Simon's amazement and clearly to Lewis's expectation, Mackenzie appears at the door. It might be an undergraduate's room, but Lewis's décor isn't like the normal middle-class kids with their ethnic throws and Radiohead posters. Lewis has proper paintings on the walls, little bits of furniture that must have come from a forgotten wing of the family pile, cut-glass wine goblets, even if the contents are still Hungarian crap. And Mackenzie is obviously familiar with the surroundings: he strolls without pausing towards the stereo and puts on a tape of Balkan folk-music, to which he sings along in fluent Serbo-Croat.

'Ah, Scharmann, good egg, about time you joined our little card game.' Sharman is panicking – will it be one of the ones he knows? Do these people play bridge? Is that too middle-class? Lewis and Mackenzie seem able to talk shop together, referring to cabinet ministers and newspaper editors by their first names. Mackenzie is never deferential or respectful to anyone, but there's a hint of courtesy towards Lewis. Simon realises that Lewis Senior is Mackenzie's editor for his weekly column in the *Sunday Telegraph*.

Mackenzie can be both angry and funny – he rages about the university: provincial, full of 'weeds' and 'nobody can fucking spell any more. How hard can that be?' He is a stream of historic narrative – the causes of the Yugoslav war, currently unfolding on television screens, seemingly part of a single conflict that had begun in Sarajevo in 1914; Thatcher's struggles as she tried to defeat communism whilst being tied down by lefties, trade unionists and spineless patricians; Rupert Murdoch as capitalist superman. Mackenzie, between anecdote and Balkan marching songs, is still able to clean up at bridge as the rest sink under the acridity of Hungarian red. At some point they're too shitfaced to play cards and Balkan folksongs have been replaced with grand opera. Simon climbs a rung or two on Mackenzie's ladder of esteem by recognising some Puccini. Gough is now swigging from the bottle, his staring eyes fixed at the ceiling. Lewis is filling glasses and Mackenzie is lying on the floor, belting out 'Anima sante'. Simon has kept it together enough to try to make a point about Puccini's meetings with Mussolini.

'Nice try, Scharmann, but you don't know what you're talking about.' It is painful, but Simon wants the pain.

He isn't a *weed* any more.

O'Brien's mention of Mackenzie has momentarily silenced Simon, but Evie steps in. 'He's certainly an intriguing character,' she says breezily, 'and his ITC is very unusual. Odd statements about how transparency must not be allowed to undermine sovereignty. Basically, it was really the International *Opacity* Commission,' she says, blushing slightly as O'Brien laughs too forcefully at the line. 'But of course the ITC carried on for a few years when Mackenzie moved to Italy. Before the Charity Commission closed it down altogether.'

Kemi, mostly silent and assiduously note-taking, leans forwards at this point. 'Is there a link to *l'Istituzione per la Sovranità Nazionale?*' she asks Evie, her Italian pronunciation seemingly flawless.

'Where did you learn Italian?' asks Simon, approvingly.

'Italy.' Kemi's reply shuts down further discussion. She turns to Evie: 'Didn't Mackenzie try to integrate the ITC with the ISN, you know the Italian national sovereignty thing?'

'Well, I think Simon knows a bit more about that.'

Kemi turns back towards him, with a sceptical look.

'I'm not going to claim huge knowledge of the *Istituzione per la Sovranità Nazionale,*' says Simon, slowing the pronunciation to limit any embarrassment. 'But I know something about Mackenzie: he was, er, I was an undergraduate under him.' Kemi and Benedict exchange what looks like a meaningful glance. 'He had acolytes and I wasn't one of them. But I followed his transition to Italy. I know people who were much closer to him, visited him there.' He shrugs. 'Mackenzie went on a bit of a journey. You know, by the end he was very in with the nat-cons, the neo-fascists there. Lamonte was a pallbearer.' Kemi nods, seemingly well aware of the presence of Italy's populist strongman, arguably the most powerful figure in the country, at Mackenzie's funeral in Rome a couple of years ago.

'Bluntly, Mackenzie looks like a reputational risk for us, given how he fell out with Oxford,' says Kemi, briskly. 'If Sidorov carried on funding him after Oxford, particularly in more recent years, that's a problem for us. So, we need to know about that. And we need to know more about Domimina.'

'What do you think, Simon, Evie?' Benedict steps in, possibly unsettled by Kemi's abrupt tone. 'Really trying to get a feel for the links here. Can you tap up your contacts? Dip into that famous network of yours?'

Simon is thinking of another network: Mackenzie's protégés, who seem to be everywhere that matters in Britain. The newspaper columnists, political apparatchiks, City whizz-kids.

He may have died a bitter, angry alcoholic, but Peter Mackenzie's people are running the country now.

Chapter 5

London

April 2022

Simon and Evie walk through Mayfair to a cavernous branch of Pret a Manger, which appears to exist solely to offer free meeting space to London's nomadic professionals. The sandwiches are stale and Simon struggles to get his teeth into the rounded end of his 'artisan baguette'. He lays out his case.

'The ITC was pure Mackenzie: pretended to be a serious foundation, but it was really there to pursue his intellectual vendettas. It was his front company.

'So, Sidorov pays the ITC – basically Mackenzie – from his special Oxford company, Domimina Holdings,' says Simon, chewing laboriously. 'But he only did it once, right? And Mackenzie had already moved to Italy at that point. The ITC was registered in Oxford, but it didn't have offices or anything. Basically, it existed wherever Mackenzie happened to be at the time. We also know that Mackenzie was increasingly into the populist-nationalist stuff. I mean, at the end he was at that Atreju conference with Bannon and the rest of them. Protecting Western civilisation from the Muslims, or whatever the hell it was. And the Russians love that stuff, 'cause it kills off Western democracy. Trump, Lamonte, Orban, Le Pen and so on, all happily linked together and funded by Putin.'

'And Sidorov has Tory friends here,' adds Evie. 'I found a donation via his wife. She paid silly money at a Tory auction for the dubious honour of a tennis match against Stafford.' The perennially dissembling secretary of state for communities, Wayne Stafford, was not an obvious athlete, but Svetlana Sidorova had paid fifty thousand pounds to play him.

'Yeah but fifty K isn't that much for those guys. All the big Russians pay for that shit. It's just their little thank you to Britain for keeping money laundering controls so slack. Only the crazies think it's a deep-state job.' There was a certain class of former intelligence officer and think-tank bore who saw a Russian plot behind every crashing computer, every Western policy failure, every Russian dying before their time. Simon had tried hard not to be a sufferer from 'Russia derangement syndrome'. He knew that lots of the Russians in London were there because the taxes were low – once you'd sorted your non-dom status – and the police were honest. Reason enough.

'Okay,' says Evie, as ever seeming to have gotten to the bottom of the issue. 'But how about this. Suppose Sidorov has been dreaming about having an Oxford college for years? He even has a special company based on an obscure Oxford joke, for God's sake. He wants to get in with the institution and decides to pay Mackenzie some money for his charity-front company thing, but the real purpose is to help get him the right contacts among the Oxford academics, start the ball rolling, so to speak.'

'Well, Evie, that makes perfect sense. Except for the fact that Mac hated Oxford and was basically kicked out. He's the last person you'd approach.'

'Well maybe, but don't forget that the politics match – populist-nationalist equals pro-Russia. And all that sovereignty stuff, right up their streets.'

'We're not going to get anywhere sitting chatting about it here,' says Simon, gesturing at the identikit café: exposed brickwork, inane slogans pasted on the walls in bold lettering. 'What we actually need to know is whether there were more payments, and from where to where.' They need hard financial intelligence. Transaction records, electronic payment instructions. This isn't going to come from talking to people in Simon's network. They need to get onto the dark web.

When asked about it by the uninformed, Simon would explain with a sigh that the dark web is not Google for bad stuff. It's Gumtree. A forum for people to buy and sell: fake passports, specially adapted weapons, kiddie porn and endless gigabytes of personal data. All of human depravity available, for a price, on the unindexed part of the internet, hidden from ordinary computer users. The product is wholesale, not retail. A million banking transactions hacked from a Luxembourg clearing house here, an Excel spreadsheet of passwords there. Access to this is available to anyone willing to log on and expose their own computer to some of the world's most accomplished hackers.

Simon and Evie are not themselves specialists in this particular aspect of inhumanity. They rely on Dylan Ifans, who lives in a remote stone cottage on a windswept mountain in mid Wales, a wizard of the dark web and computer hacking generally. Like many IT experts, Dylan is obsessed with security and insists they keep no record of his name on any computer. For this reason, they refer to him as the Welsh Wizard.

The Wizard's real magic is that he has figured out a way to hack the hackers: where others were buying with Bitcoin, he mostly steels from the thieves. He had spent years infiltrating the forums, working up to become administrator of several of them, giving him special access over certain file arrangements. He is now the equivalent of an online police supergrass, except he refused to work for any government or law enforcement. Ever since the Wizard had stormed out of GCHQ in protest at the Iraq war, he decided that he would co-operate with people he believed shared his values. He would send information about child sex abusers to contacts at certain NGOs and details of corrupt politicians to reliable journalists. As a rule, he didn't talk to commercial intelligence people – mercenaries, in his view – but when he was still at GCHQ, he and Simon worked together to break up an international child sexual exploitation ring, so he was prepared to work with Simon when the objective appeared acceptable.

Later that day, once Simon and Evie have jumped through the various hoops insisted on by the Wizard – dedicated, 'clean' computers, double-VPN connections and a voice scrambler – the three of them find themselves in the same 'room', meaning that a fuzzy image of Dylan, Evie and Simon appears on different bits of their respective computer screens as they sit at home, physical disconnection being the key feature of an ultra-connected world. Their voices are deliberately distorted to throw the GCHQ voice-recognition system off the scent. The Wizard is pretty sure this works, as he invented the GCHQ system ten years earlier.

'Four-two, Four-seven.' The Wizard insists on assigning his contacts numerical identifiers. Simon can't remember why he is forty-seven or why Evie is forty-two, but if the Wizard's triple layers of encryption have been broken by some elite intelligence unit, the listeners would never hear the names of the people he is speaking to. If any of his interlocutors committed the cardinal sin of calling him 'Dylan' on a call, the connection would immediately be cut and that person black-balled.

'What's up?' he asks, his myopic eyes blinking behind heavy black spectacles.

Some people obviously curated their video-conference backgrounds: erudite books on a shelf, or the corner of an ancestral portrait in a handsome gilt frame. The Wizard's wall is rough, dark stone, which makes sense for a cottage in the Welsh mountains. There is a corner of a poster visible, which Simon has spent many hours trying to identify. There's bold colours, simple shapes, but never enough to be able to tell what they depict. He has wondered about David Hockney and Matisse. His current theory is Peppa Pig.

'Sidorov,' says Simon. The Wizard isn't very interested in small talk. 'Russian oligarch. Need to know if there's anything on your boards.'

The Wizard is, appropriately for a tech geek, extravagantly bearded. When he is interested by something, he scratches his hirsute chin. He isn't scratching.

Evie picks up the thread. 'Usual story, ex–SVR, owns some banks. Everyone's running away from Russian money now. But there's an interesting link to a former Oxford don who was involved in the populist-nationalist scene, Peter Mackenzie. You know what I mean, euro-fascism. Hungary, Italy, France, Sweden. Russia paying for it all.' The Wizard cares about this: he had grown up in a post-mining valley in South Wales. Men who'd given their lives and their health to digging coal out of the ground had turned to increasingly extreme politics and conspiracy theories as their communities died around them. A few years earlier he had been part of a 'white hat' hacking group that had obtained and released a list of far-right European politicians that had attended a supposedly secret meeting with Putin at his favourite Black Sea resort. So the Wizard is scratching now, a slight nod of the head demonstrating his intrigue.

Evie continues: 'I'll send you background, but we know that Sidorov paid Mackenzie's foundation once, from Domimina Holdings, a BVI company. Perhaps for a sort of consultancy. What we want to know is if he kept doing it. Was there a long-term financial connection?'

–

The Wizard comes back to them a few days later, once Simon has transferred the requisite amount of Bitcoin, to be billed back to O'Brien as 'office expenses'. Evie had been through the laborious process of decrypting the Wizard's report.

'Sorry, Si, nothing more from Domimina to ITC,' says Evie, on a secure Signal call.

'Are we sure?' Simon has already imagined an established relationship between the two. He has constructed a pre-determined narrative inside his head. Mackenzie was a neo-fascist taking money from wealthy Russians to promote his ghastly politics.

'There's nothing with ITC, Si,' says Evie, apologetically. Simon realises she is showing him compassion and he briefly feels a surge of gratitude. 'But there's something else. Might actually be bigger than the ITC stuff. Remember how I found the original Domimina payment? In one of those online leaks from MMB? Well, the Wizard has got hold of the entire reconciliation logs for the bank. Nothing to ITC, except that one payment.'

Simon feels deflated. Maybe there isn't any story here. Sidorov is a slightly pretentious Russian who paid a little bit of money to an Oxford don because he dreamed of having a college named after him. So what?

'Yeah, there's possibly something more important.' Evie's voice is bright. But maybe she is just stringing Simon along, trying to keep him buoyant. 'The Domimina account with MMB goes back a long way. Right back to 1984, in fact. It had a different name, but it's the same account number. And remember, before all the privatisations, MMB was the KGB's bank. I mean, that's how Sidorov ended up owning it: he was basically holding it for the SVR leadership. So, from the late eighties onwards there are payments from MMB to something called "Flood 19 Limited". A company registered in Malta.'

'What's Flood 19?'

'You tell me. I can't find anything about it. The payments go every month, from 1988. They vary, but it's always big amounts. Twenty grand, fifty grand, never less than five. Over the years, millions of dollars have been paid to Flood 19.'

'And then what?' Simon doesn't feel he is getting anywhere.

'One day, it suddenly stops. In September 2017. You know what else happened in September 2017?'

'I got divorced for the second time?'

'As important as that no doubt is, Si, I was thinking of something else. I just checked the obits. The years of drinking heavily took their toll. Peter Mackenzie died in September 2017.'

Chapter 6

Oxford

1993

Mackenzie drank, all day, every day. And then there were his parties. There had been hundreds. Sharman is only invited to one, somehow making the cut thanks to clerical error, for which Mackenzie was well known. A handwritten card *From Professor Peter Mackenzie* with the Jesus College crest tells him to appear at the professor's rooms with bottle – *fizz or Scotch* – at nine p.m. on the last Thursday of term.

Simon invests far too much time in choosing the drink; the good single malts are so expensive whereas the Tesco champagne looks the part and is still the real thing. Then, what to wear. The look would be young fogey-casual: blazers, Jermyn Street shirts and leather brogues. And timing: the party is starting at a suitably louche late hour, but it wouldn't do to arrive on time, and nor is it good to come in late with everyone already drunk and the groups already formed. He opts for nine-fifteen arrival: earlier than the smarter guests but it would give him time to remind Mackenzie who the hell he was.

This proves a smart choice. On arrival, Mackenzie pauses, frowns and for a terrible split-second Simon thinks he is about to be shooed away as an NFI. But then the Mackenzie's frown turns to a grin and, 'Ach, *Scharmann*! Have you met *Scharmann*?' he says to a beautiful long-limbed blonde who is smoking, bored. 'His people are big-shot tailors, or something,' offers Mackenzie, before turning back towards the door and a thickening stream of more glamourous arrivals.

43

But for the tricky opening, Simon holds the memory of that party as one of the most magical nights of his Oxford life. The room is lit entirely by candles and the log fire. Arrivals clutching champagne – and a poor few who came with cava, for which they were mercilessly accused of parsimony – are directed to pour their fizz into an immense silver punchbowl that must have become college property hundreds of years earlier, perhaps a rare silver survival of the Civil War.

Everybody who is anybody is there. There are aristocrats such as Arthur Something, whose surname is difficult because it depends on which title he is using, and whose father is an actual duke. Being generally cleverer, the German toffs are better represented, their manners exquisite and their nobiliary particles bouncing around the room. The grandest of them all, Heinrich Von der Wittenberg, appears to have stepped straight off a Prussian parade ground. There are those brothers, Nick and Peter, who claim to be Croatian royalty, although nobody in Croatia seems to have heard of them. The girl whose father owns a whole district of London and, it is rumoured, has paid for a library to ensure her entry to Oxford. This being Mackenzie, the room is also full of would-be Tory politicians: union hacks, and stiffs from the Conservative Association. Tom Harkness is there, always boring on about the European Community, as is Lewis.

There is a tiny sprinkling of diversity. Kamran Patel is probably used to being the only non-white face in whichever room he finds himself. But his South Asian heritage is the only thing about him that is diverse within this group: he is a forceful advocate of right-wing ideologies. There is even a token lefty: Ben Archbold's fiery speeches at the Oxford Union in favour of world socialism belie his public-school education and stockbroker father.

Then there are the undercover agents. Not secret servants of the British state but those who, like Simon, live in blandly middle-class bits of middle England and have assumed a new identity in order to be at the smart parties in Oxford. People whose parents are never to be found in *Who's Who* or on the back pages of *Tatler*. The ones that have gone to minor public schools but wanted you to think they'd been to Eton. The ones who have gone to grammar schools but want you to think they have boarded. In later years, when being on Her Majesty's Secret Service regularly required him to pretend to be someone he wasn't, at the risk of torture and death if discovered, Simon attributes his ability to his years undercover at Oxford, watching, imitating, role-playing.

And Sarah. Sarah du Cane, with her long soft brown hair, huge brown eyes and perpetual air of slight bemusement at the fact that heads are constantly turned in her direction. In a university seemingly full of women from the Home Counties who ride ponies, she seems infinitely sophisticated, fluent in several languages, and dressed with continental elegance. Someone has said she is an Italian aristocrat, but her pale complexion supports the alternative theory that she is the scion of an improbably named Swedish dynasty. Her father is rumoured to be a globetrotting trouble-shooter for the United Nations, flown into war zones to negotiate between fearsome militias. When terms ended and British under-graduates travelled home to London, or even Worcestershire, Du Cane flew to join her parents in Ethiopia, or at an international conference in Brazil.

Sarah is famously beautiful, more talked about than talked to. Simon has watched her across the Radcliffe Camera Reading Room, inventing reasons to pore over the bookshelves next to the table where she was working, never summoning the courage to strike up a conversation. Rumoured to be the 'cleverest under-graduate in Oxford', she is studying Slavonic languages. That evening at the party she can be overheard making little jokes with Mackenzie in Serbian or Bulgarian.

And, in the middle of all of them, is Rory Gough, who doesn't give a fuck what you think about him. Simon has finally found out that he is from Carlisle, a niche accent that he'd have never guessed. He attended a local state school, his dad a middling businessman of some kind. Rory seems entirely comfortable in his own, spikey skin, not bothered about what fake Croatian royalty think of him.

And Mackenzie loves him for it. 'Gough here is our man of iron. What does he care for the rules that apply to the rest of us?' Mackenzie is holding court to a small group that includes Sarah. Simon is at the periphery, straining for an entrée. 'Isn't that right, Gough? Shoot first, ask later. Who will need democracy when brilliant minds like Gough can tell us what to do?' Simon can't understand if Mackenzie is teasing or egging him on. What does he see in the grumpy, scruffy weirdo that is Rory?

'Right, prof,' Rory always calls Mackenzie 'prof', without any sign of self-consciousness. 'We're still evolving. That's the point. Not everyone can complete the evolution; or the revolution. Some get left behind.' He pauses for effect. 'Fuck 'em, I guess.'

Mackenzie throws back his head, coughing out his smoker's laugh. As he brings his head back down, he catches sight of Simon. 'Now here's a thing, Scharmann.' A pause for a swig from the tumbler of whisky. No ice, no mixer. 'I was talking to Gough about this the other day. Hitler fucked everything up. Why? Antisemitism. But he wasn't wrong about *Untermenschen*, was he? He was just wrong when he picked the Jews, the greatest master race of them all! Ha ha ha.' But his delight is cut short by Sarah, who stiffens her shoulders, visible in a halter-necked dress, and lashes out a stream of angry words in a language seemingly known only to her and Mackenzie, possibly Hungarian. There's a split second where it isn't clear whether she's going to slap him for good measure. But she turns round, angry, nostrils flaring, eyes narrowed, and storms out of the room.

'Women: they lose it so easily,' Mackenzie mutters with false bravado, turning away to find a new audience.

And then Simon does the cleverest thing of his entire life. A thing so brilliant that he will summon the memory of it at any future moment and briefly feel a wave of satisfaction. He follows her out of the door.

On the stone-cold landing outside he finds her smoking a cigarette with furious elegance, ignoring a couple snogging on the staircase. 'Thank you,' says Simon, seized with a tiny flash of pure courage. 'I'm afraid I have no idea what you said to him, but thank you.'

'God! He's such a ghastly idiot, isn't he?' Simon realises he's never really heard her speak English. He sort of expects her to have a Sophia Loren accent, but it is blandly BBC. 'I mean, how could he say that to you? Or to me? And with Zak here too.' Zak Camondo, heir to a European banking dynasty, is snorting coke somewhere in Mackenzie's rooms.

Simon's act of brilliance has been to remember that in Mackenzie's company he isn't a pseudo country gent, he is the son of a Jewish tailor.

'He's drunk, I guess. And you hear this stuff everywhere. I'm sure you've had more than your fair share.' He's having a conversation with Sarah du Cane about their shared experience of antisemitism and the elation and adrenaline is coursing through his body. As well as the feeling of deep transgression: how has he ended up being categorised as Jewish? Perhaps more importantly, how long can he keep this going for? 'I didn't realise you were Jewish.'

'Yes. My mother...' She flashes with irritation. 'He's always bloody drunk... I don't know what I'm doing here.' She turns, as if to leave. In the background, someone changes the CD from grand opera to Whitney Houston. Simon is a man on a winning streak. He doesn't know why he's doing it, but he knows it will work.

'Sarah, if we walk away they carry on doing this stuff to us. It's us against them.' She turns her brown eyes on Simon, who realises she hasn't looked directly at him until now. The staircase is ill-lit, and her pupils are dilated. 'Why don't we go back inside and dance to Whitney?' On another day, she would have huffed, said 'no thanks', and that would have been it. But not on this day. The regal cheekbones crease into a smile and she reaches her arm out, linking with Scharmann's.

'What a good idea.'

The rest of the party is blurred, partly because of the ecstatic denouement but mostly thanks to the punchbowl. Simon remembers 'I Wanna Dance with Somebody' and he and Sarah laughing, twisting together. There was also 'Gangsta's Paradise': *'Power and the money, money and the power...'* It made sense at the time.

Another image – he staggers towards the punchbowl and sees Rory laughing maniacally as he empties an entire bottle of vodka into the mix. Sharman fills two glasses and takes a gulp of the noxious fluid and thinks, 'that tastes *grand*'. The party is deafening now. He passes a glass to Sarah and shouts, 'have this, it's *excellent*!' She sips, grimaces and then smiles.

'Simon Scharmann, this is the most disgusting thing I have ever tasted,' she grins. He knows it can't go wrong now, even though it has to go wrong because it always does.

'Shall we go?' she asks him at some point, and he plays it cool but not cold, finds her cashmere coat and puts it on her like her normally *bon chic, bon genre* lovers would, and they tackle the perilous staircase and then the short walk to Lincoln, her college, clutching one another. And soon he's in her room and they're kissing the way drunk people do and mercifully she doesn't say anything and mercifully he doesn't make a mess of things and isn't sick and they're probably both tired but it did happen.

And Scharmann woke up in her bed knowing he'd done the cleverest thing of his entire life.

–

They are never lovers again, but nor are they people that can't look at or talk to one another. Perhaps because of the improbability of the coupling, or the fact that Simon did the right things, respectfully, they remain friends. A sort of platonic friendship where some people think Sarah is Simon's beard, or possibly the other way round. Except that Simon loves her and dreams about her and fantasises sexually about her and decides that he won't bother with women any more because after Sarah, what's the point, really?

And she introduces him to a different world. A world where you learn a new language if you find an author interesting, because who reads translations? A world where your opinion of what's happening in Bosnia is informed by the last conversation you had with the UN's senior negotiator with the Bosnian Serbs, who just happens to be your father. Simon remembers when Stefan du Cane was in town, a flying visit between Kinshasa and Banja Luka. Simon was too starstruck to admit it, but he had decided that he wanted to try for the Foreign Office and was desperate to meet Sarah's father. She takes him as her plus-one to lunch with Papa at Brown's. They talk in English, Simon assumes for his benefit, although sometimes there are little bits of Italian and Swedish. Having admired Sarah from a distance because she is glamourous and unattainable, Simon now loves her because she is kind, something that few people are in his world.

'Papa, Simon wants to get into the diplomatic world.'

'Ah, Simon, well it has kept me out of mischief, so they say. And we all want different from our parents, don't we? I suppose you didn't fancy tailoring?' Simon has never talked about his family to Sarah, so she only has Mackenzie's fanciful stereotyping to go on and she still thinks his father is a Jewish tailor on Savile Row. It's one of those awkward messes that Simon hasn't quite got round to clearing up. 'Sarah, *mia cara*, is completely uninterested in my world. For her, the academy: the morphophonemic alternations in early Slavonic, isn't that right?'

'Papa, silly, you know I'm so proud of what you do.' She kisses Stefan's cheek. Simon wishes his family, stiff with middle-England awkwardness, could have been like this.

'Now, Simon – have you spoken to Douglas?' Simon is momentarily confused about the identity of the mysterious Douglas, until he realises Stefan is talking about the Foreign Secretary. 'People say he's a little pedestrian, but I like him, he's… *angenehm*.' Years later, as a student of German, Simon realised this was carefully chosen faint praise. 'Perhaps a little more pro-Serbian than we would want, but we Swedes feel these things differently.'

Simon is charmed, if slightly bitter, at the thought that he and 'Douglas' might have a little chat about his prospects in the diplomatic service. Of course, that was exactly the sort of thing that Mackenzie did for his protégés. Tom Harkness was doing research for Conservative MPs about how the European Exchange Rate Mechanism was going to bring about the end the Bank of England, or something like that. During the last vacation Rory Gough had disappeared off to Prague, something to do with a foundation that was working to bring democratic capitalism to Russia, another Mackenzie obsession. But Simon can't ask Sarah to get her papa to give him an introduction to the upper reaches of international diplomacy, because his persona with Sarah is that he hates that cosy world of élite influence networks. He hates it because he isn't in it. And Sarah is other-worldly – where it really doesn't matter that she's a stunning Italian-Swedish aristocrat with a globetrotting father whose day-job is saving the world. She doesn't care about status because she has so much of it.

Chapter 7

Oxford

1993

It's the end of that magical summer, Trinity Term of the second year. There are no exams to write, Oxford's buildings glow golden in the June sunshine and undergraduates discover that punts are for kissing in. For Simon, it is a heavenly time: Sarah is no longer a distant vision across the Reading Room; she's his friend. But their lives are not intertwined: she has many other suitors. In any case there are garden parties to go to, plays to be watched, Pimm's to be drunk. Even for Simon, inclined to depression, life is beautiful and full of diversions.

But there is still anxiety. Students are building their careers. The all-important middle-year summer vacation is looming. The lawyers are all doing something called a mini-pupillage, which sounds like a primary school activity. Would-be bankers are heading into the City. And Simon hasn't got his act together. The scheme for Foreign Office wannabes is full of complex requirements: can he demonstrate that he is from an underserved community, his Jewishness notwithstanding? Is he from a university that has not been able to send many of its graduates to the Foreign Office in the past? Not exactly. Simon finds himself caught between his suspicion that other people are getting a leg up, and British institutions that are trying to tackle centuries of unfairness.

He has seen little of Mackenzie since the night of the party the previous term. This is not by design: Simon is not one of his acolytes and the tutorials shared with Rory had been for one term only. But Simon is an interesting, if hardly original, student and Mackenzie had on a few occasions offered him qualified praise. And being thought of as Jewish might help: only the week before, Mackenzie's regular column in the *Sunday Telegraph* had been an exhortation to Israel to 'finish the job' with a full military invasion of South Lebanon to root out 'Hezbollah fanatics'. He writes a carefully worded note to Mackenzie asking if he would offer some advice. It has a touch of levity, a dash of wit and seems to do the job as a reply appears a couple of days later offering '6 p.m., my rooms'.

Simon arrives at the appointed hour, on time, because this was a meeting, not a social engagement. He had overthought like the intelligence officer he is yet to become; what is the objective of the meeting? What would he wear? What would he say? What small–talk would kick things off? It is all about belief, he concludes. Mackenzie needs to know that Simon shares his worldview: angry, caustic, obsessed by intellect, power and a sense that the world did not fully appreciate his genius.

He knocks, nervous but prepared.

'Come.' The voice is always gravelly, but it sounds slurred, even though there are hours left of midsummer daylight. Simon pushes open the door, and finds Mackenzie slouched in an armchair, wearing only a dressing-gown that is worryingly short. He stretches his head up and frowns. '*Scharmann?* What brings you here?'

'Umm, I asked if I could come round… get some advice? You'd said this was a good time.'

'Advice? Fuck you want my advice for? I'm on the scrapheap. Fucking useless.' He confirms this point by taking a long swig from the mug in his hand, which must have contained whisky, since he and the room stank of it.

Simon sits down, in the absence of any invitation, but wishes he hadn't because he can now see more of Mackenzie's dressing gown and it is clear he has nothing on underneath. 'I might be the Regius fucking Professor, but they don't actually pay you anything. They tell you to mark useless papers written by weeds who can't spell and they don't like the fact that I actually know people who matter. Margaret Thatcher reads my columns. Kissinger wrote to me about my last book. D'you think Kissinger wrote to Professor Trilling about his *seminal* fucking work on French kingship in the 1330s? Like fuck he did. And now, they're threatening me with the door because the fucking politically correct brigade can't deal with the fact that I have a drink at lunchtime and haven't come across that many women who are actually intelligent.'

Simon's trying to take it all in, not sure whether the career chat is still happening. 'You're leaving Oxford?' he asks.

'Frankly, I can't fucking wait to get out. Useless provincial backwater. This country is finished anyway. You could tell that the day they got rid of Margaret. I'm going to find a way out of here. I will go somewhere I might actually be appreciated for my scholarship, not persecuted for my *delinquent behaviour.*'

'I'm so sorry,' Simon begins to find his groove. 'It's outrageous, actually. Oxford can't afford to lose you.'

'Well, Scharmann, you might say so. Good egg. But that's what it is. Grab yourself a drink, anyway.' As he says this he reaches into the open flap of his dressing gown and gives his bollocks a hearty scratch. 'Sorry... was I expecting you? I've lost track of the diary.' It is obvious that he has been drinking all day.

'Yes. But I can see it's not a good time. I can understand... In fact, I'm still trying to get my head around it. What were they thinking?' Simon can sense vulnerability, an opening.

'Yes, yes, but what is it? Why are you here?' As he says this he is gesturing drunkenly to the seat right next to his armchair, so that Simon, drink in hand, is inches away from Mackenzie's naked legs. They are grey-white, with thick dark hair all over them. They are also fat, even swollen.

53

'Well, I can see it isn't a good time, but I was hoping to get some career advice from you.'

He can't manage a laugh, but gets out a snort. 'Career advice? From me? Barking up the wrong tree there, young man. Only advice I can give is don't work for a British university.' He leans towards Simon, his flabby chest showing through the front of his dressing gown, moobs wobbling. As he speaks he bares his smoker-yellow teeth.

This isn't unfolding the way Simon has planned. 'I suppose,' he says, 'I was wondering…' Mackenzie's head is on one side, quizzical, sceptical, even. 'I want to get into the Foreign Office,' Simon blurts out. 'I was wondering if you had any suggestions. Of people I should contact about it.'

There is a glint in Mackenzie's eye. 'Suggestions? I suggest you contact the fucking Foreign Office. There's a bloke called Douglas.' He grins at his own witticism. Maybe it is a leer. He leans very close to Simon, who can now see rows of fillings inside Mackenzie's mouth. His breath is foul. 'Or is it that you want *me* to call up Douglas? Or the foreign desk at the *Telegraph*? Or the chair of the Foreign Affairs Committee? Is that it? "I've got this terribly good egg, Jewish but not one of the tiresome ones, name of Scharmann, we should find something for him to do." Is that it? Is that what I'm supposed to *suggest*?' His face is almost touching Simon, who has frozen, unable to speak. 'And what do *you* suggest I ask? What are you planning to do for me?'

As he says this he grabs Simon's hand and puts it at the top of his hairy, flabby thigh. It is surprisingly warm. Simon's heart seems to be about to explode out of his chest and his throat is tightening. Mackenzie's grip is firm. Simon is staring at a single wooden tile of the parquet floor by Mackenzie's bare feet, willing the world to disappear. Mackenzie shifts in the chair, pushing Simon's hand right up into his groin so that it touches the edge of his pubic hair, and leans back, letting out a gurgling sigh as his eyes float upwards. The hairs have a prickly feeling on the back of Simon's hand.

For a tiny flash of time, a mere synaptic pulse, Simon wonders whether he should just do it. Maybe this is what it takes. It would happen, it would end, and he could get what he wanted. Over the coming years, this single byte of his hard-drive memory, the moment when it was possible that he would give Mackenzie a hand-job, will grow in his mind from a split-second into hours, days, weeks, months, years of shame and disgust.

And then he has a physical reaction, a shudder of repulsion. He rips his hand free of Mackenzie's grip and jumps up, dropping his undrunk tumbler of whisky. His memory of this moment is silent, but there must have been the smash and rattle of the glass shattering and spreading across the shiny floor.

'What?' Mackenzie's head has jerked forwards. 'What? You scared, Scharmann? Don't like something as big and powerful as this?' He has spread his legs out, and the dressing gown is no longer a fig leaf. His wrinkled cock has flopped into view. 'You fucking think I don't know you're queer? No shame in that: I should know.'

Simon can't speak, he thinks he might burst into tears if he tries. He shakes his head. 'So I'm supposed to think you're fucking that Sarah du Cane? You're a big, straight, red-blooded Casanova, are you?' He guffaws, as if it is the stupidest idea ever. 'Talk about out of your league. I know a fucking beard when I see one.'

The mention of Sarah has a catalytic effect: Simon suddenly wants, more than anything else in the world, to see her, to hold her, to feel her arms around his neck, to put his hands on the familiar edges of her ribcage, to smell her scent. He turns round and walks out of the room at what he hopes is a dignified pace.

'Okay, I get it. Fuck off, then. Just remember, we're all grown-ups here, we all know what we're doing.'

–

Simon walks as fast as he can without breaking into a run across the front quad of Jesus College. He has an irrational fear that

Mackenzie will be following him, even though he left him slurring drunk in a deep armchair, almost naked. All he wants in the world is to see Sarah, whose room is two minutes away. He realises he's feeling tearful, his throat aching with anxiety.

His other feeling is humiliation. Mackenzie seemed perfectly happy to do favours for the *jeunesse d'orée* that he liked to have around him. If you were well-connected, clever, politically in the right place and, ideally, beautiful, Mackenzie would open doors for you. It was impossible that he was getting sexual favours from the likes of Lewis and Camondo. So why me? Simon thought of himself as reasonably clever, and he could play along with the right-wing stuff if he needed to. Perhaps he is beautiful? Except he isn't even that. He is just attractive enough for an old man who has spent the entire day drinking whisky to want a quick hand-job. In Mackenzie's world, he is a fall-back. Plan B. No downside, no consequence: he doesn't matter.

Simon stands still on the street outside Lincoln College. His mind is racing, revolving around the same awful moment when he wondered whether he was going to give Mackenzie what he wanted. In spite of the warm summer evening he realises he is shivering, and a physical revulsion leads him to clench and unclench his fists repeatedly. He tries closing his eyes, squeezing them hard shut and opening again. His desire to cry is being replaced by a need to be sick. He can't see Sarah like this. He can't let her see so much shame.

He takes a huge breath and looks upwards. The sky is the pale blue of a midsummer evening that still has hours of light. Just as he is about to walk through the archway into Sarah's college he hears a familiar voice.

'Sharm! Oi. Over here.' Behind him. With deep reluctance Simon turns to see Rory Gough's snow-white blond hair shining in the evening light. He's t-shirted in the summer weather, leaning against the wall on the street corner, clutching a book. It is as if he's been waiting for Simon.

'Come to the Turl. Have a drink.' This is unusual. Rory has never proactively sought Simon's company.

Simon is flustered. He has just got enough of his shit together, but not enough for this. *Rory* isn't Mackenzie's whore. *Rory* doesn't get asked 'what do *you* suggest?' He is on a different level. Simon wants to say something, but the words won't come out.

'Sharm? I'm talking to you. Turl? Drink? I'm buying.'

The thought of spending time with Rory, all sneering competitiveness, as opposed to Sarah, is awful. Simon feels like crying, above all. But for some reason he can't bring himself to say that he is going to see Sarah. Simon's world is spinning, and his immediate fear is that Rory will destroy everything. *Sarah? You still hanging around her like a needy puppy? You know she's shagging Camondo, don't you?* Simon opts for evasion. 'I'm just, er, on the way to something,' he says unconvincingly.

'Sounds to me like "something" can wait. Come on, I'm buying.'

Rory barely ever bought his own drinks, let alone anyone else's. And part of Sharman still wanted this world: where people like Gough and Lewis and Harkness and yes, even Mackenzie, sought out his company.

–

The small courtyard inside the Turl is full, but luckily not with anyone Simon knows well enough to need to talk to. As he carries his pint glass he realises that his hand is shaking. In any case, Rory chooses a quiet corner that gives him a full view of comings and goings. Simon is forced to sit opposite, with no view except of Rory. An irrational fear that Mackenzie will appear standing behind him begins to form, and Simon keeps looking over his shoulder.

'You expecting someone?' Gough asks.

'No, no. Just thought I saw someone I know,' he lies, improbably.

'So, what are you up to?'

'Well, like I said I was on my way—'

'No, *idiot*. I mean what are you doing in the vac? Only, I know that you were chatting to Mackenzie about it.'

Simon realises that his face is colouring and he can feel his heartbeat racing. Did Gough know? Maybe he was watching. Maybe he and Mackenzie sat together, laughing about Simon and his needy, apologetic little attempts to get a leg-up into their world. 'You following me around, Rory?' he asks, trying to sound nonchalant.

'As if. Listen, *dickweed*. I was round there the other day and noticed your note to him. Just wondering what your plans are.' For a man who is never very interested in anyone except Metternich, Rory is suddenly extraordinarily curious about Simon. Is there a nervousness in Rory's voice, possibly a slightly higher pitch than usual?

At another time, Simon might have tried to make something of this. Why would it matter to Rory? But he is too exhausted, too shaken by the awful memory of Mackenzie, leering in his dressing gown. 'Listen, Rory, not sure why you're bothered, but we had a pretty crap meeting, actually. He was shitfaced. Couldn't get any sense out of him, as a matter of fact.'

Rory frowns, sceptical. 'If there's one thing we know about Mac, it's that he can talk sense however much he has drunk. It's almost his superpower...' He pauses, as if searching for the right words. 'Is he going to introduce you to anyone?'

Ordinarily, Simon would want to know what Rory is getting at. But in this moment, he doesn't really care. 'Seriously, Rory, I've no idea if he was thinking about helping me, but you know he's thinking of leaving Oxford? That's all he could talk about.'

'Oh, okay.' Rory seems to be satisfied, slightly relaxed. Simon feels he has to stay the course, since Rory has bought him the drink. Conversation turns to their academic work. Rory has spent a term with Mackenzie doing a special subject on Russia. He is a torrent of ideas, concepts, thoughts. You sort of had to admire it, and Simon begins to be grateful for the chance to have a drink and not say very much.

Rory isn't all that bad. And maybe explaining to Sarah what happened would have been a bit embarrassing anyway. There's no need to tell Sarah. Or anyone. It's only shameful when you have to talk about it.

Once they've finished their pints, Simon surprises himself by suggesting another. Letting Rory do his ranting is strangely comforting. But he insists he doesn't want one and has some things that need sorting out. Rory and Simon walk out onto the High Street together. Simon, raising his voice to be heard over the thundering traffic, says, 'You didn't say what you were doing over the vac.'

Rory looks momentarily uncomfortable, then grins. 'Mac has fixed me up.' He is talking about the career-enhancing opportunity that Mackenzie has arranged for him. But Simon isn't really listening: his mind has slipped back to the hideous memory of Mackenzie's flaccid penis flopping out of his dressing gown.

Why me? he thinks with shame and resentment. Then he steadies himself, hoping that Rory hasn't noticed anything.

'Anyway, have a good break.'

They part, promising to be in touch in October. In fact, they do not see one another again for nearly thirty years.

Chapter 8

London

April 2022

Simon is poring over Evie's latest report. She has been digging into Mackenzie and the mysterious Flood 19 Limited, recipient of millions of pounds from Russian intelligence. It all makes sense, thinks Simon.

Except it doesn't.

Nothing appears to link Peter Mackenzie to Flood 19 Limited. It is an entirely opaque shell company, registered in Malta. Its sole director is a trust registered in the Isle of Man called Costello. Simon pulls some strings to find out who owned this Costello Trust. The answer: Flood 19 Limited in Malta. It is an infinite ownership loop. An irrational incorporation.

Simon takes a look at the receiving bank for the payments to Flood 19. It, too, is a black box. A tiny Lichtenstein bank with a single branch known for utmost secrecy. Not even the Wizard has anything on it: it is rumoured that they do everything on paper, which is then fed into a furnace. Unhackable.

Simon decides to try the Isle of Man. On the flight over, he is unnerved when the small turboprop plane appears to be attempting to ditch into a grey, choppy Irish Sea. Seemingly at the last moment, it banks hard to starboard and makes a bumpy landing at Ronaldsway airport. The passengers bend their bodies into the offshore wind as they trudge across the apron to the terminal. Simon jumps into a taxi and visits the corporate service provider that administers Costello from a small office in a back-street of Douglas. It is a shabby outfit that knows next to nothing about either Flood 19 or Costello except for the address of the lawyers that instruct them and pay the fees on time. These are a similarly second-rate firm with offices on the Loch Promenade, Douglas's windswept *corniche*.

Simon speaks to an old boy who has done the business-lunch circuit in Douglas for thirty years and knows everyone. He explains that Cain, Quilliam and Kerruish are the sort of lawyers that are glad for any instruction, take payment in cash from mysterious foreigners, and generally are popular with people who have things to bury. He heads back to the airport realising he is getting nowhere.

Simon had started to wonder if there is a clue in the name. Flood 19. There is only one flood worth wondering about. Simon, not a religious man, decides to find his Bible. It had been given to him by his mother who optimistically hoped that he might find meaning in it. This hadn't worked especially well, as she died the following day in a car accident, indelibly linking the Bible in his mind with loss and tragedy. Simon sits down one evening at his home in Kilburn, after a surprisingly pleasant bottle of Crozes-Hermitage, and starts working through the book. With unpractised fingers he leafs through Genesis, looking for Noah's Ark. And then he sees it. Genesis, chapter seven, verse nineteen: 'And the waters prevailed exceedingly upon the earth; and all the high hills, that were under the whole heaven, were covered.'

Living on his own, Simon sometimes finds that the bottle of wine, unshared, is a barrier to effective work. But on this occasion it has given him the insight he needs. He is sure that he is onto something. The nineteenth verse of the chapter is the key, the moment when the whole world is submerged in the Great Flood. That has to be the meaning of the company's name. Whoever had chosen that name was thinking of a world submerged, swept away. This is Mackenzie's worldview: the impatience with the standard order, with the normal run of things. A belief in the power of great men to shape events, to bring about incredible change in a short period of time through great destruction. It is Leninism.

It is obvious: Sidorov was paying Mackenzie, through an untraceable shell company he had set up. And he paid him millions. He didn't yet know why, but he knew what.

Excitedly, he calls Evie. 'I think I've figured it out! Genesis seven, verse nineteen: "And the waters prevailed exceedingly upon the earth; and all the high hills, that were under the whole heaven, were covered". I mean, I wouldn't have known it until a few minutes ago. Unless you're a proper God-squadder it's just some obscure verse. But think about it: Flood 19. The waters of the biblical flood, covering everything. Obliterating everything.'

'Yes?'

'Don't you see, Evie?'

'See what?'

'Well, if it was Mackenzie's company, this was the point behind the name. It's like his personal manifesto.'

'Simon?'

'Yes.'

'Let's talk about this tomorrow.'

–

The following morning at eight, Evie calls Simon. Through his thick, red-wine hangover, he can hear a sort of brightness in her voice. *Schadenfreude*.

'Oh. Hi, Evie. How are you?'

'I'm great, Si. Have you opened your curtains? It's a beautiful day.' Of course she knows that he wouldn't have done any such thing.

Instead, he grunts.

'Do you want to talk about Noah's Ark? You know, the animals went in two-by-two. And there's a mysterious company called Flood 19 which proves... what? It proves that Mackenzie is in the pay of Russia? I mean, you knew him, not me, but last time I checked he was an out-and-out Tory, anti-communist to his fingertips and also we have no evidence beyond a largely explicable single payment from Sidorov. We know nothing at all about Flood 19 and your little bit of Bible scholarship has not changed that.'

Simon sighs. She is right. With a bottle of wine inside him, Flood 19 had made perfect sense. With a thick head and a desire for sweet tea, it is a crackpot idea. Devoid of any logic. Devoid of anything, really. Simon has hit a dead end. With the greatest reluctance, he realises he will have to contact the Pole.

–

The problem with being a former British intelligence officer was that you really are former. The gates at the Pole clanged shut as he left, and almost nothing seeped out afterwards. The only circumstances in which 'formers' like Simon got anything from the Pole was if they brought something to the table. Sometimes, Simon's relationship with the Wizard gave him morsels to trade: paedo networks busted, drugs smugglers hacked, extremists unmasked. The Wizard let him do this purely on the basis that it was work he had completed, with no government input or oversight. In return, Simon would try to cajole whichever increasingly junior officer they sent into giving him something useful from the inside. It didn't often deliver much of value, but it was all he had.

The meeting arrangements were baroque; the meeting was puritan. Occasionally Simon wondered whether they put all their formers through this extraordinary rigmarole. Or was it just him who was expected to ring a certain number – which wasn't answered – from a public call box; walk to St James's Park where a chalk mark on a tree observed exactly thirty minutes after the unanswered call signified a meeting going ahead; then use a complex numerical code relating to the date and month to determine which bench in the park he should sit on? For Simon, ever sensitive to any question regarding the quality of his tradecraft, there was a lingering fear that the complex dance around St James's Park was put on for the amusement of a bunch of Pole officers. His paranoid mind imagined that they would wander out of their office across Trafalgar Square and into the park just for the fun of watching Simon try to calculate a complex formula for benches.

If they are doing this, they blended in well. Simon knows that he is a good spotter and he has seen no surveillance on this particular trip. There are possibles: the mother pushing a pram that doesn't obviously contain a baby; the older guy sitting on a bench, apparently fascinated by his copy of *Metro* – in real life, nobody is fascinated by *Metro*, a thin newspaper given out for free to commuters. Simon finds his way to the requisite spot and waits for a young man of military bearing and public school vowels – they always were – to sit down next to him. He feels a wave of frustration as a middle-aged, rotund Asian woman sits down. There is a protocol for this, but it is just more complication: you had to move to a new bench for a fall-back exactly ten minutes later. He is just about to get up to leave when she says, loud enough to be completely audible to him, but definitely not to anyone else, 'Hello STOKESAY.' This is his personal codeword. His meeting is underway.

'Sorry. I didn't expect...'

'No. They don't, usually,' she replies, matter-of-factly. She shifts on the bench, as if to make herself comfortable. 'So, what can we do for you?'

'Well, I was thinking you might find this article interesting,' says Simon, handing over a copy of the *Economist*. Simon had taped a USB stick containing the latest Wizardry to one of the inside pages.

'I'm sure we will,' she replies. That was the easy bit. Getting blood out of the stone was the challenge. In general, what Simon found worked best was to suggest that he knew much more than he actually did. This would sometimes trick them into letting on more than they meant to.

'So I have been doing some research on FLIGHTING. Check the codeword. Back in the nineties he was an SVR officer here in London. We took a look at him then, but he seemed pretty inactive. More recently I think I've found evidence of payments made from him to a senior academic at Oxford.' Simon decides to freelance, knowing that he needs to get someone inside the Pole to take notice. 'I think this academic may have been a recruited agent, paid through a Malta company called Flood 19. His name was Peter Mackenzie.'

There was no reason to expect the duty officer sent out to meet Simon on a bench to have any knowledge of either Sidorov or Mackenzie. But Simon has dangled enough that someone would get back to him.

'Right. I'll feed that back. We'll let you know.' She – and of course he didn't know her name, even a workname – speaks in an unhurried monotone. The possibility that the SVR had a recruited agent would be enough to generate a response.

–

Talking of FLIGHTING on a St James's Park bench had made Simon wonder about those surveillance runs by Titch he had organised on Sidorov nearly thirty years earlier. Sidorov's regular attendance at the Oxford Diplomatic Forum could have had nothing to do with Mackenzie. The Forum's defenders would have called it leftist, idealistic, possibly other-worldly. Mackenzie would have agreed with all of that and added with special scorn, 'woolly minded, bloody crypto-Marxist bedwetters'. From their investigations of him at the time, Sidorov didn't do anything else when he visited Oxford. Even if he had sat down on a bench with someone for a few seconds, or cleared a dead-letter box, they would have clocked it. And he hadn't.

Simon decides he has to go back to Oxford. He isn't sure what the point is, but he feels that he has to walk the ground, to get a feel for Sidorov's route.

It is a spring day, out of term time, and Oxford's student tribe has been replaced with tourists. Open-top buses are thronging the streets and the pavements are littered with brightly coloured electric scooters, part of a new scheme involving a clever app that allowed you, judging from what Simon can see, to steal the scooter and throw it into the canal.

Simon walks out of the station with the proprietorial air of an Oxford graduate returning to 'his' city. Of course, some of the landmarks have changed: the Said Business School, monument to Britain's love of supplying Arab despots with deadly weapons, has sprung up next to the station. The shabby Westgate is now a gleaming 'retail destination'. But the street plan of Oxford has not changed since Alfred the Great's times, allowing Simon to walk on autopilot. To reach Wadham College from the station is basically a straight line, and he strides purposefully towards Beaumont Street. He has almost got to Worcester College when he remembers that the whole point of the visit is to retrace Sidorov's steps. As Titch had laboriously reported, Sidorov had gone the other way, past the green mound of Oxford Castle towards Carfax.

Simon walks back to the station and restarts, repeating Sidorov's route. The first thing that strikes him is that it is the less direct route. The second thing, odd for someone that was supposedly a lover of Oxford, is that it would have taken Sidorov through some of Oxford's least charming streets. Why does someone voluntarily miss the elegance of Beaumont Street, the sweep of St Giles, the pathos of the Martyrs' Memorial, for the back-end of the rundown Westgate shopping centre? Perhaps, muses Simon as he reaches Carfax, it is for the compensation of looking down the High Street, gently curving past Queen's College towards Magdalen? The finest street in Europe, someone had said.

Once again, Simon's autopilot has kicked in, and he strides enthusiastically towards Radcliffe Square, one of his favourite places in all the world. It is only as he reaches the corner of Turl Street that he realises two things: the first is that it was strange of Sidorov to take Turl Street as opposed to Radcliffe Square. The former a narrow, unremarkable cut-through, the latter a perfect assemblage of incredible buildings: the spire of the University Church, the elegant rotunda of the Radcliffe Camera, the looming bulk of the Old Bodleian. The second thing that Simon realises is his own natural aversion to Turl Street. It contains three little colleges and a few touristy shops. And then, almost opposite, is Jesus College, where Mackenzie had been based. As he retraces Sidorov's steps, he finds that he has stopped involuntarily outside the corner of the college building, staring up at what had been the window of Mackenzie's rooms.

Up until this point the Mackenzie who had featured in the Sidorov investigation was subtly different to the Mackenzie that Simon had known. It was as if he had yet to associate the intellectual puzzle with the visceral personal experience. But now they are one and the same. For all the painful memories, he finds he is thinking of something else: the highpoint of his career as a professional intelligence officer. Simon is oblivious to the people scurrying across that busy corner of Turl Street; in his mind, he is back in Vienna, twenty years earlier.

Chapter 9

Vienna

2002

A serving GRU officer reporting faithfully as an agent of British intelligence is a rare and precious thing. Vasya Morozov, code-named WADDINGTON, was just that thing. The story of his recruitment had become a legend told by tipsy veterans from the Pole, a case study of brilliant intelligence work. As such, it had many of the common features of success: luck; an agent that was ready to be recruited; a ready-made system for running the case. Nevertheless, it remained Simon's best effort, his *tour de force*, the first line of his service obituary and the point from which everything else would continue to be a bit of a let-down.

It is the early noughties, between the end of the Cold War and the start of the next one, and Vasya, a Ninth Directorate science and technology officer, is operating under cover from the UN nuclear inspectorate in Vienna, Europe's espionage hub. His day job sees him pretend to administrate a team of inspectors as they are sent off to places like Iraq and Libya to inspect atomic research programmes for any sign of forbidden activity. This undemanding task gives him plenty of time to talent spot among the scientists, engineers and technical specialists that operate in and out of the endless alphabet soup of United Nations agencies to be found in Vienna. The Cold War might have ended, but the spy game continues.

Vasya is a natural. He attributes this to his Armenian mother, who gave him a mercurial charm that contrasted with his dour

Muscovite father, a military man, if not quite GRU material. Vasya networks brilliantly across the delegations, embassies and missions, scooping up the disaffected and the indebted. He turns some of these into willing sources, happy to trade their access to classified material for payments into some of Austria's most discreet private banks. Others prove tougher, requiring a little blackmail to get them over the line: an unpleasant business for everyone, but giving Vasya an important element of control over his sources.

—

Alan Ferguson is an engineer specialising in the wonderfully obscure field of hydro-acoustics – underwater sounds. He is British but has little affection for the country of his birth, having been made redundant from his job in the Marine Accident Investigations Branch when the government thought it would be a good idea to privatise the agency. Luckily for him, he is able to get a job in Vienna where his unusual expertise is turned to using a network of undersea sensors to monitor illegal nuclear weapons tests. If North Korea or Pakistan decided to launch a missile, Alan is one of the first people in the world to know about it. Perhaps more importantly, when Russia was testing its stealth missile technologies, it was vitally important that people like Alan did not know about it.

When Alan had taken up his post, he thought that his wife and children might all move with him. But the post-Habsburg charms of Vienna are lost on Doreen and the teenagers. They don't speak German, and Sadie has a boyfriend at her sixth-form college in Southampton. They agree that Alan will try to come home on weekends and they will join him in Vienna during school holidays. It works at first, but then Alan, a keen runner, becomes active in a friendly Hash House Harriers group. He soon finds that the appeal of the Wienerwald trails are rather greater than the suburban dreariness of jogging round Shirley Pond. He also soon finds that the young Katya, a waif-like Moldovan who works as a secretary in the UN's pensions office, is rather more accommodating of his middle-aged fantasies than Doreen ever has been. She laughs at his jokes, takes a remarkable interest in hydro-acoustics and does amazing things to him in the bedroom of his sad little bachelor apartment.

Alan knows it is all too good to be true and is wondering when it might end. So he is almost relieved when, in the middle of a particularly vigorous session with Katya, two men in dark leather jackets walk calmly into his bedroom as if it were the most normal thing in the world. Wordlessly, Katya jumps off him and the men step aside to let her pass. The fleeting glimpse of her slim body disappearing down the corridor behind the two unexpected visitors, her long blonde hair stretching down her back, is the last Alan ever sees of her. Given that her discarded clothes are still on the floor of the bedroom, there had clearly been some prior planning involved.

Lying naked on his bed with two sinister and uninvited men in his bedroom staring maliciously at him, his improbable lover having disappeared, Alan does not feel that he is in a strong position to disagree with anything they are about to say. He pulls the sheet over his flabby body and stares expectantly. They look like the sort of men that might chop you up and feed your body into the incinerator at the Russian consulate. But Alan can't see any reason why they would choose to do that to him.

One of the men pulls a smartphone out of his pocket and fiddles with the screen, before leaning forwards and holding it in front of Alan's face. He doesn't say anything but the image on the screen sends Alan a clear message. The video is black and white, slightly fuzzy, but there is no doubting what is going on. Because of the position of the camera, and the position of Katya, he can only see the top of her head, not her face. Alan, sprawled under her, is clearly recognisable, hopeless and helpless.

'So, you're going to send it to my wife, unless I pay you how much? That's how this works, isn't it? I guess you and Katya all work together.'

'No, Alan.' The one without the phone, still standing at the end of the bed, speaks perfect English with an obviously Russian accent. He smiles, his wide Slavic face accentuating his grin. 'We're not going to send it to Doreen, *and* we're going to pay *you*. You see what a good deal this is?'

Although Alan never knows this, Vasya calls his newly recruited source HORIZONTAL, in deference to the pose they find him in at their first meeting. In spite of the awkwardness of the introduction, Alan quickly becomes a solid agent: he is an unsentimental, practical thinker. He reasons that he was doing nothing directly against the UK, as he passes UN information to Russia. And he enjoys the engineering challenge. To avoid the risk of regular meetings in a city full of spies watching one another, Vasya presents Alan with an object not much larger than a cigarette box with rows of buttons on the front. This is the DKM-S, a GRU invention that can send a squirt of encrypted signal in a split second to a receiving device nearby. The burst transmission is so fast that it cannot be intercepted and Alan and Vasya never have to be seen together.

An engineer to his boots, Alan takes pride in uploading the readings from his undersea sensors onto the transmitter, and then walking past Vasya at exactly the right time every Friday to make the transmission. Vasya reports to Moscow that HORIZONTAL is proving an excellent and reliable agent, and regular payments for Alan are deposited into a compliant private bank in Graz.

–

It is Alan's military precision and love of routine that let him down. He started his working life in the Royal Navy and it is with chronometric accuracy, every Friday morning at exactly 11:07, he walks down Dafingerstrasse, a quiet street containing some apartments and the Syrian Embassy. His fastidiousness is appreciated by the similarly disciplined Vasya, who heads in the opposite direction down the other side of the street at the same time, allowing their two transmitters to connect for the milliseconds it takes to exchange coded messages. What neither of them know is that the British and Austrian secret services are running a joint operation, which involves an observation post in a building overlooking the Syrian Embassy. There's nothing observers like more than a routine. They've seen a suspected GRU officer walk down Dafingerstrasse three times at exactly 11:07 on a Friday morning, and noticed another person walk in the opposite direction at same time. This is enough for the Austrian watchers to invite Simon, who is a year into his posting in Vienna under diplomatic cover, to come and watch the show the following week.

'We Austrians like punctuality,' says Dieter, at 11:06, to Simon as they stand in the attic room purloined by the watchers. 'That's why we think this is an interesting prospect.' Dieter checks his watch, says, 'Forty-five seconds,' and shepherds Simon over to the dormer window looking down onto the street below. Right on cue, a middle-aged man, athletic build but with a belly that shows a liking for Austrian beer, strides with naval purposefulness down the street. He is clutching a leather satchel and appears focused, a clear task laid out before him. Dieter taps Simon's shoulder and points up the street, where a slightly younger man, with a wide Russian face and a dark leather jacket, no bag, walks in the opposite direction on the other pavement, disappearing from their view as he passes along the pavement underneath them.

It takes them only a few days to figure out who Alan is: his residency application and UN ID file contain numerous photos. Simon does his research and finds him to be a minor fixture on the British expat scene, with a little scuttlebutt out there about an improbably good-looking young girlfriend that had been seen hanging around with him.

–

The following Friday, Simon is waiting for Alan a few blocks down from the Syrian Embassy.

'Alan, hi, Alan. It's me, Peter. From the Hash?'

Alan frowns slightly, pauses and then dives in. 'Peter? Peter. Sorry, I don't think I've seen you at a meet for a little while.' He is not hiding the fact very well that he has no idea who 'Peter' is. But this doesn't matter. It's enough for Simon to fall into step with him.

'Actually, Alan, I'm wondering if you can help me and my friends understand something.' Alan looks confused, slightly worried, but he's talking to a well-spoken Englishman in sensible business clothes, so is there any reason to be concerned?

'Umm. How can I help? Sorry, what did you say your name was?'

'Peter.' Simon is now walking very close to Alan's side, on the inside of the pavement. Up ahead is a Mercedes people-carrier, its wheels mounted on the pavement, forcing them to slow their pace at the narrowing. 'Alan,' Simon says in his best, smiling, nothing-to-worry-about voice, 'why do you walk past the Syrian Embassy at exactly 11:07 every Friday morning?' As he asks this, Simon gently nudges Alan towards the people-carrier, whose side door slides open with a startling whoosh.

Dieter reaches his arm out of the van, says, 'Hi, Alan,' and bundles him into the vehicle. The whole operation is over in seconds.

–

If Alan had been strangely calm when Vasya and his sidekick had appeared in his apartment, he is no such thing now. He had been dragged into the people-carrier in a sort of trance, but once the door banged shut he starts.

'What the fuck is this?' He grabs at the door, but it has been centrally locked by Henning, who is up front, driving.

Simon, sitting opposite him on a bench seat with his back to the driver, is at his most reassuring. 'Nothing to worry about, Alan. I can show you ID. These chaps are all legit.' Their ID cards are 'legitimate', it is true, albeit not in their real names. 'We just want to know why you need to walk past the embassy at exactly the same time every week.'

'I'm a creature of habit,' he shouts defiantly, already realising that he is not waving, but drowning. 'I will report you. The police, the embassy. They will hear about this.'

'I'm sure they will, Alan,' Simon winks at Dieter. Alan looked from one to the other. 'Bloody strange habit, Alan, if you ask me, walking down this particular street, not near your office, not near your flat, same time down to the minute every Friday. Shall we take a look inside the bag?'

'I'm going to report you to the UN security office.' There isn't much energy in Alan's voice.

'Right. Course you are. Is this UN business, by the way? You walking around in downtown Vienna? Something the UN should know about? Come on, Alan. The bag.'

Miserably, Alan holds it out. Simon has never liked the bit of his job that involves other people's personal possessions. The satchel contains a small lunchbox, some anodyne papers, and lots of pathos. There is also an oblong object apparently shoved into a sock. With a smile, Simon squeezes the sock and out comes the DKM-S. Dieter gives a fist-pump of satisfaction. Henning looks over his shoulder and smiles.

They drive straight to a debrief in a safe house run by the Austrians. Alan is alternately tearful and angry as he explains the fleeting relationship with Katya, the threat of blackmail and his regular comms schedule with Vasya, via his burst transmitter. Simon is all calm reassurance. He emphasises that they will not be bringing any charges, or questioning his right to remain in Austria, or even informing the UN about what happened. 'In fact,' Simon says, 'all you need to do is let us programme this,' he is waving the DKM-S around, 'before you do your next Friday walk-past. No big deal.' Alan can hardly believe that he is going to get off so easily.

-

The next stage of WADDINGTON is what Simon is most proud of. Working with Dieter and two British colleagues, with instructions from Alan, they construct messages similar in style, content and tone to the ones that he had been sending week-by-week. The only difference is that everything they send to Vasya is fake. Fake sensor readings, fake messages from Alan, fake responses to Vasya's curt instructions. It is a perfect double-cross system. Alan is permitted to have the DKM-S only for the moment he walks down Dafingerstrasse, to prevent him from sending any distress signal. On one occasion, Alan's message told Vasya that a test of a new Russian stealth missile in the Arctic Ocean had not registered on the UN's sensor network. This was received with jubilation in the GRU headquarters. Russia is developing a new generation of stealth weaponry and believed that it was invisible to the outside world. In fact, it had been picked up both by the UN and NATO.

After three months and hundreds of hours of painstaking work creating convincing chickenfeed for the weekly transmission, Alan unwittingly carries a different kind of message. It explains to Vasya that the previous three month's messages were fake, that HORIZONTAL was being run against him by British intelligence as a disinformation agent and that Vasya had a week to plan his response. He could refuse to co-operate, in which case Vasya's embarrassing failure would be leaked to his boss, the head of the GRU station, with a file of photos of him and Alan making their walk-past and a transcript of their messages. Or, he could agree to a meeting to 'discuss his options'.

–

As he waits for the next Friday and Vasya's response, Simon finds it hard to sleep, like a child anticipating his birthday. The truth is that almost nobody has ever managed to recruit a GRU officer. They are tough, ruthless and committed. Vasya could chance his arm, could delete the incriminating message and tell his superiors that he believed Alan had been turned, he could play along whilst keeping his masters in the loop, to draw out the other side. Most plausible outcomes would result in it not working out. But there is a chance. If Simon can pull this off, still a young officer making his name in the Pole, it will be a genuine intelligence coup, talked about for decades.

On Friday morning, Simon checks and re-checks the DKM-S, confirms his plans with his boss and carries out a complicated anti-surveillance route to a predetermined meeting point with Alan. Separately, a counter-surveillance team have been tracking Alan all morning, making sure that he isn't being followed or watched.

Simon has to make a physical effort not to show his excitement and nervousness. It is imperative that Alan doesn't think there is anything special about today, or do anything different to normal.

'Okay, Alan, we'll meet you straight afterwards in the safe house.'

'Yes, Simon, like usual.' Alan looks in annoyance at Simon restating the obvious. He is a diminished figure. He knows enough of the world to sense that his regular monthly stipend from his new Russian friends will be coming to an end. But 'Peter' and his people aren't telling him anything either, just handing him the DKM-S and telling him to do his usual Friday-morning walk.

As usual, Dieter's counter-surveillance team is on the lookout for any suspicious activity. But everything goes to plan. Alan walks past Vasya and, after the all-clear from the surveillance team, is picked up by Dieter three blocks later and taken to the safe house.

As Simon eagerly grabs the DKM-S from Alan's satchel, he realises his hands are shaking. There is a new message. Because of his nerves, Simon miskeys the decrypt code a couple of times. And then he is able to read the message. A single line of numbers.

48.254494, 16.265908 1230

It's game on.

Chapter 10

Vienna

2002

Human intelligence is all about control. Is the case officer controlling the agent? Is it the other way round? When one intelligence officer attempts to recruit another, it's unclear who is running whom. Vasya's message contained the latitude and longitude of a quiet corner of the Vienna woods, the Wienerwald. By agreeing to a meeting at all, Vasya is accepting that Simon has a hold over him. By setting the location and time of their meeting, Vasya is trying to regain a measure of control.

He had given Simon only one hour to figure out the location and decide whether it was safe for him to attend. Vasya knew that it would mean there was little or no time for Simon to get a counter-surveillance team in place. If the meeting was a GRU provocation, they would control the ground. But a compromised, serving GRU officer willing to meet a counterpart from British intelligence is worth taking a risk for, reasons Simon. He requisitions his Glock from the station armoury, and Dieter and his men rush to look the part as a random collection of joggers, walkers and wanderers, all just happening to be in that part of the woods on a Friday afternoon.

Dieter, who knows the Wienerwald intimately, briefs Simon that he is headed for a sort of Wendy house. It's a twenty-minute walk from the car park through forested glades, at the end of which, in a clearing in the woods, is a little ornamental building. It's yellow, white, and pretty, as if it has been the set for a

Hansel und Gretel movie. Nearer the car park the Friday afternoon strollers and joggers are out in force, but by the time he reaches the hut, he can only see the occasional streak of one of Dieter's men, trying with little success to blend into the surroundings.

Simon strains to look normal, relaxed even, as he strolls up to the hut. He knows that Dieter will call his cellphone, pretending to tell him that his plumbing problem has been fixed, if any surveillance is spotted. Nevertheless, he has a powerful sense of being watched.

The building has two storeys. The ground floor is closed, but an external staircase leads up to a wooden balcony. Simon can't see anyone, but this is definitely the right place. Feeling self-conscious, he pulls out his handgun, enjoying the familiar, secure feeling of the web of his hand against the grip, tucked under the tang.

He reaches the balcony, wincing as the timbers creak on the stairs. There is an open doorway into the upper floor of the hut. He still can't see anyone, so stands completely still, straining to hear the sound of breathing. He inches forwards along the balcony, leaning against the wall, trying to lighten his step. Remembering his Cardross training, Simon stops about four feet short of the doorway and starts to step outwards, away from the wall, each step giving him a wider view into the room. As he swings through the apex angle he sees nobody. The room is clear. He relaxes slightly and steps back out onto the balcony. A man is standing by the top of the staircase, leaning on the balustrade and looking out at the forested hills.

'You won't need the gun,' he says, without looking round. He speaks good English, obvious Russian accent, but his grammar is near-perfect. 'But if you had needed it, I would have got you as you came back out. You cleared the room, good, but then you dropped your guard.'

Simon holsters his Glock with a mixture of embarrassment and indignation and takes his place on the balcony, alongside Vasya.

'*Spetsnaz*. Ten years. But you have beat me in the intelligence work.'

78

'The mistake was the accuracy,' says Simon. 'You and Alan. You were always walking past at exactly the same minute. We noticed that.'

Vasya smiles ruefully. '*Spetsnaz*. Ten years,' he repeats. There is a pause. 'I liked your Double-Cross. We studied that one. The original.'

He's talking about a wartime MI5 operation: German agents in Britain were turned and sent fake messages back to Germany using the radios provided them by their Nazi case officers. It's gratifying to be in this company.

'So,' says Simon. 'You continue to run Alan as your agent. That's the cover. But we run you, too. We continue to use the transmitters. We will never meet in this country, but when you take a vacation – Cyprus? South of France? – we will see you there.' He pauses. Simon has often wondered if he would recruit a Russian intelligence officer in his career. He is doing it now, and feels that he has to say something bigger, appropriate to the occasion. 'We respect your service and your country as worthy adversaries. Keeping our agents safe is what we're best at.'

Vasya remains impassive, staring out into the forest. Then he nods slowly. 'I know the rules of this game,' he says. 'I hope you are a good player. That's all.'

Vasya turns and walks down the stairway. Simon remains on the balcony looking out across the forested hills. He has joined the intelligence elite.

Helsinki, February 2014

A Baltic snowstorm is raging outside, but the building is insulated in that Nordic way that excludes winter entirely. Holed up in an anonymous hotel room in Helsinki, Simon is debriefing Vasya on the unfolding crisis in Ukraine. Vasya is still supposedly a key source for the Pole on Russia's increasingly threatening behaviour. He recounts that one of his oldest comrades, still in the service, has been spending the past four weeks in Crimea, under commercial cover, posing as an engineer with a big Russian construction business. This friend is undertaking a close recce of all the key communications links, power lines, strategic locations and Ukrainian military posts in Crimea.

'Why the sudden interest in Crimea?' Simon asks, his bloodhound instincts sure that he is on to something.

'You tell me,' responds Vasya. 'But remember,' he adds, 'Crimea is Russian. Always was, always will be. And, if we're really being honest, Ukraine isn't a thing. They're just Russians with a soft spot for Nazis.' Simon decides to ignore the casual racism.

He isn't sure what all this means, but he knows it's important. Excitedly he sends his report back to headquarters, but gets a dismissive response.

'A Russian spook is pretending to be an engineer and mooching around Crimea looking at road junctions. Interesting, but hardly important,' reads the encrypted email. The fact that Simon gets this brush-off from an analyst half his age who's never met an actual intelligence source only increases his frustration. Simon is sure that something big is happening. *Russia is taking an aggressive interest in a territory it regards as its own. This is the same Russia that invaded Georgia in 2008. In a couple of days they'd seized half the country.*

But London is not interested. The problem is that Vasya's stock in the Pole has been falling. Since leaving the GRU he has gone into business with some of the less savoury oligarchs – basically gangsters – and management in the Pole doesn't like them. They also think that Vasya is giving too much of the Kremlin line these days.

'He's become a Kremlin agent of influence – feeding us lines they want us to hear,' writes the analyst in his feedback on the report. Simon is furious, but he's about to be mortified. According to the Pole's Big Data team, all spotty twentysomethings who never stop staring at their laptops, Vasya's friend cannot be checking out the infrastructure in Crimea because he has been seen in a photo on a Russian social media site attending a medal ceremony in Siberia for Special Forces veterans. It's a long way from Siberia to Crimea and Vasya has been caught red-handed spinning a disinformation line designed to sow panic in Western capitals. So the Pole files the report under the heading of 'Disinfo/No Further Action'. Simon is left wondering why he spent several hours shivering in Helsinki under a false identity ensuring he didn't have a tail, if Vasya's intel no longer makes the cut.

A few weeks later, the Little Green Men overrun Crimea, no doubt drawing on the careful recce notes compiled by Vasya's friend, who seemed not to be in Siberia after all. This takes the Pole by surprise, as it does most Western intelligence agencies. But Simon isn't in the Pole to witness it: on his return from Helsinki he had fired off his resignation and never stepped inside the headquarters again. Simon sees a rampant Russia annexing sovereign territory and a West that is apparently powerless to respond. He also sees the Russians buying up the best properties in London and enthusiastically laundering their money with the help of the City and the compliance of regulators. He decides he has given enough of his life in service to a state that appears unable to defend its most basic interests.

There is something else: like so many things in Simon's life, he feels that the WADDINGTON case has been a disappointment. It was the thing that was supposed to have transformed his reputation, defined him as one of the office's high-flyers, propelled him into the inner circle at the Pole. And yet, somehow, it has never delivered for him. His decision to leave Her Majesty's Secret Service is dressed up as disillusionment with Britain and her policies, but a lot of the disillusionment is with himself.

For his part, Vasya, a servant of two masters, decided to make a complicated life simpler. He cut his relationship with British intelligence. If the case management committee at the Pole was being asked, they might claim that they had made the decision first, 'after several years' mounting unease at apparent disinform-ation appearing in the WADDINGTON material.' For Vasya, his British friends no longer appear to believe his reports and have shown themselves incapable of acting on the intelligence anyway. When he had taken the decision to meet Simon in a little hut in the Wienerwald, Britain was still a major global power. A key player in the Western alliance, influential in Europe, London an aspirational city of culture and glamour. By 2014, things are very different: the transatlantic alliance has withered, the country is increasingly obsessed with attacking its European allies and Scots are planning independence.

As far as Mother Russia is concerned, Vasya had remained a loyal servant of the GRU for thirty years. He has good contacts in Russia's business community, debts of gratitude he can call in, and networks all over the world. Within six months of his retirement, Vasya is living in Geneva, acting as a broker of commercial information on the former Soviet Union and its satellites. Most of his buyers are Westerners with plans to make money from seedy oligarchs.

Vasya realises quickly that the things he'd been told by his case officers at the Pole, that Britain was a clean country where the law applied equally to all, are not actually true. His Geneva office becomes busy with British bankers, lawyers and investors, including many a former politician now getting rich in 'Advisory Services', all desperate to cut deals. If there is one thing he knows as a Russian, it is where the really dirty money is. That doesn't seem to bother his British clients, who swarm into the shadiest corners of the Russian economy like bees to honey.

Vasya and Simon maintain a discreet contact. They are both exiles from their own services and share a similarly cynical view of the world. Simon notices that Vasya seems to be the better businessman, progressing from a pleasant apartment in Geneva to a beautiful chalet in an outstation of Crans-Montana, the ski resort of choice for Russian intelligence. Vasya has also become an increasingly firm advocate of the work of Vladimir Putin. A man who has a clear vision of where Russia wants to be, takes firm action, and is giving back pride to a great country. He and Simon agree to differ there, but Simon can see where he is coming from.

Chapter 11

Oxford
April 2022

Simon realises why he is standing on Turl Street, staring at the handsome gothic stone windows on the corner of Jesus College. The windows of Mackenzie's study. The glory days of Vienna are distant memories. What he feels now is rage, sadness and disgust.

After the recruitment in a Wendy house in the woods, Vasya and Alan had continued their Friday-morning walks in opposite directions along Dafingerstrasse, maintaining their routine. Over time, they varied the routes and timings, and Simon began to run Vasya directly. The methodology also changed: Vasya would walk under the window of Simon's apartment at an agreed time. Exactly as Sidorov had walked under the windows of Mackenzie's rooms at Jesus College, once every term.

Sidorov's inexplicable route through Oxford now made sense. And why he had repeated it on every visit. He and Mackenzie were communicating via DKM-S.

–

Simon explains his Turl Street revelation to Evie on a summery evening, a few days after his visit to Oxford. London is going through an early spring heatwave and people have flocked into the streets, thronging pavement cafes and pretending they are in Italy. Evie is soignée in a loose summer dress and sunglasses pushed up over her forehead. They have defeated most of a bottle of rosé and the conversation flows.

'Mackenzie would have been a terrible agent,' Simon points out. 'He was late for everything, would forget appointments, get drunk, oversleep. You name it. Also, he was very noticeable in Oxford. Everyone knew him. But there's no doubting his intelligence and I remember him being computer literate, so I assume he could deal with a DKM-S.'

'You sure about this? I mean —' Evie is enjoying the tease '— we've had a few other theories, haven't we?'

Simon feels suitably ashamed of his brief, wine-fuelled flirtation with Noah's Ark numerology. 'Okay, Flood 19, I agree that might not be a biblical reference. We haven't yet figured that out. But this one, Evie, this one is for real. I know how these things work. No Russian intel officer does something without a reason. Sidorov walked a bizarre and pointless route through Oxford in order that he could pass under Mackenzie's window. Burst transmission was their thing. They were under real surveillance pressure so they couldn't meet their agents directly. In the old days they'd've had a network of commies dotted around Oxford ready to courier messages and so on. But not after the end of the Cold War. So they relied on this stuff. We could never track it; it was perfect for them. All it needed was for Mackenzie to be in his room, with the transmitter ready to go. He could even leave it on his desk or whatever. As long as it was there, when Sidorov walked past, it would trigger and exchange messages. It has to be what was going on.'

'Si, have you ever stopped to think what Mackenzie's actual motivation is here? I mean, I was reading up on him. He was a *fanatical* anti-communist. You know he smuggled a dissident out of Poland in the boot of his car, back in the seventies. Risked everything. It just doesn't make sense that he could have been a KGB asset.'

'I wondered about that too. But the Poland thing — that's simple. I've seen a photo of the guy. Beautiful young artistic bloke. Mackenzie would do anything for a pretty boy. That wasn't ideology. That was opportunity.' Simon's pulse quickened as he said this, a memory he'd rather forget vying for his attention.

'Okay, but actually spying for them? It doesn't add up.'

'Well,' Simon is rehearsing a theory, still not sure if it works. 'He was a lifelong contrarian. He loved to disagree, dispute, argue. He also hated mediocrity, above all. The idea of being the secret spider at the centre of a web would have massively appealed to him.'

'But still, Russia? Really? He was a committed Thatcherite.'

'Yes, he was, but he was also an angry outsider. He wasn't from the Old Etonian mafia. He was always going on about how the West had failed, its moral bankruptcy, lack of valour and grit. Particularly the wets, the upper classes. And the other thing was he didn't have money, and he hated that.'

'It's still pretty weird.'

'Okay, Evie, we know that he received money from Sidorov. We know that Sidorov made regular journeys that would have enabled them to exchange secret messages. And there is a high probability, with Flood 19, that he was also receiving huge sums of money over many years from the Russian services' favourite bank. The payments carrying on until the month of his death. Then suddenly stopping. And we're still arguing about his political views? That's a lot of evidence that needs explaining.'

Evie nods, and they move on to other things. Simon is trying to work out if she is still job-hunting. She is much more interested in talking about the amazing resistance of the Ukrainian military, knocking out Russian tanks with Javelin missiles.

‑

A couple of weeks later, a notification lands on Simon's phone that looks like a confirmation of an Amazon delivery. In fact, it is a code used by the Pole to request his presence at a park bench in Central London. On the appointed day, Simon carries out an anti-surveillance route through Westminster. No followers: he is clean. As a final check, he cuts through Queen Ann's Gate, always a good place to get a look around. As he does so, he thinks he can see Benedict O'Brien at the far end of the street, talking in a small huddle of young, besuited men.

Simon makes some rapid calculations: O'Brien doesn't appear to have seen him. Indeed, he appears to be particularly engrossed in the conversation. His presence on a street that is full of over-priced 'professional services' firms is nothing suspicious. Simon decides not to abort the meeting.

At the required bench, a familiar face awaits. She is slightly more animated than the previous time, when he had been given the clear impression that meeting him was a major chore.

'STOKESAY.'

'Hello,' says Simon. 'What shall I call you?'

'How about Devi?'

'Hello, Devi,' says Simon, happy that she has offered a name, even if it is almost certainly not her real one.

'We had a good look at the Mackenzie stuff.' She smiles, but Simon is wary. It's a kind smile, the sort that you reserve for someone who hasn't got the job.

'Good. Thank you. Much appreciated. What's the news?' Simon is wondering whether being very polite would have the effect of making the news better.

'Well, I'm afraid to say —' his heart sinks '— that we're sure there's nothing there.'

'Meaning what, exactly.'

'Meaning there's nothing there. What do *you* mean?' Devi gives him a quizzical look, as if to point out that there aren't many alternative meanings for 'there's nothing there'.

'I suppose I mean, are you saying "there's nothing there in our files at the Pole"? Or are you saying, "there's nothing there", as in, "this isn't a thing"? Because some of these things are completely provable. Flood 19. That's a real entity. I can prove that. It's definitely "there". I would be happy to go over the details for you. Once you put the pieces together this becomes a big deal. This could be a major Russian intel network operating in this country that's been completely missed. And now doesn't feel like the right moment to be ignoring that.'

'Like I said, STOKESAY, we've looked and there's nothing there.' There's now a slight edge to her voice. She has been given a message to deliver and is neither authorised nor inclined to get into a discussion.

Simon has not come to be given a *line*. He can imagine a group of self-satisfied desk warriors sitting around agreeing the 'form of words' that would just about be true, whilst also closing down his options. He knows he is being fobbed off and Devi's deliberate phrasing is the proof.

'Okay, Devi,' says Simon, hoping that he is sounding calm, reasonable. 'We can go round these houses where you repeat the line and I ask silly questions to see if I can persuade you to say anything more. But is that going to be a waste of our time?'

'Yes, it is. Going to be a waste of your time. Not mine. I'm doing my job right now, Simon.'

Her use of his real name has the desired effect. Simon realises that he isn't getting anywhere, and that Devi is determined that he should know that. But he feels he has to give it one last try.

'Devi, I get that you're doing your job. But this is definitely serious intel, and there's probably more to come. It doesn't make sense for you guys to ignore it. I mean, Russian agents on British soil. Just at the moment we decide to take the Russian threat properly seriously. You can't afford to ignore that.'

Devi leans back into the bench and turns to look straight into Simon's eyes. 'Simon, word of advice.' Her tone is sharper, insistent. 'From me. Colleague to colleague. Let it drop. This isn't something you want to get into.'

She means to be helpful, but Simon has allowed himself to get annoyed. 'Is that supposed to be a warning?'

She doesn't respond.

He wants to deliver a parting shot as he gets up to leave. 'Right. But when this all comes out, everyone will be asking the government what they knew.'

'Thanks, STOKESAY. That's all, I think.' Devi has returned to the monotone of their first meeting. Dismissed.

Chapter 12

Simon draws two conclusions. The first is that he is definitely on to something. That's why Devi said 'there's nothing there'. The second is that the Pole would be hoping they'd scared him off. For Simon, this is the incentive he needs: it isn't a competition, of course, but he would take great pleasure in proving that he could get to the answer more effectively than his stodgily bureaucratic former employer.

Over the next few days a third conclusion begins to develop in his mind. Like all people in his world, he is professionally paranoid. But some things need explaining. A document he is typing on his computer about Mackenzie seems to need manually resaving, as if it has been altered remotely. Or is that just some Microsoft annoyance? He has WhatsApp on his laptop, synced with his phone, but it keeps logging out. Perhaps his VPN is playing up?

Then he starts seeing people.

Simon lives in a small flat on the first floor of an undistinguished house in Kilburn. Estate agents have been generously describing his neighbourhood as 'up and coming' for decades, but the fried chicken joints are sub-Kentucky and the food shops do not sell sourdough.

Simon's professional instincts mean that he is a keen observer of neighbourhood luminaries. He knows the friendly drunkard who occupies a strategic location just down from the tube station.

There is the pallid minicab driver who never seems to have a fare, his car suspiciously immobile. And a group of young Black guys that congregates at a barbershop. Simon tells himself they are probably God-fearing boys who were just trying to figure out what to do with their lives. But he is embarrassed by the nervousness he feels around them, a double strike against his liberalism and his manliness.

Simon starts to notice new additions: an extra member of staff at the tube station. A parking warden who appears improbably keen to check the cars on his street, several times over. A new distributor of throwaway newspapers. In Simon's experience, if it looks odd, something is wrong. He starts to feel different: a nauseous lightness in his stomach and a constant, mild headache – feelings he associates with the hyper-vigilance of real intelligence work.

If Sidorov is still close to Putin, there is a chance he will be sanctioned pretty soon. The EU has surprised the world by imposing sanctions on long lists of pro-Kremlin oligarchs and the UK is generally following suit. Sidorov might well be in the next tranche. This is the sort of thing that Simon's research is supposed to identify – Oxford University would then be taking money that turned out to be not just unpalatable, but illegal. There is a euphemistic landing-zone expected: '*Sidorov, whilst well-connected, is not in Putin's inner circle. But, given the changing geopolitical context, it may no longer be prudent to accept his donation.*' This is the sort of thing that is supposed to appear in his report. It would give everyone enough cover to have been about to take Sidorov's money in the first place, whilst also giving them the excuse that 'enhanced due diligence' now made it impossible.

But now, Simon is looking at something completely different: Sidorov as Mackenzie's case officer. Mackenzie, adviser to Thatcher, friend to Reagan. A Russian agent at the heart of the British establishment, for *decades*? Things were getting serious, and fiddling around on the Internet didn't cut it. At a certain point, the only way to find out about a Russian intelligence officer is to speak to another Russian intelligence officer. Simon needs to speak to Vasya.

Since 2014 and their parting of ways, Vasya has passed Simon titbits of business information from Russia, but 'national security' has always been off the agenda. Vasya decided what national security meant, but Simon was pretty sure that it extended to the details of a Russian recruitment of a prominent academic at the heart of the British establishment, even if that academic was now deceased. And that was before the invasion of Ukraine, which had put every Russian ex-intelligence officer into a state of high paranoia. If Simon is to get anything from Vasya other than the Kremlin party line, he needs Vasya to understand this is something much bigger than the topics covered in their occasional phone calls. He needs to pay a visit to Vasya's palatial chalet in Crans-Montana. But Simon has seen enough: he knows he is under surveillance. The only question is whether it is Russians, or the Pole. Or both.

This would have to be 'Moscow Rules': a ghost visit. Unlike fictional spies, Simon does not have a drawer full of false passports: you had to give up your cover identities on leaving the Pole. So he has to go low-tech. Like an escaped prisoner of war, Simon will have to walk over the frontier into Switzerland, through the mountain passes. He just needs to get to the Alps.

–

A couple of nights later, he walks out of his flat in a pair of hiking boots, with a rucksack on his back. He has turned off his phone and put it inside a Faraday pouch, ensuring that he cannot be tracked. He walks an elaborate route he has memorised across north London to Hackney. He makes extensive use of pedestrian-only cut-throughs and canal towpaths, crossing a couple of parks en route. At the end of this dry-cleaning exercise he is confident he has not been followed to the shabby house in Dalston, another bit of London taking its time over gentrification.

He knocks on the door to find a man roughly his age eagerly awaiting his arrival. Simon has drawn five hundred pounds in cash from O'Brien and with this he pays David, an old friend and penniless writer. The fee is for driving him overnight from London to Bernex, a mountain village on the French side of the frontier above Lake Geneva. David is delighted to have the money and the frisson of being involved in something rather more exciting than his usual life of pitching articles to websites that pay fifty quid a go. So the two of them sit in David's beat-up Ford Fiesta, hoping it will survive the journey down through Europe.

Post-Brexit, they can't avoid being stamped in by European frontier police. So they take the ferry to the Netherlands and cross two more unmanned frontiers to get to France. It's not ideal, but he reckons neither the Russians nor the Pole will have a reason to be hacking into Dutch government systems. Obviously, the car would have been caught on various cameras on the way. But David only spent cash and they avoided the autoroutes and their busy *péages*, rigged with cameras. Simon wore a baseball cap pulled down low over his face and only left the car for essential pee stops beside quiet roads. He let David buy the necessary coffees and fuel, always from filling stations at the edges of small towns.

Their destination, Bernex, is perfect: it is early summer and the village is thick with tourists. There are plenty of middle-aged male hikers wearing baseball caps, minding their own business. Simon can easily blend in, and the tourist crowds extend up to the hiking trails and the cable cars. Before dismissing him, Simon sent David into the Spar, with a shopping list. Baguettes, salami, tins of beer. For good measure he'd added a few oranges and two litres of water. His rucksack rather heavier than he'd hoped, Simon strolls through the village, passing tempting *auberges* and *chambres d'hôtes*. As the settlement gives way to open country, the track is unpaved, passing through woods and across pastures. He heads straight up the valley, walking in the direction of the Dent D'Oche, a craggy mountain at its head.

These are not the snow-capped high peaks of the Massif du Mont Blanc. In the lower Alpes du Léman, the only visible snow is in small patches in shady parts of north faces. Most of the landscape under the rocky peaks is a brilliant green, studded with alpine flowers. Luscious meadows dotted with brown cows swinging their bells alternate with the darker green brushstrokes of the pine forests.

Simon has not rested well in David's Fiesta, but the mountain air is refreshing. The contrast with London is beguiling and initially energising. In an hour of uphill walking he has passed several chalets promising hearty meals. At the third of these, on a hillside in a forest clearing, surrounded by statuesque trees and overhung by dramatic crags, Simon's resolve fails him. A mountain chalet is well off the beaten track of any normal investigator, he reasons, and so he takes a table outside, his cap pulled far down over his eyes.

He spends a happy afternoon at Chalet la Fétiuère, gorging on the Menu Savoyard and the invigorating vin de pays. It is an appropriate choice, as eighty years earlier the family owners of the refuge had bravely sheltered Jews escaping Nazi-occupied France. On the wall is an old map, marked with little dotted lines that show the back paths across the mountainsides into Switzerland used to lead the escapees to safety. Simon takes careful note, and after dozing a little to aid digestion of his *assiette du pays*, he resumes his climb, up into the forest, the clean smell of pine sap on the air, the roar of distant waterfalls in the background.

After another ninety minutes of hiking up a steep track, he is above the tree line, in a hanging valley, facing Les Portes d'Oche: a gap in the mountain ridge. It is now later afternoon, and at the higher altitude a cool breeze is beginning to breathe through the gap between the peaks and onto the meadows where Simon is standing. The only surveillance seems to be from the Alpine choughs flying overhead and a possible sighting of a chamois on the skyline. There is a mountain refuge on the ridge above, but it is not visible from where Simon is stood.

After searching for a few minutes, he finds a perfect bivouac spot: a flat space in front of a large boulder, offering shelter from the prevailing wind. He pulls out his sleeping bag and mat, plus his Gore-Tex bivi sack, and makes himself comfortable with a nightcap of a couple of beer cans.

In front of him is a stupendous view back to Bernex and across the Haute-Savoie. As dusk falls, the cooling air is accompanied by the lights of the village, far below. As the sun disappears behind the horizon it throws its last rays onto the Dent D'Oche, bathing the rock in an improbable pink alpenglow. He concentrates hard. Can he hear anything, any sign of human activity? Only the beckoning silence. Cocooned in his sleeping bag, he begins to doze off.

Then he hears it. The noise of disturbed stones. The sound is below him, still distant: not an avalanche, but a clatter of small rocks dislodged underfoot. It could be chamois skittering down loose ground, or late hikers searching for a bivouac spot. But Simon instinctively feels danger. He is prepared for a swift departure. Within a few seconds he has wriggled out of his sleeping bag, stuffed it into his rucksack and folded his mat. Now he can see two lights, bobbing in and out of vision somewhere on the dark hillside below. He laces his boots methodically and shoulders his pack, squinting as he tries to get a good sightline in the gloaming. He clambers up above the path, treading as lightly and as quickly as possible. He can hear more clattering, closer now. After a short scramble, Simon is able to squirm behind a large boulder. He has a view down towards the bobbing lights and he focuses on controlling his breathing, in spite of the adrenaline pounding through his body.

They are right below him now, two dark shapes with little circles of light from the headlamps on their foreheads. Two men: slim, athletic build, small backpacks. All as you'd expect for a surveillance or black-ops team. They have paused at the flat area of Simon's bivouac spot. He can hear low voices and concentrates hard, trying to tune in to the language. They are speaking French, panting from the steep climb below.

'He would have come this way.' It is a deep voice, gravelly. Simon guesses in his fifties, ex-smoker. Probably gave up when he left the Foreign Legion.

'You sure? Not the ridge above?' Younger, the slighter of the two figures, also taller. Perhaps DGSE, France's feared paramilitary intelligence service?

'Definitely. I mean, we know he's a mountaineer, but he's not here on holiday this time, is he?'

At those words, Simon has to suppress a gasp. They have obviously been given a dossier on him – photos, description of relevant interests. He begins to go back over the journey in David's car. Where had they clocked him? He suspects it was the Pole's London team, right from the start of his journey, who then passed the file onto their French partners. He blinks hard, refocusing on the two figures below, trying to block out of his mind the question of where he had fucked up. He can go back to that later.

'But would he have bivouacked?' asks the younger man.

'I don't think so, too risky. We're talking about a real survivor here. Someone who doesn't take chances unless he has to.' Simon is feeling furious with himself, wishing he had continued through the night like the 'real survivor' he was supposed to be. His afternoon eating cured meats at the chalet had been a schoolboy error.

'Well, my boy, we have to carry on if we're doing this properly.'

Odd, that. 'My boy'. Maybe they'd been working together for years?

There is a pause: all Simon can hear is the two men, still breathing heavily.

'You're right. It's just amazing to think he was here, one night in '42. I'm really glad we did this. You know, repeat his route, to honour him.' It sounds as though the younger one is making a small concession: perhaps he'd been a sceptic at the start of the outing.

'Weird to think that neither of us would be here if he hadn't made it to Switzerland.'

And then it clicks. Simon wants to groan with the absurdity of the situation. But if he shows himself now, he'll end up being reported to the police for his bizarre behaviour.

'Well,' the older man speaks, gentle but commanding, 'let's keep going. See if we can make it in one push, like Grandpapa.'

The two lights disappear from view behind the boulder, but Simon can hear the trudging sound as the men repeat the route their forebear had taken in 1942, escaping Nazism to freedom and safety. Simon lets out a sigh and thinks how nice it would be to have the sort of family that celebrated its ancestors in simple, practical ways. And then he feels stupidly embarrassed. His paranoia had got the better of him.

'Idiot.'

The mountains didn't respond.

Chapter 13

Les Alpes du Léman
May 2022

Simon awakes around dawn. His face is slightly cold, but the rest of him has been comfortable during what was left of the night. He breakfasts on oranges, salami and bread and gulps some of his water. He stuffs his sleeping kit back into his rucksack and sets off towards the col. It is not yet six in the morning. By seven he is heading down the other side, breathing in a new vista towards Lake Geneva as he pants in the thin air. Another hour sees Simon pass through tiny settlements — summer pastures dotted with deserted stone chalets. He descends a steep mountainside, climbs back up to another col and then down a long winding path to the crystal blue waters of the Lac de Tanay. There, already sweating in the morning sun, he stops for an enervating swim. Then he continues down switchback lanes to Vouvry, a nondescript Swiss village sitting in the flatlands of the Rhône valley. He walks confidently into a campsite at the edge of the village and uses their showers, changing into clean shirt and slacks.

He had successfully entered Switzerland as a ghost. No immigration authority, no CCTV camera, no airline, car hire or hotel had any record of his arrival, either in France or Switzerland. This means that there was no way that Vasya can know he will be coming. But it also means that the Pole has no idea where he is. Since the disturbing meeting with Devi this seems more important. They don't want him digging into the Mackenzie issue. That is clear. What he still doesn't know: why?

Vasya will be monitored, both by the Pole and by Moscow Centre. Any contact between him and Simon will be picked up with particular interest. Simon's ability to get to him unnoticed is essential. Once they have met, it will be a different matter. The Pole, or Moscow, can rush out a surveillance team, but they won't be able to cover the meeting. They will have missed their chance.

Simon's other priority is not to alert Vasya to his intentions. If Vasya is a disinformation agent, he doesn't want him to have the chance to get his latest instructions from Moscow. They have not communicated since a perfunctory exchange of New Year greetings several months earlier. In the light of the Ukraine invasion, Simon has twice composed an angry message to Vasya, only to delete it before sending.

There is every chance that he might not be at his blingy chalet in Crans-Montana. But Vasya has not passed on his canny intelligence instincts to his daughter, Alina. A would-be social-media influencer, she is fond of posting pictures of herself by the pool at the chalet, or pouting at the mirror in her bedroom or some overpriced restaurant. Vasya, a hopelessly doting father, is an occasional presence in these Instagram posts, sometimes in posed #Daddysgirl shots of the two of them, on other occasions in the background around the pool. Two days ago, Alina had posted an image of the family enjoying #caviar at Pasha, a restaurant popular with Crans-Montana's oligarch community.

At Vouvry's single-platform train station, Simon buys a ticket for Sierre, paid for with cash fed into the machine. Simon has planned his arrival in Switzerland to be a Sunday morning, and things are suitably quiet. The station appears to be unmanned, as does most of Vouvry. A deep-voiced bell tolls for mass and a few doughty widows can be seen heading for church. A young family, absorbed with keeping their toddler off the railway tracks, is busy at the far end of the platform. The wrong profile for surveillants: never work with children. Although, maybe that is what they want him to think… When the train arrives, Simon has most of a carriage to himself. As before, he keeps his cap pulled down low.

At Sierre, Simon transfers onto that most Swiss thing imaginable, a gleaming funicular railway that whirs him up from the valley floor, past winding roads and terraced vineyards. It is lunchtime when he reaches Crans and the town is busy with vulgarians looking for things to spend their money on. It is a beautiful summery day and Simon reasons that Vasya will be having a family lunch around the pool. The chalet, on a quiet hillside road, is a vast, architecturally illiterate mess of stone and timbers, bristling with gables and balconies, newly built. Directly above the building, after a small stretch of grass hillside, the pine forest sweeps up the mountainside. Simon walks a route across the top of the town, following the open ground cut into the forest for skiers' pistes, incongruous swathes of grass in summer. By contouring round the hillside, Simon reaches the strand of forest directly above Vasya's chalet. There, concealed behind thick spruce trunks at the edge of the woods looking down at the house, he watches through binoculars, finishing the rest of his food as he does so.

Initially he sees no movement. For a long hour he curses the bad luck that has brought him to Crans the day after Vasya and family have departed for some undisclosed location. But then it arrives: the black Range Rover, dark windows gleaming in the sunlight, winding its way up the switchback road. It disappears into a garage built into the hillside below the house. Simon knows from a previous visit that an elevator takes passengers up to the house. He waits a few more minutes and two people walk out onto one of the wide balconies. Vasya, in polo shirt and jeans; Alina, hot pants and sunglasses, staring at her vast smartphone. There is no sign of the teenage boy looking awkward in his glasses who occasionally appears on the edges of the Instagram posts; nor Anna, who happened to be the mother of these children and Vasya's current wife. Simon assumes they are still inside: perhaps taking a nap? Vasya is laughing about something. They have clearly been enjoying a boozy lunch out.

Simon waits: Alina goes back inside and Vasya sprawls out on a lounger facing into the sun. Anna appears briefly on the balcony, holding what looks like a beer bottle and hands it to Vasya, before tottering back inside on her absurdly high heels. Simon waits a few more minutes to ensure that Vasya is not about to be disturbed again before pulling out an unused burner phone from his rucksack. He sends Vasya a message on the Signal secure messaging app, using his workname from Vienna days, warning that he will call in one minute. It was important to exert some control.

Simon cannot hear Vasya's phone ring, but he can see him hold it up to his ear.

'*Tovarisch.*' Simon liked to call Vasya 'comrade', which sat somewhere in tone between formality and irony.

'Mikhail?' Vasya's English is excellent, but he has always used the Russian version of Michael – the alias name that Simon had given him when they first met, in Vienna.

At this point Vasya is breezy geniality, but with a touch of concern, as you might expect from an unanticipated call from an unfamiliar number. 'Mikhail? New number? Nice to hear from you. What's up?'

'Vasya. A lot is up. We need to meet. There's lots to talk about.'

'Mikhail.' Vasya's voice is calmer, slower. 'Of course we should meet,' he says in a tone that suggests he has no intention of it. 'When I'm next down from my mountain I'll let you know. Would be *great* to see you.'

'We need to meet today, *tovarisch.*'

'Mikhail. What are you talking about? Are you in Crans?'

Simon had walked out of the woods and is now less than a hundred meters from the chalet, still on higher ground, standing in the open. Vasya has stood up from his lounger and is pacing down the balcony, his back to Simon.

'It's a lovely view from the balcony, Vasya.' Simon can see Vasya's physical reaction as he says this. 'Turn round,' he orders.

Vasya spins on his heels and looks up, immediately catching sight of Simon, the two men facing one another, phones held to their ears, modern-day duellers.

'You did well.' Vasya's voice is calm, the tone is low, almost in defeat.

'We need to speak, Vasya. Privately.'

Simon can see Vasya looking round, as if hoping for a way out, then shrug. 'Meet me outside the casino in twenty minutes. Black Range Rover.'

—

Vasya had taken the time to collect himself. Simon climbs into the Range Rover, feeling a cold blast of excessive air conditioning as he settles into the white leather seat. The usual embrace, or even a handshake, is absent. They are driving up the mountainside, on roads that are only passable in summer. The view across the valley opens up, over the Rhone and south to the high peaks of the Valais, the Dent d'Herens and the Matterhorn.

'To what do we owe the pleasure, Misha?' asks Vasya.

Simon tries to play it as cool as possible. 'Oh, you know. Just want to pick your brains about something.'

Vasya laughs, unconvincingly. 'Oh sure, Misha. So you don't call me? Or schedule a meeting? And you call on a new number?' His voice is rising slightly. 'You think I'm some kind of fucking moron now? You think I've forgotten how this stuff is working? You think I haven't noticed there's a fucking war on?'

'Exactly. These are sensitive times, you know.'

'I'll tell you what I know: once a Chekist always a Chekist. And it's no different for your people. Sure, you call me on your regular phone to chat about commercial work, we fix meetings all normal. But suddenly you appear outside my house on a different number a few weeks after a war breaks out? You think I don't know what's going on here? Your people, how you say? The *Pole*? This is from them, isn't it? Reactivation. Don't treat me like I came out of the Conservatory yesterday. There's a war on. I have noticed.'

On the face of it, Vasya is completely wrong. Simon is under no instructions from the Pole. In fact, they seem to be trying to stop him. But there is a kind of truth to it. Simon still has something to prove. And this is also true for Vasya. He knew that he had never really had 'the indirect ear of the British prime minister', as Simon had assured him in the early days. That was just the hot air they had blown up his arse.

When the Pole had decided it had heard enough of Vasya's 'pro-Putin agitprop', as one senior analyst characterised it, Simon had been sent to deliver the news to Vasya. The prime minister was no longer hanging on Vasya's words. Even the lowly analysts had decided he was just a Kremlin mouthpiece, best ignored when you could just as easily watch RT. And Vasya felt as if he had failed. He had not been the spider at the centre of a web between the UK and Russia, manipulating and controlling events. He had been no more than a snout, passing titbits of information, much of it disregarded as unreliable. Vasya, like Simon, had still wanted to prove that he could be the Penkovsky of his generation: the spy who saved the world.

And now there is a war on.

Simon shakes his head slowly. 'This isn't reactivation, Vasya. That story has finished.' Vasya nods, his eyes fixed on the winding road. 'This is a private job.'

'Ah, yes, mercenaries. We're all mercenaries, aren't we? Blackwater, Wagner and little old Misha, or do I call you Simon now? I guess that depends who is paying. Which takes me back to the start: what is this? You act like you're back at the Pole and then you tell me it's just another private job, but you creep out of the mountain forest without calling ahead.'

'It might not be *just another*. That's the thing. I've been looking into Georgy Sidorov.'

Vasya's voice is level, almost bored. 'You know his story: SVR, London, then banking. Keeps himself out of trouble. Putin likes him, but he's Moscow, not St Petersburg, so he'll never be right on the inside. You could have sent me a WhatsApp to find that out.' Vasya has pulled the Range Rover onto a passing place that juts out like a balcony over the mountainside. 'Come on,' he says, 'let's walk a little. Mountain air, good for both of us.' They climb down from the car and continue along the road, little more than a track at this point. On their right hand side the slope falls away, steep grass for a few metres then tumbling into a rocky cliff. By virtue of having been passenger, Simon is on the outside edge.

'Why do you want to know, anyway?'

'He was funding a college in Oxford. And the university is worried about his money. After Ukraine. You know, sanctions risk.'

Vasya throws back his head and laughs. A ribald, rib-cracking laugh of the sort a drunk man lets out when told a particularly dirty joke. Vasya shakes his head at the mirth of it all.

'So, let's just get this straight. Your ancient, prestigious university wants to take our dirty Russian money. But to make sure our dirty Russian money is not too much like shit, you pay a dirty ex-spook to talk to a dirty Russian collaborator to make everyone feel better about the dirty Russians? And meanwhile you're trying to fuck my country with extreme sanctions so that we can no longer eat, or buy medicines, but you still might like a bit of our money in your university. Have I got that right? But wait a minute, Mr Simon Sharman, former officer of the Most Secret Service of them all, where are all the British entrepreneurs that love their country so much they want to pay for a nice college in Oxford?'

Simon doesn't answer this rhetorical question.

Vasya is shouting now. 'I'll tell you where. They've buried their money in vaults in your little empire that exists solely for the ongoing purpose of laundering money. The Virgin Islands. Or Cayman. Or, if you don't like the hot weather, the Isle of Man. That's where your great British patriots have put their fucking money! And you've come to tell me there's a problem with our

Russian money because we're all corrupt, aren't we? We're always stealing. Not like those nice British bankers who are so good at washing it all. Or like your new friends the Ukrainians. No corruption there,' he says with heavy sarcasm.

'Vasya, I didn't make the system. Don't pretend to me that yours is any better.'

Vasya doesn't answer.

'What I really want to know about is Sidorov when he was in the service. He used to go up to Oxford three times every year. Once a term. And he would walk the same route every time. And we both know from Vienna what that means...'

'What now, Misha?' Vasya's voice is raised, and he turns towards Simon. Physically he is a slight man, wiry, overweight at the belly but still powerful. 'Are we going to talk about burst transmitters again?' There is a slight undertone of menace in his voice.

'Vasya, I believe Sidorov was running an agent in Oxford. By DKM-S. Professor Peter Mackenzie. Prominent historian, featured in newspapers, on TV interviews. That sort of thing. Did you ever hear anything about that?'

Vasya is now smiling again. He lifts his hands in an exaggerated gesture. 'Misha, Misha! Come on! You know our game! Even when I was in, it was impossible to get agent IDs. Only the case officer knows the real name.' Vasya is smiling at the absurdity of the question. 'And if I did know, would I tell you now? With our country fighting a war for survival against NATO and Ukrainian Nazis? Seriously?'

Simon had told himself that he wouldn't get dragged into an argument with Vasya about Ukraine, an argument he knew would go nowhere. So, like generations of intelligence officers before him whose sources hold views they find abhorrent, he ignores this, and ploughs on. 'He was well-known in Russia – spoke the language, would appear on TV.'

'Not really my kind of thing,' mutters Vasya unconvincingly.

As they walk, they have come to a part where the road narrows. The grass verge has disappeared altogether and the side of the track is delineated by a sheer cliff, dropping a few hundred feet onto forested talus. Simon can feel an airiness. If Vasya chooses to shoulder him hard, he'll fall off the edge. Would he do that? Neither of them speak, as if considering the likelihood. Simon flexes his toes to improve his grip, like a rugby player facing a tackle.

'Vasya, it's not a reactivation. But we need to know this. This isn't about the money stuff, all that bullshit. This is the old days. These are big questions and the answers make a difference and the person with the answers is the one that matters. The man who is actually in the arena.'

And then Vasya has surged forwards and grabbed Simon by his shirt, pushing him towards the edge. The heels of Simon's boots are hanging over the cliff and time slows down. He can feel a breezy updraught. It's pleasantly cool and he wonders how long he'll be in the air. Will his arms and legs flail around like they do in the movies? Or just drop limply, like a sack of potatoes?

Time speeds up. He's flapping his arms, uselessly. He can't get purchase on his toes and he realises that if he grabs Vasya they will both go down. Two bodies, flailing in a deadly embrace.

'Don't fucking lie to me!' shouts Vasya. 'You people fucked me for years. Tell me now: what is this about?'

Simon can feel the ridge of the cliff-edge catching on a groove in the soles of his boots. A few millimetres of rubber keeping him alive. He stares into Vasya's eyes.

'I swear to God, Vasya. On all that is holy. This Oxford thing is big. I think it's got something to do with the government, but I don't know. If it was anything less I wouldn't have stalked you here like this.'

Vasya grinds his teeth and snarls.

This is it, thinks Simon. It had to end at some point. Odd, because nobody knows he's here. *I guess it'll take them a while to figure it out.* And then he realises his body is being dragged forwards and his feet are on flat ground and Vasya's snarling jerk has turned into an embrace. He can feel Vasya's body heaving with sobs.

'*Misha*... Misha, I gave you guys everything because you told me it *mattered*. The way to help Russia out of its hole was to make sure the West really understood it. That was what you told me. And I believed it. You said the prime minister read my intel. Yeah, right. Then you fucked off because Russia got out of its hole and you didn't like that. And now you're back telling me this matters again but you don't want us out of our hole. You want Russia to lose. You're going to humiliate us in Ukraine and you want us to beg you again, like we had to in the nineties.'

Adrenaline is now surging through Simon's body, a delayed reaction. His knees are buckling, shaking. His stomach heaves.

'Fuck, man. FUCK.' Vasya has released him from his embrace and Simon drops into a squatting position, hyperventilating. 'Okay. Vasya I don't know what this is. But I don't think it's about Ukraine. Let's not get into that. I think I stumbled on something important. This man Mackenzie was at the top of the political tree. He was connected to the newspaper editors, the Tory MPs, he knew everyone. I realise you wouldn't know if he was an agent. But was something going on in Oxford? Did you ever hear about SVR operations there? Early nineties? Even just a rumour? This might be the biggest secret you ever tell me.' Simon is almost pleading.

Then he pulls himself into a stand, closes his eyes, sighs.

Vasya has turned away, as if he cannot bear to look at Simon. And then he turns back and he has narrowed his eyes, frowning. It is a gesture that Simon recognises from countless agent debriefs. It is as if Vasya cannot decide whether to tell him something interesting, some real gold. And then he nods, which means he is about to tell him something that matters. It means that Vasya is the man who is actually in the arena.

'Misha. We need to talk about COSTELLO.'

Chapter 14

'COSTELLO. Some claim they worked on it – and if they say that you know they're full of shit. Now and then you hear a reference here, a mention there. You nod and try not to stop the flow, in case you might learn a little more. But most people just don't believe in it. It's a myth. A fairy story for Russian spies.' Vasya has shoved his hands into his pockets, thrusting his shoulders forwards as he does so. It's his posture of determination, focus, action. They have walked past the narrowing and are now at the edge of a broad alp. Cows are grazing the summer meadows, dotted with ancient *mazots*.

COSTELLO, thinks Simon. *Like the Isle of Man shell company?*

'We all know the story of the Cambridge ring. Philby, Blunt, Burgess, Maclean and Cairncross. Our greatest triumph. Exposing the rotting core of your decadent, crumbling empire. They were all men of class, connections, high education. Britain's greatest strength is its tight-knit establishment, you all know each other from school and university. And it turns out to be its greatest weakness. It was easier for you to let Philby just carry on than expose a good chap. One of us? Rather not, *old bean*.'

'Yes, Vasya, I have actually heard this story before.' Simon feels calmer, but still wobbly. He is desperate not to show this. To pretend that being held over the edge of a cliff was just a normal thing.

'Right. And have you wondered why there's only a Cambridge ring? I mean, you have Oxford and Cambridge everything else,

106

don't you? Boat races, football matches, that club in Pall Mall where they kick out Russians for using their mobile phones. Why should Oxford be left out?'

Simon has, of course, wondered about this. Why was there a Cambridge spy ring and no Oxford equivalent? Explanations varied from superiority to the idea that Oxford was more conservative than Cambridge, less likely to be a fruitful hunting-ground for youthful communists. After a career in the infuriatingly unpredictable world of human intelligence, Simon believed that the most likely answer was contingency: sheer luck.

'You know our world, Vasya. Arnold Deutsch, the guy who recruited them, was in the right place at the right time. He got lucky. We all need luck.' Simon left unspoken the thought that luck had delivered Vasya to him in Vienna.

'Yes, maybe. But maybe there *was* an Oxford ring. A group of young men recruited for their talent and ambition, to rise into positions of power and influence. That's COSTELLO.'

There is a silence. Each willing the other to speak. Simon folded.

'But was it real? Vasya, I need to know.'

'Who knows? Like I said, it's probably a myth. We tell the story so we can feel better about ourselves.'

'But there must have been case officers, support, couriers, all that. You know how this stuff is: you can't run a network without a team. Eventually, the word gets out. People talk, they boast. And wouldn't the defectors know about it? Gordievsky, Mitrokhin. Wouldn't they have blown the operations?'

Another pause as they walk onwards. Simon can hear Vasya's laboured breathing. Is he taking his time because of the thin air at two thousand metres? Or is he figuring out how much he is willing to say?

'One of the things Moscow Centre learned from the Cambridge ring was that too many people ended up being in the know. Every bloody defector seemed to know there were agents, where they worked, and so on. So, two things came from that.

One was that the intelligence had to be buried in other reporting. No more of this, "we have an agent inside the Foreign Office, here's what he can tell us". No single-source reporting. All of it meshed in with other analysis to protect the *existence* of a source, let alone his identity.'

'Makes sense. The other thing?'

'To have a completely separate organisation to operate the networks. These are not officers from GRU, SVR or FSB who are assigned to a certain operation. It's a totally different group, recruited separately, trained, organised, funded separately. Reporting directly to the presidential executive office, not to the security council. That way, nobody from the other agencies can find out about it.'

Simon can't believe what he's hearing. An entirely separate Russian intelligence organisation, one that nobody has heard of, to recruit and run the most sensitive cases. 'So that's what happened with COSTELLO?'

'It's what I would do.'

'That's the answer to a different question. Anyway, if this is what happened, how would you know? Like you said, it's a fairy story.' Simon is realising it is too good to be true.

'Yes, but even a completely separate organisation might need to make use of the regular channels now and then. Maybe Sidorov has to walk past your professor's room every few months, carrying a transceiver. He's told the route to walk, but probably he doesn't know who the agent is, where on the route the messages will transmit. He just knows he has to follow the trail. And when he receives the message he can't decrypt it, but sends it back encoded to Moscow. That's how COSTELLO would work.'

'Would work. *Would*. But did it? The rumours, the myths. They had to start from somewhere.'

'Do you remember Kleshnyov? Valery. We tried to stitch him up in Prague.'

'The defence attaché?' About a decade earlier, Vasya and Simon had tried to blackmail Kleshnyov who was running a lucrative kickbacks scheme in Prague. The plan had failed because both the Czech minister of defence and the Russian ambassador were in on the scam. It's impossible to blackmail people who have no shame.

'You know that I was, er, friendly with his wife?'

Vasya and Irina Kleshnyova had been lovers. 'What's this got to do with COSTELLO?' asks Simon, irritated by Vasya's attempt to change the subject.

'Well, Kleshnyov left the service, went into the oil business. I lost touch with him. Irina and I had ended it.' He pauses. They have stopped walking now. Vasya is leaning against a rock that has been warmed by the afternoon sun. 'A few years later, Irina contacts me. I haven't heard from her in years and she's calling and leaving messages saying it's urgent. I remember well because I had just married Anna. And it was, basically, inconvenient. To get calls from a former lover. One who was, how you say, *undeclared*.

'Anyway, I find a quiet moment and call her. She's bawling, hysterical. Valery had gone missing. He'd said he was going to Italy. Milan. But then he'd just not come back. His mobile is switched off. She calls the hotel, no Mister Kleshnyov staying here thanks very much. She calls the Russian consulate. *Niet*. No Russian citizen called Kleshnyov recorded as missing. She makes a fuss, the consulate people eventually call the police. No Kleshnyov. Nowhere.'

'So he'd lied,' says Simon. 'He hadn't gone to Milan, but that was the cover story. We've all done that.' Simon has two failed marriages to prove his point. Vasya is on his third, at least.

'No, Simon, she had spoken to him in Milan two days before. On his phone, video call. He was definitely there. The thing I like about Irina is she is smart. Razor sharp. Mathematician. Not some floozy with fake tits pouting all day long.' He seems to be describing his current wife, Anna, at this point. 'If she said he was in Milan, he was in Milan. End of.'

'So how do you explain it?'

'This is the point: I promised Irina, you know, for old times' sakes, I promised her that I would try to find out what happened.

So I sent one of my guys to take a look. He knew all the police across north Italy. No Russian citizen was logged as going missing, dead or anything else at that time. So I say, try the usual B-list. You know, the easy passports that we can all make in the office: Malta, Cyprus, even Montenegro, for fuck's sake. Nothing. But Irina assures me that he was in Milan. So I say to my guy – just find any reported foreigners dying in Milan. Narrowed down of course: middle-aged men. And then we find something. A middle-aged, European man with a St Kitts passport had been knocked down and killed by a tram. St Kitts. What even is that? One of your empire outposts where you sell passports, launder money, what else? It's your show.'

'I dunno, Vasya. Never been there. Was it him?'

'Yes. Eventually my guy goes to the morgue, sends me a photo. His face was pretty mashed up by the tram. But I can make it out. It's Valery.' Vasya pauses with a mixture of guilt and guile.

'But, you see, the thing with a St Kitts passport is there's no consulate. Nobody to call when an upstanding citizen of St Kitts is tragically killed in an unnecessary accident. None of his addresses or credit cards seem to lead anywhere beyond offshore black boxes. A St Kitts citizen is the perfect platform from which someone can disappear right off the map. Puff.' Vasya moves his hand like a magician making a card disappear. 'The only clue is the name on the passport. Walter Pinsent.'

'How does that help?'

'Misha, come on. Is your Russian getting rusty? Kleshnyov. You know what is *kleshnya*? It means "pincer". Pincer, Pinsent. Valery, Wally, Walter. It's a typical alias.'

'Okay, so Kleshnyov was running an alias op and came to a nasty end. These things happen.'

'Yes, but it wasn't a GRU op. I checked back with our people. Then I checked with the SVR. Nope. We don't have any other Russian services running alias operations.'

'Maybe the Israelis were running him. They might use a St Kitts passport. Frankly, anyone can buy a bloody St Kitts passport. Could be anyone.'

'Yes. Could be. That's what I said to Irina. She didn't like that. Said her Valery would only serve Mother Russia. Begged me to try to find out more. I guess I find it hard to say no to her. In or out of the bedroom.'

'What'd you do?'

'What's that English phrase? We threw the bathtub at it.'

'The kitchen sink.'

'Also. I got my guys to look into the bookings for the hotel, we hacked a CCTV server at the police HQ, we paid off one of the Albanians who runs all the brothels, to see if he had paid for any *entertainments*. We tried everything. And finally there was a lead. On the CCTV we get an image of Mister Pinsent entering the Principe Hotel. He wasn't staying there, but he'd visited, middle of the day. So we get onto the CCTV at the hotel. And we find the footage. He walks straight in, seems to know where he's going, has a key card already, goes up to the sixth floor. We can see him walking down the corridor and going into a room. But because of the angle of the camera we can't tell exactly which. It's one of two rooms. Look to see who's booked those two rooms. One is Doctor Robert J Schatz. He's a vascular surgeon from Connecticut, travelling with his wife and attending a conference. Easy to confirm, he's listed as a speaker on the conference website.'

'Right. Sounds unlikely. The other room?'

'The other room,' says Vasya, smiling, folding his arms and squinting into the sunlight. 'The other room had been booked for five days by a trust, based in the Cayman Islands. There you go, your British Empire, again, always there to help civilise the world. So, it's a dead-end. Cayman Islands trust. You give up trying to find out what's going on there.'

'So you never figured out what he was up to?'

'No. But, Misha, did I mention the name of the trust?' Vasya is grinning broadly. It's like the best of the old days, when Misha and Vasya would get drunk together and laugh at the absurdities of their collective masters. Misha and Vasya, *contra mundum*. Had he tried to kill Simon only minutes earlier? Maybe that was a strange dream.

'Come on, Vas, the name. What was it?'

Vasya has put on his best Terry-Thomas English accent. 'It is Administered by Appleton, Appleton (Cayman) Limited. Esteemed Solicitors and Commissioners for Oaths. The name? The Costello Trust.'

COSTELLO.

'Fuck.'

'Yes. Fuck.'

'Fuck, Vasya.' Simon's mind is racing, his intelligence officer instincts trying to figure out what was going on. 'What was Kleshnyov doing? What was this?' Simon is organising different structures in his mind. The Costello Trust, Cayman. Costello Limited, in the Isle of Man, that paid money to the mysterious Flood 19.

There is no need to tell Vasya any of this.

'Well, you tell me what Kleshnyov was doing,' replies Vasya. 'But if there was another Russian intel organisation, a third one that did overseas operations, alias passports, all that, and it existed to run a top-secret network, and that network was called COSTELLO... Wouldn't it look a lot like this?'

The sun is lowering in the sky, ready to dip behind the wall of the Valais peaks. The two friends turn and walk back towards the Range Rover. They pass the narrow section, where the cliff-edge juts against the track, in silence.

Vasya drops Simon off in the middle of Crans. As he climbs out of the car, he turns to Vasya, who is struggling for the right words. 'Misha, make sure this matters to someone.'

'I will, Vasya, I will,' he promises.

–

In the descending funicular, a canoodling couple giggle joyfully. Simon is elated, his mind surging with thoughts, connections. An Oxford spy ring with Mackenzie at the centre of it. Called COSTELLO. Run by a third intelligence agency nobody has ever heard of. And Vasya, still believing in the power of intelligence to change events, and make history. Still wanting to be heard by people in power.

Simon was too caught up with the amazing possibilities to notice the couple taking careful note as he bought a train ticket to Zurich airport.

Chapter 15

London

May 2022

Simon is only five minutes from the Heathrow Express when he sits down with Evie in a Lebanese cafe in Paddington to begin their research. The Costello Trust existed, administered by Cayman lawyers. That was easy enough to confirm. To learn any more he will probably have to organise a break-in at the office in Cayman, and even that would be unlikely to tell him very much. He had also tried to trace Mackenzie's movements on the specific date of Walter Pinsent's final journey. Early July 2006. Mackenzie had moved to Italy several years earlier. He was increasingly associated with the far-right Lega Nord, appearing at several of their conferences, speaking in fluent Italian with a Scottish accent. By scouring old Facebook posts, Simon confirms that there had been a Lega conference in Milan that week. Mackenzie would have had a cover reason for being in the city.

But it is Evie who strikes gold: on YouTube, with dodgy spelling and terrible sound quality, a video entitled *Il professor Pietro Macqensi si rivolge alla Lega*. It is a recording of a speech given by Mackenzie to the Lega's conference on the eighth of July 2006. It seems to be about the threat of the European Union to indigenous Christian culture and traditional values, although neither Evie nor Simon speak good Italian. Nor do they feel sufficiently inspired by the subject matter to persevere to the end of the video.

Simon's excitement is palpable. It is Evie who brings him back to earth.

'Si, this project isn't really anything to do with Sidorov any more, is it?'

'Sidorov? Well, it seems to go a lot further than him. This might be bigger than just that one guy.'

'Except that we're being paid to look at Sidorov. The exam question is whether Sidorov was financially connected to Mackenzie. As far as we can tell, he wasn't. And we haven't managed to figure out about Flood 19. What are we planning to tell O'Brien at our next meeting?'

This is deflating, but entirely correct.

—

Simon and Evie went to their briefing with O'Brien with some trepidation. They had dug deep and found no evidence of a lasting financial relationship between Sidorov and Mackenzie. Why would the 'project office' feel the need to pay for more? That meant the end of Simon and Evie's lucrative commission.

'So, what we're seeing,' says O'Brien, in his best chairman-summary voice, 'is no linkage: Sidorov was not, as far as this intelligence goes, in a sustained and direct financial relationship with Mackenzie.' There is a strange formality in O'Brien's language, even though the only people in the room with him are Simon, Evie and Kemi. As if he is speaking for the benefit of an invisible audience. O'Brien pauses, purses his lips and then turns towards Simon. 'Forgive me, Simon, but if I can offer some *feedback*, that's more or less what you told us last time. Just want to clarify what your new collection efforts have turned up?' O'Brien is all smiles, as he delivers this 'feedback'.

Simon cannot tell him about COSTELLO. 'Well, a lot of this is about what we know was *not* happening.' He chooses his words carefully. 'We have shown there was no *direct* contact between Sidorov and Mackenzie. I have this on excellent authority. Further, during Mackenzie's time in Italy there is no evidence of direct payments.'

'And Flood 19?' Kemi asks pointedly. 'What do you say about that?'

'I say,' replies Simon, grappling for the right formulation, 'that Sidorov's bank may well have made payments that were ultimately on behalf of some kind of Russian government entity to Flood 19. But that is about Mackenzie, not Sidorov.' Simon throws out a scrap of bait. 'Unless you're actually investigating Mackenzie, I can't really see why this should matter.'

Do Kemi and O'Brien exchange a glance? Simon is sure that some wordless message has passed between them.

'Exactly,' says O'Brien, almost too forcefully. 'As you say, this only matters if we're focused on Mackenzie, which we aren't. But I think, for *completeness'* sake, it would be good to have a, er, summary of your findings there.'

'Of course,' promises Simon. 'We'll get something to you by the middle of next week.'

They have five days.

–

'What are you going to tell them?' asks Evie, as they sit in a pub, debriefing over mid-afternoon pints.

'We can't mention COSTELLO. I need to get that to the Pole. But they don't seem to want to talk to me.'

'Surely we need to find out about the others? The basic concept is that Mackenzie is the talent-spotter, isn't he? Who did he spot? I mean, you were *there*, Si? Did he spot you?'

Simon feels a flash of anxiety. 'No, not me. I mean, I don't think I was his type. I wasn't in his *orbit*.'

He is sure that he sounds unconvincing, but Evie seems to take it at face value. 'But others? It's a network, right? Who's in the network? Who was Mackenzie favouring, helping? You must have had contemporaries that were relying on Mackenzie for introductions, opportunities, all that.'

Simon wants to answer, but something stops him from saying the name. It's not that he has any desire to protect or deflect attention. It's the enormity of it. A man who has the ear of the prime minister. An influential donor. Someone who is on the inside, a man who wants to transform government, reduce the bureaucracy that gets in the way of his hedge funds. Who, it is reported, is increasingly taking an interest in the activities of the armed forces, the intelligence services.

It's too much to think about. So he doesn't.

'What we need to remember, Evie, is no system is completely secure. They did a pretty good job with their COSTELLO organisation, but they still had to rely on regular structures from time to time.'

She gives him a quizzical look.

'Put it this way: Sidorov has to make a trip from the embassy up to Oxford every term to service the link with Mackenzie, even if he had no direct role in COSTELLO. There must be other stuff like this, where the regular SVR guys get involved, even if they don't know the ultimate purpose.'

'So what you're saying, Si, is *all* we need to do is get intel on the SVR. That should be nice and straightforward.'

Simon can see her point.

—

Later that evening, Simon is sitting at home, drinking a little bit too much red wine and watching the news. He does this whilst doom scrolling Twitter and trying to figure out if someone who seemed to be enjoying looking at Evie in the pub garden earlier on was a surveillant or a bloke who enjoyed looking at an attractive young woman. Or both.

The phone rang, interrupting Simon's Twitter screen. It is Evie.

'We need to go to Prague.'

'Huh? Why?'

'Because, Si, there's a guy there who helped with Skripal, who might be able to help us.'

Evie is part of a group of 'Open-Source Intelligence' – *OSINT* – activists. This bunch of youngsters glued to their laptops had identified the assassins who had poisoned Sergei Skripal, a Russian defector living in the UK. A loosely organised collective had done what MI5 and the CIA had been unable to, ferreting deep secrets of the Russian state from social media websites.

'What's Skripal got to do with this?' asks Simon, sceptically.

'Nothing. But you know how it is: we do these big OSINT projects but sometimes we need actual sources. I mean your type of sources. People on the inside. A lot of this stuff isn't online. It's stuff we can get because someone is giving it to us.'

'But who is "we" here?' Simon has never quite managed to get his head around this world.

'That's the thing: we – I'm including myself – we are a collective. This is crowd-sourced. "*We*" can be almost anyone.' It is so far from Simon's experience, where intelligence operations are run by small, tightly organised teams whose members are carefully vetted. 'But there are one or two people who have access to special things that were necessary for the investigation. Like immigration data.'

'Okay, that makes sense. And who's this guy in Prague?'

'Name's Rudi von Pannwitz. He seems to be good at getting information from corrupt Russian officials.'

Chapter 16

Prague
May 2022

A familiar face?

Simon, as ever, is on the lookout. As the sun dips below Prague's gothic skyline, he's trying to work out if he spotted the young man earlier: tight jeans, 1980s style. The rest of the outfit has changed, but those skin-tights are probably too hard to pull off in a hurry.

At the station there are Ukrainian refugees standing in a defensive huddle, surrounded by piles of bulging bags, dark circles of exhaustion around their eyes. Some of the children still have the energy to cry, but most of them, and all of the adults, stare listlessly at the Brutalist architecture. Simon feels he has to look away.

The city has fewer tourists than usual. There are still visitors in the Old Town Square and the narrow streets leading down to the Charles Bridge, but the crowds that usually leave the visitor standing still, as if in a queue, are absent. The Mandarin Oriental appears pathetically grateful for the presence of two business travellers, even if they are in standard rooms without any extras. Simon is pathetically grateful for the fact that he has been able to call up O'Brien, who agreed to charge the whole trip to his mysterious foundation office.

Pannwitz has agreed to a meeting, at his home, 'after dinner'. Evie is in charge.

'Leave this with me,' she says, as they warm up with a drink in the hotel lobby. 'We've never met in person, but I've interacted with him lots online. He's a bit of an oddball, but fine. I know what we need.' Evie has none of Simon's weary caution: she seems to be floating on a cushion of excitement and enthusiasm, which serves only to make Simon more nervous.

Pannwitz lives in a garret in the maze of streets beneath the castle. Evie had explained that his family was engaged in a protracted lawsuit against the Czech government for the restitution of the ancient land-holdings of the Von Pannwitz dynasty. If successful, most of the district they are walking through will become theirs, as well as a few thousand acres of Czech countryside. For the moment, they own only a grey stone building around a courtyard behind the Albanian Embassy, most of which is let out as apartments. Simon and Evie approach through a small wooden door set into a larger gate that looks as though it hasn't opened in decades. Inside, tall facades loom over a cobbled courtyard, poorly lit by lantern lamps that hang on the wall. The whole thing has been added, accreted and squeezed together over hundreds of years. In the gloom, Simon can make out windows of different sizes and styles appearing at random intervals. There are lights on in some of them, others are dark, shutters closed. External stone stairways lead to assorted corners of the building. As Simon cranes his neck up towards the twilight of a summer evening he can see balconies and galleries. A hopeful cat purrs, rubbing itself against his legs.

Evie is energised by the atmospheric setting. 'Rudi said the stairway opposite the entrance, up to the top floor.' She walks ahead, confident and excited, bounding up the uneven stone steps, her shoulders bare in a floral summer dress. Prague is hot, even after nine at night.

As they climb upwards, Simon thinks he sees a shadow, a presence, no more, moving at one of the dark windows. He pauses, letting Evie go several steps ahead of him and turns round, pretending to be taking in the surroundings. There's nothing. He's just a middle-aged spy who's scared of the dark.

They reach the top floor, panting slightly, and a sturdy, ancient door studded with black bolts. Evie looks at Simon, grins with girlish excitement and bangs a black ring knocker that sits on a cast-iron lion's head. The door opens, but thanks to the dark outside, Simon can only make out the backlit shape of a head. It belongs to a tall figure, slim, not powerful.

'Evie? Mr Sharman?' It's a Germanic voice, plummy. 'Please do come in.' He sounds courteous, ingratiating even.

He turns, and Simon can now see, fully lit, an aquiline nose under a shock of brown hair. He's probably in his late forties, and well dressed for an informal meeting on a summer night: smart shirt, brightly coloured trousers, brown suede brogues, sockless. It's the euro-aristo look that would fit anywhere from Aarhus to Zug. Rudi leads them down a long corridor painted a bold, deep scarlet. Much of this wall is covered with ancestral portraits in heavy gilt frames, antique prints of Bohemian hunting lodges and maps of kingdoms lost to history.

They reach a library that opens into a vaulted ceiling under the eaves of the building. The walls are lined with tall bookshelves filled with rows of handsome, leather-bound volumes that Simon suspects are little read. The real focus is in the middle of the room. On a large table are various powerful-looking computers and several screens. The office chair in front of it is like a throne. But Rudi leads them to another corner, where three armchairs are arranged around a drinks table. Out of the small windows Simon can see floodlit rooftops and distant spires.

'Whisky? Cognac? Please, make yourselves comfortable.' Rudi has a strange formality, as if he's stepped out of a period drama. 'I'm going to have some *slivovice*; it is made from the plums on our family property. Perhaps Evie has told you,' Rudi says, turning towards Simon, 'I am in a protracted, ah, *negotiation* with the Czech government. But we still have a few little orchards.' He pours three small shot-type glasses and hands one each to Evie and Simon, before sitting in a chair and gesturing them to do likewise.

Rudi smiles at Evie. 'So, Evie, such a pleasure to meet finally in person. It's been a good few days, with the Transnistria work, no?' In her spare time, Evie has been working with a loose international collective of open-source researchers to uncover a network of GRU agents in Moldova.

'Hasn't it just, Rudi? And thanks for seeing us. Really grateful.'

'My pleasure. And Simon –' he flashes a smile '– I've always respected the English gentleman spies. You are both most welcome. What can I do to make your journey to Prague worthwhile?' He reaches for his glass and sips the *slivovice*. Simon feels the obligation to follow suit. He braces for fire-water and is pleasantly surprised by the warm, fruity flavour, something between Cognac, Scotch and Oloroso sherry. He feels the alcohol surge to the head almost instantly.

Evie has also taken a sip. More of a gulp, actually, which appears to have made her eyes water slightly. She starts talking. There's a hint of nervousness in her voice, but also intensity.

'Okay, we might as well jump straight in. In the Moldova thing we managed a lot because of your sources. Movements of Russian officials at certain times, stuff about different GRU units. I know you've got access to things.' She pauses. Rudi is smiling, inscrutably. 'We're working on something, Simon and me. Simon and I. And I've had an idea, where I think you could help.' She pauses again, flustered by her grammatical slip. 'Meeting records. Did certain SVR officers meet certain people at a certain time? I know that any meeting that took place would be logged, for security reasons. A contact note would be filed, that sort of thing.'

'I have never managed to get access to the contact reports, if that's what you want,' says Rudi.

'No, not the reports. Just logs of meetings. My understanding is that on every SVR officer's file there's a log of all foreign contacts. It's part of their counter-intelligence system, isn't it?'

'That's true.' Rudi pauses. 'I might have access. It depends on the years, countries and so on. When we get these data dumps, they can be annoyingly incomplete. As you know, my focus was primarily Europe. I am unlikely to have much from officers that worked in Asia or Africa.'

Simon has been watching, learning. At one level he is amazed: a random Teutonic aristocrat appears to have access to more intelligence on Russia than most Western intelligence agencies. But his intelligence officer antennae are twitching violently. Who is this guy? Why and how does he have this stuff? Has Evie really understood what she's getting into here?

Simon clears his throat apologetically. 'I'm really sorry to jump in here, guys, but can we, just for my benefit, of course, sort of clarify where everyone's coming from? I mean, Evie and I are looking at possible Russian espionage activity in the UK. That's our interest. But what's your story, Rudi? How do you come to be in this game?'

Rudi looks at Evie, smiles, and looks back at Simon, with a slight frown. Simon notices that his forehead is very high, as if he has more brain in there than most people.

'Simon, my story is about family history. One branch of my family was here in Prague. Another was further east, in the German-Polish borderlands. Am I allowed to call it Prussia? My grand-uncle led a force of anti-communist Cossacks that fought against Stalin. At the end of the war, even though he had surrendered to the British, Count von Pannwitz was handed over by your people to the Russians, sent to Moscow and executed. About fifty thousand Cossacks who had fought against Stalinist Russia were also handed over and sent to the gulag. Most died, of course. But among those that survived the gulag, some were rehabilitated after Stalin's death, and some even ended up with the KGB. These people revered their general, Von Pannwitz. We have kept these networks alive.'

Rudi stops talking. Outside, Prague's hundreds of churches are striking ten o'clock. A medley of bells.

Simon realises he knows what Rudi is talking about. 'These people were fighting for the Nazis, weren't they?'

'That's easy for you to say,' objects Rudi, unhappy at the reference. 'I would say they were fighting to be free from Russian imperialism. Rather like the Ukrainians, and the Russians call them Nazis, too. As for my grand-uncle, he was a German Army officer. And here's the thing. On your little island, you British seem to think you weren't invaded in the war because you were superior, braver, more principled. Has it ever occurred to you what would have happened if Hitler had launched Operation Sea Lion? If Britain had fallen? Would there have been collaborators? A British division of the Waffen–SS, perhaps? English aristocrats in the Gestapo? What do you really think? I mean, I know you're *now* doing your Brexit because you are superior to the rest of us. You don't need us, you keep saying. You won the war, you keep reminding us.

'So, yes, my ancestor led a force of Cossacks that fought against Stalin's Russia. And if your family had lived in the same lands for generations, but those lands changed rulers every few decades depending on who won the last war, you would see these things differently. Perhaps your idea of nationalism wouldn't be quite so clear-cut if you had experienced this? Something I've noticed about the British: you all have very strong opinions about history, which is something you read about in books. Here on the Continent, history is something that happened to us.' His voice has risen in frustration.

'I'm sorry. I'm not here to judge you or your family. We're all on the same side here.' Simon feels stupid for having led the conversation in an awkward direction. It is clear that Evie is also pissed off.

'Rudi,' she volunteers. 'Simon and I think we might be about to crack open quite an important Russian operation. We're not here to talk history. We just want help with that, if you can. SVR stuff. That's all.' She empties her glass and holds it out to Rudi, smiling. 'This stuff is brilliant. Got any more?'

Whether it was Evie's charming candour or Simon's apology, Rudi mirrors Evie's smile and tops up all three glasses.

'Meeting logs,' Evie continues, taking another gulp. 'What we are really looking for are the logs for Georgy Sidorov, during his SVR posting in London. Early nineties.'

'Sidorov? Like, the MMB guy?' Rudi knows exactly who he was. 'It's possible that we can get something on that. There was a backup drive that one of my people managed to get a hold of. You know how it is in Russia today: everything is for sale. You just have to know who to ask. That's where I come in. I managed to get terrabytes of admin data from the Russian foreign office. A lot of it is meaningless, unusable. But some files can be extracted. Things that seem rather uninteresting on the face of it, barely sensitive at all, can turn out to be rather revealing. Embassy visitor logs, for example.'

With rising admiration Simon has started to realise what Evie's game is.

'So, how does this work?' asks Evie. 'Can you send us something?'

Rudi laughs dismissively. 'Evie, the only way this works is that you leave here tonight with a data stick. We can never communicate about this stuff. Not on any platform – even the secure ones, Signal, Threema, doesn't matter. Don't trust them. I just have to do a data sort on one of my spreadsheets and save that for you. That's how it works.'

To Simon, this sounds too easy. Too good to be true? 'Rudi, can we pay you for your time? Or research costs?'

'Simon, I have spent thousands of hours working on this stuff. I doubt you can pay for that. What you can do is assure me that none of this will reach the British government.'

Simon has not expected this stipulation. It isn't a particularly onerous restriction. Except that Simon has already decided that the Pole need to know. Because he, an outsider that many of his former colleagues don't take particularly seriously, is about to blow open the biggest secret in Russian espionage since the unmasking of George Blake as a KGB agent.

'Why would that be, Rudi? I mean, I'm not here to defend any of those people. But on the Russia stuff, we're all on the same team, right?'

'Spoken like a true bureaucrat.' Simon feels his hackles rising at Rudi's dismissive tone. 'You see, Simon, you probably think that the world of government human–intelligence operations is similar to my world. You build up relationships with sources, *personal* relationships, create an alignment of interests where they want to give you the intelligence that you need. Isn't that your game?'

'Well, something like that,' Simon answers, unsure where Rudi is taking him.

'Yes, *but*. In your world it's actually a myth: you create these fake friendships but you are working for an institution. You are instrumentalising relationships on Her Majesty's Secret Service. The person thinks that you are their great friend, the one person that really gets them. But it's just another betrayal in lives that have been full of them. At any point your precious agent can be traded away by a politician who needs a diplomatic deal, or by an analyst who decides he doesn't like the intel he's reading any more. Or by an army that has an alliance to maintain.' He pauses, and looks at a portrait hanging on the wall of a military man in Cossack uniform. Count Helmuth von Pannwitz.

'My work is actually based on human relationships. *Real* human relationships, between *real* people. Actual friends. Not some sordid fake arranged by an intelligence agency. The people I am dealing with have been fighting Stalinism and its nasty little successor, *Putain*, for generations.' He deliberately mispronounces the Russian president's name. 'I actually care about these people on a personal level. These people are not "assets". That is why I don't deal with governments.'

'Okay,' says Simon, chastened. 'I'm not saying I agree, but you've made yourself clear.' Simon's immediate thought is: *fuck him, how will he know?*

'And if you're thinking, "fuck him, how will he know?" I can assure you I will.'

Simon gulps at his *slivovice*.

Evie steps in. 'Rudi, Simon here is ex. *Very* ex, I'd say. I have never been in government. There really isn't anything to worry about there. We're doing this because the government can't or won't. Or both.' She has leaned forwards and is looking at Rudi pleadingly, idly toying with her empty glass. There's a pause when nobody says anything for a bit too long. And then Rudi stands up and walks towards his computer table. There are hums and whirs as the machines come to life, multiple screens lighting up with new information. Simon and Evie sit awkwardly, waiting whilst Rudi's fingers flash across the keyboard. A few minutes later he walks back over to them, holding a USB stick, which he hands to Evie.

'It's a text document, no metadata, but it'll be self-explanatory.'

Evie turns it over in her hands and then puts it in her handbag. She turns to Rudi and throws her arms round him. He looks surprised and delighted in equal measure. She steps back and turns to Simon, smiling. 'Gentlemen, I think we should drink a toast. To the Cossacks!' Rudi obliges with a refill and they knock back their glasses. As they are all on their feet it is easier for Simon to move as if to depart. He is uneasy about Rudi.

'We've taken too much of your time,' observes Simon. 'And it's been a pretty long day for us.' He ushers the tipsy Evie out of the room and back down the corridor. As they turn to make their farewell, Simon's eyes lock with Rudi's. A wordless exchange. They are challenging, and questioning, one another.

Simon thrusts out his hand. 'Rudi, great pleasure. We must do this again.'

Evie leans forwards and kisses him on both cheeks. And they are back outside on the stairs.

Simon is alert, watching windows for any sign of movement. He sees nothing. But he feels. His spine is tingling. Maybe it's just the *slivovice*.

They walk down narrow, ill-lit cobbled streets. It is nearly midnight and mostly deserted. But there are still dark figures moving around: revellers returning home, tourists with jet-lag, common-or-garden night owls. All possibles, but he can't see a team. He doesn't think there's a follower.

They pass an inviting cellar bar.

'Nightcap, Si? I think we might have things to celebrate!' Evie is happy, even ecstatic. Inside, it's nearly empty, although the music is still at high volume. A few drunken couples are trying to work out if they are going to have sex. But it's late, so if they're still in the bar, it's probably not going to happen. Evie asks for a Scotch and soda. Simon likes that she drinks 'proper' drinks. After all the *slivovice*, Simon is thirsty and orders a large Staropramen, gulping down the cool lager. Evie sips her Scotch slowly, shaking the ice-cubes around the glass. Simon orders a second beer, but he's forced to wait as the barman has stepped away to make a call.

'I think I have some catching up to do,' says Simon. He's sure Evie has done something rather brilliant, but he's not exactly clear what.

Evie is smiling, sitting opposite him on a small corner table. Her eyes are wide in the dimly lit bar. 'Yes, Simon. I'm sorry. I didn't want to say too much before, in case we didn't get anywhere.'

'Have we got anywhere?'

'Okay,' says Evie, sounding more serious and not even slightly tipsy. 'Let me start at the beginning. Mackenzie. He's a talent-spotter, right? His job is to identify suitable candidates who are then passed on to someone else in the COSTELLO system to be run as agents of Russia. But Mackenzie, well, from everything you've said and everything I've read, he's a pretty erratic guy. I mean, could easily nominate someone because he's shitfaced, or because he likes the look of him, or because the person's dad is a Tory bigwig. So they'd need a kind of quality control, before taking the risk of them actually meeting the COSTELLO people, wouldn't they?'

'Yes, that makes sense.'

'Right. So, you have to assume Mackenzie sends them to someone for a once-over. We already know that Sidorov is involved. And he has cover in terms of his attendance at the Oxford Diplomatic Forum.'

'Yes,' says Simon, 'carry on.'

'So here's the hypothesis: Mackenzie talent-spots, sends them to Sidorov, who has a "cultural-academic" cover job at the embassy and therefore a reason to be meeting Oxford types with an interest in Russia. So –' and now Evie is grinning, leaning excitedly towards Simon across the table '– now that we have meeting logs, we check through to see if anyone going to meet Sidorov was a contact of Mackenzie. And we start to find the COSTELLO ring.'

Suddenly, Simon wants to cheer in sheer delight. The stress and ambiguity of the past few hours have subsided. He can feel as happy as Evie. He stops caring whether they're being followed – it's just the old paranoia of his trade. They never are. Evie leans towards him to make a certain point, but he gets in first.

'That's fantastic, Evie. Bloody hell. So good. I can't tell you how impressed I am.' The second beer on a stomach full of *slivovice* leaves Simon feeling suddenly elated, maybe giddy.

Evie has folded her arms on the table and laid her head on them, sideways. She looks tired, but happy. They talk more, but not about Mackenzie, or Rudi. About Evie's childhood with a Russian mother in England, trips to visit relatives in Krasnoyarsk, swimming in Lake Baikal. Simon finds himself reminiscing about his Oxford days. But these are carefully edited memories: neither Mackenzie nor Sarah du Cane are mentioned. They have one for the road and the conversation descends into 'top five songs', 'top five films' and other trivia. They both seem to find lots of things to laugh about. Simon notices there is only one other couple in the bar, silent, looking bored with one another, checking their phones. Simon feels a bit like he's on a date that's going well, although he can't really remember what those are like. But he knows that he and Evie aren't attracted to one another, and that makes it better. They are just two people who are on the verge of the greatest intelligence coup of their era.

They get up to leave. They walk in silence to the hotel, both happily submerged in their own thoughts. Outside the gateway they pause. Simon can feel his phone buzzing in his pocket, which is a surprise as it's a burner and nobody is supposed to know he's in Prague. He pulls it out with an apologetic look to Evie, turning away from her, as if embarrassed by the intrusion.

In his peripheral vision, Simon can see a shadow of Evie, swaying slightly with the alcohol, wandering down a narrow street by the side of the hotel. He is feeling slightly annoyed as he wonders whether to take the call from an unknown number. Probably just junk, so he ignores it, turning back to follow Evie.

As he does so, something clicks. A momentary glimpse of a face he has seen already that evening. Simon knows that he has drunk too much and feels a rush of vertigo. He's trying to take in too many bits of information at once and he seems to be processing everything too slowly. *Weird phone call. Evie drunk, probably needs taking care of. A face he has seen already. Surveillance. Who is following? Which side are they from?*

The face belongs to one of a tourist couple. Simon realises they are both familiar: they were in the bar bored, checking their phones. Now they are turning away, apparently changing direction just as he spots them. Simon has a flashback to the barman making him wait for his drink while he made a phone-call. Things are coming into place. Simon turns back towards Evie and he can see her back disappearing down the dark street. He follows. Should he call out to her? He thinks not: she's drunker than he is and might need a little space. He will keep a respectful distance. But he will make sure she's safe.

Evie has reached a junction. She's standing under a streetlamp and Simon has a clear view of her back, maybe fifty metres ahead of him. Simon can't see any followers and he begins to wonder if he's got in a muddle again. Maybe the couple in the bar were just heading back to their hotel?

Evie is looking up and down the street, as if unsure what to do. Then she starts to cross the road junction. It is quiet. Suddenly there is a screech of tyres, an engine screaming in low gear. A car appears from the left, slamming into Evie. Her body is tossed upwards. Everything slows down: Simon watches her arms flail uselessly as if she's swimming through the air. Then her body slams down on the ground. The car reverses, smashing her prone body with a sickening crunch, before swinging forwards again in a sharp turn. The headlights are now pointing at Simon, blindingly.

The engine is screaming as the car speeds towards him. The street is narrow: just a car's width and no pavement. Simon has nowhere to go. He feels surprisingly calm. He can see tyres, the specific shape of the headlights: modern LED-type. He wonders what make it is. As a boy he knew all the makes.

The car is on him now. Breathe out.

Chapter 17

Prague
May 2022

He feels his legs being jerked sideways, falling. His shoulder bangs painfully on some kind of brick ledge. He has landed on top of someone. It's dark, and cool. He's in a kind of cellar. The stars in his eyes clear and he sees a coal hatch leading to the street above, the scream of a speeding car ringing in his ears. A dark figure slams the hatch shut.

A light has been switched on. It's a bare bulb hanging in the ceiling of a cellar, directly above Simon's head. His eyes adjust to the reality of what's happening: he's not dead, his shoulder hurts and he's lying on the floor of a cellar, staring at a lightbulb which is hurting his eyes. Simon turns his head and sees three people: two of them are the couple from the bar. The third is Rudi von Pannwitz, who kneels down and offers a hand to Simon, pulling him back onto his feet.

Rudi looks deadly serious. 'That was too close. I didn't think we'd be able to get you in time.' He pauses, looks away, and then turns back to Simon. 'I'm so sorry about Evie, we were too late for her.'

Evie. Later, Simon recalls that he simply denied the possibility of what he had witnessed moments earlier. But in that moment, he has no consciousness of his surroundings or what he is doing. He hears Rudi say, 'Yes, I am afraid so,' so he must have said something before that. Perhaps it was Rudi's reply that caused him to believe what he was hearing. At that point he slumps against a wall, both hands clutching his throbbing head.

And then he is sick on the floor.

This shocks everyone into action. Pavel and Alena, the couple from the bar, show him to a dank toilet in the complex of cellars where he tries to clean himself up with his head over the sink. Rudi reappears whilst he is doing this.

'Simon, we have to move. They'll figure out where we are pretty quickly.'

Simon has only just managed to piece together the preceding minutes. The car would have hit him if he hadn't been pulled down off the street into a coal chute by Pavel. He is feeling despair and rising fury with himself: he had spotted surveillance. In his trade that meant one thing: you abort the meeting. But he had ignored it because he had allowed himself to be caught up in the excitement and wanting it to go well for Evie.

Evie.

He can't stop thinking of the awful sight of her body spinning through the air.

'Simon?' Rudi is shaking his shoulder as he leans over the sink. 'We need to go, *now!*'

Rudi leads the four of them into a long dark corridor. A flight of stairs is visible at one end, dimly illuminated. Pavel is carrying a CZ 75, a Czech handgun. There is the bang of a door being forced open and a flood of light being thrown onto the stairs. Footsteps pound down the staircase and Simon sees several pairs of legs descending, their features opaque from the backlighting. Rudi spins round, frantically signalling with his hand. They turn and run away from the stairs into the darkness of the unlit corridor. Simon can't see where he's going, he's just running blindly, aware of dim shapes ahead of him. Rudi shoves a door to the left with his shoulder. As Simon follows, a shot rings out from behind. There is the familiar whooshing sound of a 9mm bullet whistling past his ear. Pavel, just behind Simon, turns and lets off a well-aimed shot down the corridor. One of the dark figures cries out, falling to the ground. With a well-drilled roll, Pavel joins them in the side room, slamming the door and throwing a bolt.

Instinctively, he and Simon start dragging items of furniture and old trunks, barricading the door with them. Rudi and Alena are crouched on the ground, fiddling with some kind of manhole cover. There's a creaking sound as they pull it open and a waft of watery stench.

'Go, *go*, GO!' shouts Pavel as Alena jumps down the hatch. He hears a slight crunch, indicating a short drop. Rudi follows. Suddenly there is sharp crack and a bullet-hole appears at head-height in the door. Simon and Pavel drop to their stomachs and roll to the side. Two more cracks follow and holes appear at a similar height. Then the pounding. With each crash, the door and its barricade shift.

Simon rolls over to the hatch and lowers himself down, bracing for a drop, but he is basically just stepping into a grimy, foul-smelling puddle. Simon can hear the pounding on the door continue, as well as more gunshots. Pavel appears to have fired back again and follows directly, pulling the cast-iron cover back into place with one hand, his CZ 75 pointing upwards in the other. Rudi pulls out his phone to use the flashlight and sets off at a jog. They are in a large brick drainage tunnel. There are puddles of effluent water in the base, but it does not appear to be in current use. As they run, the tunnel curves and Simon can see an opening, a change of tone in the darkness. With a surge of relief, Simon realises this is the outflow into the Vltava. They reach the opening and stand on a stone ledge just above the fast-flowing water. Across the river, Simon can see the lights of Prague on a summer night, taxis and trams moving along, everything normal.

Pavel, bringing up the rear, holds up his hand. They wait and Simon can hear four exhausted adults panting for breath. After what feels like an eternity, but is probably half a minute, Pavel announces, 'They're not coming.'

'Who were they?' asks Simon.

'Chechens,' says Alena, as if it is the most obvious thing in the world.

Simon sighs, and turns to Rudi. 'How did you know your way around there?' he asks, gesturing back into the tunnel.

'When you have spent the last decade in a protracted legal battle to regain your property rights, you spend a lot of time looking at maps, plans and all that.' He pauses. 'Come on, let's get out of here.' They walk along a stone quay until they reach a rusty ladder that is bolted to the wall of the riverbank.

Rudi has climbed first and is gesturing to the others. Simon reaches up to the ladder with a shaking hand. He reaches the parapet and pulls himself over. He's standing in a sort of park but all he can think about is Evie. Rudi motions them towards a bench and the two of them sit. Pavel says, 'I'll get the car,' and he sets off at a jogging pace. Alena heads off in a different direction.

Simon puts his head in his hands. 'Fuck. Tell me what I need to know, Rudi.'

'Basically, two things were on my mind this evening: one was meeting you guys earlier. The other was that one of my sources in Moscow told me a Chechen hit squad was in town.'

'Never a good sign,' says Simon, grimly familiar with the use of Chechen gangsters by Russian intelligence to carry out their dirty work.

'Damn it!' Rudi is suddenly furious, slamming a fist against his leg in frustration. 'The thing I failed at was to connect the two things. The Chechens were here for you guys. I didn't see that.'

Simon's head is still in his hands. He feels an emptiness and deep guilt about Evie. When he speaks it is in a low, miserable voice. 'It was my fault,' he says. 'I *felt* surveillance. I should have aborted our meeting. Gone back to the hotel. They probably wouldn't have come for us there.' Simon takes a deep breath and then stands up. 'Okay. We've gotta go now.'

'Yes, Pavel is bringing a car.'

'Evie. I have to deal with her body.' As he says the last word his voice cracks.

Rudi puts his hand on Simon's arm. 'Simon,' he says, 'you have to think about this very carefully. Moscow Centre sent a hit squad here for you guys. As you know very well, the Russians have a major presence here in Prague. And they also have plenty of police, judges, politicians on their payroll. The moment you go to a police station you won't come out.'

'What are we going to do about Evie?'

'Alena is sorting it out. She has good contacts and will make sure the British Embassy are on the case. We have to get you out of the country, fast. Do you have your passport on you? Phone? Wallet?' Simon nods. In a lifetime as a fieldman he never went anywhere without a passport, even if it had often not been a passport in his real name.

They walk to the edge of the park, avoiding the straggling tourists that have yet to go home. By the kerb in a side street is a large, dark Škoda saloon. The headlights are off but the powerful engine is purring in anticipation. Pavel climbs out from the driver's door and opens the boot. He looks apologetically at Simon.

'At least it's spacious,' says Rudi. And there are a couple of blankets and some water.

Simon thinks to himself – there are two options here: the first is that these guys are part of an elaborate plot to kidnap me after killing Evie. Or, these guys have just saved my life because they have devoted their lives to fighting Stalinism and its modern variants. And whichever it is, he realises he has run out of energy to do anything about it. So he climbs into the boot, curls into a foetal position and shuts his eyes, hoping the world will disappear.

–

Simon is in a house by a lake. He is sure he recognises the surroundings although there is nothing familiar about them. The room is bright: white walls and sunlight streaming in. The furniture is also white. The brightness is almost a strain to the eyes.

Evie is lying on a white chaise longue, sleeping. Behind her head the sun glistens on the water of the lake. Simon wonders if he is in Sweden.

Evie is trying to say something but Simon can't hear her over a resonant banging sound, a bit like a gong. He's sure that she is trying to explain something very important but her voice is inaudible. The banging seems to have been going on for hours, ruining this important moment.

—.

Bang. *Bang*. BANG. Firm knuckles are tapping on the boot of the car.

'*Hallo!*'

Simon wakes suddenly, ripped from his dream. Bright light is streaming into his eyes as the boot opens. He has a pounding headache and can only make out two dark shapes. Momentarily, he can't remember where he is, or why. Then it floods back, with a sinking feeling: Evie is dead, and he is on the run.

'Just a moment,' he calls out, but his voice isn't working. He clears his throat and tries again: 'Hi, guys.' Croaky, but audible. His eyes are starting to be able to make out the shapes looming over him in the early morning light. It is Rudi and Pavel, looking solicitous. Pavel's powerful forearm reaches down and helps Simon out. He shakes his head and blinks, realising that he is in a layby truck stop. There is a dowdy-looking cafe that has not been altered since the 1970s, a row of spherical orange lampshades visible in the window. From the road signs, Simon guesses he is in Germany or Austria.

'You need breakfast,' declares Rudi, setting off towards the cafe without waiting for an answer. Pavel grins and follows. Simon, unsteady on cramped legs, totters after them. The only other customers are a few long-distance lorry drivers. They sit in a discreet booth and Simon's mouth waters at the smell of fresh bread and coffee. Soon he is stuffing a buttered roll into his mouth between gulps of coffee and orange juice.

'So, Simon, damage limitation. How did Moscow Centre know to send the Chechens?'

Vasya?

'I don't know,' he answers.

'We've had a few sources look at this,' Rudi continues.

Simon is still unsure what to make of him, or Pavel. In fact, he realises he doesn't even know where he is or what has happened, beyond the fact that Evie is dead. But the coffee is beginning to work, and the dehydration headache is morphing into a low, caffeinated buzz at the front of his skull. 'Okay,' says Simon with more energy in his voice. 'Let's start from the beginning. How much did Evie tell you about what we were doing?'

'Told me nothing, beyond investigation into Russian intelligence activity,' replies Rudi. 'I mean, aren't we all doing that?'

'Right. So we've been investigating a possible Russian intel agent ring in the UK. And we reckoned Sidorov had been involved in some way, back in the day. Our hypothesis was that Sidorov was screening potential candidates for recruitment. Hence wanting his meeting logs from the embassy. Which were on the USB in Evie's handbag.'

'I'm not too worried about that,' Rudi says. 'They were password protected. After four tries the files delete themselves.'

'But you never gave us the password,' notes Simon, momentarily annoyed.

Rudi smiles. 'I knew that you'd find out the docs were protected and then contact me. If I'd given you the password at the beginning you would have written it somewhere and had that scrap of paper, or disguised message, with you. Everyone does it.'

Rudi's phone beeps. He fiddles with it. 'We were definitely right to get you out,' he confirms. 'Czech police are searching for you. They haven't put out a European arrest warrant because they are trying to keep it low profile, for now.'

'You haven't actually told me where we are.'

'Ah yes, so rude of me,' replies Rudi, as if he's committed a social faux pas. 'We're near Frankfurt. The border police may have been looking for you. There was an unexpected check when we drove through – that border's usually completely unmanned. But I think two things got us through. Pavel, show him.' He turns to Pavel who is clearly a man of few words, and fewer English words. Pavel obliges by pulling up his left sleeve to show a tattoo, depicting the insignia of 601st Group, the Czech Special Forces unit. 'There's not many Czech police who'll stop a man with that tattoo,' smiles Rudi.

'What was the other thing?' asked Simon.

'They had a sniffer dog so I fed it one of my cookies. Stopped it from sniffing you in the trunk of the car. That could have been complicated.'

'Okay, so what do you think, Rudi, am I safe to fly out of Frankfurt?'

'I'm not sure. You might be a murder suspect. We have contacts. We can delay things for as long as possible. You probably have three days, no more.'

Simon is starting to think in straighter lines. Without Evie he can see only one option: he has to press on, whatever the risks. 'Okay, but I need the visitor logs again. How are we going to do that?'

'We'll make a second copy, do a brush contact in Frankfurt tomorrow. But is there more you can tell us about the case? What is it we're looking for?'

Simon hesitates. He can't work out whether Vasya has betrayed him or just been clumsy. Either way, the presence of the Chechens feels like pretty strong evidence that the Russian government is trying to protect one of its deepest secrets. He prefers to believe the latter. But it would be hard to question the loyalties of Rudi and Pavel, after all they had done.

'There was an academic based at Oxford, back in the early nineties, who was talent-spotting candidates, we think for recruitment by Moscow Centre, and sending them to Sidorov for vetting.'

'An Oxford spy ring? Like the Cambridge Five?' Rudi is suddenly animated, excited.

'Possibly.' Simon is still cautious, mistrustful even.

'The Oxford spy ring.' Rudi shakes his head in wonderment as he says it. 'Everyone is looking for it, and you think you've found it? That would be something.'

Simon has a flash of pride: this could be the intelligence coup of the century, and he's done it from outside the Pole. 'With the visitor logs and some other stuff we could figure out who the likely members were. But there's something else: you seem to have a handle on Russian citizens' movements. I'm guessing you have a source in Russian immigration.'

Rudi smiles. 'Perhaps. I can usually figure out when Russians leave or enter their country.'

'Okay. So what can you tell me about the movements of Valery Kleshnyov in July 2006? He was in Italy that month under the alias of Walter Pinsent, false flag using a St Kitts passport. But did he leave Russia in his Kleshnyov identity and switch it later? Or did he leave Russia as Mister Pinsent? Because I suspect there are some other St Kitts passports in the mix here.'

'Anything else?' Rudi is eagerly typing notes into his phone.

Simon shakes his head. He wants to mention COSTELLO, Flood 19 and the whole story, but he has realised he can only risk a small part of the whole tale. So much is at stake and he has to stay alive.

They agree the protocols for the upcoming brush contact.

Rudi and Pavel get up to leave. Before stepping out of the booth, Rudi grabs Simon's hand in both of his and says, with fierce feeling, 'Simon, I was proud to work with Evie. She has given her life for something vital.' Both their eyes are watering. Pavel says nothing, but the vice-like grip of his handshake says enough. And then they depart.

Simon stays at the table. He is now completely alone, a likely murder suspect on the run from a deadly adversary.

Chapter 18

Frankfurt

May 2022

Simon has no margin for error. He needs to plan every move knowing he can't afford a single mistake. His phone battery failed not long after they had exited the tunnel by the River Vltava, so he has no reason to fear that he is giving away his location, as long as he doesn't switch it back on. But if the resources of the Russian state are arrayed against him, they could hack CCTV cameras and use facial recognition software to search for a match on his face. The risk will be in public places, train stations, airports. Cameras in shops or private businesses are likely to be safe, simply because the Russians won't know which ones to hack.

And then there's the Pole. Since his curt dismissal by Devi from the bench in St James's Park, he had concluded that they too have had a team following him. Surely they would have known about the Chechens? They could easily have warned Simon, but had chosen not to. It's easier not to think about it.

The cafe is on the outskirts of Hanau, a satellite town of Frankfurt. Simon is in a liminal zone of industrial estates, car showrooms and supermarkets. His clothes, chosen for a business-travel jaunt to Prague, are now manky and unsuitable. His first stop is to a discount supermarket where he acquires a clean t-shirt, a hooded top and a baseball cap, paid for in cash. He also buys a new pair of shoes. He then walks to a local rail station and boards the first train heading roughly in the direction of Frankfurt. It's not important exactly where it's going: he has time to kill and wants to see if anyone changes carriages and platforms with him. After a couple of stops he gets off, crosses the rail line and rides in the opposite direction. He then switches back to his original trajectory.

Simon has to avoid the main stations, which have concourses lined with a web of surveillance cameras. He gets off at one of the outer stations of Frankfurt and walks a circuitous route into the centre of the city, frequently crossing streets, where playing the cautious pedestrian looking round for traffic affords an excellent opportunity to check for a surveillance team. He's heading for Frankfurt's notorious red-light district, clustered in the blocks east of the main railway station. Simon is not in the mood to sample the services on offer. But these streets are places where a monosyllabic single man who pays for a cheap hotel room in cash doesn't stand out. And the hoteliers don't make a habit of being helpful to inquisitive outsiders.

Few people would ever have described the Hotel Anna as perfect, but in this specific context it is. The grey-skinned receptionist is too bored to look at Simon's passport, merely asking him to fill in the registration slip himself, which Simon does in exquisite, fictitious detail. After paying his cash up front, he's handed a key, off which hangs a heavy, bulbous metal fob. It occurs to Simon, in a practical moment, that the fob could be a useful weapon. The receptionist grunts and indicates the lift with his thumb, before returning his diligent attention to the porn movie playing on his battered laptop. The lift is at the end of a passageway where the lino floor has scuffed and is torn in places. The faux-wood wallpaper is peeling and travel posters offer a different, wholesome Germany to the one being sought by the hotel's clientele. The lift is claustrophobic and, like the rest of the hotel, smells of cigarette smoke; something of an achievement in a country that outlawed indoor smoking years earlier. In another context, with a single bed pushed against a corner made up with a thin blanket on polyester sheets, Simon's bedroom could be called monastic. As there are large brothels in the two neighbouring buildings, this description doesn't quite match.

This part of Frankfurt is also the sort of place where internet cafes still exist, run by bored Turkish men and mostly used by lonely travellers researching sex workers and avoiding leaving an embarrassing trail on their phones. After checking into his room, Simon goes online to see whether he can find anything about Evie's death. There are no reports. The Czech police are still keeping it quiet. Satisfied that he is, for the moment at least, off the radar, he makes a reconnaissance of the brush contact to take place the following day.

It's a classic 'Moscow-rules' setup: no communications before, during or after, old-school safety signal, purely brush contact. Satisfied with the layout, Simon heads back to his hotel, all the while using elaborate routes that would have made the Cardross instructors proud. He wanders into a minimart and buys essential supplies: chewing gum, a six-pack of Weißbier and a tote bag to hold it all. He picks up a doner kebab on the way, and spends a restless afternoon wondering whether he is going to hear a violent banging on the door. After six bottles of beer, Simon drifts into a troubled sleep.

He spends a lot of the time thinking about Evie. If he hadn't been momentarily distracted, she would not have walked off alone. But would the car then have come for the two of them? These thoughts are occasionally interrupted by the rhythmic thud of a nearby nightclub and the too-loud television in the next-door room. Unsurprisingly, the walls in the Hotel Anna are the thinnest plasterboard.

–

Simon wakes, hungover and depressed. He knows that he has to get up and walk to the Grüneburgpark for the brush contact, but part of him just wants to lie in bed for the rest of the day, staring at the ceiling, where the peeling paint between two panels has become an object of obsessive fascination.

It is the thought of Evie that makes Simon haul himself out of bed and drink disgusting tea made with a little hotel kettle on his bedside table. Not for the first time he wonders if Sir Thomas Lipton was a real person and what he made of terrible tea being named after him. Then he sets off.

His route is a textbook anti-surveillance trail, using the contrast between crowded and quiet areas to force out followers. He walks past large plate-glass shopfronts, using the natural mirror to check who's behind. He cuts through alleyways where any single tail would instantly be suspect. And he judges that he is clean. There are plenty of possibles: the Turkish-looking man with the vacant stare who Simon sees twice, the second time talking into his phone. Could easily be a Russian, maybe from the North Caucasus. There's a guy who appears to follow him round three corners in the middle of the city, but he's far too tall. Surveillants have to look like everyman, forgettable. There are mothers with children, but you can always rule them out: fantastic cover, but children are too unpredictable to be used operationally, even unwittingly. Younger women on their own fit the profile. There's one that makes Simon pause, so he doubles back, acting like someone who's just remembered to go into a shop fifty metres back, to see if she will change direction with him. She doesn't, instead marching grimly onwards, her large bottom inside a tracksuit bouncing out of view. And then there are the Ukrainian refugees. Waiting for nothing, listlessly, their lives upended, their futures now uncertain. He wonders whether he should be cautious around them, but concludes that those made homeless by Russia's invasion are unlikely to be Russian agents.

As he passes through Frankfurt's financial district, the profiles change. He's now looking for young men in suits, but not the really smart ones. The surveillants will be guys dressed *as* bankers. But they can't actually afford to dress *like* bankers. Another possible: male, twenties, slicked-back hair, aviator sunglasses. Probably too good-looking to be working for the Russian intelligence services. But Simon isn't taking chances, so he boards a tram for a few stops to shake him off.

Finally, he reaches the Grüneburgpark, a large splash of *rus in urbe*, full of quiet meadows and wooded glades.

The plan for the contact is simple. He will walk through to a quiet, shady area where there is a mossy bench that sees little traffic. As there is no surveillance spotted en route, he leaves the safety signal, telling the contact to make the brush-past.

He is walking and chewing gum: he takes the blob out of his mouth and presses it onto the top of a litter bin, like a nipple on the green plastic dome. Nasty habit, but effective as a signal because nobody else will touch someone's pre-chewed gum. He reaches the bench and sits down, pulling out a copy of *Der Spiegel*, which he starts to read laboriously with his schoolboy German. With this recognition signal in place, he waits, his tote bag propped open on the floor between his legs. A few people walk past, and Simon ignores them.

After about ten minutes, had he looked up, Simon would have seen a young woman, mousy hair, studenty clothes, carrying a battered rucksack. Of course, he didn't look up. And she neither slows down nor looks at Simon but walks past. Like a true millennial she is clutching her smartphone in one hand, head down, reading something, apparently unaware of her surroundings. Had an observer followed her at a close distance, it's just possible they would have noticed a small object slip from her free hand just as she passed Simon. If that observer was filming the moment, perhaps they could then go back, frame-by-frame, and make out the tiny USB drive slipping out of her fingers into the open tote bag.

But there was nobody. Even Simon appeared not to have noticed, carrying on reading his magazine for another fifteen minutes. Only then, with nobody on the path, does he replace the magazine in the bag, allowing himself a rummage with his hand for the reassuring shape of the USB stick.

He has the files. Time to get out.

–

Simon has spent his life in the intelligence world managing risk. But sometimes you just have to hope that things will be okay. So he decides to fly back to London: not obviously a bold move. But one that necessarily will give the Russians a chance to zero in on him. Speed and deception are key. He walks into the main railway station in Frankfurt, his face suddenly visible on hundreds of Deutsche Bahn CCTV cameras. He buys a ticket to Cologne, paying with a credit card, triggering a false trail to deploy a team to intercept him there. On the train he plugs in his phone and buys a ticket on a flight to London that leaves in just over two hours. After about ten minutes the train stops at Frankfurt's airport. Simon gets off and heads into the terminal. The only risk he now faces is from a European arrest warrant, not Russian intelligence. With this in mind, he has bought a ticket to Gatwick, which people in his world know to have the sleepiest of border police. If there's one British airport where you can rely on your passport being largely ignored, it's Gatwick.

Simon walks through the immigration lane feeling numb. If the Czechs have asked the Germans to lift him, they'll do it now. Since he can easily prove he had nothing to do with Evie's death, it's not the fear of legal consequences that animates, rather the fear of being stuck in the Czech legal system for weeks as COSTELLO covers its tracks. A border guard waves him through, uninterested in his passport. Perhaps they'll do it at the departure lounge, once they know he's checked in.

Simon takes a close interest in the staff at the service desk, taking calls, rechecking tickets and passports, calling certain passengers over for additional screening. He waits for his call, but none comes. Boarding is announced, but it is only once the flight has taken off, wheels up, that he really believes that things are going to work out.

–

Arrival in Britain is not safe harbour. He is pretty sure the Pole is tracking his movements. But he is equally sure they won't do anything to harm him. The Russians are another matter. They will not try to kill a British former official on British soil, Simon reasons. Probably too risky. But they will follow his every move. The Russians have moved on from sending out their own surveillants onto British streets. Nowadays they rely on the finest British private investigators. Those who dare to shed light on London's money laundromat, journalists, lawyers, activists and politicians have all been targeted by British private investigators in the pay of the Russian oligarchs. Most of these surveillants are 'patriotic' former MI5, Special Branch or Intelligence Corps operatives offering 'bespoke' security services from Mayfair offices, as if harassing members of the media was akin to stitching together a fine suit.

Simon knows that his purchase of a flight ticket would have been picked up within a few hours by the Russians. They wouldn't have had time to get to him in Frankfurt, but they had plenty of time to do something in the UK. As a result, from the moment of his arrival he has to go dark. Returning to his flat is out of the question. Instead, from the Gatwick Express at Victoria station, he heads to a justifiably anonymous hotel, located within a four-storey terraced stucco house. Pimlico, land of lonely husbands, commercial travellers and hotels that are improbably unappealing, given their proximity to central London and handsome architecture.

En route from the station, Simon stops in a computer shop to buy the cheapest laptop available, for cash. The sales assistant is confused by Simon's complete lack of interest in technical features, beyond a quixotic request for a computer 'that doesn't connect to the internet'. There being no such machine, Simon leaves the confused salesman in the shop a few minutes later with a basic model under his arm and a new burner phone that he loads up with credit. In the hotel he impatiently pulls the new device out of its box, discards the instruction manuals and waits for it to awake for the first time, ignoring repeated requests that he register his purchase. As soon as the computer will allow him, he plunges the USB stick into the side and opens the files.

Nothing has prepared him for what he finds.

Chapter 19

London

May 2022

Rudi had sent two Excel files. Simon opens them with a password sent in an encrypted message to a burner phone. The first is a table of dates, names and a description of the visitor, all written in Cyrillic. To the uninitiated, it could have been a spreadsheet from any Russian business. The visitor logs of those that had appointments with Georgy Sidorov at the Russian Embassy had little that was unexpected. But Simon's quickening heart knows that it is much, much more than that. He is sitting in a shabby bedroom in one of Pimlico's worst hotels, with a passing train shaking the bedframe every five minutes. But he is shaking with excitement. He has realised that he is on the verge of one of the great revelations in intelligence history. An undiscovered Russian spy network could be hiding in this mundane office document.

But first he must plough through the names transliterated into Cyrillic lettering and their corresponding Russian descriptor. Most of these names obviously have no link to Mackenzie. Sidorov had a cover job at the embassy that put him in academic and cultural circles. The list is full of professors looking to attend conferences in Russia, as well as a few business types. It is painstaking work for Simon with his rusty Russian.

A strange sort of mania has overtaken. He works his way through the names seeking only those whose descriptor is 'student' or 'scholar'. Some can easily be transliterated back into English. Others require fiddling with alternative spellings to make them recognisable. And rather like a picture very slowly coming into focus, he starts to see them. Names long forgotten flooding back to remembrance, others that have been playing on his mind from the moment Mackenzie re-entered his consciousness. And one, more than any other. Unbelievable, yet strangely inevitable.

Рори Гоф: Rori Gof.

Rory Gough. Hedge-fund manager and Conservative-party donor. 'The discreet financial genius believed to have a direct line to half the Cabinet,' fawned a lengthy profile in a Sunday newspaper. 'Is this the most influential man you've never heard of?', asked the *Daily Mail* in a sceptical, yet admiring piece that also, true to form, stated the market value of his house. 'The one fundraiser they actually listen to', says another lengthy analysis, this one on a Conservative activists' blog widely read for its insider perspective. Rory Gough, the most powerful Tory member outside the Houses of Parliament. Rory Gough, informal adviser to the prime minister.

And before Gough had been any of these things, before Gough had risen to become the business figure senior politicians fell over themselves to impress, increasingly believed to be influential not just in economic affairs but in defence, security, intelligence and foreign policy; before any of this, 'Rory Gough, Oxford Scholar' had an appointment to meet one Georgy Sidorov, SVR officer at the Russian Embassy in London. Mackenzie was the talent-spotter, Sidorov would vet the candidates.

COSTELLO would run them.

Rory Gough, more feared than admired.

Thinker, businessman, culture warrior… *spy*?

Simon has a jolt of memory: a drink with Rory at the end of a summer term in Oxford. It was the 1990s and Rory was talking about Russia. About how it was going through a revolutionary phase no less important than the Bolshevik revolution itself. 'This is the thing about change: people think it's linear, but actually it's logarithmic.' Vintage Rory: Simon couldn't tell if it was genius, or utter bollocks. Rory's later success launching algorithmic trading platforms offered support to the latter view. 'Sometimes nothing happens in decades,' he had said, 'and sometimes decades happen in weeks. I'm talking Lenin there – the Russian, not the Beatle – the right people with the right resources can seize the opportunities generated by creative destruction. That's what's happening in Russia right now. Obviously it's not socialism this time. But socialism was never the objective, it was the means. The objective is power. That's always the objective.'

Gough had tried to find out what Simon and Mackenzie had spoken about. They hadn't really spoken about anything: Mackenzie had made a pass at Simon who fled in dismay and disgust. Whereas Gough seemed to have got just what he needed out of Mackenzie.

'*Moscow. I'm off to Moscow. Mac has fixed me up...*'

Mac had fixed him up. With a meeting with a Russian intelligence officer?

Simon thinks he'd better ask Evie what she makes of it. Whether there is an alternative explanation. And then the deadening reminder that Evie has gone. How could he have forgotten? So he is alone, grappling for answers. Perhaps there was some kind of cultural exchange in place? Perhaps Gough had gone to the Russian Embassy to apply for a scholarship, or to get his visa sorted? Except, none of these explanations worked: Sidorov wasn't involved with visas. Sidorov's meeting logs had only a tiny number of students on them. There was nothing *normal* about a student having a meeting with Sidorov. But Gough had had a meeting.

The meeting was abnormal, but it wasn't unique. Mackenzie's job was not to make an appointment but to talent-spot. As Simon and Evie had agreed, Mackenzie's judgement was often questionable. There was always the possibility Mackenzie's choice was driven by drunken lecherousness, not a keen assessment of his target's intellect and character. But some names of those from Mackenzie's circle who had been sent to meet Sidorov stand out to Simon. Not for who they were, but for who they are now.

Tom Harkness, the prophet of Euroscepticism, a cause he had embraced as a student, when people barely recognised the word, eventually becoming a leading figure in the Brexit campaign.

Zak Camondo, who Simon remembers from Mackenzie's parties as a coke-snorting Eurotrasher, now head of one of Europe's largest private banks. His family foundation had spearheaded investment into Eastern Europe and Russia after the Iron Curtain came down.

Heinrich Von der Wittenberg, a stiff, aristocratic German whose formal manners as an undergraduate seemed to have come from a Prussian military academy. Now a leading politician in his home country, tipped to become defence minister. Known for his speeches about NATO's need to 'find a way of working with' Russia.

Kamran Patel, iconoclastic professor of history at Cambridge whose revisionist account of the wonders of the British Empire, a doctorate supervised by Mackenzie, had the academic consensus up in arms. All the more so because its author was the son of Indian immigrants who had arrived penniless in England thirty years earlier.

Ben Archbold, leftist agitator, *Guardian* columnist and Labour Party strategist. Often on the airwaves attacking the Western security consensus, blaming NATO for Russia's invasion of Ukraine, putting 'the other side of the argument', which seemed to involve defending Russia, mostly.

And Rory Gough, party donor and informal adviser to the prime minister.

The magnificent six. The COSTELLO Ring.

Simon's head is ringing with a tension headache, the product of little sleep, trauma and fear. Part of him is gainsaying: *you don't know that any of this is true. It's all supposition.* He can hear the scoffing in the canteen at the Pole: '*Sharman got ahead of himself. Most of this was dreamed up inside his brain. It's Bermuda Triangle stuff.*' And then he looks again at the spreadsheet: hundreds of names and only six of them had been students of Mackenzie. And he remembers the payments: Sidorov's bank to Flood 19 Limited, the Costello Trusts in the Isle of Man and Cayman. He remembers Vasya's discoveries in Milan.

And he remembers that this was a tried and tested methodology, stretching back to the 1930s. Identify and recruit promising 'future leaders' at the top universities. Help them to find their way into positions of power and influence in the British establishment. Reap the harvest from this careful seeding. Kim Philby, tipped as a future Chief of MI6. Anthony Blunt, trusted by the Royal Family with the delicate task of retrieving the Duke of Windsor's correspondence with Hitler. John Cairncross, scoring the highest marks in the civil service entrance exam before rising through the ranks of the Treasury and Foreign Office. All recruited as Cambridge undergraduates by the KGB in the 1930s; all operating undiscovered as Russian agents for decades.

And then Simon remembers that he's in hiding, staying at a hotel under a false name, his room paid for in cash, using a burner phone and an unregistered laptop, suspected of murder in the Czech Republic and spurned by his former associates in government service, who probably have him under surveillance. He has made the most important intelligence discovery in Britain since the end of the Cold War and he can't tell anyone about it. His head is swirling with memories from Oxford – Mackenzie, Gough.

And memories of Sarah du Cane. Professor of Slavonic Studies at the University of Oxford, author of well-regarded works on orthography in early Slavonic languages. Admired by her colleagues, feared by her students. But her life as an academic was only half of her story. Very few people knew of Sarah's connection with British intelligence, which was how she liked it. Soon after Simon had joined the Pole, Sarah had, surprisingly, made the same choice. Her own government career was, according to official records, very brief. She spent a couple of years in an obscure analytical role before leaving to return to postgraduate studies, where she excelled. Most of her official biographies make no mention of it at all, at most noting a couple of years as a 'civil servant'.

In fact, Sarah had led a double life ever since her return to academia. Not for her the operational world, recruiting and running intelligence sources. Her forte was strategy. Her ability to imbibe intelligence, reporting, news, history and analysis and use this to think inside the Russians' heads, had made her an invaluable member of Britain's national security system. She might be professor of Slavonic Languages at Christ Church, Oxford. But she was also chief Russia strategist for the British government, frequently called upon by Britain's closest allies in Australia, Canada and Norway and of course the United States. No British prime minister would consider attending a summit with Russia before a private briefing from Sarah. When the US National Security Adviser visited Britain, when a NATO summit with Russia was underway, when the United Nations Security Council was facing a showdown with Russia over Syria or Libya, it was to Sarah they turned for advice.

And Simon realises he, too, needs her advice. When he had first been commissioned to look into Sidorov, Simon had wanted to contact Sarah. But the self-doubt had kicked in: *why would Sarah be interested in my little commercial project when she's busy advising the prime minister on global strategy?* If he had contacted her, perhaps he would have realised just how serious this all was? Perhaps he would not have exposed Evie to fatal danger? He tries to put the thought out of his mind. He must contact Sarah.

But first, he still has another file from Rudi to look at. He had asked Rudi about Valery Kleshnyov, who travelled to Milan as Walter Pinsent on a St Kitts passport, on COSTELLO business. The question was, did Kleshnyov leave Russia in his own name, or in his St Kitts identity? And the answer, in another spreadsheet, was a long list of trips in and out of Russia at different times by Kleshnyov, somehow accessed by Rudi from Russian immigration data. It made sense: if someone speaking native Russian was travelling through Moscow airport on a St Kitts passport, this could arouse the attention of any curious-minded immigration official. Far more sensible to travel on an entirely normal Russian passport, like millions of your compatriots. But this meant that there would have to be a switch at some point. It also means that Simon now has a list of dates for when Kleshnyov had travelled, including his final journey to Milan. There is good reason to believe that many of these journeys could have been COSTELLO business. So now Simon tries to figure whether any of the dates could be matched to Gough's pattern of travel over the years.

Chapter 20

London

May 2022

Simon spends the rest of the day planning his visit to Sarah. Since his return to England he has not contacted anyone in the country nor used any of his normal communications methods. Sarah is no different. He could not call her or signpost his plans in any way. He studies the Oxford University lecture schedule online and can see that Sarah is due to give a seminar in Christ Church on 'Kyivan Rus' and its Ethnogenesis in Soviet and Post-Soviet Literature'. As thrilling as this sounded, Simon is not taking an interest in the subject matter, however topical. But he knows that she will be at the seminar room in college at ten o'clock in the morning on Thursday, in two days' time. It is likely that she will then return to her office within the college grounds. In the worst case, if Simon can get into the college, he can blend in for long enough before Sarah reappears. He just needs to get there unnoticed.

He also needs to know whether the Czech police are after him. To do that, he resorts to an old-school spying methodology; also the most secure. The phone box. Few still exist, but he manages to find one on a Pimlico side street. Stepping into the iconic cast-iron red phonebooth is like stepping into a forgotten era. The interior is plastered with strangely anachronistic postcards luridly depicting available sex workers, just a phone call away. There is a nostalgic odour of stale urine. Simon wonders whether the only users of public phone booths are men buying sex whilst urinating, and men contacting espionage associates. Being the latter, he makes an international call to the Czech Republic, made possible by a carefully prepared pile of pound coins balanced on top of the phone cabinet.

The first call is to Charles Quint, the Pole's man in Prague. Quint was not someone that Simon would normally seek out. Most people agreed he had been given the Prague posting to keep him out of trouble and as a reward for having toughed it out for a few years at the NATO airbase in Kandahar. He was a bureaucrat's bureaucrat, preferring to find the easy option that kept his life quiet and let him enjoy the perquisites of his job. Not ruffling the feathers of his liaison contacts at Czech intelligence would be his number-one priority. Taking a phone-call from Simon, likely to be a wanted man in Prague, would be a long way down the list.

'*Christ*, Simon. Everybody here is talking about you. Where the hell are you?'

In the movies the guy standing in a room full of computer screens and nameless analysts only has to keep the target on the phone for a couple of minutes and the supercomputers can then locate the caller. In real life, Simon knows that Quint will have no means of locating his call from his ill-equipped office in a corner of the British Embassy in Prague.

'I'm out of your way, Charles, that's where I am. Many miles from Prague. Not your problem.'

'I can assure you that you *are* my problem,' says Charles, peevishly. 'I was summoned to the BIS headquarters a couple of days ago. Let me tell you, I was completely *sideswiped* by what they told me. I had *no idea* that you were in Prague. And you might well be a suspect in the death of Evie Howard. I mean, *really*, Simon? What were you thinking?' He sounds like a teacher scolding a recidivist child. Detention for the rest of term. 'Well. Thanks to the *very* strong relationship I have built up there, I think I *may* have been able to convince them it was very unlikely that you were in the business of killing your young colleague. But they're going to want to question you. It's not exactly the behaviour of a blameless man, disappearing like that.'

'Charles — let's get to the point,' says Simon tersely. 'I was in Prague with Evie, doing an investigation into Russian activity. Obviously, there's only so much I can say about that, but, point is, she was killed by a Chechen hit squad working to the Kremlin's orders. The car that hit her missed me by inches. The reason I didn't hang around, Charles, is that I would not have lived to tell the tale,' he says with bitter understatement. 'And I think we both know that bits of the Czech system, including some of your friends at the BIS, are rather closer to the Russians than we would want. And I'm not even going to get into the thought that you guys at the Pole probably knew what the Chechens were planning.'

Simon hears a splutter: Charles won't hear a word said against his Czech hosts and wants to deny that half the BIS is on the Russian payroll. 'Simon, I can assure you we had no inkling, not a scintilla, of this awful thing being in the works. As for the locals, some of them might be closer to Russia than you or me, but that doesn't mean they're completely unreliable. I mean, we're running some pretty good joint ops with them.'

'No doubt. You've always been an operator.' Simon strokes his ego, as much as it feels distasteful. 'But you have to understand, I was a split-second from ending up in the same situation as Evie.'

Charles appears to have calmed a little. 'How did you get away?'

'I had help from some friends. But I'm not going to talk about them on this line.' In truth, Simon is not going to talk to Charles about Rudi, Pavel and Alena on any line, or even in person. 'But I need you to set the record straight there. I disappeared because I was a target, not a suspect. Any investigation will show that I was more than fifty metres away when the car hit her...' He still has to pause as he utters these words. 'And I definitely wasn't the driver.'

'Yes, of course, Simon. But can I tell them you'll answer questions?' Simon realises that this is mostly about Charles making himself look useful to his Czech interlocutors.

'Course you can. But I'm not coming out of hiding so it would need to be via a secure link or whatever. And can you do something for me? I want to put Evie's father in touch with you. Solid chap, ex–Guards officer. He needs someone to be a point of contact.'

'This is going to be a lot of work!' says Charles. It is supposed to sound like a complaint, but in reality he is delighted that he has something to be self-important about.

'Well I know it's in the right hands,' says Simon before ending with banal courtesies and promises to keep in touch, like two former colleagues having a gossipy lunch, rather than a man on the run from ruthless global assassins.

–

The next call is far harder to make. In fact, Simon had wanted not to make it at all, but he could put it off no longer. Now that he has his lines cleared in the Czech Republic, he knows that he has to call Evie's parents. He knew a certain amount about them: her father had been an army officer and then worked for BP most of his life. He had met Evie's Russian mother whilst in Baku, Azerbaijan, and the two of them enjoyed a conventionally comfortable retirement in Wiltshire. Simon wanted nothing less in the world than a conversation with a bereaved father, but it was also his duty. And he didn't want to be misunderstood.

He realises his fingers are shaking as he dials the number. He wills nobody to answer, so that he can leave a short and respectful voicemail. But he is not so lucky.

'Henry Howard,' says a clipped military voice.

'Mister Howard, I'm Simon Sharman, Evie's colleague.'

There is a long silence. Can he hear a stifled sob? Then, in a collected sort of way, as if military discipline is coming into play: 'Well, Simon, it's good to hear from you, I suppose. I was rather surprised that you, er, disappeared.'

Simon has said the lines in his head several times. But they still don't seem to come out quite right. 'I am very, very sorry about what happened to Evie. The people that killed her are also targeting me, and that's the reason I had to get out of Prague immediately.'

'May I ask where you are now?' Howard sounds weary. The unimaginable pain of losing a child, bearing down on all of his years of being a straight-backed man of 'duty'.

'I'm really sorry, but I can't say. It's just not safe at the moment.'

'Was it safe for Evie? Did she know what she was getting into?'

'I take full responsibility, sir. But Evie probably knew more about our adversary than I did. She had a brilliant mind.' Simon feels tears forming in his eyes. 'I had no idea that we were being targeted in such an aggressive way. I think we both missed that.' He stops talking because his voice is cracking. There is a pause. Neither party feels like talking.

'It's very difficult,' says Howard, breaking the silence, 'trying to arrange everything. Repatriation, you know.'

'Yes, I want to help with that,' says Simon, desperate to make it better, but knowing it never would be. 'There's a good man at the embassy. Charles Quint.' Simon reads out Charles's details. 'He knows the right people, is expecting your call. He will sort it out.'

Simon stops again. He is getting flashbacks to the awful sight of Evie's body cartwheeling in the air, having been smashed by the car.

'Sir, I should like, once the coast is clear, so to speak, to come to pay my respects, tell you more about what your wonderful daughter did.'

Howard lets out a huge sigh. Clearly with some effort, he says, 'We would like that. Thank you. I know she loved the work she did with you.'

This is as much as Simon can bear to hear. He ends the call as quickly as is polite and leans against the side of the phone box, tears streaming down his cheeks.

—

Simon's pile of pound coins is much diminished, and he doesn't want to be in one place for too long. He returns to the hotel, via a circuitous route designed to smoke out surveillance. He thinks he has seen a possible: an older woman who keeps popping up in different places. But he has not slept properly for weeks and sees hostile surveillance everywhere. And he can't stop thinking about Evie's parents, preparing to bury their child.

–

Thursday comes. Simon has not left his hotel room for an entire day. He reasons that the COSTELLO organisation probably does not know where he is, but the moment he goes to Paddington for the train he could easily trigger an alert via a hacked CCTV camera. He wonders about getting a dodgy minicab to take him most of the way, but concludes that the lowest risk is to get there quickly in a train. At Reading, he switches platforms, deliberately leaving his burner phone on the first train to act as a decoy. But he hangs on to his unregistered laptop.

A bald man, thick-set with an Eastern European, wide face and a shabby denim jacket is standing in a queue at a coffee kiosk on the platform. He seems to flash a glance at Simon before looking away, too quickly. Simon christens him Igor and takes a look at his shoes – navy blue Converse, new, the white rubber sole gleaming in the dull light. Remember the shoes. They never change.

He picks up the shoes, and their owner, later on. Igor's associates, Reg and Usha make a surveillance box that follows Simon to Christ Church. They know he's in Oxford, but do they know what he's doing? Who he's meeting?

–

The door to Sarah du Cane's rooms swings open and Simon suddenly realises he is nervous. A long time ago, as her friend, confidant and onetime lover, he had always felt butterfly-stomach excitement when with her. He knew that she was out of his league, that their friendship was basically improbable. Other people regularly reminded him of this fact.

'Well, hello, Si. I *wondered* when we'd be seeing you.' Sarah has aged, of course, but she still has the magnetic brown eyes and luscious long hair that she plays with, absent-mindedly. Features that Simon had stared at for months before he'd ever spoken a word to her. The only clue to her secret secondary career is her clothing: she's dressed smarter than the average academic, in a black suit jacket and collared shirt. You could mistake her for a lawyer. Not for the first time in her presence, Simon is dumbstruck. What is he doing here? And how does she know to expect him? He doesn't have answers to either question.

'Er. You don't seem surprised to see me.'

She is all elegant poise and he is wearing clothes he picked up from a Pimlico market stall to avoid going inside any shops. Simon isn't sure if he should be kissing her on the cheeks, hugging her or shaking hands. There is an awkward pause.

'Come here,' she says, putting out both arms and pulling Simon into a hug. He feels relief and release. Deep, painful emotion from days of stress, Evie's death, the chase through Prague's sewers, travelling in a car boot, constant hiding, watching his back, thinking twice before he takes any action and not being able to communicate with anyone he cares about. And now someone who has loved him is holding him tight and he feels like crying.

They walk into Sarah's study, a classic Oxford don's room with high ceilings, thousands of books on cream-painted shelves and leather furniture. Simon flops into an armchair without waiting to be invited, involuntarily letting out a deep sigh.

'Cup of tea?' Sarah asks, busying herself with a kettle.

'Got anything stronger?' replies Simon, who has stretched out his legs, trying to squeeze the tension out of his body.

Sarah says nothing but hands him a tumbler of whisky. Simon recognises the soft fruitiness of Glenmorangie. He takes a sip and lets out another sigh, that is almost a sob. Sarah has sat down, opposite him. Simon realises he's in the chair that students would sit in for their tutorials with Professor du Cane, and she is in hers. And it dawns on him that he is here to present his assignment.

Sarah confirms this: 'Simon. I know you're here to talk about Sidorov, Mackenzie and Gough. Where do you want to start?' Her voice has the calm authority that he had always found so attractive.

Perhaps the whisky is doing its job: things are clicking together in Simon's brain. Has he been working for Peebles and O'Brien, or has he, all along, been working for Sarah? 'O'Brien, he was yours, wasn't he?' asks Simon, recalling his notional client.

'No, he's Marcus's. Well, I think we paid him a day-rate, sort of bonus. Kemi is ours.' Of course. Kemi, who had never given Simon her surname, clearly the brains of the operation: cool, sharp as a knife. Not so different to Sarah, really.

Simon has spent his life devising sophisticated intelligence operations, designed to mislead targets, to manipulate them into doing something for him. And now he has been the target of a sophisticated intelligence operation. And he can't figure out how much of it fooled him.

'Is Oxford even reviewing Sidorov's donation?'

'Sidorov? They bloody well should be, but I doubt it,' says Sarah. 'I mean, that was about the only risk: that you'd get a source telling you the university definitely wasn't planning on handing anything back. But in general, the cover fitted well: everyone is talking about whether it's still acceptable.' Sarah says this as if it were an interesting question, worthy of further study, rather than a burning geopolitical controversy.

And how many people knew he'd been fooled? That was almost the worst part: the thought of a group of people at the Pole, watching Simon as if from behind a two-way mirror. 'Does Marcus Peebles know all this?' he asks, a sudden sharpness in his voice. The thought of Marcus being part of some complicated scheme to mislead him is particularly frustrating.

'Marcus is an important supporter of this work: like I said, O'Brien is one of his. I told him we were lending him someone.

He had to admit to Kemi if anyone asked, but she didn't even go to his office. You never met them at Grosvenor's offices, did you? He probably thinks you were conscious to the operation from the start.' Simon feels the annoyance rise inside him: he realises now that they had never discussed the Sidorov work in Marcus's normal office, and he hadn't figured out that something else was going on.

'What about the Pole?' For some reason, the answer to this matters more than the others.

'Well that's where it gets a little complicated. They seem to think you've gone rogue.'

Simon wants to be in control of the conversation. 'Well, it seems like you know it all already. Is there anything I have to tell you?'

'Simon.' Sarah's voice is firm, but also patient, perhaps the tone that she takes with bolshie students. The ones she knows are worth the trouble. 'I only know what you have said to Kemi, and that's only a small part of the story. I knew that you wouldn't tell her or O'Brien the things that you felt were national security issues. So, please, I am listening.'

Simon tells her everything, from the beginning. He tells her about Sidorov's strange walks through Oxford, on an inexplicable route past Mackenzie's window. He tells her about the payments from something called Costello Limited in the Isle of Man to Mackenzie's company, Flood 19, payments that stopped the month Mackenzie died. He tells her about his secret journey to Switzerland, and Vasya's account of Kleshnyov, visiting a hotel room booked by the Costello Trust. And the existence of a completely unknown Russian intelligence organisation that existed solely to run the COSTELLO network.

He tells her that the Pole tried to get him to drop it. Which was when he knew he was on to something. And when he started to see people. Were they the Pole's or COSTELLO's?

And then he tells her about Prague. About the snatched sightings of followers, and about his failure to do anything about it. And then he stops. He doesn't tell her about the last hours with Evie. He doesn't tell her about the sight of Evie's back disappearing down a narrow street and the awful seconds that followed.

There is a silence. Simon has stopped talking. 'We know about Evie Howard,' says Sarah. 'I am very sorry.' She pauses again. 'I doubt it will help very much, but we made sure the embassy did the right thing. They're sorting out the repatriation.'

Simon gulps at his whisky, trying to banish the mental image of Evie's body, floating through the Prague air on its final flight.

Sarah regains focus. 'Carry on, Simon.'

And Simon realises that the intelligence agencies have done what they always do: they use, they discard and they move on. Evie had played a role. Britain was grateful for her service. But the job needed completing. And Simon wants to show that he can complete it. Wants to show Sarah that he is tough, focused. Ruthless, if necessary. He feels desperate pain whenever he thinks about Evie. But he is determined not to show it. He is also determined that Sarah learns what else he has figured out. He, too, wants to complete the job.

So he tells her about Rudi and his network. And about the brush contact in Frankfurt. And, finally, he tells her about Sidorov's visitor logs.

He gets to the names.

Sarah, who has been taking notes and nodding along, politely interested, is now leaning forward, her shoulders stiffened, her usually soft eyes narrowed, sharper. Simon mentions Von der Wittenberg and she nods, knowingly. Camondo, who pursued Sarah as a lover during their time in Oxford, elicits a frisson. But she doesn't say anything. Simon gets to Patel. Perhaps because he's a fellow academic, she breaks her silence.

'Kamran? Really?'

'Don't forget, these are just the meetings. We don't know whether they became full COSTELLO agents.' He continues, mentioning Archbold and Harkness. 'Well, I don't think there's much of a surprise with Ben: he was always defending Russia, calling NATO a neo-colonialist militaristic alliance, or blaming the Ukrainians for being too aggressive. And Harkness: think about it, which world leader was popping the champagne corks on the morning of the Brexit result? It was a victory for Putin. And back when he got into this stuff as an undergraduate, the whole "British sovereignty" campaign, it seemed like a joke in those days. Only a few ancient Tories and folk who hated foreigners were anti-Europeans at that time. How did someone back in the early nineties think that this would be a thing to get into? Unless someone was *telling* them to get into it.'

'Carry on,' says Sarah. This is still the part of the tutorial where the student gives his presentation. Her feedback comes later.

'And then there's Gough. I know that Mackenzie set him up with some kind of job in Moscow, because he told me so. Over a pint in Turl Street. But we now know that Rory had a meeting with Sidorov at the embassy, before he went out to Russia.

'So, what remains to figure out? I still don't understand the significance of Flood 19. And we have the dates of Kleshnyov's travel – so we have to see if that matches with the travel patterns of any of the COSTELLO people. But –' Simon is reaching the end of his presentation and has to stop himself from saying, *in conclusion,* like a pompous undergraduate '– we have confirmed the existence of a Russian intelligence network based around Sidorov and Mackenzie, called COSTELLO and including Rory Gough among its likely members.' Simon folds his arms and looks up expectantly.

There is a long pause. Then Sarah starts speaking. Is Simon supposed to take notes? She's got a lecture-room delivery, her eyes focused on an imaginary audience member in the middle distance.

'Simon, let's start with genesis. Small "g",' she clarifies unnecessarily. 'About a year ago I was invited to talk to the parliamentary Intelligence and Security Committee about Russian influence in the UK. Secret meeting. You know the background: they did a report on all the Russian interference here, the fact the government wasn't taking it seriously. The fact that the government never even *asked* MI5 to investigate the Russians' interference activities over Brexit. And they asked for my views. Well, that coincided with some discussions I'd been having in various bits of the secret state.'

Simon knows what she is going to say next. 'This is the fact that the politicians are too dependent on Russian donors to do anything serious about their influence.'

'Yes, Simon, that's right. But there's more: Gough. He's the problem. Makes no secret of the fact he's had lots of investments in Russia, but he's pretty evasive about what he did when he lived there. Who he worked for, what interactions he had with the authorities, that sort of thing. And when you scratch the surface, there are some pretty troubling details: all the people he worked for in Russia had a link to the intelligence world. You know, so-called "former" KGB officers in a country where nobody gets to be former anything. Plenty of people passed through Russia at that time, looking for adventure and fortune. But most of them weren't in business with the intelligence services.

'At the beginning, we thought it might be containable. Gough's just a party donor – doesn't have any official position. But the government kept bringing him onto things! You know they actually gave him a Number Ten email address? He has this business card calling him a "senior adviser" in the Prime Minister's Office but he's never been vetted, doesn't have a formal job, or a line manager, or anything. Basically, nobody knows anything about him. He seems to believe that the entire British system has to be torn apart – just to make it easier for his bloody hedge fund to keep printing money. He wants to reshape the Civil Service, privatise the BBC, sell off the NHS. And then he starts getting interested in high-security stuff. Porton Down, SAS, SBS, Cardross. Talks to the prime minister about "reshaping national security architecture so it's leaner, more results-oriented". And the prime minister bloody listens! That's the bad bit. Gough was all over the strategic defence review. Has ideas that the nuclear deterrent can be run by a private consortium, for God's sake. And nobody actually knows anything about him!'

Sarah's lecture-room voice has risen. She was always coolly unflappable, but now Simon can feel her frustration. 'In any normal situation,' she continues, 'MI5 would take a look. Full investigation, get to the bottom of things. But this isn't normal. MI5 won't touch it without a clear directive from the Cabinet Office. Cabinet Office says they need a specific instruction from the National Security Adviser. The National Security Adviser says, well, he says nothing, in fact. Because he's too busy trying not to be fired. Because all it takes now is a nod from Gough. And everybody knows the PM doesn't do difficult decisions and is short of money. And some of the people keeping the PM's head above water happen to be strangely generous Russian oligarchs, who have invested in Gough's funds.' She pauses, frowns slightly, and Simon is wondering if he's supposed to say something. But she fills the gap. 'And then Ukraine happened. And that's when I knew we had to do something. Gough is running credit structures that are funding the Russian war machine. It's all behind shell companies and cut-outs, but we know what it is. So we, the people in government who care about the integrity of our national security, we decide to get to the bottom of what Gough is up to without the official structures knowing about it.'

'So you hired me? Keep it off the government's books?'

'Well, yes. That's it. Some of the people on the Committee were able to establish a discreet funding mechanism. And they lent me one of their people. That's Kemi. And then I got Marcus to lend me O'Brien.'

'But how did you know that I'd end up coming to you?'

Sarah clicked out of lecture-hall mode, put her head slightly to one side and fiddled with her long hair so that it was falling in front of one shoulder. Looking directly at Simon, she smiled. Nothing really needed saying.

'But that's all admin, really. It's what you've found that matters. COSTELLO. I mean,' she almost chuckles, 'it's an incredible

168

piece of intelligence work. I don't know what else I can say. Brilliant.'

Simon needs this validation, pushes his luck. 'Working mostly alone, I figured out more than the Pole have managed in years. They'll wish they never let me go. This is bigger than anything they've got.'

Sarah looks impatient. 'Simon, this doesn't have to be about you. Or the Pole. Or about who is better. The point is what do we do with this intelligence? How do we complete the job?'

And then they start talking practicalities, just like in the old days. They're back in that brief, happy period when Sarah had worked at the Pole as an analyst and Simon was the young operations officer.

'Who knows you're here today?' asks Sarah.

'Nobody. Except for Moscow Centre,' replies Simon with a grimace. He explains that since he had travelled back to the UK he had gone dark. But he had seen a surveillance team out in Oxford today. Clearly not Russians – except possibly Igor. 'Probably just contractors working for some kind of COSTELLO cut-out, but I think there's a reasonable chance they'll eventually connect my visit to Christ Church with you. And the Pole seems to want me off the scent, too.'

'We can't rule out the possibility that Gough has already stitched up the Pole. That would explain them trying to get you to drop it,' she adds, calmly, as if the hobbling of one of Britain's key intelligence organisations was just another data point. 'What are the intelligence leads we need to chase down?'

'It's the travel dates, plus Flood 19. I still can't figure that one. But more than that – we have to show that Gough is in the network. We have to find some kind of smoking gun. He could tough all of this out. What's your endgame?'

Sarah shuts her eyes briefly, pauses and then looks at Simon. 'It's a very good question,' she acknowledges. 'There's a group: the Intelligence and Security Committee chairman – not all of the members, I assure you, but the chairman's sound – chief of

MI6, director-gen at the Pole, head of GCHQ, chief of defence staff. As I say, there's a group, and if we can present then with a compelling case, they will take action. MI5 is wobbly. Cabinet Office, Number Ten, hopeless. I'm not sure about the Pole. But if we get that group in one place with a complete file on Gough, they can't ignore it. They'll do it.'

'Do what?'

'Confront the PM. It's the only way this thing can end.'

'And what if the PM says no? What if he says, "actually, I'm not buying this, Gough's a bloody good bloke and we do need to reframe the way the national security stuff works in this country". What if he says that?'

'He won't, Simon. Come on, we're talking about an actual Russian spy while there's a war on. No British prime minister is going to ignore compelling evidence that there is a Russian spy at the top of his administration. The challenge is: it has to be compelling.'

'Don't forget that this prime minister went straight from a NATO summit to an orgy hosted by a former KGB officer. He may not actually care.'

Sarah seems to have decided to ignore this comment. Some things are too difficult. 'Okay. I'm going to get Kemi to come up tomorrow. Where are you staying?' She asks this with an absent-minded professor air.

'Sarah, I'm not *staying* anywhere. I'm on the run. A gang of Chechens nearly killed me. I think that was less than a week ago, except I have slept so little that I am not sure what day that was.'

'Well, Christ Church is big enough. We'll find space for you here.' She pauses. 'And I will *have* to get you out of those awful clothes.'

Simon is remembering why he has loved this woman, largely unrequitedly, for a quarter of a century.

Chapter 21

Oxford

May 2022

Kemi Williams's youth does not limit her self-confidence. She speaks sharply, directly and quickly. There is a slight flare of her nostril as she listens to Simon, who feels rather stupid. He tells her the COSTELLO case history not as a meandering narrative of the sort he had shared with Sarah, but as a military briefing. What follows is an interrogation: Kemi fires off direct, specific questions that don't allow for hesitation, deviation or repetition.

'Why do you believe Gough is part of the network?' she demands.

Simon admits that he can't prove that. 'That's the bit we have to figure out,' he acknowledges. 'We only know he had the meeting at the embassy with Sidorov and then went to Russia. But Sarah's told us that he worked with intelligence people in Russia. And COSTELLO operates as a network focused on Oxford. We know that. So, with the Kleshnyov file we might be able to find the dates of the meetings, track travel, who was there, so on.'

'Yes, but Kleshnyov died in 2006. What about now? Who's running this stuff now?'

It is another one of Kemi's difficult questions, to which Simon has no answer. But then he has an idea. 'The one thing we know about Kleshnyov is that he travelled on a genuine St Kitts passport. And you have to buy them. Kleshnyov can't have been the only one using one of these. Maybe all the COSTELLO operatives used them.'

'So we need to find out which other Russians acquired alias passports from St Kitts?'

They huddle round the shiny laptop that Kemi has brought with her. There are a variety of licensed operators offering 'citizenship advisory services' and, inevitably, 'solutions'. Most of them have offices in Mayfair and slick websites full of pictures of exquisite Caribbean beaches and attractive, successful people with lots to smile about. What this means in practice is companies taking a cut on the messy business of selling passports to whoever is buying. And who buys passports?

'You start out a pariah, from Russia, Iran, Venezuela, whatever,' explains Simon, although he's sure his audience already knows, 'and come out a proud citizen of St Kitts. A small, blameless country whose citizens get to travel visa-free throughout Europe.'

Citizenship by investment, they call it.

'Can we find who's selling the Russians their passports?' asks Kemi, getting straight to the point. As usual, asking all the right questions. But Simon still has something to offer: he has sources. A lifetime of networking, cultivating relationships, means that he can still do what he is best at: find someone who has the information they need.

'The man we need to talk to is Iain Radcliffe,' says Simon.

'Who's he?'

'I knew him at the Pole. He had joined from private banking. All smooth hair and tailored suits. Good with people, but even better with money. So he got out once he'd made enough connections and got into the passport-sales business. I'll need to go and see Radcliffe, find out how this whole racket works.'

'What, in the Caribbean?' Kemi sounds incredulous.

'No, in Dorking.' The highly profitable work of selling passports had enabled Radcliffe to play country squire in a village at the foot of Leith Hill, in Surrey.

Simon is staying in a college guest room that Sarah has arranged for him, a garret at the top of a winding staircase. As Christ Church is a large college, with plenty of visiting scholars and hundreds of students living on site, it is easy for him to blend into his surroundings, particularly once Sarah has provided him with suitably 'Oxford' clothes. She has also provided him with a university ID card that suggests he is a graduate researcher in the Slavonic Studies Institute. Simon likes that: a bit of him wishes he'd been an Oxford don.

Since their initial meeting Simon has not seen much of Sarah. She had sent him to his guest room and told him to be ready for Kemi the following morning. She had then apologised for having a full lecture schedule over the coming days and disappeared. Simon knows that he can't risk appearing in the Senior Common Room as her guest, arousing the curiosity of some of Oxford's keenest minds. Repeated visits to her rooms would also not be a good idea. So, he spends the evenings alone in his garret, dreaming about a tumbler of whisky with Sarah for company, and consoling himself with just the tumbler of whisky.

He makes a point of rarely leaving his room and not leaving the college gates. There was no way the Russians could mount a surveillance operation outside a busy, well-secured site like Christ Church, particularly not twenty-four-seven. So Simon concludes he can leave the college unobserved, with a little forward planning. And, as a senior academic, Sarah has access to one of the most coveted possessions in all of Oxford: a parking space inside college grounds.

The following morning, wearing a cap and dark glasses, Simon drives Sarah's car out of the side gate of Christ Church and is quickly on the motorway heading towards London. On the car radio he listens to the news. The prime minister is explaining how 'global Britain' is fully sovereign and independent. No foreign bureaucracy could interfere with its laws or governance. It was free to navigate the waves of global trade. Mobility, agility, sovereignty. These are the watchwords of the new Britain. Simon switches channels.

Radcliffe lives in an Old Rectory that has very expensively been given the country-casual makeover. In all probability, none of the old rectors would recognise the place. Outside, Simon has to be buzzed through a tall, impenetrable iron-railing gate which slides open noiselessly. As he sweeps down the drive Simon notices an incongruous ornamental well and expensively coiffured topiary, surrounded by perfectly white gravel, not a protruding weed in sight. A vast 'orangery' is plugged onto one side in architecturally illiterate fashion. Radcliffe greets Simon at the door, gleaming stone floors stretching out behind him. He is dressed in bright pink moleskin trousers and blue suede loafers that he wears without socks. His white shirt is crisp and his complexion glows with a tan that reflects a combination of regular business travel to the Caribbean and ownership of a chalet in Verbier.

'Simon, old boy, how *wonderful* to see you,' he lies. They have never been close. But prior service at the Pole is a sort of honour code: you always give your former colleague the time of day, if not much more. 'And what brings you to my little patch of rural heaven?' he asks, theatrically signalling the manicured surroundings.

'A little bit of work. Trying to understand your business, actually.'

'Is this for one of your clients? Or for Her Majesty's Service? I'm not going to give you the crown jewels so you can set up in competition, am I?' He is trying to sound jolly, with a hint of menace.

'Oh God, no, Iain. Her Majesty is asking.'

Radcliffe nods, satisfied.

He leads Simon through a spacious hallway into the orangery, a vast, light-filled room laid out with wicker furniture. Although it is a grey day outside, it is disconcertingly warm, as if Radcliffe wants to show off his indifference to vast energy bills. A housekeeper brings coffee and *faux rustique* cookies, before removing herself from earshot.

Simon has struggled to stay abreast of Radcliffe's revolving-door approach to personal relationships, so he chooses his words carefully. 'How are things in the Radcliffe household?'

'Oh, good, very good in fact. We're all very well,' Radcliffe replies, not offering Simon much to go on. Safer to get Radcliffe to talk about himself and about work, his two favourite subjects.

'So, passports flying off the shelves?'

'They certainly are!' exclaims Radcliffe with unexpected verve. 'Tell you what, we are banking the Brexit dividend. Bet you didn't expect to hear me say that.'

'Can't say I did, Iain,' says Simon, trying his best to sound impressed.

'The one market we never thought we'd have was the Brits themselves. Used to be one of the best passports, the British. Opened a lot of doors. Not any more,' he cries, with a pantomime flourish, as if this is the most amusing thing in the world.

'What, so Brits are buying St Kitts passports?' asks Simon, sceptical.

'God no! Ha ha ha. No, no. The St Kitts passport, whilst an excellent product, is not our prestige option. That's Malta. Full EU member, right to live and work anywhere in Europe, yours for a million Euros. You have to pretend to live there for a bit, but we have ways round that, of course. All of a sudden, super-wealthy Brits are quietly sorting out their European options. Half of them probably voted for Brexit, but, you know, money talks.'

'So is that the mainstay now? EU passports?'

'Not really,' says Radcliffe, warming to his theme, 'it all depends what you're after. The Caribbean is still of incredible value. Only one hundred grand for St Kitts. If you're Chinese, Russian, Iranian, that's a real bonus, gets you into Europe, the UK and so on. And you know the best thing about the St Kitts passport? It doesn't list your place of birth. Once you've got it, nobody needs to know where you're really from.'

'So you could turn up as a Russian called, for the sake of argu-ment, Valery Kleshnyov, and emerge as a Kittitian called Walter

Pinsent and nobody would have any documentary evidence that you were ever Russian?'

Radcliffe seems to catch on something, narrowing his eyes and looking quizzically at Simon. 'That's about right, Simon, old son. You can see the attraction.'

'You done a lot of Russians, Iain?'

'We did, Simon, we did.' There's a slight uneasiness slipping into Radcliffe's usual bonhomie. 'And Ukrainians, for that matter. Not taking sides.'

Perhaps you should take a fucking side, thinks Simon. But he keeps his voice level. 'What's your *impression* of them? Trustworthy people? Or Kremlin stooges?'

Radcliffe assumes a priestly air, as if he is intoning an important religious text. 'Simon, our role is merely to market the *product* and process the applications. It is the responsibility of the St Kitts government to ensure that their new citizens will bring credit to their country.' He could not have sounded more pious if he had chanted it in plainsong.

'So, for the sake of argument, some dodgy oligarch shows up, links to sanctioned businesses, clearly close to the Kremlin, you wouldn't get in the way of that?'

'Not our job, old boy,' says Radcliffe, as if this is the most obvious thing imaginable. 'Now, strictly *entre nous*, these dodgy ones aren't good for the brand. The Americans have been kicking up about the St Kitts passport for a while, now, going on about "reputation laundering". It's all bullshit, of course: Florida is full of Colombian drug barons who have bought their residency status and you don't hear much about that. But the Yanks find it easy to have a go at one of the world's smallest countries. So I take the opportunity to pass on the message when I'm with Max Holford, the PM of St Kitts.'

'"Passing on the message" might not be having the impact you're looking for,' observes Simon.

'Like I said, not our job. Since the invasion I think the Yanks will probably stop the Russians getting any more passports anyway. Not that it stops the ones who've already got them.' Radcliffe is starting to sound testy. He looks at his watch. 'Is there something specific you're after, Simon? Only, the one thing about this business is, our clients and our suppliers – also known as countries – are in pretty much every timezone. So there's almost always a conference call.'

Simon pauses. Frowns. Moves his coffee cup on the wicker-frame table, the saucer squeaking on the glass top. Looks up. And then looks Radcliffe in the eyes. He'd not noticed previously what an extraordinarily pale shade of blue they are. Duck egg blue.

'Suppose Moscow Centre got a job lot of St Kitts passports for their hoods. Say, about twenty of them. You'd kind of notice that, wouldn't you?'

Radcliffe folds his arms and sighs, impatiently. 'I don't like to deal in supposition, Simon. What're you getting at here?'

'Shall I spell it out for you?' Simon replies, losing patience. 'Did you process a job lot of Russians that weren't obviously indi-vidually wealthy oligarchs? One of them called Valery Kleshnyov, took a St Kitts passport in the name of Walter Pinsent. No suppos-ition needed, Iain, just an answer.'

Radcliffe stands up and turns his back, gazing out over his sloping garden and the carefully preserved wilds of the Surrey Hills beyond. Simon knows he is pushing his luck, but Radcliffe's oleaginous self-interest has got the better of him.

'All right, Simon, here's how this works: if you can show me evidence that they're doing something illegal, or directly undermining British interests, then fine. I'll be happy to help the *appropriate* authorities. But I know what you people are like. You're desperate for there to be a new Cold War. You see a Russian threat everywhere, but in the real world, this is business. Everything we do is within the rules. If we don't provide these services, others will, others who are much less ethical.'

'Hang on a minute, Iain, are you telling me that it's good that you're selling passports to Russian intelligence because if you didn't someone else might do it?'

'No, I'm telling you that you need to give me the names you're interested in and explain what crime you suspect them of involvement with. Otherwise, I am bound by my confidentiality agreements with my clients, which, as you might imagine, are pretty fucking tight!' His voice rises. Is it frustration or anger? 'So, would you like to outline in some detail what Mister Kleshnyov is suspected of doing?' He is now sneering through a smile. 'Because I'd need to know that before I'd even *consider* sharing anything from our confidential database.'

Simon has heard enough. 'Fuck you, Iain.' He gestures around himself at the grand orangery, the manicured garden, the genteel Old Rectory. 'Pretty obvious what's paying for all of this. I think we know whose side you're on.'

'Lovely to see you, as ever,' sneers Iain, his back turned. 'You'll let yourself out, won't you?' he calls as he disappears down a long echoing hallway.

He is heading straight for his study, to make a call to some people Iain would describe as 'key clients' and everyone else would call 'Kremlin assets'.

Chapter 22

Surrey

May 2022

As Simon drives the winding road down from Leith Hill towards Dorking he feels rage coursing through his body. Inside the private metal box of Sarah's car he allows himself a bellow of anger: shouting at an imaginary Radcliffe who has the misfortune to be sitting in the passenger seat.

Radcliffe's smug privilege, his knowing cynicism, his willingness to make money from the most suspect clients. These are all considerable faults. But what grated most was Radcliffe's faux-respectability, his self-image as a perfect English gentleman. An upstanding, patriotic pillar of the British establishment. Chairman of the parish council. Stalwart of the village church. Generous donor to the Surrey Conservative Party. Radcliffe sees no contradiction between his self-image and the reality of supplying dodgy passports to international criminals, financed by offshore money, most of it stolen.

Don't get mad, get even.

By the time Simon has reached the motorway he has the outline of an idea. The traffic is clear and he makes good progress with his journey and his thinking. The answer is straightforward: if Radcliffe won't give him the information he needs, he will steal it by hacking his computer. The principle of a phishing attack is to send an email that the recipient believes to be from a real entity. The target opens the email, exposing themselves to the threat. Most computer hacks failed due to the hacker lacking sufficient information about the target. In Radcliffe's case, Simon has plenty of information. As he drives, he formulates a plan.

Spoofing a message from a family member would be tricky: Radcliffe has been married and partners appear to come and go. He knows there were children, but Simon doesn't know the details of how they communicate and would too easily be found out if the tone of the messages isn't perfect. On the other hand, both he and Simon are members of a secretive club, the qualification for membership of which was previous employment in Britain's intelligence and special forces community. The club regularly sent out messages to its members drawing attention to events and other important news. An email purporting to be from the club would likely be opened so long as its contents were sufficiently interesting. Simon reasons that the definition of 'interesting' is something that appeals to Radcliffe's vanity. A round-robin email isn't enough: it needs to be direct to Radcliffe, requesting his involvement in some kind of high-status activity.

By the time Simon has reached Oxford he has most of a plan in his mind. He needs to talk to his Welsh wizard of the dark web. Once he has got through the laborious security protocols the Wizard insists on, they are able to see one another over an ultra-secure video-link. As usual, the Wizard is sitting in front of a slate-dark stone wall.

'Four-seven,' says the Wizard, using the code-number assigned to Simon.

Simon lays out his plan, technically fairly straightforward and the Wizard nods along, fiddling with his heavy spectacles as he does so.

'To be honest, Simon, I can do the trojan malware – we'll have full access to all of his files if he opens the attachment, but you'll have to make it worth him clicking on it. So it's down to you to get the phishing email just right.'

Simon notes that, in common with IT specialists everywhere in the world, the Wizard is ensuring that if the project fails, it will be Simon's fault for creating an insufficiently enticing phishing email; if it succeeds, it will be thanks to the Wizard's superior hacking skills. Fortified with this responsibility, Simon spends the rest of the day trawling through old emails from the club, imbibing the style, nomenclature and layout, and playing around with dummy versions on his laptop. After a while, Simon has got pretty close to what is needed. The email appears to come from the club secretary and addresses Radcliffe in a familiar, but ingratiating tone.

Re: The Incorrigibles' Club, invitation to join Business Advisory Board

Dear Iain

The Incorrigibles' Club has decided to establish a Business Advisory Board. Its purpose will be to draw on the considerable commercial expertise present among our membership. We hope to help the club secure its financial future with the advice of our most successful members. We would be delighted and honoured if you would consider joining our team, given your history of public service, international business success and active club membership.

Should this be of interest I'd be most grateful if you could click on the link below to our online calendar to help us to establish the most convenient date for the first meeting of the advisory board. We expect the club's patron, HRH Prince Michael of Kent, to attend the first meeting.

We look forward to welcoming you on board.

Simon plays around with the text a little more until he is happy with it. After double-encrypting it he sends it off to the Wizard, who will make it appear – to Radcliffe – to have come from the club secretary's email. The trojan will only load onto Radcliffe's computer if he clicks on the link to the online calendar. From almost any other source, Radcliffe would ignore an invitation to click on an unexpected link, but the combination of the club and the involvement of minor royalty should be enough to get him across the line. Simon feels a small wave of satisfaction lapping over him. He had begun the day with a low opinion of Radcliffe, which had plummeted further still during their short meeting. Now he is going to fuck him up a little, and this feels good.

He decides to give Sarah a call from the internal phone in his room that connects via the college network. It is unlikely that anyone has a tap on this internal line. On the pretext of returning her car keys he ascertains that Sarah is in her rooms, not expecting other visitors and not dining at High Table that evening. At this point Simon realises that he no longer knows anything about Sarah's personal life. There had been a short, unsuccessful marriage about fifteen years ago, but he has no idea what has happened since.

It is early evening. Sarah greets him at the door of her office with her mobile phone held to her ear, gesturing apologetically as she finishes a call, apparently to an academic publisher. Expertly, with one hand, she provides him with a tumbler of whisky and motions him to sit down. Simon slouches on her sofa and enjoys watching her move around the room. She is about to publish a *magnum opus* on the languages of the Caucasus and seems to be in dispute with her publisher over whether it was strictly necessary to have a section on the language of the Svan people.

'Honestly, I know it's only about fifteen thousand but there really isn't any other language that has the archaic Kartvelian grammar. It would be *such* a shame not to include that, don't you think?'

A pause, whilst the publisher, Simon assumes, offers his views on archaic Kartvelian grammar.

'Yes. Eighteen vowels. I know you know this, but it really wouldn't be a complete survey without including it.'

Simon can tell they both want to agree with one another. This conversation may be a sort of formal engagement, a bit like a traditional Svaneti dance, in which each party stands in their own space in the knowledge that they will eventually have to meet the other halfway. He can tell that they are winding up the conversation and realises he is feeling excited, and nervous to be talking to Sarah again. He is trying to figure out the nature of their relationship.

Sarah is apologising, fixing herself a drink and asking Simon about progress. Simon launches into a diatribe about Radcliffe, his lack of patriotism, his laundering of dodgy identities, his cynicism and his poor taste.

Sarah, almost absent-mindedly, says: 'It may not matter. We might be able to find it some other way.'

And then Simon announces his triumph: 'No need. I'm going to hack him. Little fucker has no idea what's coming his way.'

Sarah smiles nervously. 'Simon, I don't think I want to hear about that. The key is Rory Gough. How are we going to find out what he has been up to?'

'That's why we need the St Kitts list. Radcliffe refused to tell me anything, but he did it in such a way that he was kind of admitting the Russians got a job lot of these St Kitts passports. For COSTELLO. So if we get the list, we can find out who the other operatives are. We know they leave Russia using their normal passports. And from Rudi we can find out when they do that. Then, all we have to do is see if that matches any of Rory's trips. If we can find them, of course.' Simon knocks back his whisky and walks over to the drinks table for a top-up. 'Rory's an abrasive character. There must be plenty of people who wouldn't mind dobbing him in.'

Sarah is twisting her long hair into a spiral, a gesture that Simon remembers from their undergraduate days as a signal that she is thinking hard. 'I've been trying to get better leads on Rory. I thought it over: someone would have noticed if he was making odd little trips to Europe now and then. You know, popping off to see Mackenzie. I've managed to get a line to his former PA. There's a rumour he bullied her.'

'Well that's the sort of thing you'd expect him to be doing.' The deep boom of Great Tom bell was chiming 101 times, an ancient Oxford tradition that used to summon the scholars of Christ Church for the evening curfew. Sarah leans back in her chair and shakes off her rather stiff-looking court shoes. 'We haven't had the chance to catch up, really. Where did the past twenty years go?' she asks, only partly in jest.

'Well, for me they didn't really go anywhere. But you're now a big fish in two ponds. And, family? Home? What's the story? I've lost track.' Simon is trying to sound casual, but he's intensely interested in the answer.

'I'd like to say it's complicated. But it isn't, really. I have an ex-husband. We don't really have much to do with one another. And we didn't have kids. I regret that. I've been very busy with work stuff in the last couple of years.' She pauses, looking around her huge office, lined with bookshelves and antique furniture. 'I live in college at the moment.'

'You live here? In these rooms?' Simon's mind is racing with possibilities.

'It's a bit pathetic, isn't it? I'm in my forties and I live in something that is basically a boarding school.' As she says this, there is a noise of young men shouting incoherently outside. The would-be upper classes of England were baying for broken glass. The distinctive sound of public schoolboys with too much alcohol inside them echoed off the limestone facades. 'And you, Simon?' He hasn't thought through the obvious point that his questions might bounce back. 'What's your story these days?'

In trying to answer, Simon finds himself thinking about Evie. 'A small flat in Kilburn that is the result of two messy divorces is far less impressive than a suite of fine rooms in Oxford's grandest college.' He gulps his whisky and decides to change tack. He looks directly at Sarah. 'Did you ever suspect Mackenzie in this way? I mean, he wasn't exactly a communist when we were at Oxford, was he?'

'Not a communist, no, but quite possibly a Leninist. By which I mean someone prepared to destroy everything to get what he

184

wanted. But no, I didn't suspect anything at all. We were all so young then.'

'I used to think of you as impossibly sophisticated. You know, with your parents saving the world and that sort of thing. You seemed to understand things much better.'

'I don't think any of us understood Mackenzie.' As Sarah says this, Simon has a flashback to that terrible moment in Mackenzie's rooms. At the time, he had wanted to find Sarah, to seek comfort and reassurance. But he had ended up bumping into Gough. Simon wonders if he can tell Sarah now. He feels ridiculously nervous.

'You know the thing about Mackenzie?'

'What, other than the thing that he was a Russian agent?'

'Well, yes, other than that. The thing was that he abused his influence. You see, you came from a connected situation. Your dad, well, he was about the most important diplomat on the planet. I'm not saying you're here –' Simon waves around him at the grand Oxford study '– thanks to him. Obviously not. But to you, the possibility that Mackenzie might introduce you to some Tory *apparatchik* was probably of no particular appeal. You already had connections at a much higher level, if you wanted them.'

Sarah chuckles, slightly embarrassed. 'I'm not sure if the prime minister of Sweden counts for much outside Stockholm,' she says. Simon had forgotten that Sarah had been born Swedish, with a hint of Italian aristocrat for good measure. She had grown up in a world where heads of state and global leaders were regular visitors to the family home. 'Anyway, what was I supposed to think about you? For the first few years we knew each other you were pretending to be Jewish.' Sarah has a mocking smile as she says this.

Simon looks awkwardly at the floor. His period of pseudo-Judaism felt like a regrettable infidelity that he couldn't undo.

'I can't defend that. But the whole thing was a very different experience for me: I was nothing and then Mac gave me that label

— *Scharmann* the Jewish tailor boy. It wasn't much, but at least I was something. Bloody stupid, I know. But at that time I thought he was the business. I wanted so much to be part of his crowd. And then... when I asked him for help... It's difficult to talk about,' says Simon, realising he is stumbling over the story. 'He, er, well, he... He tried to sexually assault me.' He says these last words quickly, as if the shame will reduce if he gets it out in a hurry. Simon can feel tears pricking his eyes. He is desperate for this not to be something that matters to him any more. But it obviously does. He blinks slowly, and continues. 'I walked out of Mackenzie's rooms and wanted to see you. Remember, at that time, we were... well you and me had something going on, I guess. And then, just because life's like that, I bumped into Gough and he took me off to the pub and he wanted to talk about Mackenzie, and his own plans to go to Russia. I guess, I haven't really processed what happened on that occasion.'

Simon wants Sarah to show empathy. But she is completely focused on the Gough story.

'What was Gough saying about Mackenzie? Is that still significant?'

Simon feels a wave of resentment sweep over him. But then he remembers that Sarah is attractive in part because of her fierce intelligence. As if the little things that troubled normal people didn't matter to her.

'It might have been significant,' he replies. 'Rory was trying to find out if Mac had been talking to me about him. At the time I thought it was just undergraduate vanity – you know, "did he mention me at all?" – but I realise now that Rory had probably just been introduced to Sidorov. By Mackenzie. He was wondering if I knew about it. It was a very long time ago, of course. The maddening thing was, at that time, I was trying not to prolong the conversation.'

'Why not?'

'Two reasons: one, didn't exactly enjoy Rory's company. The second: I was actually hoping to go and see you. That felt more important.' Perhaps the whisky is helping Simon.

'Well, perhaps it was, at that time.' Sarah seems keen to locate the event in the distant past.

Simon has got the message. There is an awkward silence and then Simon is saved by a ping on his phone. It's a coded message from the Wizard. Radcliffe had clicked on the link in the phishing email.

'Good news: we have access to Radcliffe's computer.'

Chapter 23

Oxford
May 2022

Simon grabs his laptop from the satchel that stayed by his side, and they log into the Wizard's secure video channel. At Simon's recommendation, Sarah keeps herself off-screen.

'Okay, so your friend obviously doesn't believe in IT security,' says the Wizard, wearily. Like all computer people, he is especially contemptuous of those that don't appear to understand computers. 'He's got a set of spreadsheets on his computer with passports from each country. Not password protected or anything. So you just need the St Kitts spreadsheet, I suppose?'

'Umm, can you give me the others?' asks Simon. Sarah, off-screen frowns at Simon and mouths, 'Why?'

'Not sure about that, four-seven. Unless you can demonstrate some kind of legal necessity. Can't be done, otherwise.'

'None of this is legal, is it?' says Simon in exasperation. 'What difference does it make?'

'As far as I'm concerned, you need the St Kitts file to prevent a crime. Do you also need the others for that purpose?'

Wearily, Simon accepts that he does not. But he is well aware what is really happening: the Wizard is reminding him that he is in charge.

'Okay, well you'll be able to download the spreadsheet from the usual location. Password via the messenger platform.'

It's a fiddly business but soon Simon is double-clicking on an Excel spreadsheet that has been lifted off Radcliffe's computer just a few minutes earlier. The laptop is sitting on Sarah's large desk, between piles of impenetrable-looking journals and monographs. Sarah is next to Simon and their two heads are close together as they press forwards to try to read the screen. The little egg-timer icon seems to be taking an inordinately long time, stretching their patience. Then it appears to freeze.

'Don't do this to us,' says Simon, rendered powerless by an inanimate computer chip.

And then it pops open. The familiar green framing of the Excel bar along the top, above a crowded page of information. Dates, names, passport number, expiry date, name at application, nationality at application, passport number of original nationality, address. And finally, a column confirming that the client had passed the stringent requirements to become a citizen of The Federation of St Christopher and Nevis, better known as St Kitts. It was one of those annoying spreadsheets where the boxes stretch much wider than a normal computer screen. Simon starts scrolling down the screen, increasing the speed until the text is just a grey blur.

'Good God,' says Sarah, gasping.

Finally, Simon reaches the bottom of the document. There are just over two thousand names. It's only a fraction of the sixteen thousand passports that St Kitts has sold over the years, but it represents millions of dollars in fees for Radcliffe. Simon clicks on the search window at the top of the spreadsheet and types in 'Kleshnyov'. He hits return and waits for Valery's passport to be highlighted. But there's nothing.

'Fuck. If Kleshnyov isn't in the document that means I've got this whole thing wrong.'

'Wait a minute,' Sarah says, reaching over Simon's hands on the keyboard. They awkwardly brush fingers and Simon shoves the laptop towards her. Carefully, she types 'Kleshnev', hits return, and a cell is highlighted, deep in the document. Simon had never realised that a small square on a computer screen could make his heart pound with excitement.

'It's the other way of spelling these names. Missing the diacritic on the "e". You often see it in passports.' Sarah slides her finger across the trackpad so that they can see the row dedicated to Kleshnyov. Dated May 2004, 'Pinsent, Walter', his St Kitts passport number, his name at application, 'Kleshnev, Valery', and his Russian passport number. And then they both look at the names in the same column as Kleshnev. Other passports, all issued on the same date. Kleshnyov is in the middle of a block. There are eighteen names, all Russian or from the former Soviet Union. All but two are men. In all of these cases, the St Kitts passport was issued in a different name, unlike all of the other names in the spreadsheet. The new names are a mixture of European styles, some as English as Walter Pinsent. Others look Spanish, French or Germanic.

'This is incredible,' says Sarah.

Simon is feeling excited, exuberant. 'You see what they've done with the aliases,' he says. 'They've all gone for Western European names. I guess you pick a name that fits your language skills.'

They both fall silent as they scan the list. Simon is half expecting to see a name he recognises. But other than Kleshnyov they're all unfamiliar to him. But not to Sarah.

'Look at that,' she says, tapping a cell on the screen with her index finger. 'Sazanovich, Sergey. St Kitts name is Steve Carpenter… Oh, wait a minute. I see what they've done.'

'Enlighten me,' asks Simon, annoyed that he can't get the reference.

'Sazan is a fish. A carp. Carpenter. Spies are the same everywhere, aren't they? Can't resist a little joke.'

'Friend of yours?' asks Simon, ironically.

'Sazanovich was in Oslo in 2003. He'd been there under diplomatic cover, pretending to be some kind of consular official. But he was actually the SVR case officer of Anders Holte. Remember him? Norwegian ministry of defence official. He was passing information about NATO's North Flank to the Russians.

'The Norwegians invited me to participate in a review, a sort of lessons-learned exercise,' says Sarah, warming to her theme. 'They asked the Brits to help them do an independent assessment of where things might have gone wrong. Bloody good idea, actually. We'd never do that,' she adds, ruefully. 'One of the key learning points was that Sazanovich had played Holte brilliantly. Identified his weaknesses, his resentments at being passed over for promotion. Holte believed his bosses were all idiots and were ignoring his work. And Sazanovich spun that round, said, "these people don't appreciate your talent, but if you talk to us, you'll finally be having the impact you deserve". Holte went for it. Classic intelligence recruitment, really. Sazanovich was really good at it.'

Simon agrees — persuading the unsung civil servant that another country's government might be more appreciative of your work was a familiar methodology. 'And what became of Sazanovich? Was he kicked out of Norway?'

'No, he was too good for that. Holte has never been convicted of anything. The Norwegians had been reporting on what they were doing, but it was from super-sensitive sources they couldn't reveal in a prosecution. So they tried to flip Holte and double-cross Sazanovich. That didn't work either: Holte wouldn't co-operate. So they then shifted Holte into a job where he had no access to sensitive information. He's still there today, for all I know, running the stationery department at the Norwegian Ministry of Defence.'

'And what became of Sazanovich?'

'Well that's what's interesting. Disappeared from view. It was one of those things that always struck me: he was clearly a talented SVR officer, withdrawn from Oslo because they knew there was heat on the Holte case. But then he vanishes. Never seen again in any of our reporting, or any reporting from any ally. That's unusual. So, what would you do if you had a really good SVR guy who needs to become invisible for a while? Assign him to the COSTELLO organisation, where he acquires a whole new identity, disappears from the SVR's books.'

Gradually, COSTELLO is taking shape. Something that, only a few weeks ago, had been a chimera, possibly a myth, was now an entity. With named, traceable operatives.

'We need to get these names to Rudi. See what the COSTELLO travel patterns were. And then we see if any of those trips can be shown to match a journey when Rory, or Harkness, Camondo, and the rest of them were travelling, look for the overlaps. This is it. We're onto them.' In his eager anticipation, Simon slaps his hand on the desk, turning towards Sarah. Thanks to her need to huddle in front of the laptop screen, their faces are surprisingly close to one another. There's a moment. Something might happen. And suddenly Simon feels self-conscious and stands up, pacing, excited and disappointed in equal measure.

'I'm sorry, Simon,' says Sarah.

Simon wants to say 'it doesn't matter' but he's not quite sure what she's sorry about.

'I'm sorry,' she repeats, with greater emphasis. 'You'll be able to find if a COSTELLO operative left Russia at a particular time, and you'll be able to see if one of Mackenzie's nominees was travelling at the same time. But millions of people get on aeroplanes every day. If two people in two completely different countries do that, it's not conclusive. Don't get me wrong, this is amazing. You've uncovered something I never believed existed… never believed would be possible. But we aren't there yet. You've come such a long way, but you haven't scored.'

You haven't scored. True on all fronts. Simon folds the laptop, thanks Sarah for the drinks and heads back to his room, feeling hollow. As he crosses the vast expanse of Tom Quad, dark figures are scurrying between the lighted doorways. He walks past a student who appears to be staring at her smartphone. But there is something not quite right about the intensity of her stare at the screen glowing in the dark. The stare of someone who is staring at their smartphone in order to look as though they are staring at their smartphone. Someone who has, moments earlier, been staring at you.

Simon curses inwardly. Christ Church might have been one of the safest places in all of England to hide away from Russian intelligence. But the twenty-first-century student at a British university, even a student at Oxford's grandest college, is likely to be financially stretched. Perhaps a Russian national, shown a picture of Simon and told to look out for him or risk negative consequences for family back home. Or a Brit, offered five hundred quid in cash and a promise of the same again for a photo proving Simon is on Christ Church grounds.

He's sure they won't try anything on him inside the college. But he needs to be more careful.

Chapter 24

Oxford

May 2022

It is a magical summer evening, the sort that would allow undergraduates to construct imagined memories for years to come. The scent of wisteria hangs heavy in the still air. It might be the middle of the week but spotty boys in their dinner jackets are escorting young women in evening dresses to some supposedly exclusive event. Simon knows he should be scornful of the privilege, the implied smugness. But he allows himself to feel charmed by the beauty of it all.

Simon rounds a corner and enters an arched passageway. This leads to the winding staircase close to the bell tower and the rooms he has inhabited for the past few days. He is padding up the stone stairs, absent-mindedly twisting the shoulder-strap of his satchel as it crosses his chest, wondering about the suspicious student he spotted earlier.

An odd clicking sound catches his attention. Instinctively, he jerks to an immediate halt, steadying himself on the cast-iron banister. He narrows his eyes to help him hear better: illogically, this seems to work. His own breathing appears excessively loud, but he can also hear the click again. The unmistakable sound of a camera shutter. Placing his feet as carefully as possible he edges over to the middle of the staircase. The steepest part of the spiral gives him a better perspective of the door to his room, looming ahead of him. Wide open.

It is a summer evening and no lights are on, but there is still enough daylight for Simon to see the legs of two men, at his eye level as he ascends the staircase, moving around in his room. His initial thought is to reverse course, to get help in apprehending these intruders. But he realises he cannot let them out of his sight. Instead, he decides to creep past the door opening, further up the staircase, so that he can observe unobtrusively.

Each step feels like an eternity. He is sure that his breathing is audible from a considerable distance, but the two men seem not to notice. They are speaking in Russian in the sort of low voices that are quieter than a whisper. As Simon edges past the open doorway he sees one of the men taking pictures of the papers that are lying around in Simon's room. These are mostly print-outs of news articles about Gough, of no intelligence value. The other man is looking in drawers, cupboards, clearly searching for something. Simon feels huge relief that his throwaway laptop is hanging in the satchel round his shoulders.

It feels like he has passed the danger zone. He is standing at the gap between door and hinge, concealed, but able to see a slice of what is happening in his room. But then he hears one man turn to the other and say a single, sharp word.

'*Tikho!*' Be quiet!

The two men look at each other and then at the open doorway. Simon is seeing their faces for the first time. He thinks he recognises one of them — was it Igor, who'd followed him into Christ Church? Shiny bald head, wide face. Igor pulls a pistol from the back of his waistband and moves towards the doorway. Simon steps backwards and moves up two steps, waiting for him to appear in the staircase.

Then everything happens quickly. Just as Igor is approaching the doorway, Great Tom, Oxford's loudest bell, strikes. The sound distracts Igor. His head appears at the doorway, less than fifty centimetres from Simon, but looking down the stairs away from him. Very slowly, Igor moves to descend the staircase, holding the pistol out in a two-handed grip, his back to Simon. The sound of the bell is briefly deafening. Simon braces one hand against the stone pillar at the centre of the spiral staircase, his other hand gripping the cast-iron bannister on the outside. Grunting with the effort, he swings his legs forwards, thrusting both feet squarely into the centre of Igor's back. This sound has caused Igor to turn backwards, but far too late. Simon catches a view of his face in profile just as his two feet crash into Igor's back. With his hands out in front clutching his pistol, Igor stands no chance of steadying himself on the steep stairs. There is a sickening crunch as he is pitched forwards, his body rolling down the stone steps, his head stretching in odd directions as his spine snaps. The second man rushes out. He makes the mistake of looking down at his comrade, allowing Simon to repeat the manoeuvre. But it is less effective this time: he is more solidly built, and Simon's feet catch him on the side of his body rather than squarely in the back. He stumbles and falls a few steps but steadies himself and draws a gun as he swings back. He surges back up the steps in pursuit of Simon, who is already racing up the staircase, the adrenaline propelling him upwards in huge strides.

There is a sharp crack as a 9mm bullet ricochets past, but the curve of the spiral staircase is protecting Simon. He bounds upwards, moving faster than his chubby pursuer. And then he has reached a low, flimsy door at the top of the spiral stairs, which looks more like a shabby cupboard, held closed by a padlock. Simon throws all his weight against the lock and finds he is barrelling out past the splintering door, falling on his shoulder onto a flat, leaded roof at the top of Christ Church. He rolls sideways just in time to see his chaser appear in the stone turret that houses the doorway, his hand holding the pistol appearing first, which he fires uselessly into the air. He has the build of a rugby prop and pauses to work his way through the narrow opening, more hatch than doorway. Simon aims a heavy kick at the pistol, which spins out of the hand and clatters on the leaded roof. The man pulls the rest of himself through just as Simon slams a plank of splintered door down on the back of his shiny bald head. Simon repeats this, aiming the protruding nails in the plank into the assailant's skull. He feels slightly queasy as he feels the nails dig in, as if he is hammering into soft wood. The main gives a low groan and rolls his eyes slightly. Then his knees buckle and he falls forwards, deceptively slowly, as if genuflecting before an invisible deity.

Simon grabs the pistol, checking for a safety catch and then remembering it's a Glock, and he shoves it into his waistband. He then tries to collect himself.

He is standing on the roof of Tom Quad, a vista of Oxford's dreaming spires before him in the evening light. There is a light breeze and the deep boom of Great Tom bell chiming the curfew, merrily ignored by the happy voices below. Simon knows he has, at best, a couple of minutes before someone spots a crumpled body at the bottom of the spiral staircase that leads to his room. His first thought is to get to Sarah, but then he realises that even she cannot make a dead body go away. So he is the one who must disappear. Again.

This disappearance needs to start with getting off the roof. Happily, Simon had spent some of his undergraduate years pursuing the esoteric sport of nocturnal stegophilism – climbing the outside of buildings at night. A well-established Oxford tradition, it usually involved the hoisting of some kind of trophy on the parapet of a well-known university landmark. Many a night had been spent trying to get a traffic cone or lavatory seat onto the roof of the Bodleian Library. As a result, Simon knows that the best way off the parapet of Tom Quad is via a drainpipe a few feet from where he is standing. That leads down onto a lower roof in the corner of the college closest to Blue Boar Street, a quiet part of the complex that is usually empty at night. The *where* is clear: what is difficult is the *how*. It is more than twenty years since Simon has climbed the outside of a building using its drainpipe, and his shoes, sensible middle-aged leather brogues that Sarah had bought him so that he would fit in the college environment, are far from ideal for the purpose.

Simon proceeds at a running crouch towards the point where he can lower himself over the gutter. He lies on his stomach to peer over. The familiar drainpipe is still there: a solid cast-iron artery leading down to a smaller roof, two floors below. Simon stretches out his arm to test the pipe, trying to shake it. It feels solid, as does the gutter he is lying on. The wall behind the drainpipe is completely flat. He remembers coming up this way, many years earlier, but not the descent. He needs to get a good grip of the pipe and swing his feet against the wall, using the pressure to keep the soles of his shoes in place. Simon takes one more look round, forlornly wondering if there's another way.

There isn't. So with a grunt he readjusts the satchel across his shoulders, puts both hands on the parapet of the gutter and, as slowly and with as much control as possible, swings first one, then another leg down, pushing his feet against the flat wall, his arms immediately taking the pressure. The gutter sags slightly with this weight, but it's not going to give way. He reaches one arm down onto the drainpipe, then the second, his biceps already feeling the strain, his heart in his mouth. The satchel swings out into the air behind his back. He works his hands downwards on the pipe, as if he is descending a fat rope, jumping his feet as he does. After six feet there is a small bracket where the drainpipe is fixed onto the wall. This gives him a chance to edge his toes on the tiny ledge, taking the strain off his arms. As he does this, he feels the pistol slip out of his waistband and watches in horror as it spins into the gloaming. He waits, his entire body tensed for the moment of impact causing a discharge, but none comes and all he hears is the dull thud of the gun landing in a flowerbed. Now pulsing with extra adrenaline, he resumes his descent, gratefully slithering the final ten feet onto the lower flat roof of a single-storey extension built against the main facade. His arms are shaking with the exertion and he realises he is completely out of shape. He edges to the side of this lower structure and jumps down into a flowerbed thick with tulips. The landing is harder than he expects and he feels a sharp pain in his left ankle. Cursing under his breath he starts fumbling around for the gun. He isn't sure he wants a weapon, but it now has his fingerprints all over it so he cannot leave it there. After a few seconds of mounting tension, rummaging with his hands among the blooms, he feels the familiar flat top of a Glock pistol.

He is about to sprint towards a gateway that leads into the quiet backwater of Blue Boar Street when he hears footsteps crunching on the gravel path. Simon, still on his knees in the flowerbed, freezes. He turns his head towards the sound and sees an amorous couple, barely two metres away; the boy in his suspiciously shiny black tie, arm round a young woman in a shimmering red dress that finishes a long way above her knee.

'Come on,' the boy is saying. 'Let's go up.' His slurred speech suggests he has had plenty to drink. He is staggering with her towards a building that looks like student halls.

'Freddy,' she sounds unsure – perhaps open to persuasion, perhaps regretting the situation. 'Let's not rush.' It's unclear whether this suggestion relates to their relationship globally or to the current moment. But they stop moving and begin kissing enthusiastically. Simon feels voyeuristic and wonders if he can creep round them: they are drunk enough not to have noticed him yet. But he is incredibly close to them. Then the boy breaks away from the embrace and turns directly towards Simon. With a huge burp he leans forwards and starts to vomit. Simon is just out of range, but the young woman has now seen him and lets out a surprised squeal.

'Don't mind me,' says Simon, trying to sound as normal as possible. 'I dropped my phone down here. Just picking it up.' The boy has finished vomiting and groans slightly. Simon has his hand over the gun. He has to trust that the darkness and the drink will stop them from identifying the dark object he is stuffing into his trouser pocket. He stands up and tries to look like a member of faculty with some responsibility for discipline. 'Young man, you look like you need to go and clean yourself up. Er, perhaps you can help him with that?' he says, turning to the woman. His suggestion is briefly authoritative, and the couple stagger off towards the accommodation block. Simon seizes his chance and sprints towards the locked wooden gates. He uses the hinge bracket to get a footing and hauls himself over the top, this time landing better on the pavement below. The little side street is empty and he dusts himself down and turns into the main road, striding purposefully like any other academic wandering through Oxford late on a summer evening.

Simon moves as quickly as he can without attracting attention towards Gloucester Green, Oxford's coach station. His plan is to board the first coach that is departing, destination unimportant. The advantage of a coach is that it stops rarely, and when it does, it is usually in a god-forsaken layby, hard for a surveillance team to monitor.

Gloucester Green is little changed from Simon's memory. It still has the standard shabbiness of bus depots all over the world. Sad people are dragging cheap suitcases towards coaches. Diesel fumes belch into the air, mixing rupture with loneliness. This is the means of travel chosen by those that cannot choose any other. Simon scans the departure board and sees that there is an imminent departure to Southampton. There is no time to consider options – he buys a ticket and stops at a phone box, pulling out his mobile to get Sarah's number, which he dials in carefully, before turning off the device so that his location is no longer traceable. Sarah picks up quickly, an urgency in her voice.

'Simon? Where are you?'

'Gloucester Green. Now, listen very carefully. First thing: this call never happened. Anyone asks, wrong number. When I got back to my room there were two guys. Russians. Armed. I think they're dead. Not sure about the second one, to be honest.' Simon hears a gasp, and decides to plough on. 'I'm going to get out of the way, but I'll call you again tomorrow.'

'Did this *really* have to happen?' asks Sarah, exasperation in her voice.

'Well, I could have let them shoot me, I guess,' says Simon.

'That's not what I'm saying,' she replies, sounding very annoyed. 'It's just, they keep popping up.' Her tone alters. 'I think I've got Gough's ex-PA to talk to me. She has a good reason to want to dump him in it. Could be a big deal. Name's Amy Cleverly. Look her up.'

'Maybe we're nearly at the end of this,' says Simon, trying to sound hopeful, even if he doesn't feel it. 'Anyway, I'm going to need some transport from Hampshire at some point in the next twenty-four hours.' Simon puts the phone down quickly, not wanting to give Sarah the chance to ask more questions. He's nervous that calls to Sarah's number might be monitored. But there's an important difference: the Russians won't kill a serving British official as high ranking as Sarah. Simon had thought they wouldn't touch him either, as a 'former'. But he was obviously wrong about that. COSTELLO is too important. Unlike Simon, Sarah is safe.

He climbs up into the strange, spaceship lighting of a long-distance coach after dark. Happily for him, not many people appear to want to travel from Oxford to Southampton on a summer's evening, and he has a double seat to himself. He leans back in the overly firm chair and places his hands on his thighs, where the bulge of the Russian's pistol is digging into his leg.

The coach pulls out of Gloucester Green and heads towards the motorway. Simon can hear sirens, and is sure that they are for him: the police alerted and on the hunt. But he sees an ambulance whizz past the coach, heading in the opposite direction. If nobody has seen him leave the college, he will have several hours' head-start. The police might try to pick him up in Southampton, but that's a problem for later. For now, Simon can try to relax as the coach heads southwards into the night.

Chapter 25

Hampshire

May 2022

Simon may have slept, but he isn't sure. The coach stops at a layby on the edge of a major road, surrounded by rolling hills looming in the dark. He climbs out into a service station. There is a Travelodge glowing perfunctorily in the night sky, a gleaming beacon of inhospitality. The sound of high-speed traffic whooshes in the background. Using his burner phone for navigation, Simon works his way round to the back of the hotel building. After a quick check for CCTV cameras, he climbs over a fence into the thick woodland behind. As he walks deeper into the forest, the sound of the road begins to fade to a dull buzz, and the crunching of twigs underfoot becomes the loudest noise. He stops, momentarily distracted by rustling foliage. In the woodland darkness he can see no movement and wonders if it's a deer. Now, the most audible sound is his own heavy breathing. An owl hoots.

He isn't sure what he's looking for, but he finds it a few minutes later: a fallen tree has created a sort of shelter; a patch of flat ground, cushioned with dried leaves and overhung by foliage. It is neither comfortable not sheltered, but it is better than nothing. Using his satchel as a pillow and with his hand resting on the gun, he lies on his back and wonders if he might sleep.

It is colder than he'd expected.

202

Simon realises that he has slept a little. He is lying on his back, staring past the forest canopy to the sky above. It is a clear morning, cool with the blue skies of the early summer. He gets stiffly to his feet and looks around the small forest clearing. The highway is audible: a low drone of traffic, punctuated by the occasional monstrous rumble of a heavy truck. The woods are undistinguished. There are few broadleaves, hardly any bluebells and a lot of pine trees. These look to have been planted for commercial timber and then forgotten. This being the south of England, owning the land was always going to be worth more in tax breaks than the tiresome business of working it.

The morning light is spreading a clean, warm glow over the tops of distant hills and the Lego-brick facade of the Travelodge, visible between the trees. Simon decides against heading back towards the building. It's the predictable choice and there will be people up and moving around. He turns his back on civilisation and heads into the forest.

But this is the south of England, and civilisation is not far in any direction. Simon is certain that he will run into another road if he works his way through the woodland in a consistent direction. His plan is to get to where there would be less traffic and fewer chances for watchers, and then call Sarah.

He falls into a sort of reverie as he picks his way through the woods, stepping over branches and working his way around fallen trunks. The dawn chorus is joyous. Not for the first time, Simon wishes he knew the names of the different birds. The noise of his feet crackling on twigs and dried leaves is getting in the way, so he stops, just to listen. He breathes out slowly; the going has been tough, his heart pumping harder than usual. Before breathing in again, he shuts his eyes to take in the sound of the forest, undisturbed.

Then, a distant crunching sound. A large animal breaking twigs as it walks. Deer? His head twitches, uselessly trying to find the source of the noise. A dark shape. Is that a person?

The shot rings through the trees with a sharp twang. The birds screech their violent objection. Instinctively, Simon runs. He has no clear idea which direction the noise has come from. But he runs, the Cardross training reminding him to weave through the trees.

Another shot. This one seems to ricochet off a tree trunk just to the right of Simon's head. He jerks away from the sound and runs into a small channel between two clear strands of pine trees. He looks over his shoulder and thinks he can see a dark shape moving through the woods towards him, also at a running pace. The pistol is bouncing around in his trouser pocket and he grabs it, throwing one arm over the opposite shoulder, pulling the trigger without breaking his stride. The trigger clicks, but no shot.

Shit. Safety catch? But it's a Glock. Simon remembers he hasn't cocked it.

He has no time to fiddle with the gun and runs onwards. He is wondering if he can reach a road on the far side of the woods. Nobody would shoot him in front of passing cars, would they? But the forest stretches ahead of him for more than a mile. He can't run that far. Another crack as a bullet whistles through the trees. His legs are surging on adrenaline. Maybe he can outrun them?

And then he catches his foot on a fallen branch, catapulting his body forwards into a slight hollow. He lands with a thud, momentarily winded, seeing stars, his satchel slamming down on his back. The gun has tumbled out of his hands under a thick holly bush. But the adrenaline is coursing and he rolls his body into the bush without thinking, grabbing at the dark object, hundreds of spiky leaves prickling into him. He lies motionless. He is sure that his surging heartbeat is audible, hammering on his ribcage. But he can't hear anything else. His assailant must have stopped moving too, momentarily confused by Simon's disappearance. With his head at ground level, Simon cranes his neck, hoping to catch sight of moving legs. But the undergrowth is too thick. Can he hear breathing? Where?

A twig snaps. Very close, but not from the direction he expects. Simon stops breathing. Imperceptibly slowly, still lying on his side, he crancs his neck towards the noise. There is a darker shade to the undergrowth, no more than four metres away. And then he hears it: heavy breathing. The dark shape begins to form an outline: a pair of legs, and a torso, obscured by foliage. Simon draws the pistol across his body so that he can hold it in both hands. As slowly as he can, he pulls back the top slide. There is a slight click as the round enters the chamber. He is holding his hand as tightly as he can over the weapon to deaden the noise. Then he waits, listening to the breathing of a man who wants to kill him, less than a car's length away.

It feels like an age, but it is probably less than ten seconds.

A male pheasant makes its loud 'cock, cock' cry, which is followed by the whirring of flapping wings. Simon had heard one earlier on, even if he wasn't sure exactly which bird it was. With this noisy distraction Simon leans upwards, aims the gun into the foliage and fires.

Everything happens at once. He hears a roar of agony and the sound of a body falling. And then more shots are ringing over his head. Simon rolls lower into the hollow and fires twice, this time aiming at ground level. Adrenaline and bloodlust are coursing through his body. Another cry of pain, this time strangulated. The shouts die down and he hears desperate breathing, someone sucking for air. Simon lies rigidly still, still hardly breathing, his heart hammering.

'Simon.' The pronunciation is foreign, probably Eastern European. The gasping returns.

It's a trick. He'll get you to stand up and double tap you.

'No trick, Simon.' He gasps again, a gurgling sound. 'I die… Help.'

Help.

Suddenly, Simon feels terrible pity.

'Who are you?'

'No important. Help.' Gasps again. Then he hears whispering, punctuated by desperate gasps. Simon strains to hear. …*ill-allahu wahdahu la shareeka lahu lah-al-mulku*… It's the *Kalimat al-tawhid*, spoken by Muslims as they face death.

Chechen.

Simon stands up, holding the pistol out in front of him in both hands, his finger taut against the trigger. He edges cautiously around the side of a bush and sees a man lying on the ground, his arms outstretched, Christlike. In the right hand, closest to Simon, another Glock, held loosely. At Simon's appearance the fingers twitch around the pistol grip and Simon feels another surge of adrenaline. But the gesture is fleeting, the hopeless instinct of a dying man.

It takes Simon a couple of seconds to take it all in. The man is wearing dark clothes, which mask the blood spreading across his trousers and jacket and pooling on the ground. Little bits of leaf are floating in the blood, turning in eddies. Fearfully, Simon walks forwards. He feels a sense of dislocation, as if the dark object behind a bush he shot at had no connection with the dying man in front of him. There are large gashes at the top of the thigh and bright red arterial blood is pulsating from his femoral onto the ground, like a hideous water feature. The second shot appears to have pierced the side of the torso. Here, darker blood is bubbling out. The man's face is already taking on a grey pallor, his naturally olive complexion fading as his life ebbs away. He is gulping and frothy blood is bubbling from his mouth.

As he approaches, Simon kicks the pistol away from the now-limp hand, before shoving his own in his waistband and crouching down. The man's lips are moving fast, but he is inaudible. With a huge effort the man's left arm reaches up and clutches Simon. Initially, Simon is alarmed, but the grip weakens almost immediately. Simon knows that the only chance of saving him would be to stop the bleeding from the femoral artery, by plunging his hand into the wound. But he doesn't do that. Is it revulsion? Cruelty? Or the realisation that he is too late? The man's eyes widen in a gesture of surprise, before rolling upwards as he appears to gasp, finally. Simon suspects he is still technically alive, albeit unconscious.

Suddenly, he appears to regain consciousness, his eyes narrowing in focus. '*O bozhe nyet.*' Oh God, no.

The grip on his arm loosens, and the hand falls limply to the ground.

Simon is surprised at his own calmness. He is thinking mostly of Evie and wondering if this man had driven the car that hit her. He stands up and returns to where he had lain as he fired the fatal shots. He searches the ground until he finds the three spent shell casings, their brass gleaming in the morning light. He knows nothing of the history of the weapon digging awkwardly into his groin, but they all leave a signature, so he shoves the casings into his pocket for disposal elsewhere.

Then he returns to the body. Using his jacket fabric to cover his fingerprints he checks the man's pockets and finds a phone. Simon turns it on, but it's password protected. He keeps it, for later destruction. There is also a car key. The man would have parked near the Travelodge. Simon wonders about taking the vehicle but concludes it's not worth the risk, so he stuffs the keys back into the dead man's pocket.

Standing up, he realises he has bloodstains on his jacket.

–

Simon continues his walk through the forest, heading for the far side and quieter roads. After about five minutes he realises his hands are shaking uncontrollably. It isn't the first time he's taken another man's life. But he has never before looked into the eyes of the man he's just killed as he utters his final prayers. He stops and leans against a large oak tree, its trunk the width of a small car. Trying to steady himself, he exhales and stares up through the canopy of juvenile leaves, their foliage brilliant green against the azure sky.

One word: how? Nobody had known where he was going. In Oxford, he had switched off his burner and only used a payphone to call Sarah. He'd said 'Hampshire', but that wasn't exactly narrowing it down. But they seemed to be on him, every time. In Prague, in Oxford, and now in remote woods by a dual carriageway in the Hampshire countryside. Is there a leak? Sarah?

He puts the thought out of his mind. It made no sense for the person orchestrating the operation to be its traitor. But the others? Kemi? He knows nothing about her. O'Brien? But he's barely involved.

Or is he just going crazy? A good surveillance team could have followed him onto the coach. No need for a mole.

You're letting the stress get to you. Stay calm. Stay logical.

And then he has a flashback to gunshots and the agonised screams of a dying man. He has to keep moving.

–

Simon is standing by a small country lane at the edge of a forest in an undistinguished corner of rural England. He has a fleeting fantasy that he could disappear back into the forest and live there in hiding, a wild man of the woods. But he knows that this isn't a real plan, that they will send someone else to find him in a few hours. He has to call Sarah, even though he doesn't want to use his phone, because there's nobody else he can trust and he's standing by a lane at the edge of a forest in rural England. With deep misgiving he fires up his phone, waiting for it to connect to the network and announce his presence to the world.

Sarah is businesslike, as if Simon's having to flee Oxford is of little importance. 'You need to get to London. You went to Hampshire, for some reason?'

Simon feels there is a lot he needs to explain but the conversation hasn't started as he had hoped. 'Sarah, I'm currently trying to escape a police investigation into two Russians found dead in Christ Church.'

'Ah yes, that was the thing. They're not dead. One is paralysed. Never going to walk again. But he's lucid. He's not willing to tell anyone what he's been up to, of course. The other is in a coma. And according to the police, only one of them was armed.'

Instinctively Simon's fingers curl around the pistol in his pocket. A wave of fear and stress sweeps over him. Is he going to be on the run for the rest of his life?

'Thames Valley Police have been asking all about you,' continues Sarah. 'I've told them I arranged a guest room for you, as a favour. Your personal life was in a mess and you needed a place to stay for a few days.' She pauses, is she enjoying this? 'Not that far from the truth, actually. Obviously, I've said I've no idea where you are. Which also happens to be true.' Sarah isn't very interested in his predicament. 'Anyway I mentioned Amy Cleverly before. You know I told you about her? Gough's ex-PA. He completely screwed her over. She's bitter. I've had a bit of a breakthrough. She's agreed to talk to me.'

'Okay.' Simon doesn't sound very impressed. He had indeed googled her on the coach journey. She seems like an admin person who won't have been party to any of Rory's deeper secrets. He still hasn't managed to tell her what has happened, and this call is going on for too long. Maybe he doesn't have to tell her? Then it won't have happened at all.

'No, Simon, this could be a big deal. This is someone he bullied out of her job. She was going to take him to a tribunal and the Cabinet Office hushed it up. Big settlement.'

'Does she know what we're looking for? Is she in the loop?'

'Well, I've no idea, but I do know that she's very keen to talk, but also very nervous. A good combination, if you see what I mean.' Sarah's ruthlessness is shining through, again. 'She's agreed to meet me tonight.'

'Where?'

'In London, on Hampstead Heath. You'll need to be there.'

Simon thinks about this for a few moments, looking around at the deserted country lane.

'Simon? You still there?'

'Yes. I'm just trying to figure out how I get to London.'

'Can't the hotel order you a taxi? You're in Hampshire, aren't you?'

To his annoyance, Simon loses his temper. 'Do you not fucking get it? I am on the run. I slept, well actually I barely slept, on the ground in the woods somewhere near Newbury. It was cold. And damp. And someone knew I was here. How did that happen?'

Even more annoyingly, Sarah seems indifferent to the outburst. 'You slept in a forest? All a bit John Buchan, isn't it?' Simon is rapidly remembering that Sarah has an incredible intellectual command of the intricacies of intelligence work, but very little practical knowledge of the realities. But she is catching up. 'Okay, I've an idea. I warned O'Brien he might need to pick you up from the Hampshire area. He'll drive you to London. Send me a pin via Signal.'

With that she ended the call. Simon has not had a chance to mention the death in the forest.

The call had taken two minutes. *Is that long enough? Will they be able to get a fix in that time?* Simon sends his location to Sarah and then powers down his phone, which he stuffs into the Faraday pouch he has in his satchel, cutting it off from any external signal. Then he sits down against a venerable tree. He breathes deeply and slowly, trying to calm his racing heart and quivering limbs. Occasionally, vehicles speed past, but none stop. It is very obvious when a white sedan slows to a halt. Simon is walking towards it as the driver door opens. O'Brien smiles awkwardly, as if they have just stepped out of a meeting at Grosvenor and Simon is underdressed.

'Hello, Simon. Bit of a change of scene,' he adds, pointlessly. 'I'm taking you to London, right?'

Simon realises he is struggling to talk and hopes that the blood on his jacket isn't obvious. 'Umm, I think I should lie down on the back seat. For your sake, so that nobody sees you with me.' The real reason is that Simon is too exhausted and doesn't want to talk.

'Right you are,' says O'Brien, opening the rear door and ushering Simon in, before clicking it shut. Simon makes himself comfortable on the bench seat, bending his legs to squeeze in.

He drifts into a sort of daydream, out of body, where he is observing himself, lying on the back seat of a nondescript car. After about an hour he feels the vehicle slow to a stop and a sudden wash of cooler air as the nearside door is opened.

Momentarily, he can't tell if the imposing figure backlit by the bright sun is O'Brien or someone else, but then a familiar voice says, 'Here we are,' and Simon clambers down onto the road. Simon looks round and sees that he is in a small lay-by near a bridge over the River Thames. Clearly not in central London, but not somewhere he recognises.

'Staines,' says O'Brien, apparently reading his mind. 'Oh, wait a minute, Sarah wanted you to have these,' he says as he rummages around in the pockets of his blazer, pulling out a credit card and a fresh phone. 'Contactless. Pay for stuff.'

'Right.' Simon is starting to catch up. Sarah's card means that he will leave a false trail for anyone tracking his movements via spending transactions. 'That's smart of her.'

O'Brien turns to him, grins, and says, 'You know where you're going, right?'

'Yes, Hampstead,' Simon replies without thinking. O'Brien gives him an awkward thumbs-up as he walks back to the car and speeds off.

Simon leans on the parapet of the bridge watching the River Thames flow lazily underneath. He reaches into his pocket and drops the three shell casings into the river. They disappear into the satisfyingly murky water. He then does the same with his old phone, which gives a little plop as it hits the river.

Simon then pulls out the new phone and messages Sarah.

What did you tell Ben? he asks, vaguely hostile.

The little checkmarks tell him that the message is read almost instantly: she has clearly been waiting for him to pop up on this new number.

Nothing. A curt response, then a longer one. *Can you do counter on Amy? She's going to go from Tufnell Park tube and walk from there. You need to be carrying, I know you've got one from the guys at Christ Church.*

In the bland language of text messaging it's as if it is the most mundane thing in the world. But the instructions send a shiver down Simon's spine to the awkward block of the weapon, still jammed into his waistband. A flashback to a memory he is already trying to bury.

Where are you going to meet her?

Lime Walk on Heath. I'll tell her to walk from station.
You make sure she's clean. I'll be on bench.

Simon feels he ought to tell her he killed someone before break-fast. But secure messaging doesn't feel like the right way to do it.

Chapter 26

London

May 2022

Simon is passing through the far west suburbs now: rows of dodgy car dealerships, furniture showrooms and shiny developments of 'luxury' flats, whose appeal is dulled by their proximity to one of the busiest roads in Europe. He uses Sarah's card to hire 'Boris bikes', the heavy red bicycles located at docking stations throughout the city.

Wearing his baseball cap with the peak pulled low over his eyeline, Simon realises that he is almost invisible when riding a bike. CCTV cameras are all configured to capture faces as they look forwards and upwards. On a bike, the rider is tilted forwards and looking down, out of view. With a credit card in a different name he could move around the city undetected by even the most sophisticated hacking team.

Simon does not rush. He rides towards Tufnell Park, avoiding main roads, zig-zagging through side streets and cut-throughs. He keeps running into dead-ends and cul-de-sacs. This is intentional, as it gives him a reason to turn round repeatedly, checking for watchers every time. He switches bikes a few times, to muddy the waters. His journey takes him past the pastel-coloured villas of the ultra-rich, followed by the stolid redbrick houses of the merely very rich. And, this being London, the other side of the road has council housing. He parks his bike in a docking station near Camden Town and continues on foot, meandering through Victorian terraces and scruffy housing estates as he climbs the hill towards Tufnell Park. He has plenty of time, allowing him to do a thorough recce of the streets leading towards the meeting place on Hampstead Heath.

Simon returns to Tufnell Park as the evening draws in. The early summer days are long but the light is dull that day, leaving no shadows and darkening prematurely. His greatest fear has been that he wouldn't recognise Amy. He has no plan to engage her directly: his role is to watch, to see whether she is being followed and to warn Sarah of any problems if she is. It is therefore vital that he can identify her, but not be identified by her. He has studied her photo on LinkedIn and done a bit of online stalking to get a feel for her character. Is she tall? Confident? How does she dress? What sorts of clothes will she likely be wearing?

He acquires a copy of the *Evening Standard* and positions himself in the classic role of anxious man awaiting date's arrival at the entrance to the Underground station. He chooses his spot carefully, having figured out he needs to be opposite the station to be out of the way of the CCTV cameras. The front page of the paper has a big splash about the 'PM's infrastructure boost'. Something to do with new power cables coming into the country from the continent to make electricity cheaper. But he isn't taking it in, focusing instead on the faces of weary commuters emerging from behind the ticket barriers.

Amy arrives on time. As promised, she is petite, pretty and looks nervous and harassed. Her Facebook page doesn't seem to describe someone who appears confident. But this makes it all the more important that she doesn't spot Simon: if she sees him now, any second sighting would leave her thinking that Simon is her follower, and she would abort the meeting. Simon buries his head in the newspaper, his cap pulled low over his eyes, and watches as Amy phones Sarah, according to their arrangement. There is a pause as she fiddles with her phone, obviously getting her maps application to start guiding her to the meeting place. And then she crosses the road, passing so close to Simon that he is sure that she has noticed him. But her head is staring at a direction arrow on her screen and she appears mercifully indifferent to her surroundings.

Simon gives her time to get a head start and then begins his follow. The streets are busy with commuters scurrying home in the early evening and the younger crowd warming up for their night out. This makes one part of his job easier: Amy is unlikely to spot him. Another part is harder: spotting her followers. His experience from Oxford has shown him that they are using outsourced teams, local talent. This is also a challenge. There is no profile to look out for. Pointless to seek out thick-set men with an Eastern European look and ill-fitting suits, like they used to in the old days. Now it could be just about anyone. And London has a huge Eastern European population anyway.

Following the arrow on her phone, Amy turns off the main road into streets full of tall, narrow houses. These streets are quieter, but a scattering of workers are heading home, enough to give Simon cover. There is a lining of parked family cars, squeezed tightly against the kerb. This gives Simon plenty of cover. He looks for people walking with purpose. In the smartphone era, many people walk whilst staring at their screens, completely oblivious to their surroundings. Simon can discount these. Then there are those that walk purposefully but overtake Amy, who exudes uncertainty and moves slowly. These are also not suspect.

That leaves the small number remaining. They walk carefully, meaningfully but ordinarily. Does the man carrying a briefcase and wearing a business suit live round here? Many like him do, but this one doesn't seem to be focused on getting home. Simon tries to think inside the head of the would-be follower: are you dawdling because you don't want to overtake Amy, or because your relationship is on the rocks and you can't face getting home to your partner? Simon looks out for tell-tale signs: the person carrying a copy of yesterday's newspaper (it's a prop, not reading matter); the person who looks away too quickly or visibly recoils if you turn in their direction. At one time you could get really close and spot the earpieces, but now everyone has a phone, so you watch to see if someone spots the target and immediately makes a call. But making calls is normal, too. Paranoia goes with the territory.

Amy is criss-crossing the quiet residential streets of Dartmouth Park before she comes to Highgate Road, busy with buses and rush-hour traffic. Simon positions himself behind a large plane tree outside a handsome terrace of Georgian houses, set back from the main road. Amy has walked up to a pedestrian crossing, fastidiously waiting for the green man before moving. Simon holds back, letting the followers reveal themselves. Young man, pale jacket, mousy hair, grey complexion. His hands are thrust into the jacket pockets above his waistband, his clenched fists making two little bulges. There's something aggressive about the pose that makes Simon nervous, so he christens him Petr, which makes things feel a bit better. He looks for the box and can't see anything. Instinctively, he twitches his waist so that he can feel the reassuring solidity of the butt of the Glock digging into his groin.

Petr is following Amy. Of that, Simon is sure. There's an intensity to his gait, tension in his neck muscles. Amy is at the entrance to the Heath. If Petr is going to try anything, he will probably wait for Amy to get to her meeting and take out both her and Sarah. Or is the objective just to identify the contact? Simon tells himself that he can let this run until Amy reaches Sarah. At that point, he will take executive action. After the events of the morning, Simon realises that his blood is running hot. He is visualising pulling out the weapon, trying to recreate muscle memories that are faint from lack of repetition.

Simon is dawdling, watching Petr and, ahead of him, Amy. She has reached the long avenue of lime trees that crosses Hampstead Heath, a tunnel of green stretching through the open space. Sarah, according to the plan, will be sitting on a bench somewhere in the middle, at the point where the avenue turns to head northwest towards Hampstead village. Petr continues to follow Amy, at a safe distance: she has made his job easy by wearing a distinctive light-coloured trench coat.

What is Petr going to do? Is he going to shoot them? Record the meeting? Simon has a sudden moment of frustration as he recalls that the Glock is not made ready. So he drops behind a lime tree to pull the pistol out of his waistband and pull back the top slide, chambering the first round. He shoves the weapon back into his groin, acutely aware of the possibility that a mistake could result in him blowing off his genitals. Ahead, Simon can see Amy nearing her target. A bench, further up the avenue, has Sarah on it, ready and waiting. Petr is keeping a fixed distance from Amy, looking like a bloke going for a walk in a bosky part of Hampstead Heath. Simon doesn't think Petr is there to kill them: COSTELLO would want to know more about the threat before neutralising it. So he must be planning to eavesdrop, or at least figure out who Amy is meeting.

Amy has reached the bench. Simon can just about make out her pale trench coat up ahead, sitting down next to Sarah. Petr, who is about fifty metres ahead of Simon, pauses. He turns towards the side of the avenue and leans against one of the huge trunks of the ancient lime trees. Petr has his focus towards Sarah and Amy, enabling Simon to observe him undisturbed. Petr appears to be rummaging in his waistband for a large, dark object, which he brings up to his eyeline.

Fuck. Wrong again. This is a wet job.

There is no time for consideration. Simon surges forwards towards Petr, fumbling in his waistband for the Glock, which he pulls up with a two-handed grip, looking for the sight picture. He trains the sights on Petr's torso and keeps running. The thud of his footsteps on the hard earth causes Petr to twitch and swerve towards Simon. As he does so he fumbles and Simon sees the dark object fall to the ground. It is a smartphone, not a weapon.

Petr takes in the sight of Simon bearing down on him, holding an automatic pistol in front of him as he does so. His eyes widen, and his mouth turns to a perfect 'O' of surprise. Instinctively, it would seem, he recoils back against the tree-trunk, his arms darting upwards in supplication. At ten metres, Simon slows his pace and lifts his left index finger to his lips, to signify a need for silence, as his right hand continues to cradle the pistol. His right index finger is still on the trigger, firmly sensing the pressure, without trying to pull.

Petr's smartphone is on the ground in front of him. Simon has come to a halt and has assumed the boxer's stance, his legs apart, ready for the fight. With his free hand he motions down to the phone on the floor, indicating that Petr needs to pick it up. Petr does so.

'Unlock your phone!' Simon says, quietly, but firmly. Petr appears to be playing dumb so Simon tries another language. 'Разблокируйте телефон!' This has the desired effect: Petr's eyebrows twitch upwards and he fiddles with his thumb. Simon can see a change in colour on the phone screen.

'Here,' says Simon, holding out his hand. He is now about five metres from Petr. He twitches his hand, as a dog-handler would to get his hound to deliver a ball or stick. With a furious grunt, Petr flings his phone towards Simon, who catches it easily with his left hand, his right still holding the gun out ahead of him.

Simon tilts the phone towards Petr and says, 'PIN?', his thumb tracing imaginary codes across the screen. He calls out, 'one, one, one, one' and Simon assumes he's deliberately talking crap – nobody has such an obvious code. But he tries it and is surprised that it works.

Simon's eyes sense movement. Petr has taken his chance and is sprinting with impressive speed away from the avenue, weaving between trees as they would have taught him at the Spetsnaz training school. Simon spins in his direction but it's pointless: he can't get a clear shot between the trees. And anyway, he was never going to fire a gun in the early evening on Hampstead Heath with dog-walkers and children out in force. And Petr knew that. Simon shoves the Glock back into his waistband, ensuring it is concealed under his jacket. He then walks as obviously and visibly as possible down the middle of the avenue, ostentatiously looking around him for other watchers. There aren't any.

Simon reaches the bench where Sarah and Amy are sitting, talking in low voices. He doesn't look at them or alter his stride, but from his peripheral vision he can see Amy turn her head towards him as he passes. Once he has moved a sufficient distance he pretends to take a phone call to give himself a reason to come to a halt, putting the phone to his ear and meandering aimlessly as he engages in fictitious conversation. He confirms that Amy has turned back to face Sarah and can no longer see him. He then tracks back along a thin path that runs parallel to the main avenue until he can lean behind a fat tree trunk, just within earshot of the two on the bench, but out of sight. He maintains his constant scan of the surroundings. There are a couple of passers-by, but none that seem likely to be a security risk. They have got away with it: the meeting can proceed. He tunes in to the conversation. Things haven't got very far: Sarah is still warming Amy up.

'...any reason? He fired you, but did he explain why?' Sarah is asking for clarification.

'Well –' Amy has a quavering, nervous voice, sounding like she's on the verge of tears. '– it was fine at the beginning, but then there was the leak inquiry. You know, the *Guardian* did a big profile on Rory and he hated it. It wasn't very complimentary, but I don't think he cared about that. There was stuff about him constantly travelling around Europe and having lots of business with Russia and him bringing in some of the Russian donor money and Rory said that some of the info had come from inside the office at Number Ten. He became obsessed with the idea that there had been a leak and insisted that we hand over our phones for an investigation. I didn't have a government phone: at my level you don't get them. So I didn't hand mine over. But then Rory said I had to anyway.'

'So what did you do?'

'The thing is, I was in a relationship, with a married man. And that man is a senior civil servant who has come under a lot of pressure from the current government. They don't like him – he's suspected of being not fully signed up to their agenda. Ideologically unsound.' She laced these last words with bitter contempt. 'And you know what's been happening, don't you?'

Sarah murmurs assent.

'They've already got rid of the Cabinet secretary, they got rid of the head of the Diplomatic Service, the national security adviser. Nobody is safe. If they had cottoned on to my guy having an affair, they'd use it against him. And against me, of course. Leaks to their friends in the press, that sort of thing. Rory's a bully. He uses information against people to get what he wants. He has his little gang of mates, people who look up to him 'cause he's so bloody rich and they all have their silly nicknames for each other. And they have names for all the women. Mostly offensive, childish. Typical schoolboy crap. Anyway, I knew I had nothing to fear from a leak inquiry. I hadn't leaked. But I couldn't let them know about my private life. I just wasn't prepared to do that. So, I said no. I said you can't see my phone which is private property. And I looked up the civil service regulations and they didn't have the right.'

'But he didn't like that?'

'No, he did not. I said they could check all my emails but my private phone was not their business. They said, "you use WhatsApp for government business" but that was only because Rory forced me to. He did everything via WhatsApp, even though it's against regulations. In fact, that's the reason he did it, because he knew it was off the books. Nothing on the record, you can cover your tracks whenever you want to. That's how he likes things.'

'But you stood your ground, didn't you?' asks Sarah, encouragingly.

'That's right. I was in an impossible position. I could give them the phone and then Richard… oh, I wasn't going to say his name … fuck, *fuck,* FUCK.' Amy is thrown off-course by her own slip of the tongue. Simon can hear a sniff and a stifled sob.

'It's okay. Nothing you say goes anywhere. We're only interested in Rory Gough, not anyone else.' Sarah's voice is calming and there's a rustle of movement from the bench. Perhaps she has put a hand on Amy's arm?

'Right, I've said it now. Richard. I was stuck between fucking up Richard's life or fucking up mine. Richard said we should move in together, that he was going to leave his wife and we'd do things properly. So I stood my ground. Richard's career was way more important: higher salary. I could find a new career outside the civil service. I'm employable, right?'

'Of course you are,' agrees Sarah.

'So I told them they had no right to my personal phone. Part of the thing was that we all knew who the source of the *Guardian* story was, anyway. It was Luigi. Well, that's his nickname 'cause he supposedly looks like the character in the game. Mario Brothers?'

Sarah, normally so composed, seems momentarily confused. 'I'm afraid I'm not very well-informed on computer games.' She sounds apologetic.

'Nor me, but they had all these nicknames and Lewis Moreton was called Luigi. You know, Luigi, Lewis. Sort of makes sense. Luigi's one of Gough's closest acolytes, with him since before he was involved with politics, I think. Gough wouldn't hear a word against him because he has that essential characteristic for advancement in Gough's world: zero capacity for independent thought. He was pure cipher. But Luigi loved to shoot the breeze with journos and they picked stuff up, inevitably. So, the heat was turned on me. I was accused of having leaked to the media and escorted from the building by police officers, like I was some fucking criminal.' Amy has stopped talking and is trying to control her breathing. 'I'm sorry,' she says, her voice cracking. 'It just makes me so angry.'

'You have every right to be angry. Tell me what happened next.'

'There isn't much to say. I knew I could challenge them at a tribunal, but you know how these things work, don't you? First you have to find the money for lawyers, and then you know they can cook up the evidence so you lose and have to pay the government's inflated legal fees, QCs and all. And then I didn't want to draw attention to Richard, knowing that we were moving in together.'

'Yes, I can see. Umm —' Sarah seems a little uncomfortable '— how are things with Richard?'

'Richard? Yes, well you might say that didn't quite pan out as originally expected.' A tone of upset has joined the fury in Amy's voice. 'He decided he was going to give his marriage a second go. So you could say he was fucking me and then he screwed me.'

'Oh, Jesus.' Sarah is sounding almost equally angry. There is a long silence. Absurdly, Simon is feeling guilty, although he is reasonably confident his own miserable love life played no part in this particular mess. 'Oh God, I'm so sorry. These things are so, so awful. Do you need anything? Do you need me to help you find another job?'

'No. Richard was decent enough to make me some introductions. Guess he was feeling guilty. Pay's better than the civil service. So I can't complain, really. But, God, I cannot tell you how much I hate Rory Gough. So, if you can guarantee none of this comes back to me, I will tell you whatever you want to know. He deserves whatever's coming his way.' Amy seems to have found her voice, her confidence and determination rising.

'I need to tell you that your security and privacy are our absolute priority,' says Sarah. Her voice is at its most velvety serious. She sounds capable, reliable and also, to Simon's ears, very sexy, although that is definitely not the important point. 'If you can help us with some ongoing, *sensitive* research into some of Gough's activities, that would be most valuable. But the things you tell us will only be used to enable us to move forwards in the research. No publicity. Nothing that can be linked back to you. That's my solemn promise.' Simon can hear a rustling sound, as if Sarah has laid her hand on Amy's arm, or made some other gesture to drive the point home.

'Okay, well, what is it you want to know? I mean, I was his PA basically. And he is so up himself he doesn't do anything normal. I mean: I sorted his dry cleaning, his presents for his godchildren, his expenses, his travel bookings. You name it, I did it.'

'Funnily enough, it's probably the travel bookings we're most into. You mentioned how the *Guardian* report had some reference to his travelling around Europe. What was that?'

'Well, in the article, it's literally no more than a quote from an unnamed source – but of course we know that was Luigi. It's just a throwaway line, something like: "Gough is hyperactive, when he's not fixing British politics he's travelling through Europe and forging alliances there", and nothing more. Because the article was focused on what he's doing here in the UK.'

'But he *was* travelling, right?' Sarah asks, politely, but there's firmness too. The meeting has moved from recruitment to debrief.

'Correct. He would quite often, I mean, at least once a month, make a business trip to a European city. Not usually a major city like Paris or Berlin. Smaller ones. Düsseldorf. Lugano, Milan one time. It was usually over a weekend. If it was anyone else, you'd totally say this is a mistress he's seeing. But Rory: no way. He's got almost no humanity – no wife, no kids, no *normal* relationships. So it was something else. Dunno what, but something.'

'Okay, so how did these trips work? They were government business? Party business? Who pays for this stuff?'

'Definitely not official business. It was all paid for by this other company. The way it worked was you had a bank card number from the other business and you used that for the reservations.'

'Can you remember the company name?'

'Course I can, I had to use it loads of times. It was called Flood 19. Weird name.'

Behind the tree, Simon has to suppress a gasp. Sarah, far more professional, murmurs agreement, that, yes, it is a weird name.

'So how did it work? Did you have any details of the company?'

'Not really, just the credit card. Gough would leave it with me to do the bookings. And then he would take the card when he had to do a trip. We never had to settle the bill or anything. It was like a magic card.'

'What bank did the card come from?'

'It was this obscure bank in Lichtenstein. Alpenbank. I once googled it because I was sort of intrigued about what was behind

223

the magic card. It doesn't even have a website. You can see it exists, but it's basically invisible.'

'But the reservations were in Gough's name?'

'Usually. Not always. Sometimes I had to book something in another name. If it was a meeting room, or something like that.'

'And what was that? What name?' There's a hint of sharpness, insistence to Sarah's question.

'The Costello Trust. Easy to remember, 'cause it's another unusual name.'

'Yes, it is, isn't it?' agrees Sarah, calmly. 'Do you know anything about that? The Costello Trust? And what was Gough doing on all these trips? Who was he meeting? What was the purpose?'

Amy sighs. 'Sorry. I don't know anything at all. Rory never gave the slightest details. People like me were just there to carry out instructions. He wouldn't discuss why he was doing something with someone like me.'

'But you have the dates? The dates he made the trips?'

'Some of them. Not all. I lost access to my work emails. But sometimes I would forward that email to a personal account if I had to do something on the weekend or in the evening. I mean, he used to make a thing of that: "expect to work weekends and evenings", was his line. You know the type: he thinks it makes him a bigger person when what it actually tells us is that he has no life outside work. He was completely empty.'

'So can you put together a list for us? It is very important – the dates of these trips.'

'I could, but I can just get it from my phone now, if that's easier. There weren't that many. I'll just WhatsApp them to you.' There's a silence as Amy fiddles with her phone. 'I'm just going to send you a message with a date in it,' she explains. 'There'll be a few of these.'

Simon hears a series of beeps as the messages arrive on Sarah's phone. There's something other-worldly about the way she hasn't turned off the noises on her smartphone, even during a secret espionage meeting.

'Any other details of the trips?' insists Sarah. 'Did you ever see the names of anyone else on a booking, or an email?'

'Oh, wait, there was one,' says Amy, clearly dragging out deep memories that have almost faded. 'Yes, there was one time he asked me to sort the bookings for three of them. Him, plus Tom Harkness. I remember that because, you know, if you work in Westminster you get to know who Harkness is. He's on TV all the time. Loves the sound of his own voice, if you ask me. But yes, there was Harkness travelling as well.'

'Anyone else?' Simon can hear that Sarah is struggling to keep the excitement out of her voice. 'Was it just Harkness?'

'No, there was another name. But I can't, for the life of me…'

'An Asian name?' asks Sarah, hopefully.

'Yes! That's right. Indian sort of name. If you say it, I'll get there.'

'Kamran Patel?'

'Patel. Kamran Patel. Definitely. I think I had to put "professor" under his title, rather than plain old "mister". Kamran Patel. Funny how the memory works, isn't it?'

'But just three names?' asks Sarah. 'No more, and just that occasion?'

'That's right,' says Amy. 'I remember when I did the extra guys, Rory said to me "this time" can you book for the others as well? The point was, it was "this time". Not every time, like it was out of the ordinary. But that's all. I don't have the date of that one. It must have been early 2016. Run-up to Brexit. I remember that 'cause Rory was so busy at that time – you know he was one of the main backers of the campaign – and I thought it was odd him going off on one of these funny Flood 19 meetings.' Amy stops talking, clearly distracted by her memories.

'Where was the meeting? Where did you do the bookings for?'

'It was one of those places you don't hear about very much. I want to say, Arkan?' There's a brief pause whilst Sarah tries to figure out what this might mean. This mysterious place called Arkan. 'It's somewhere in Germany,' Amy adds helpfully.

'*Aachen*. Yes, of course, they would meet there.'

'I'm not really very good at languages,' says Amy, apologetically.

'Is there anything else we should know about?' asks Sarah.

'Yes. One thing. I said I didn't know what he was doing on those trips. That's true. But there was a word that was important. Berezina. I don't know what that is. But occasionally he would come back from his trips and would spend ages on his iPad writing some kind of report. It wasn't ever a government thing – that was why he was using the iPad rather than the government computer. I mean, usually those sorts of rules meant nothing to him. But he was punctilious about this stuff. He would get me to do the bookings, sure, but he was making pretty damn sure I didn't know what it was about. But sometimes he would call me over to do something for him and I noticed that the file was always entitled "Berezina" and then a number. He always took care to ensure I couldn't see inside the document. But it was easy to see the filename. Berezina. No idea if that's important or not. But I thought I'd tell you, anyway.'

Berezina.

There's a rustling sound as if Amy is checking the time. 'I have to get going,' she says, apologetically.

'You have been incredibly helpful,' says Sarah. 'I can't emphasise how valuable this will be.'

'I just want people like him to stop getting away with it. They always seem to be winning. Why can't we win? I mean, normal people who pay their taxes and don't think they're above the rules. The ones who think that politicians should actually be doing something for the right reasons, not just to make their friends rich. The ones who believe the civil service are doing their best for the country, not a lazy bunch of pen-pushers. Why can't we win any more? Why is politics always the arseholes winning, by being arseholes?'

'It's a good question, Amy. I'm not sure I have the answer. But I can promise you that what you've told us about Gough may

226

mean he stops getting away with it.' Sarah has stood up. 'I want you to take a taxi home. And if you ever need to contact me, you know how to get hold of me. Don't hesitate. But please, take a taxi, to your front door. I'll pay.'

'Don't be silly,' she replies. 'Nice to have the excuse. It feels like money well spent, if you can nail him.'

Simon has edged his head round so that he can see. The two women are sharing a brief hug and then Amy sets off back towards Highgate Road. Simon waits for a few seconds and follows. It is dusk and harder to spot the followers, if there are any. Amy is walking faster, more confidently, no longer having to follow a phone screen. The Heath is quieter, as is Highgate Road. But there are plenty of black cabs and Amy climbs into one after a short wait. Is the woman with a pushchair a watcher? Normally, Simon rules these out, but there's something about her that doesn't feel right. He pretends to make a call and takes a photo of her as Amy's cab disappears on its journey south.

Chapter 27

Simon is waiting for a text message on his burner from Sarah. He has the second mobile phone in his pocket, which he had taken from Petr. He realises that this could lead Petr and his associates straight to him, but it will also be a mine of useful intelligence. He opens the phone and scans the WhatsApp messages. There are several in a group that contains an image of Amy, which looks as though it was swiped from her LinkedIn profile, and a link to a Google maps pin. He touches the link and it opens in Google maps, showing a location in the City of London, which Simon guesses is Amy's workplace. Petr and his team would have followed her from work as far as the Heath. He goes back to the messages. They are in broken English. Is this because it was a multinational team, or to throw anyone who sees them off course? Or both? He checks the saved names in the phone. There are only a few numbers, all saved with initials. There is no email installed, and the internet browser is on private mode, so there is no history. Simon shrugs and powers down the phone, before removing the SIM card, just to be sure.

Sarah has messaged with instructions to meet her on the other side of the Heath. Simon sets off on foot, tracking back through the avenue and past murky ponds where hardy souls brave frigid water to swim outdoors. But the ponds are empty in the early evening and the ducks have taken back control. Simon reaches Sarah's car, in a car park on the edge of the Heath. She is sitting in the gloaming, no lights on, apparently motionless. For a crazy moment Simon wonders if she is dead and then he opens the passenger door and the light comes on.

Sarah turns towards him, very much alive. She stretches out her hand towards Simon and squeezes his arm. 'We've done it, Si. We have the details of Rory Gough's long-term treachery to this country, as an agent of Russian intelligence. And we've also got Archbold, Harkness and Patel. It's incredible if you think about it.'

'Yep,' says Simon, heaving himself into the passenger seat. 'We've nailed him. But they're onto us, too. I don't know if it's a leak or extra-heavy surveillance effort. Amy was followed tonight,' he says as he pulls out the Glock and clears the round in the chamber before sticking the weapon back in his waistband.

'Really?' Sarah is pulling the car onto East Heath Road, sounding slightly distracted. Is she distracted by the traffic, or the revelation that the watchers were out for Amy?

'Yes. I'm not exactly sure about the size of the team but I tracked one guy, for sure. Youngish, strong neck muscles. Very alert. He followed Amy right to the avenue. He was trying to photograph the two of you on the bench. I pulled the gun on him, actually.'

'You *what*?'

'Split-second decision. He took an object out of his pocket and put it up to his eyeline. I wasn't sure if he was about to shoot you. I pulled the gun and he turned round, and then I realised it was his phone. So I forced him to give it to me and he scarpered.'

'You've got his phone?' Sarah is sounding more incredulous than grateful.

'Yes. I've checked it. Not much on it. Definitely a burner. Probably just used by the surveillance team. Doesn't seem to have any other function.'

'You're sure he was a surveillant? I mean, he could have just been some creepy guy who decided to take a picture of two women for his Instagram. You know, hashtag Hampstead Heath beauty or something like that.'

Simon feels his blood rising. He had saved a crucial source meeting and now he's being given a hard time for it. And he hasn't even told her about what had happened in the woods in Hampshire. 'Sarah, I shouted at him in Russian, and he clearly understood.'

'A Russian in Hampstead? Where have you been, Simon? They're the only ones that can afford the property prices these days. We're trying to stay below the radar, not bloody well get arrested.'

Simon is about raise his voice, but stops himself. The car is edging along in crawling traffic around the perimeter of the Heath. He takes a deep breath and speaks in a low monotone, suppressing his anger. 'Sarah, the other thing I haven't yet had the chance to mention is that I was pursued through a forest in Hampshire this morning by a Chechen assassin. He's dead, by the way. And less than a week ago I was running from another group of Chechens in Prague, with my colleague lying dead on the street a few meters away. In my shoes, you might feel a bit differently about this. I am not going to switch on his phone again, but he was obviously part of a surveillance team and the handset proves it. We have a leak.'

'Wait, what? Someone died this morning,' says Sarah, sounding almost as annoyed as Simon.

'Yes. I shot him. He was armed. I was lucky, I suppose.'

'Why didn't you mention it before?' She sounds affronted.

Simon allows himself another deep breath, the tide of his anger ebbing slightly. The traffic is also flowing better. 'Sarah, a lot has been going on. Not much time to cover everything… Can we just go back to the beginning? Evie and I were followed in Prague. We later learned that it was a Chechen hit squad that had a prior association with the Kremlin. They killed Evie and came pretty fucking close with me. Then, while I was coming to find you in Oxford, there was at least a three-man team on the ground. Probably bigger: they would have had backup, a van, maybe a drone. Now, that team in Oxford had to be ultimately working for Moscow Centre, not Gough.'

'How do you know?'

'Simple: Gough knows that you're at Christ Church and that you do more than just study Slavonic languages. He knows that you're the government adviser on Russia strategy. Moscow Centre might know that too, thanks to Gough, but the information won't be widely held. Particularly with what we know about how tightly they are managing COSTELLO in Moscow. If the team tonight had been reporting directly to Rory, it would have been you they were following, not her. But that's not what happened, is it? So that shows it's from the Centre. Maybe they got the lead from some kind of technical surveillance. They've hacked Amy's phone, or computer, or something. The fact the surveillant tried to take a picture suggests he didn't know who you were. But he knew who Amy was because he had a photo of her in his WhatsApp: I saw that on his phone.'

'Well, I don't think I saw any surveillance today,' agrees Sarah.

'And then there's another point: I was followed to Christ Church, but they couldn't get inside. So they bribe a student and manage to get in a day later. Two guys in my room. Not bothering you, following me. Again, this morning, someone manages to track me. Can't work out if it's my burner or my laptop. Or a leak.'

Sarah concedes. 'I think I owe you an apology, Simon. That was good work today.'

'There's a lot we need to do,' Simon continues, 'first, check that Amy got home okay.'

Sarah shuffles in her seat and pulls out a battered phone. 'I was using this. It's got a burner SIM in it. Why don't you message her?'

Simon taps a message on WhatsApp, taking care to mimic the style of earlier messages in the thread. He is relieved to see it landing and the blue ticks confirming it has been read. But has it been read by Amy? The reply seems monosyllabic, possibly guarded. Is this someone using Amy's phone, having killed her?

'Sarah, we can't rely on messages. You need to hear her voice.'

'Okay,' says Sarah impatiently. Simon taps the dial button and holds the phone, on speaker setting, close to Sarah's ear.

'Hello?' Amy has picked up and sounds perfectly normal. The lack of background noise suggests she is inside.

'Oh hello, just checking that you got back okay?'

'Didn't you see my message?'

'I didn't. I'm actually driving so it was easier to call,' she lied fluently.

'It's all fine. Should I be worried about anything?'

'You shouldn't,' says Sarah, firmly. 'But let's keep in touch over the coming days. If you notice anything unusual: you know, odd people hanging around your flat, or anything strange with your phone or computer, promise you'll let me know straight away? Nothing to worry about, just sensible precautions,' she says, contradictorily, before letting Simon end the call.

She turns to Simon. 'There, you see. Nothing doing. Let's not make this more complicated than it needs to be.'

'Sarah, we have just proved the existence of a Russian spy ring at the heart of the British Establishment. And our work is only about two paces away from being uncovered by Moscow Centre. This is really fucking complicated. We can't get round that.' Simon pauses, then asks the obvious question. 'What do we do now?'

'We have something to eat. I'm starving.'

–

They pull off the M40 at Stokenchurch, a village high on the Chiltern ridge. It's a strangely charmless place: in spite of a village green and a few pubs it feels cold and empty. The sort of place you don't stop at unless you really have to. It is therefore ideally equipped with a nearly empty curry house, the Tripadvisor hygiene rating of which was completely accurate and a disappointment to its proprietors. Simon takes the gun from the glovebox, not because he is expecting trouble, but because it looks as though they have parked in a car-crime hotspot. In a booth near the back of the restaurant they tuck into their Kingfisher beers and papadums as they wait for the curries to arrive.

Simon feels heavy flashbacks to undergraduate dates. 'A bit like the old days,' he says. 'You, me, a curry and an incredible story.'

'I don't think there were ever any incredible stories,' says Sarah, smiling. There is twangy sitar muzak in the background and the carpets and walls are a uniform fuzzy nylon. The waiter, used to catering to couples having affairs and requiring unobtrusive service, does an excellent job. The chef is rather less skilled. But to Simon the food seems delicious. Or maybe he's just hungry.

'Sarah, what's the plan here? What are they trying to do?'

'What do you mean?'

'I mean, what's the *overall* plan? They can scoop up students here or there, but what are these people trying to achieve? There's no ideology any more. So what's it about? This isn't like Blake or Philby. Whatever we think of those guys, they believed. They wanted a communist victory and were prepared to work for it. None of these people can possibly be mistaken for communists. What is a Russian victory, after all?'

'I've been thinking about that. A lot. And you're right, of course. The Russians have no ideology that someone can sign up to these days. I mean, even if you're a fully committed super-ideological capitalist, nobody is going to hold up Russia as an exemplar.'

'So what's going on?'

'Well, I think the biggest difference is between agents and agents of influence. I mean, you know this already. Blake and Philby were *agents*. They took direct instructions from their case officers, and ultimately regarded themselves as officers within the KGB. In fact, they were both given an official KGB rank. They saw their job as passing onto Russia any intelligence they could get hold of and, of course, ensuring that any intel operations on their own side failed. Philby betrayed all the agents he sent into Albania, Blake betrayed the Berlin Tunnel. That was the system.'

'And you think this group is different?'

'Yes, I do. You know what really showed me the difference? It was Harkness. He's such a one-trick pony. The only thing he's cared about his *entire life* is getting Britain out of Europe. You remember, back at Oxford? He had those leaflets and some people wondered if it was some kind of weird joke. It seemed so implausible. But, whatever the reason, he has believed in this his entire adult life.'

'Tell me about it,' says Simon wearily. The transformation of Tom Harkness from a marginal figure of fun propounding a fringe theory to a key figure in the current government had been one of the many depressing elements of recent political history.

'Right. And if you're a true believer, you will work with anyone to achieve your goal. No relationship too toxic. That's true of the IRA getting weapons from Libya just as much as it's true of Harkness and the Eurosceptics. So, from his perspective, at some point in his young life, imagine that he was given an opportunity to get funding, support, perhaps influence, to further his goal. I mean, thinking about it, political funding is so badly regulated in this country, channelling money to him would have been the easiest thing in the world. Harkness probably didn't even know it was Russia supporting him at first. Or, by the time he realised, he had rationalised it as acceptable – his enemy's enemy, that sort of thing.'

There is a pause as the waiter offers to bring more drinks.

'So, that's Harkness. From Russia's perspective, the whole talent-spotter thing is a brilliant, low-budget strategic play. Mackenzie sends them for vetting, and then the Kremlin can pick and choose. Put yourself back into the early nineties: you have some young fogey called Harkness out of Oxford banging on about Europe. You know that a weaker European Community is in Russia's interests. At that time, the prospect of Brexit is way over the horizon. But, for the paltry sum of funding Harkness to promote anti-Europe attitudes in Britain, you can weaken Europe as a political entity. Their willingness to play this stuff long is part of their success.'

'Okay. What about Gough?'

'He's a bit different. He's a fanatic, but the fanaticism appears to be about himself, rather than a specific political objective. So, with Gough it's about someone who admires Russia in quirky ways. He goes on about their scientific prowess, and he loves the ruthless drama of Bolshevism. But it's harder to figure out what he's actually trying to achieve in the UK, beyond get incredibly rich. He hates anything regulating his funds so he hates Europe, hates Whitehall bureaucracy. But I think it's more about the psychology of a raging ego. The one thing about Gough is that he's absolutely convinced he's the cleverest person in the room, whatever the room. He likes to believe he's pulling the strings behind the scenes. And he probably thinks he can turn everyone to serve his financial interests – whether it's the British state or the Russian one. But, figuring out the ultimate objective? That's buried in his psyche.'

'And Moscow Centre? What do they get?'

'I think what they have is not a useful idiot, but a useful psychopath. My guess is at first he was just a bit of a punt, both in the financial sense and strategically. Loads of the Kremlin *obshchak* gets washed through his funds. And he has been hugely influential in ways that are helpful to them, lobbying behind the scenes against sanctions, or making sure that the ones they do bring in are full of loopholes. And then he's attacking NATO as bureaucratic, calling for a lower military budget because he's convinced he can outsource all this stuff for a fraction of the cost. And Scotland. You know he goes on about how we shouldn't "bail out the Scottish", so support for independence is at an all-time high. All of that is music to Moscow's ears. But Ukraine has upset the apple cart.'

'How so?' Simon feels like a marathon runner struggling to stay with the leader of the pack.

'Well, now you can't be mildly pro-Russian any more, the way Gough has been for years. And the sanctions are making everything harder. So he'll be having to unwind a lot of his business arrangements, trying to cover his tracks. But I know that he's part of a shadow finance network that is keeping things like the aluminium and energy sectors afloat in Russia. Channelling their oil into Europe in spite of the sanctions. All part of their war effort. And look at what he's saying now: he can't defend Russia publicly after the invasion so he's arguing about the risk of nuclear war and the economic pain from sanctions. Saying that Ukraine is "irrelevant". He's walking a very careful line.'

'And the others? Patel? Von der Wittenberg?'

'Well, we're never going to know the whole story with all of them. Some of these people might just have had brief entanglements with the Russians, nothing more. Patel is a neo-imperialist. Completely on board with the clash of civilisations stuff. These people say that the biggest threats to the West are China and Islam. So therefore Russia, an Orthodox Christian country, is your ally, in the grand strategic sense. "We might disagree with them over Crimea. But on the big picture, from this viewpoint, they are part of the Christian-European cultural world." Patel loves this stuff. You can find the crap he writes along those lines in all the usual places. And they lap it up because he's a man whose parents arrived in this country as Indian immigrants so nobody can accuse him of racism.

'As for Wittenberg, that's easy. There's always been a strong Russophilia in certain circles in Germany. It's their mercantilist, pacifist urge. They just want good relations, as long as they can sell them Mercedes cars and so on. And particularly in Wittenberg's party, the FDP. Whatever Russia does, their response is, "well, we must try to de-escalate, see if we can work with them". So it would make perfect sense to find that Wittenberg has been working for them all along. He was one of the biggest advocates of the Nordstream pipelines, both of them.' This is a gas pipeline that took Russian gas and deposited it in Germany, deliberately cutting off gas-dependent Poland en route. Sarah, content that she has made her point, scoops some lamb jalfrezi onto her plate.

There's one name Simon hasn't mentioned. Sarah gets there first. 'You haven't asked me about Camondo,' she says, blandly. 'Is that because I went out with him?'

'I don't know. I suppose I wasn't sure what the situation was there.'

'The situation was that he was very briefly my boyfriend more than twenty years ago. Not a particularly significant factor, I'd say.'

'Well, it's slightly more significant to me, given that I was sort of trying to be your boyfriend at the same time.'

Sarah shrugs, as if it is the least significant thing imaginable. 'Camondo is a more interesting case. Do you know about Fee Marco?'

'Free Marco? Who's that?'

'No, Simon. F-I-M-A-C-O. FIMACO Limited.'

Simon's blank face shows he has no idea what she's talking about.

'You really are operational, aren't you?'

'What's that supposed to mean?' says Simon, aware that this might not have been a compliment.

'It's supposed to mean that I have no doubt that you are good at running intelligence operations, recruiting agents, that sort of thing. But you don't really know very much about the underlying subject, do you?' She ploughs on, ignoring Simon's spluttering on his second Kingfisher. 'FIMACO was a company set up by the Russian *siloviki* around 1990. It was designed to channel the Russian Communist Party's assets out of the country after the party lost power. The company was registered in Jersey, by which I mean the British Crown Dependency, not the US state. The British money-laundering empire playing its role, as ever. But that's just a brass plate, shell company. The real activity was taking place in Switzerland. The Russian Central Bank was running a secret ledger for FIMACO: funds being sent out of the country into the Western banking system for laundering. And the main bank used for these transfers? Banque Camondo Genève.'

'I think I had heard about that,' says Simon with a vagueness that Sarah finds infuriating. 'But Zak was still just a student when that all began.'

'Zak was probably still at Eton. Or did he go to Aiglon? Anyway, the Camondo relationship with Russia goes back to the nineteenth century. They were originally the big bankers in Istanbul: "the Rothschilds of the East". Moved to Switzerland around the time of the collapse of the Ottoman Empire, and the Russian revolution, for that matter. Well, right after the revolution, the USSR still had to have relations with Western banks. They had to borrow money. And Banque Camondo was always there for them. So, you could say that Zak was born into a relationship with Moscow Centre. When he went to see Sidorov at the embassy, he was picking up an existing thread, not starting something new. But what's new is the relationship with Gough. Most of his funds and projects have some link with Banque Camondo. Their financial interests are bound tightly together.'

'I suppose what you're saying is that everyone brought something to the table: Harkness was politically useful in a direct way, as was Archbold, on the left; Patel is fighting the battle of ideas; Von der Wittenberg is dragging Germany closer to Moscow, helping connect the Russians to Europe's biggest gas market. Camondo is banking the whole show. And Gough? Well, he's being Gough. Making millions whilst believing he can control Britain, Russia, God knows what else.'

'That's about it, Si,' says Sarah, chewing determinedly on her mutton.

–

They pay the bill and step out into the chill of an early summer night. There is the last of a glow in the sky but the objects on the ground, parked cars, a man on the other side of the street dog-walking, are dark shapes, indistinct. Simon finds himself shoving his hand into his jacket pocket where the Glock is a reassuring weight. The dog-walker seems to be loitering. Is that for the animal to mark a lamppost or so that he can get a sight of Sarah and Simon returning to the car?

Chapter 28

They're standing outside the car, awkward with an air of expectation. She throws him the keys and climbs into the passenger seat.
Simon joins her on the driver's side and immediately feels that
strange intimacy of two people sitting in a car at night.

'What happens now?' asks Simon, hopefully, as he edges the
car onto the main road.

'You can't go back to Christ Church, obviously.'

This isn't quite the issue that Simon wants to discuss. But it is
important.

'If you can stay below the radar for a couple of days,' Sarah
expands, 'you'll probably be out of the woods.'

'Speaking of the woods, aren't we forgetting something?'

'I don't see why? From what you said, you were fairly deep in
the forest when you dropped him. It's a shooting area so nobody's
going to take an interest in gunshots, even off-season. And they're
not exactly going to report one of their goons missing, are they?
So, as long as your dry-cleaning was solid, it seems to me we're
fine for the moment. Speaking of dry-cleaning, you do need
to get rid of that jacket, though. I noticed the bloodspots over
dinner.'

Not for the first time, Simon is impressed with her cold effi-
ciency.

There is a brief silence.

'We should talk about leaks.' Simon had wanted to bring up the subject at an appropriate moment, but it feels like a crunching gear-change.

'I thought you said it was Moscow Centre. Big surveillance teams, so on.' There's a hint of defensiveness to Sarah's response.

'Yes, that's my assumption,' he answers, keeping his voice as level as he can manage. 'But I find it a bit weird the way these goons keep popping up every time we try to do something. Prague, Oxford, some bloody woods in Hampshire. Every-fucking-where, basically.'

'Yes, but that's what they do at Moscow Centre: they throw proper resources at it. Unless you think you have an alternative explanation? I mean, did you tell anyone you were going to Prague?'

'O'Brien. I had to tell him, 'cause it was on his expenses account – or that's what I was led to believe,' replies Simon with a hint of resentment. 'He had to sign off the flights, hotel, that stuff.' Until that moment, Simon has not wanted to put a name to it. But now it seems to make sense. Unlike Kemi and Sarah, O'Brien is a weak link in the chain: he isn't quite on the team, just some chinless wonder working for Peebles, paid as a contractor to help out on the case.

'So you're saying O'Brien reported back to Moscow Centre?'

'You tell me. You know much more about him than I do.'

Simon had not wanted to turn this into an accusation. But it seems to have ended up that way. Sarah has lapsed into a sullen silence. Simon continues, remorselessly.

'Because O'Brien knew I'd gone to Hampshire, didn't he?'

'Hampshire?' Sarah sounds incredulous. 'That wasn't exactly narrowing it down, was it? I mean, I noticed you didn't actually tell me where you were going.'

He pauses, blinking as he thinks hard.

'But you knew I was at Gloucester Green. Coach station. Did you tell O'Brien?'

'Er...' It is unusual to hear Sarah flounder slightly. But it is unmistakable. 'I might have. I mean, incidentally. You know:

"Simon's just called from Gloucester Green, he'll be needing some kind of transport tomorrow from Hampshire." How is that giving anything away?'

'Because Gloucester Green means coaches. So you look at coaches from Oxford to Hampshire. Turns out there's only one on a Thursday night, to Southampton. Once you know that, you scramble a car, catch up with the coach, watch to see where it stops and, bingo! "There's that Sharman bloke. We're on him."'

There is a long silence. Simon decides to fill it.

'What do we know about O'Brien?'

'We know,' says Sarah, evidently annoyed, 'that he's nothing very special, but he comes with Marcus's complete confidence. Marcus was at Sandhurst with O'Brien Senior.'

Simon wants to scoff, but Marcus Peebles is the ultimate insider. If he'd endorsed O'Brien, that ought to be enough.

'Fine,' he replies gracelessly. 'But can we at least keep O'Brien at arm's length from now on? Safety first.'

Sarah makes a sniffing noise that means she agrees, reluctantly.

'And Marcus?'

'Oh come *on*, Simon. Now this is getting ridiculous. Marcus? We've known him forever and always. He was pushing me to do this thing from the outset.' Simon knows she is right: Marcus is pompous and incredibly pleased with himself, but he is definitely on the right side.

'Now,' she announces briskly, 'have you got any friends, Simon?'

It takes him a couple of moments to figure out what she means. 'You mean, somewhere I can stay?'

'Exactly. Just while I sort stuff out in Whitehall. You know: rural, out of the way.'

I do know, thinks Simon, an idea forming in his mind.

—

At his insistence he drives Sarah to the gates of Christ Church, even though Oxford city centre is busy – an unlikely spot for a hit squad. He pulls into a little sideroad just below the college entrance. Neither of them has spoken for some time and there's an odd tension in the air.

'This is it, then,' says Simon, unnecessarily. He turns his head towards Sarah and is surprised that she has leaned towards him. He can see the gleam of moving headlights reflected in her deep brown eyes. There is the sound of her breathing and a familiar scent, but he has no idea what it's called. They kiss, like lovers, and he realises that his heart is racing. She pulls away.

'Simon, we have to sort this thing out. Before you and me try to sort anything out. Know what I mean?'

Sarah is, as usual, completely correct. She climbs out of the car, wordlessly. He watches her walk towards the college gate and then, with a physical effort, forces himself to reverse the car and head off into the night.

Chapter 29

Carlisle
May 2022

Simon has driven overnight and pulled off the motorway to grab some sleep in a windswept layby. He is thirsty and has a nauseating headache from several days without a proper night of sleep. It is a grey morning, with high clouds streaked across the sky.

Using his latest burner phone for a hotspot he fires up the laptop he has dragged around the country for the past few days. He's been cautious about connecting this computer to the internet, but he knows he is coming towards the end of his journey, whatever the final destination. Simon and Rudi have a comms protocol which involves the two of them logging into the same anonymous account on a little-known email service. They then leave cryptic messages in the email drafts folder. The last from Simon had been the hacked files from Radcliffe's computer, the spreadsheet of Russian names and their St Kitts aliases, which he had sent on the coach ride out of Oxford. Although just over a day ago, it already felt like a different era. He needs to find the dates the COSTELLO operatives had travelled to Europe. This was where Rudi's access to Russian immigration data came in. Painfully slowly, thanks to his phone struggling with rural connectivity, he waits to see if Rudi has responded. The blank browser screen and the little turning wheel are the epitome of modern mundanity. And yet, Simon knows that this could be the final piece of the jigsaw.

Eventually, the page starts to load: a bold hyperlink tells him there's a new message. Another click, more turning wheel.

Simon's heart is racing. *Come on!* Obligingly, a little spurt of 4G data gives him what he wants. The message contains an attached file, and a single word.

Volltreffer!

'Yes!' Simon surprises himself with an exclamation of joy and a pump of the fist, as if West Brom had just sealed an improbable victory. Without even opening the attachment, he sends the file to Kemi and leans back in the car seat, letting out a huge sigh. He has it. The final piece of the jigsaw.

There is a shabby transport cafe that operates a twenty-four-hour service. Simon still hasn't sorted out the bloodspots on his jacket, so he leaves that on the car seat as he climbs out of Sarah's Maserati. It is still very early, and cold, and he shivers in a biting wind. He strolls into the cafe and is immediately struck by the distinctive Cumbrian accent. It's one he's heard before, many years ago. He may be on the run, again, but he is feeling positive. They have got their case. The Oxford Spy Ring, COSTELLO, has ceased to be a theory and become a fact. And his self-defence against armed Russian assassins will be entirely justifiable. Something the police will not need to make a big deal about. It's just a question of time. So, Simon decides to start the day with a large breakfast, an immense confection of fried food that must have contributed to the deaths of numerous truck drivers from heart failure over the years.

Fortified, he returns to the car clutching a large takeaway coffee. He drives into the North Pennines, England's last wilderness, a trackless expanse of high moorlands, isolated farms and austere beauty. Above all, it is empty. The sun has burned through the grey clouds and the Pennines are at their finest in the early summer sunshine. Simon can see lambs skipping in the small, walled meadows. Old stone barns dot the landscape. The road passes craggy streams and isolated farmhouses surrounded by flowering blackthorn, late to bloom on this higher ground. He keeps an eye open for followers but sees nothing.

The Maserati winds up a narrow valley towards the ridge of the Pennines. After a few hundred meters Simon reaches what he was looking for. Little more than a widened bend in the road, a big enough passing place. He eases the car to a halt and switches off the engine. It is a bright, chilly day, but out of the wind the car is warm, the windscreen starting to mist up, clouding the magnificent views stretching out over the fells. The only sound is the bleating of newborn lambs – spring comes later this far north – and the occasional squeal of a hopeful buzzard. Simon slouches in his seat and tells himself he mustn't fall asleep. Positioning his mobile in the cup holder and the laptop on the dashboard, he waits for the call: a three-way video session via Signal, the secure messaging app that is still, to the best of his knowledge, out of reach of either British or Russian interceptors.

–

He has dozed off and is jerked awake by the blittering of the Signal ringtone. He doesn't have time to check whether he looks respectable, fumbling to click on the icon to accept the call. Two faces float into view on the laptop screen, the standard setting for a modern office meeting. Simon hasn't looked at Sarah since their passionate kiss. He has a little flash of desire as he sees her face on the screen. Kemi seems unfazed by the fact that Simon is on the run, jumping straight into the issue.

'Yes. So, the latest from Rudi – you know, the travel information. There's a whole load of data. I've uploaded those onto a spreadsheet and I'm now cross-referencing that with the dates that Amy gave us for Gough's trips to Europe. And…' Even Kemi allows herself a pause for effect. 'I've got a hit on almost every one.'

'Wow.' Intelligence is supposed to define the argument, not be led by the argument. But Simon realises how much he has wanted this answer.

'Amy gave us nine separate dates when Gough is travelling on his Flood 19 credit card,' Kemi continues. 'On eight of those dates, at least one of the guys that we know had a St Kitts passport is logged as leaving Russia. One of those dates matches a trip by Kleshnyov, that's Walter Pinsent. There's another by Sazan-ovich, aka Carpenter. A few others here, highlighted in red,' says Kemi, pointing at a printed spreadsheet she is holding up to the screen. 'So, what we can show is that on almost every occa-sion that Gough travelled on COSTELLO business, a Russian COSTELLO operative was travelling at the same time.'

Sarah's image floats forwards on the laptop screen. 'What about the one Amy told us about? With Harkness, Patel and Gough travelling together. Early 2016, Aachen.'

'Yeah. We've got a Sazanovich trip out of Russia in February 2016.'

'The symbolism of it,' muses Sarah. 'Aachen – Europe's first capital. Charlemagne's palace. You can see that appealing to them. They go to the heart of Europe to plot its downfall.'

Simon takes a big gulp of his cold coffee. '*Volltreffer.*' Bullseye. Unusually, Kemi doesn't seem to know what he means. But she takes up the thread.

'The other thing is Berezina. Amy mentioned it – the files that Rory kept to himself. And I think we've found something. It relates to the old question about Gough's business. Is he a brilliant fund manager who has succeeded with his hi-tech trading algorithms? Or is he a guy who helps Russian oligarchs get their wealth into the Western financial system and avoid sanctions?'

'I think I know the answer,' offers Simon.

'But even if he's the second,' interjects Sarah, 'that alone doesn't make him a COSTELLO agent. We all know that London is the world's laundromat. But Berezina's much more than that.'

'That's right,' says Kemi, a hint of impatience in her voice. 'There's a company called Berezina in the Paradise Papers leak, and one of its directors is Jeremy Rathbone. He's Gough's CFO: fronts for him on all kinds of things. So that's basically proof that Gough is involved with the business.'

'So what?' Gough has literally hundreds of businesses, shell companies incorporated in different tax havens, all serving some purpose, mostly invisible to the outside world. And Rathbone is often the frontman.

'So this: the major shareholder of that Berezina is a holding company based in Luxembourg, which also owns Powerstream. You do know what Powerstream is, don't you?' Kemi asks this question with an undertone of incredulity at Simon's ignorance.

Sarah comes to the rescue. 'Powerstream, Si, is an interconnector project. It's basically an enormous underwater electricity cable from Northumberland to north Germany. And it'll have a data cable too. So the idea is that the UK and Germany, two biggest power and data users in Europe, can sort of balance each other out depending on demand. And connecting the UK to the continental data grid is also important. But you can see how—'

Whatever Sarah was going to say, she didn't get to say it. Because Simon had a sudden moment of recollection. 'Yes!' he exclaims. 'I know this story!'

Chapter 30

London

2015

The first thing that strikes the visitor to the Boyar Lounge is the lighting. Mostly, the lack of it. As Simon's eyes adjust to the gloom he begins to make out shapes: these are people. He scans the space, trying to identify his host. The room has heavy wood panelling, fake bookshelves and leather armchairs, but this affectation of clubland tradition is offset by a huge iconic Union flag painted on one wall and a profusion of gold paint. Alongside the high-tempo bass beat, another exception to clubland tradition are the many young women dotted around the room. There is a look – glossy hair, tiny dresses, vertiginous heels, and a pout of boredom. This is reasonable, as they are mostly at work and their job involves pretending to enjoy the company of overweight men laughing loudly at their own jokes. Most speak English, but Simon also picks up plenty of Russian. And finally, on a leather banquette, he finds Vasya, looking equally bored, flanked by a young woman whose short white dress and chemically whitened teeth glowed in the ultraviolet.

He greets Simon with a relieved warmth. These are the early days of Vasya's life on the outside and he has made a habit of offering Simon extravagant hospitality whenever passing through London, to show how well he is doing. The Boyar Lounge is *the* place in Mayfair for oligarchs and their impersonators to waste money on Cristal and caviar. Vasya puts in an immediate order.

'Mischa! It is wonderful to see you. I am disgustingly well. Business in booming and your wonderful country has made it easy for us to do business. Sanctions? Only an idiot gets caught up with those!'

Vasya releases a torrent on his fantastically successful business, his stunning new girlfriend – not to be confused with his wife, or the 'hostess' sitting next to them staring at her vast smartphone – and the chalet he is building in Crans-Montana. And a running commentary on the clientele spread around the room. Vasya's desire to be part of the crowd is reflected in his obsessive interest in those that already are. There's the baby-garch whose father runs the Russian railways. The lugubrious oil-trader who owns the world's largest sailing yacht but had failed to protect it in his divorce proceedings. Lots of bankers, some friends of the Kremlin, others accused of corruption and seeking protection from it.

'Isn't it a bit of a security issue,' asks Simon, feeling stupid that he hadn't raised it earlier, 'you know, me and you appearing in the open like this?'

Vasya gulps some Cristal before letting out a dismissive guffaw.

'Mischa, you know that pretty much everyone in this room has a tame little James Bond working for him? MI6, MI5, the Pole – you people are – what's the phrase? – two a penny. Guns for hire.' Turning to more important matters, Vasya points out Arkady, in the premier league of oligarchs, on the strength of the fact that the football team he owns plays in that division. Simon lets the story of Arkady's complex business empire wash over him. Just another billionaire stripping his country bare and using Simon's to launder the spoils.

And then Simon realises that Vasya is asking him a question and he has allowed himself to drift off. 'Meaning what, exactly?' he replies, noncommittally.

'Meaning, don't you think your country would care that a consortium of Russians with links to the Kremlin is about to own a crucial power and data interconnector? Not my problem, Mischa, but I would have thought it was yours.'

Simon is wondering about the two things that always matter most in conversations with Vasya: what is he talking about and why is he talking about it? Vasya has long given up worrying about Britain's national interest, so it must be a commercial issue. 'Sorry, Vasya, who did you say was behind this? Just wanna check I heard it right.'

'You know, the St Petersburg crowd. *Botoks* and his mates. Arkady, Shevchenko, the Danes.' Vasya is describing a group close to the cosmetically enhanced president and his former employer, the Russian foreign intelligence agency. This is a closed network to Vasya whose connections run through the GRU, a separate entity. Which is why he is telling Simon: being stuck on the outside of the deal gives him an interest in its failure.

Simon is underwhelmed. 'To be honest, Vasya, these things get talked about all the time and it rarely comes to much. There'll be some hurdle. It'll never actually happen.' Deflated, Vasya turns towards Natalia, reaching his arm around her.

The North Pennines, May 2022

Simon has been told this story before, but hadn't realised why it would matter.

Sarah has been thinking hard. Simon knows this because he can see her on screen, playing with her long hair, twisting and untwisting it into a ponytail. She sighs, pauses and then speaks. 'I always thought it was more than just the money-laundering. There had to be a plan.'

Kemi nods sagely. 'With a power interconnector you can manipulate the energy price during peak demand. It's like a gun to the head. Send a whole load of businesses to the wall, or just switch the lights off in some major city. Not to mention the data link. I can't believe they've got away with this.'

'Yeah but surely not now? Everybody's getting off Russian gas supplies.'

Kemi sighs. 'Simon – this has nothing to do with Russian gas, or Ukraine. The interconnector allows you to restrict supply, just when demand is highest. It doesn't matter if the power comes from Russian gas or North Sea wind farms. In fact, without gas, there'll be more fluctuations – so it gives them even more power.'

'It's like a hedge for Moscow against the loss of their energy markets,' observes Sarah. She pauses, then smiles. 'You've both done an amazing job.'

Simon feels a powerful sense of gratification. Kemi's feet may be rather closer to the ground. 'This wouldn't stand up in court without a confession,' she points out. 'And you're not going to get that from Gough. They'll just say it's held independently by an investment board. Usual stuff.'

'Kemi, we're not looking for a confession,' says Sarah. 'Berezina is enough for me to go to the Six and they can make the necessary arrangements. We just need to get Gough and the others away from the chain of command. And away from the prime minister's ear. And then they can do a proper investigation, damage assessment, all that.' The Six was the closest thing that Britain had to a secret government. A committee of the six most senior public servants: Cabinet Secretary, National Security Adviser, Chief of Defence Staff, and the Chiefs of MI5, MI6, and the Pole. As a formal structure, the Six did not actually exist. But at various points of crisis in British history, it had come together to make necessary decisions in the national interest, as it would need to do now.

'Okay, so we need to get our shit together to make a presentation to the Six. When can we do that?' Simon has put this question to both Sarah and Kemi. They both look awkward.

It's Sarah who speaks. 'Um, Simon. You won't be at the meeting. Just me and Kemi. I'm sorry.' Kemi is studying something off-screen with an intensity that is designed to cover her embarrassment.

Simon is about to protest and then he sees it: Sarah and Kemi are insiders. They are trusted parts of Whitehall's secret machine. He, on the other hand, is an outsider, instantly suspect. And, worse, he is an outsider known to have opinions, to have disagreed operationally with his bosses. A cantankerous fieldman getting fed up with head office. So, in spite of playing a crucial role in uncovering the most significant act of Russian espionage against the UK since the end of the Cold War, Simon will not be in the room where it happens.

'Funny how, even when you've done the thing that nobody on the inside could possibly have figured out, you are still treated as an outsider.'

'Fuck's sake, Simon. Do you not see that we're trying to help you? I have been trying to hose down a lot of fires. Thames Valley Police will probably let it drop, but that doesn't mean you're out of the woods.' Sarah's rebuke is bracing. 'This is bigger than all of us. You have done your bit, excelled even. Now, let us do ours.'

'Yes, fine,' says Simon, channelling an obstinate undergraduate. 'You'll let me know how it goes,' he adds, logging off the call.

–

Simon climbs out of the car, needing to stretch his legs. And get his thoughts in order. He has often found he is better able to think through a complex issue when he is walking, especially if he is walking uphill in beautiful surroundings. Something about the oxygenation of his synapses that promotes clarity of thought.

He rehearses the story in his head, as if he was briefing the Six.

Start at the beginning. Even when someone is lying to you, they might be telling you something important.

Peebles had told him from the outset that this was about Sidorov wanting to endow an Oxford college. That wasn't true: as far as Simon knew, Sidorov hadn't been there in years. But it *was* Sidorov's specific route through Oxford, picking up the encoded signals, that proved he was Mackenzie's case officer.

Mackenzie was the Russian agent, Sidorov his case officer. Mackenzie talent-spotted Oxford students for further vetting at the Russian Embassy. Gough, Harkness, Patel, Camondo, Wittenberg, Archbold.

He pauses at a stile, clambering cautiously over a dry-stone wall.

The Russians set up a parallel intelligence agency to run this network, called COSTELLO. The case officers are provided with St Kitts passports to enable them to travel around Europe unnoticed.

A company called Flood 19, owned by the Costello Trust, receives monthly payments from the KGB's bank. Flood 19 pays for trips to Europe. Trips which coincide exactly with COSTELLO operatives travelling out of Russia. And who makes these trips? Harkness, Patel. But most of all, Rory Gough. The man who is supposedly a hedge fund manager but has a business card calling him *Senior Adviser* to the prime minister, whatever that means. The advocate of the slimmed down state. The sceptic of NATO, warning against nuclear war with Russia. Dismissing Ukraine as irrelevant. The frontman of Berezina.

Volltreffer.

He's at the top of the ridge now, and he has a 360-degree view of the harsh, beautiful countryside. Despite the exertion of the climb, he feels the chill wind in this exposed spot. In the far distance he can see a single farmhouse limned against the skyline, cowering behind a strand of trees bent by the prevailing wind. Who lives here, in this upland desert? Does it matter to them if a bunch of cynical, connected people have some inexplicable relationship with the Russian government?

Simon screws his eyes tight shut and inhales the cold mountain wind. Desperately he tries to get his thoughts into order.

Suddenly, pathetically fallacious, the wind drops, knowing he has reached an epiphany. He is trying to save Britain, but from whom? Why?

From itself.

Because, in spite of everything, he has a deep, unrequited love for his country.

Chapter 31

The North Pennines
May 2022

Simon returns to the car and begins to drive. He descends from the Pennines into the borderlands, once a contested, lawless country. There are few villages: for centuries this was a difficult place to live safely. But there are still, every few miles, large stone houses, some with towers, some fully castles, some in ruins. In this unfashionable corner of England, these ancient remnants of a more violent time are not much modernised. He speeds along straight roads, bounded by conifer plantations, the regimented rows of trees flickering by mesmerically.

He slows the car and turns in to a gateway. Barely visible, behind encroaching thornbushes, are two stone pillars with lions regardant, struggling to see through the foliage.

The Maserati bounces on the unmade driveway, groaning noisy objections as the undercarriage scrapes on the grass strip in the centre. The drive twists into a valley and then he sees the house, for the first time in more than twenty years. It is three storeys high, built from a reddish sandstone, a large wing with Tudor mullioned windows protruding from a squat tower that is clearly much older, surmounted by battlements. Roses are waving in the late morning breeze. Simon steps out.

There is no obvious sign of occupation, but it's a vast building, with rooms that go for days without being used. He bangs a black cast-iron knocker in the shape of a lion's head in the centre of a vast oak door. It thuds, resoundingly. He waits. No sound. Simon is feeling rather stupid, standing holding a small satchel in beat-up city clothes and damp suede loafers. Is he standing outside an empty castle in the middle of nowhere? He looks up, and sees smoke rising from a chimney towards the back. And then he recalls that in posh houses nobody uses the front door except on special occasions. He follows a path around the side of the building. At the rear he sees a jumble of low buildings, the accretions of centuries of adaptation, before it became a listed building that must not be altered in any way. He finds what he is looking for: a stable-style door, the top panel propped slightly open. He leans his head in and sees a large kitchen, stone floor, heavy oak furniture, a huge Aga in an enormous inglenook, walls darkened by centuries of smoky cooking. And a tall, slender figure, stooped over a large white square sink, scrubbing something with an angry intensity.

'Sebastian?'

The figure turns. A pair of owlish eyes behind heavy tortoise-shell spectacles blink twice. 'Simon? Was I expecting you?'

'No, Sebastian. I don't think you were. I have just, er, showed up.'

'Well, that's interesting.'

Interesting. Is that good? wonders Simon.

'Shall we have tea?' asks Sebastian, brightly, pulling a chair from the large kitchen table and pushing the kettle onto the hot plate on the Aga. An ageing border collie is snoozing in a basket on the floor.

Sebastian busies himself with tea and Simon sits, happy that he is close to the Aga. The rest of the room seems to be terribly cold, in spite of it being early summer.

'I should explain,' says Simon. 'I found myself near Carlisle. Slightly unexpectedly. Seemed like a good opportunity to look you up. Been meaning to come here for ages. Amazing spot, really.'

Sebastian is too polite to point out that it might have been more conventionally good mannered to announce his visit in advance. 'Are you, er, here for long?' he inquires, a hint of anxiety in his voice.

'I definitely don't want to be a nuisance,' says Simon.

'Not a nuisance at all. Sprogs are all away at school. Cecily has gone to see her mother in Wiltshire. Rather good timing, actually. I was rattling around here on my own.'

There's an awkward silence as the blindingly obvious question hangs over the two of them. 'I suppose you're wondering why I'm here.' Simon doesn't quite know the answer to this question. Why is he sitting in the ancient kitchen of Ereby Hall, drinking tea with its hereditary owner, Sebastian Ereby?

'Well, I quite understand if it's hush–hush.' Sebastian, like most of Simon's university contemporaries, knows that Simon has done 'something to do with intelligence'. Sebastian's identity is bound up with complicated self-perceptions of duty, honour and patriotism. This came naturally to someone whose family had owned the same patch of borderland for centuries. Self-important, if not actually important.

'Seb, it's not really super-secret, but I do need to be out of the way. Just for couple of days. Didn't want to set any hares running by calling you, so I thought I'd drop by. If you were out, I'd have gone somewhere else. No biggie.'

Sebastian is clearly excited by this news. 'Goodness! So you're here *undercover*, so to speak?'

'You could say that, I suppose. This seems like a good place if you don't want to be noticed.'

'It certainly is, old boy. Not for nothing do we have a priest-hole,' he adds, grinning. 'It's like we're back to recusancy. We can keep the whole thing completely hidden from prying eyes.'

'But let me make myself useful. Dig the garden. Chop logs. You tell me.'

'Of course, of course. But I suppose we should hide your car first. Spy satellites.' He says these final two words with exaggerated emphasis and taps the side of his nose in a knowing fashion.

'Er, right. Good idea.'

'So, where's your bag, then?'

'I don't have one.'

'Gosh, you really are on the run.' Sebastian has a little bit of childish excitement in his voice. 'Do I need to get the shotgun out?'

Instinctively, Simon shifts in his seat as the pistol in his pocket digs into his thigh. 'I very much doubt that'll be necessary. I can't promise any excitement at all, I'm afraid. Anyway, don't let me get in the way of whatever you had planned at the moment. Just let me know if there's anything I can do to be helpful.'

'I have to repair a pig-pen this morning. Little buggers keep escaping. You could hold the pliers, or something.' At university, Sebastian had been a studious linguist and still had the slender stoop of someone more at home in the library than in the pig-pen. In his work boots and scratched Barbour he still looks like an academic cosplaying an agricultural labourer, rather than an actual labourer.

The pig-pen is behind the house against a range of outbuildings filled with ancient farm machinery and a cobwebby Land Rover. The state of the fence gives further weight to the idea that Sebastian is not a natural farmer. Simon borrows wellies and a threadbare shooting jacket that has been hanging on a peg in the cloakroom, relieved to take off the blood-spotted blazer. As was always the case when in close contact with pigs, Simon finds himself very sad at the thought of eating these obviously intelligent animals. A murder of crows swirls above them, mocking their work with cackling laughs. But, for the first time since travelling to Prague, Simon feels almost safe.

Inevitably, conversation turns to their university contemporaries. Simon avoids mentioning Sarah, but Sebastian brings her up, unbidden. Simon steers the conversation away from her, disingenuously.

'I've not seen her in years,' he says, leaning against her car as they assemble the fencing tools. He steers the conversation in a different direction. 'What about Rory Gough, remember him?'

'He's the last person you'd expect to have become such a big success, don't you think? I mean, he was such an invisible, grumpy sort of chap in the old days. I never knew why anyone would invite him to *anything*.' There is an implicit snobbery in Sebastian's words: Gough as undergraduate had no social capital. But Sebastian is obsessively interested in observing power, perhaps because he is so far from it in his remote manor house.

'I think everyone's pretty surprised at how well he's done,' agrees Simon, trying not be drawn as he holds the barbed wire strand while Sebastian hammers it into a rickety fencepost with heavy steel staples.

'People are saying that he might be one of the few people the prime minister actually listens to. *Ow!*' Sebastian is distracted by a hammer blow on his thumb. 'Extraordinary, if you think about it. He just seemed like a weirdo.'

'Yes, well, like I said, I haven't really been following him that closely. I didn't realise you knew him.' Simon steps sideways and towards the next fencepost. A large sow grunts placidly behind them.

'Well, he's not exactly a *close* friend,' clarifies Sebastian, keen to put a little class distance between them. 'But you know he's practically a neighbour?' he continues, picking up his bucket of staples and hammers. Simon frowns, wondering what this means exactly. For very posh people, 'practically a neighbour' suggests anything within a thirty-mile radius of any of their houses.

'I didn't know that. Or I'd forgotten. Where does he live?' He tries to sound not very interested in the answer.

'His family have a farm just off the motorway. He went to school in Carlisle. Some totally unknown place.' As an Old Etonian, Sebastian is very generous to all the people in the world who had the misfortune to have been educated elsewhere. He pauses to position a staple over the wire on the next fencepost, taking more care than earlier.

'I'd completely forgotten he was from Carlisle. Presumably you never see him round here, though?'

'Now and then. He's an only child with no extended family or other connections, as far as I can make out. All that money and he doesn't appear to have anything to do with it. Nice problem to have,' adds Sebastian, looking around at various bits of the ancestral home in need of repair. 'He seems to visit his parents fairly often, most weekends.' Sebastian pauses, his tongue sticking out to one side as he aims his hammer. 'There's not a huge amount of company in these parts.' As if to emphasise the point, the crows overhead start to cackle particularly loudly.

—

After they've finished in the pig-pen, Sebastian, who tries to fund the endless upkeep of Ereby Hall by translating legal documents, says he has work to do. They eat some lunch and Simon announces he is going to drive to the nearest village. He tells Sebastian he is going to look at the church, supposedly sporting one of the best Norman towers in the county. To Sebastian, this is entirely believable. In fact, he is not sure if he can even trust his burner any more and he needs to find a phone box and a place to leave Sarah's car. On a windswept village green he finds the first of these and dials Sarah via the Porters' Lodge at Christ Church. He gives his name as Rory Gough and is put through immediately.

'Rory?' Sarah is sounding somewhere between nervous and intrigued. She seems relieved when she hears Simon's voice, and slightly disappointed.

'I knew you'd pick up a call you thought had come from him.'

'I was thinking he'd somehow found out about my meeting with the Six.'

'How did it go?'

There's a pause. Simon wonders if she's not heard him.

'Still there?'

'Yes… It's not going.'

'What?'

'I don't suppose you've been reading much news lately.'

'Not exactly.'

'We're too late. Cabinet secretary and the national security adviser have resigned. Well, I assume they've *been* resigned. Rory's people are crowing about a "deep state clear-out".'

'Fuck.'

'I knew this was coming,' says Sarah. She usually sounds composed, on top of things. But right now she is flustered, speaking in disjointed phrases. 'This is why you're doing it. I mean, this risk. That's what led me to get you working on this in the first place... But I thought we had more time. Particularly with Butler.' She is talking about Will Butler, the now-former national security adviser, highly regarded throughout Whitehall.

'What about the others? The chiefs? Defence and intelligence. That's a pretty powerful line-up.' Simon is clutching at straws.

'They're all operational, Si. Super important, yes, but operational. Without the cabinet secretary and NSA, you don't have anyone who can talk to the PM about something that is politically sensitive.'

'Head of the Foreign Office? That's kind of the next in line, isn't it?'

'He's gone too.'

'What?'

'He was pushed out a week ago. In all the craziness, I forgot to mention it.'

'It's a slow-motion coup, isn't it?' says Simon, amazed.

'You might say that,' answers Sarah archly. 'It seems like we took a week too long.'

'So, that's it?' asks Simon. 'All this work and just at the point we can actually prove the existence of the Oxford spy ring, it's "oh well, nothing to be done here, just have to live with it". I'm not settling for that. There's a bigger issue here. This isn't the country I grew up in. I'm not going to let them do that.'

'Okay, but what we have is an intelligence case: not a legal one. And there's something else you need to know.' She pauses. 'Radcliffe is dead.'

Simon gulps. Should he feel bad about this? He's not sure that he does.

'His body was pulled out of the well in his garden this morning. He'd obviously been tortured.'

'Oh. I thought it was just ornamental.'

'What?'

'I thought the well was just ornamental.' Even as he says this, Simon realises it's not very important.

There's a silence as Sarah seems unsure what to make of this.

'It feels like someone's covering their tracks,' she says. 'That's what I'm getting at: threat's very real at the moment.'

'So, are we really saying these people control everything? That nothing can be done to stop them?' Up to this point, Sarah has been in control. More than that, she has been the puppet-master, pulling the strings from the beginning: setting up the cover for Simon to think he was working for Peebles and Grosvenor Advisory; seconding Kemi into Peebles' organisation. But her plan had not provided for a situation where the furthest inner workings of the British state were compromised.

'So, I spoke to Butler... And he just confirmed how bad things are.' She pauses, again, trying to work out the best way to deliver a difficult message. 'You know, the way the Russian money is everywhere now. The donors. Russian oligarchs, giving huge amounts to the party, buying the superprime properties, major share listings, you name it. Even with the Ukraine sanctions, it's buried deep in the system. Can't be changed overnight.'

'But nobody's accusing them of anything,' exclaims Simon in frustration. 'I mean, you can be pissed off about the oligarchs and their tennis matches with Cabinet ministers. But that's not the same as spying for Moscow Centre.'

'That's true, but I just hadn't realised how far this had gone. Their money has changed the way people think about this stuff. The money is the bit we *can* see. What we *can't* see is what they have been able to buy with it. There's a hold they have. Maybe there are glamourous parties in foreign villas, mistresses, offshore accounts. British politicians don't tend to be very rich. A little Russian money goes a long way.'

'Okay, but someone must want to do something about Rory, right?'

'On the strength of what Butler said, I'm not sure anyone does. As long as they don't ask the questions, they don't have to face answers they don't want to hear. We carry on sending weapons to Kyiv and hope that nobody stops the City doing its thing.'

Simon can't believe what he is hearing. 'I'm not sure I've understood properly,' he says. 'Why wouldn't they care? Why would anyone ignore this stuff?'

'It's not about caring. It's about fear. You've got to remember: even the last PM, straight as a die by all accounts, auctioned off a "girls night out" with the oligarchs, just like the rest of them. But they hounded her out of office anyway. And she was terrified of them, of the whole crowd.'

'So what do we do now?'

'Well, you keep hearing phrases like, "it's a can of worms", and "be careful what you wish for".'

'What about the deep state?' asks Simon with only a little irony. 'Surely Butler doesn't think we just pretend this isn't happening? Thames House? The Pole? Someone has to take this on.'

'They'll all find a way round it. They'll tell themselves that they don't want to get dragged into "politics" and that will be their excuse for ignoring it. And they'll try to talk down the seriousness of it all. You know: "Worst case, Gough is a bit too close to one or two Russian businessmen". That's how Whitehall is rationalising this. And in the case of the Pole, I'm not even sure they aren't working to Gough's directives already.'

Simon has a flashback to a pallid face breathing his last in a wooded glade. What if that was a Pole operative, not COSTELLO? And who had killed off Radcliffe? But they wouldn't go after one of their own, would they? He's no longer sure. Nothing seems to make sense any more.

'The thing is,' Sarah continues, 'Gough's not really party to deep-state secrets, it's the strategy stuff.'

'But it's Gough's *strategy* that's killing us!' Simon realises that he has raised his voice inside the phone booth, an old-style red box with a heavy door. A passer-by walking a dog turns her head to look at the man shouting into the phone. Their eyes briefly meet before she looks away quickly, clearly embarrassed at breaking the English taboo of taking too much interest in strangers. 'This is where the Russians are winning: they're not wasting time trying to get our encryption or recruit some mid-level intel guy. Identify our sources. What's the fucking point of that any more? It's the grand strategy where they're winning. Get the UK out of the EU. Get Scotland out of the UK. Then England won't be a nuclear power any more because we don't have access to Faslane. So you get British nukes out of NATO. Make the UK desperate for deregulation because it hasn't got any industries left. Have it dependent on global finance and the laundromat for Russian money keeps humming away. How can they not see that this is Gough's strategy? Moscow Centre's strategy? We castrate our hard power and provide concierge services for their funny money. It's killing Britain!'

'They can't see it, Simon, because that requires them to admit that their signature policy has been a total disaster. Having to admit their pet project is unpatriotic. It's a religion, and that's heresy.'

'So, after all we found out, they won't do anything about Rory? They're just going to sit on it, because it doesn't conform to the tenets of their fucking crazy religion?' Another silence. 'Sarah? Still there?'

'Yes, I'm here, Simon. Just trying to figure out what I think. And the answer's yes, anyhow. Yes, they're going to sit on it. What I'm saying is: this is not something that can be fixed, unless we can prove Berezina. And I don't see how we can do that.'

Simon is starting to think through the implications. 'I guess this means that the police investigation into me is not going to be hushed up. I am so fucked. So that's it, is it? We stop here?' Sarah doesn't say anything, and Simon fills the void. 'Because right now I am on the run from the police, my close colleague and friend is dead, another body just got dragged out of the bottom of a well and you seem to be telling me that all this was for nothing. And, if I remember correctly, it was you who started this whole thing.'

That seems to silence her. Simon decides he will wait for her to fill the silence. She gets there eventually. 'I am genuinely sorry, Simon. I'd no idea that it would lead here.'

There is another pause. He can hear her breathing. Almost sighing.

'We found COSTELLO and nobody is prepared to do anything about it,' she says.

'Yes, but at the end of the day, you're still the professor of Slavonic Languages and Fellow of Christ Church, which I seem to recall is Oxford's grandest college. Meanwhile, I have lost everything.' Simon wants to feel anger, but what he really feels is incredible stress. Up until this point, he had believed that there would be some kind of resolution. Sarah, about the most capable person he knows, would see to that. And now she is telling him they've run out of road. 'What do you actually suggest I do? Where do I go?'

He hears Sarah take a deep breath. 'Simon,' she is doing that slow speaking thing that people use when they're about to tell you that someone has died. 'You're running out of time. I know that the police are still looking. And someone at MI5 has been asking about you. I've been putting them off, but I can't keep this going much longer, so I agreed to meet them tomorrow night.'

In spite of his anger, Simon can see she's still trying to help. When the project started, Sarah had a clear mandate from the most powerful people in Britain's secret state. None of them had expected that their findings would end up in the too-difficult tray, and the most powerful people had themselves been shoved aside; perhaps not quite as powerful as they believed. But for Simon, the problem is more immediate: he has endured, believing he was in a tunnel and would eventually see light at the other end. But he now finds himself in a cave whose entrance has been blocked off.

Perhaps the only option is to blast a way out of the cave.

'So what do you suggest,' he asks, calmer, accepting the inevitable.

'I've thought about it. By the time I meet him I need to be able to tell the MI5 guy that I don't know where you are. And what I need to know is that you're not in the country. All the airports will have you on a watchlist. So you're going to have to leave by boat. There's a few arrangements I'll need to make. I'm going to get Blondie.' She was talking about Blondie Phillips, a former SBS commander who had watched Simon's back in Baghdad more than a decade ago. Simon feels mild relief at the thought of being in Blondie's steady hands. 'But you've got twenty-four hours at most.'

Twenty-four hours.

Chapter 32

The North Pennines
May 2022

Simon has left Sarah's Maserati in the village pay-and-display, ensuring the parking was paid for the next three days, and hidden the key behind the front wheel. He can no longer afford to be driving a car associated with Sarah, which would lead straight to him. He had then stomped back to Ereby Hall, energised by adrenaline and anger. He wants to finish the job. But does he have enough time?

He finds Sebastian finished with his work for the day, pottering around his kitchen.

'Ah, Simon, ah, what're your plans?' asks Sebastian, chopping carrots with an apologetic air.

'Umm, I'm sort of figuring that out,' Simon answers, cautiously.

'It's just that, ah, Cecily, is due back tomorrow.' Sebastian sounds uncomfortable. It's obvious that Mrs Ereby might not be as open-minded as Sebastian was about an unexpected guest who is on the run from a murderous secret service.

'Right, yes. I was going to say,' lies Simon, 'that I was planning to head off tomorrow. Good timing, actually.'

'Not rushing you out, am I?' Sebastian wants to pin down Simon's departure.

'Not at all, quite the reverse, actually.' Simon knows what he has to do, but he hasn't yet figured out the how. What he really needs is a vehicle unconnected to him, Sarah or anyone else who has worked on the case. In the meantime, with the awkwardness of Simon's length of stay now out of the way Sebastian seems to be relishing having a visitor and has pulled a brace of pheasants out of his freezer, the gamey scent sending his dog crazy with anticipation. Perhaps unsurprisingly for a man living in the middle of nowhere and often alone, a bottle of claret has been opened and appears to function as a thirst-quencher. Sebastian is loosening up: the stereo is tuned to Radio 3 and a Beethoven quartet is fighting to be heard over the sound of a sizzling pan. Simon joins him on the wine but is trying to pace himself.

They cook a game stew and repair to the Great Hall, where Sebastian lights a fire from some damp logs that hiss and fizzle with moisture, throwing out a faint, smoky heat into the room. Although it is early summer, there is little daylight making it through the heavy mullioned windows. Sebastian doesn't appear to believe in excessive electric lighting either: a small table lamp has made little impression on the vast, vaulted room. Spectral shadows are spread across the dusty gilt frames of long-dead ancestors, high on the walls.

Sebastian is in an expansive mood, talking about family history, his academic work, classical music. They turn to politics (the prime minister had been at 'School' a few years ahead of Sebastian). Sebastian is anti-Brexit, concerned that his lamb and beef prices will fall and his farm subsidies eventually dry up. But Sebastian's instinctive loyalty to a fellow Etonian prevents Simon from any real discussion of the PM.

Increasingly, Sebastian is babbling through his drink. After they have eaten, they retreat to a small drawing room behind the fireplace in the Great Hall, probably the original solar of Ereby's earliest inhabitants. There, around a smaller chimneypiece and a smaller fire, Sebastian starts on the single malt, which Simon encourages, topping up his glass and encouraging him to tell his anecdotes about long-forgotten incidents at Oxford and memorable bags during the last shooting season. Sebastian obliges, segueing from talkative to garrulous. The sun has set and deep, dark-sky blackness pervades the house. Simon is acting the grateful guest, attentive to his talkative host. In truth, he feels frantic. Time is running out, he has to make his move and cannot do so until Sebastian is asleep. But, for all the wine and whisky, Sebastian seems to be full of energy. And, just when Simon is resigned to the failure of his plan and ready to drain his own generous measure, Sebastian has the sudden change of energy that drunk people often have. He stands, carefully as if he isn't sure whether his feet still work properly, and remembers that he has not shown Simon where he will sleep. Relieved, Simon assures him that he's happy in the made-up bed in one of the kid's rooms and watches Sebastian stagger up a narrow, twisting staircase to his own bed. Simon pulls himself up onto the deep window-ledge on the main landing and sits silently in the quiet night. After several minutes, he hears a loud, inebriated snoring noise, which is his signal to head downstairs again.

He has fifteen hours left.

His first stop is the library, decked out with rows of leather-bound volumes that have not been consulted in decades. There's a computer sitting anachronistically on the edge of an ancient oak desk. He taps the trackpad and is relieved, but unsurprised, to find that there is no password. Quickly he opens a web browser and navigates to a little-known secure messaging site where he fires off a short, carefully worded note. He isn't sure if the recipient will answer, but it's worth a try. On lower shelves around the room are the useful items, including rows of folded Ordnance Survey maps, which Simon had noticed earlier in the day. After searching around for a few minutes, he finds what he needs. Then he walks to an old wall-mounted landline phone, its rotary dialler and Bakelite casing proving it's vintage. He picks up the handset and calls Sarah's cell phone, taking a couple of tense attempts to recall the number correctly.

He only tells her one thing – the place he will meet her and Blondie Phillips in his boat. The rest of his plan he keeps to himself.

Sarah ends the call with a warning. 'You can't be late, and we can't wait for you. There isn't enough time.'

Simon is exhausted, the accumulated tiredness and stress of several days buzzing in a persistent headache. He finds his way to a downstairs cloakroom that has a shower cubicle and gives himself a bracing blast of freezing cold water. He has spotted some clothes hanging on a drying rack in the warren of utility rooms that run behind the kitchen. Clothed in Sebastian's shirt and clean underwear, he feels cold, but wide awake. He takes his grimy, bloody blazer and throws it into the fireplace. It blazes with a satisfying surge of yellow flames, throwing dancing light around the hammerbeam roof of the Great Hall. He pulls on the old shooting jacket for warmth.

Off the kitchen there is a door leading into a small side room, a sort of butler's pantry, equipped with a deep stainless-steel sink and shelves full of ancient-looking glassware. Earlier in the day, Simon had noticed Sebastian replace a key on a small board mounted on the wall. After a bit of searching Simon finds the one for the Land Rover. He also takes the solid black lump of the Škoda key – Sebastian's regular car. Simon grabs a torch from a shelf on the dresser and heads out of the kitchen, his hand slowly pushing the stable door, braced for creaks or clicks. The dog, asleep in her bed by the Aga, makes a deep growling sound. Simon freezes, but the animal appears to be fast asleep, the sounds part of a happy dream in which nobody stops her from chasing squirrels.

Outside, Simon uses the torch beam to guide him to the truck. The driver's door is unlocked and the door hinge makes the groaning sound you get with all Land Rovers. No light comes on and he is certain the vehicle will not start, but he tries the key nonetheless. Nothing: the battery is dead. He jumps out and props open the bonnet, before walking over to the Škoda. He then searches around for jump leads and quickly finds them in the back of the Land Rover, which he connects up to the Škoda's battery. Leaving the car ticking over he returns to the kitchen, where the dog stirs and then relaxes after a few strokes.

Simon finds a scrap of paper and jots a note to Sebastian:

Sebastian, old chap

    It really was way beyond the call to put me up for the night out of the blue. Much enjoyed the chance to catch up. Sadly I have had to make a bit of a rushed departure to carry out an essential task in the national interest, so for minimum disruption I have borrowed the Land Rover. I assure you it will be returned to you in better condition than I found it in.

    My love to Cecily,
    S

He leaves the note on the kitchen table and returns outside and opens the Land Rover door, his feet crunching guiltily on the gravel. This time the interior light comes on and he climbs into the driver's seat. The key turns in the ignition and a starter motor stutters stiffly. But it is turning and after a few seconds the engine fires into life, belching smoke out behind the vehicle. Simon is certain it is too loud and pushes the choke in as far as he dares, but he sees no evidence of stirring in the hall. As quickly as he can manage, he disconnects the jump leads, returning the Škoda to its parking place. He then replaces the Škoda key on the appropriate hook, before tiptoeing past the dog for a final time and heading outside, carefully pulling the door shut behind him as he goes.

    He jogs back to the Land Rover and switches on the sidelights. The dashboard light also illuminates, showing him that he has a quarter of a tank of fuel. With infinite care he puts it into gear, jerkily but without any excess noise, his arms reacquainting themselves with the heavy steering. The driveway has a slight downhill slope, so he lets her roll to minimise engine noise, the unforgiving suspension bouncing over the potholes and hummocks. Within a few seconds he is swinging onto the road. He resists the temptation to use the headlights until he is out of sight of Ereby Hall, at which point he fires up the heating and guns the engine in the hope of recharging the battery. He drives for about an hour until he is in the car park of a service station, where he beds down in the back of the little truck, glad of an old blanket that has a distinctly doggy smell. Time is limited, but Simon cannot do anything until daylight, so he gives himself a few hours' sleep.

–

Shortly after dawn, Simon wakes and drives in to the filling station. He fills the car's tank with petrol and his own with coffee and soggy croissants. It is still very early, and he snoozes for about an hour, lying on the flatbed in the rear. Once he feels a little more awake he sets off, driving on small lanes that wind between high hedgerows through windswept villages. After about thirty minutes he parks in an area of scrubby woodland and walks down a metalled track towards a tiny settlement. Simon has the car blanket slung over his shoulder.

And he still has the pistol in his pocket.

He can see a farm complex. There is a white-painted farm-house with a stone barn built onto the side. Typically Cumbrian, albeit not a particularly distinguished specimen, with plastic windows and an incongruous conservatory sprouting out of one side. He strolls around to find a footpath that allows him a vantage point overlooking the front of the house and the two cars parked outside. There is a large, modern SUV and an expensive-looking saloon more at home in Belgravia than Cumbria. It is a Saturday morning and Simon knows what will happen next, if he waits patiently. Sure enough, an elderly couple soon emerges from the house. They have all the fussy routine of two well-established creatures of habit. They are carrying matching reusable shopping bags and wearing sensible country clothes in muddy green shades. They climb into the SUV and drive in the direction of Carlisle, a retired couple out to do the weekend shop.

Simon is less certain about the next step. He creeps closer to the house, standing behind a tall tree that juts out of the hedge. He wants to move quickly, but forces himself to wait half an hour, using the blanket to give him something to kneel on behind the hedge, his shoulder leaning against the tree. This proves a good decision: after about twenty minutes the front door opens for a second time and a single figure emerges, holding a dog on a lead. This person is younger, wearing scruffy tracksuit bottoms and a baggy navy hooded top. The hood is down, revealing very fair hair, almost white-blond. Simon thinks he can make out white earbuds, no cable. The figure ambles out of the gateway and onto the lane. It isn't immediately clear whether the person is leading the dog, or vice versa. Simon gets a clear sight of his profile as he heads down the lane towards the nearest village.

He is looking at Rory Gough.

Chapter 33

Practically every retired couple in the country goes shopping on a Saturday morning, bickering as they carry out their long-established routine. This is part of the plan, to get Rory on his own. But now Rory had also gone out.

It's a gamble. Rory might be out for a major hike, although nothing about his clothing suggests this. The parents might come back first. But Simon reckons he has Rory where he wants him, and as soon as Rory is out of sight of the house, he heads straight for the building. Simon does a circuit. The conservatory door is not locked, but the inner door is. He walks round to the front door: a heavy, old farmhouse number – solid oak with black bolts under an overhanging porch. Rory has clicked it shut on the Yale lock. He won't have set the alarm. Simon jiggles the door to see how well the lock sits in the doorframe. There is little movement. No chance of an entry here.

Simon walks backwards to get a better view of the building. There is a first-floor window open on a latch, just above the porch. It offers a possibility. Simon puts his foot on the low side-wall of the porch and reaches up to the curly wrought-iron bracket that holds up the porch roof. With the grunt of someone who is still not in shape, in spite of his escape from Christ Church a couple of days earlier, he pulls himself up and places both feet on the wall. He then performs an ungainly move like someone getting out of a swimming pool, squirming over onto the flat roof of the porch. He feels the little pieces of gravel on the roofing felt scraping against his wrists as he brings his feet up. It's surprisingly painful. He rolls forwards onto his stomach and wriggles his legs onto the little roof, no bigger than a coffee table. Eventually he is in balance and can stand up to reach the open window above. A small steel latch with a row of holes holds the window in place at the bottom of the frame. A sharp blow flips the latch out of its housing and the window swings idly in the breeze. Simon reaches up with both arms and executes an ugly pull-up, his feet scrabbling against the wall, making a mess of a climbing rose as he does so.

He pitches forwards into the opening, the window frame digging into his stomach. His torso knocks some small plastic figurines off the inside windowsill which fall lightly onto a carpeted floor. He follows, awkwardly pitching forwards onto an outstretched hand and wriggling his legs into the room. Somehow, Simon hasn't quite got this manoeuvre right, and his hand slips, his face plunging into the carpet. It's an ungainly mess; Simon is happy not to have any spectators. With his eyes at carpet-level, Simon realises that the figurines are Star Wars characters: he is staring at C-3PO, Luke Skywalker and Darth Vader, whose lightsabre appears to have been chewed many years ago by a family pet.

Rolling onto his side, Simon stands up, rubbing his sore tummy. He is in a little boy's bedroom. There are more Star Wars figurines arranged on the windowsill. On top of a bookshelf he recognises a large model of the *Millennium Falcon*. The single bed has a faded Batman duvet cover. The walls are covered in a range of film posters from the 1980s and school photographs with faded Kodachrome colours. A young Rory Gough, somehow innocent and vulnerable in his ill-fitting blazer and stripey tie, snow-white hair, grinning geekily at the future. Rory, an only child, friendless, weird, bullied. His juvenile bedroom lovingly preserved by ageing parents whom he visits every weekend he can. Against all his instincts, Simon feels a wave of empathy.

And then he snaps back to the task at hand. He grabs the figures from the floor and rearranges them carefully on the windowsill, replacing the latch on the window-frame. He peers down at the climbing rose. It has mostly sprung back into place. A professional intelligence officer would notice the difference, but probably not Rory. Simon pads down the narrow staircase and does a quick survey of the ground floor. There is a burglar alarm, but Rory hasn't set it for a short dog-walk. The only risk is that his parents return home first. But Simon doesn't think that likely – a Saturday shopping trip is rarely a swift enterprise. He positions himself in an armchair in the sitting room, next to a French window. As a precaution he has unlocked this, after hunting for a little key that hangs on a hook under the drawn curtain. If the parents arrive first, he can slip out into the garden, leaving them to argue about who left the windows open.

It's a small room, humble and chintzy. In this temple to Little England Simon sits, trying to locate Rory, multimillion-aire maven of international finance. The swirly deep pile carpet, floral pattern sofa, ducks flying unironically across the wall, no books. A large shelving unit is filled with DVD box sets: nature documentaries and costume dramas. Rory, or more properly, the cynical adult that is Rory Gough, creature of Mayfair and the hedge-fund scene, is nowhere to be seen. More than that, it feels improbable that he could ever be present in this room.

And now Simon just has to wait. An ersatz cabinet clock on the mantelpiece, shiny faux-veneer, ticks noisily. He's down to his last six hours.

Simon checks and re-checks the gun on his lap. He double checks the door into the garden, figuring his line of retreat, invisible from the front door of the house.

And the waiting continues.

After what feels like a lifetime, but is actually only twenty-six minutes, he hears the crunch of footsteps on the gravel driveway. It's now or never: Simon has run out of options. This is his final move. He doesn't really know what he is going to achieve, but he does know that the other option is to wait for the police to track him down. At least he is taking the initiative. But now the moment is on him he feels nervous, regretful, even. Somehow, Rory's childhood home feels like the wrong place to do this. Some would say distasteful.

In a way, he can feel proud to have got this far at all. He's proved something to the doubters. The people at the Pole who didn't think he really cut it. And all those smug public schoolboys running the country into the ground whilst lining their own pockets. And he did it mostly on his own, against the hardest of targets. Perhaps, in those places the spooks go to drink and share stories, people will say that eventually, after the shock has subsided: 'It's amazing he got there at all, if you think about it. Terrible, yes, but impressive, in a way.'

He pulls out the gun from the shooting jacket and cocks it, checking the brass round is properly chambered. The footsteps on the gravel are getting lounder and closer to the front door. He hears the clicking of a key turning a lock and the whine of a dog, eager to get inside. There is the sound of the opening door and rustling. Perhaps someone is removing a coat. And then he hears the voice: 'C'mon Raf,' it says to the dog. A distinctive, Cumbrian accent, a little blunted by years in high financial circles. Although Simon has not heard him in the flesh in many years, there is no doubt who it is.

Rory Gough. Now, or never.

'Rory.' Simon tries his best to sound calm, as if he has every right to be there. He is summoning, not asking. But he has reckoned without the dog. At this sole word, Simon hears rushing paws and a cascade of barks. Before any sign of Rory, a large golden Labrador rushes into the sitting room. True to his breed, he is no guard-dog, but desperate for attention and affection. Ordinarily, Simon would be happy to provide these things, but he is also trying to be ready for the appearance of Rory. Simon is still seated and wants to remain so, to give the appearance of control and relaxation. But he is having to focus one hand on the dog, stroking him to keep him happy.

And then Rory appears, slowly, his head tentatively poking around the door frame. The round face is fuller than he remembers. The hair is still albino-blond, but rather thinner. It shouldn't be a surprise: Simon has seen numerous photos of Rory, video clips of him talking to journalists, even caricatures in the weekend papers. But none of these are Rory in Simon's head. That person is someone Simon had known more than twenty years earlier, with a hollow face and floppy hair. With his right hand still stroking the head of the dog, now happily wagging his tail and sitting at the foot of the armchair, Simon raises his left hand, holding the gun, as Rory enters the room, an expression of confused terror on his face. Simon has seen this face before in other places, on other operations. Rory's trying to figure out if he should turn around, run away, stand his ground, or charge Simon. He is also trying to figure out who the hell Simon is. And whether his life is about to end.

Simon stands up, motioning with the gun for Rory to stand in the centre of the room. Simon can let go of the dog, who is still hanging around eagerly, probably hoping for a treat for good behaviour. Rory's mouth, initially a little triangle of surprise, is now firmly closed, his jaws biting with the tension. It's obvious he has realised exactly who Simon is. He has probably been receiving regular updates from his Russian friends on the attempts to track down and kill him. Or from the Pole? This thought, and the thought of Evie's body cartwheeling through the air in Prague, sends a sudden surge of determined anger coursing through Simon, helping him to refocus. He pats the dog and sends him trotting out of the room. Then, flattening himself against the wall of the sitting room so that Rory cannot get too close to him, he issues the first instruction. A test of his power.

'Out. French window. It's unlocked.' There's a momentary pause. Is he going to do what he's told? Or is this going to have to end even quicker than planned? But Rory seems to have resigned himself to co-operate.

'Yeah, no problem, Simon,' he says calmly, as if he was agreeing to do some minor favour. Simon lets Rory step onto the grass of the lawn, a few feet from the house, before following him out and pushing the French window shut behind him. The dog has reappeared, looking plaintive at being left out of this interesting activity. But he doesn't bark, choosing to lie down by the window instead, no doubt hoping to be invited outside momentarily. Rory has turned to face Simon, his hands apart, palms upwards, like a maître d' welcoming diners to a tourist-trap restaurant.

'You need to give me your phone,' says Simon, matter-of-factly.

'My what?'

'Phone. Come on. Hold it out in front of you.' Simon waggles the barrel of the pistol at Rory to make his point, his other hand outstretched to receive. Rory, clearly very reluctant, passes Simon a large, new-looking iPhone that is so far up the range that Simon isn't sure he's ever actually held one like it before. He shoves it in his back pocket, but it doesn't fit very well.

'Right. Walk. Round to the front of the house.' This is the most exposed part of Simon's plan. If Rory's parents return home at this point, Simon might have to start shooting. But the SUV does not reappear and the two men walk in a strange crocodile back towards the strand of trees where Simon has parked the Land Rover. Simon can now hear the dog barking, angry to have been left out of all the fun. Simon wants Rory comfortable. He wants to ease him in to talking about himself, a subject on which he never usually lacks things to say.

They follow the long, straight lane back up the hill towards the scrubby patch of woodland. Simon keeps the gun trained on Rory as they walk. After all the madness of the past few days, Simon now has Rory Gough in his control. It's the end of the line, but he can't quite work out exactly how to play it. Weeks of tension, moments of panic. He now feels strangely calm. Simon begins to talk.

'I expect you're wondering what the hell this is all about.' He doesn't really think Rory is wondering at all, but it seems polite to offer the possibility. Simon is really just filling a void, a warm-up act.

Rory is playing it very cool. 'Yeah, well, some kind of explanation is probably in order. I mean, I'm going to have to explain to the police, aren't I? Either that, or you're going to kill me, in which case you don't need to bother, I suppose.'

'I could talk for hours, but in the end it's pretty simple. I need an explanation for various things. I reckon you can give that to me. So that's what we're going to do. No need for it to get nasty.'

'Simon.' Rory turns his head to look straight at him. 'It is Simon, isn't it? Just, I mean, you could say this has already got pretty fockin nasty.' In his tension, Rory's Cumbrian accent has thickened. 'The bit where you broke into my parents' house with a gun and kidnapped me. That was nasty.' Rory is trying to make light of the situation, but Simon can tell that he is on edge. But has he figured out Simon's plan?

They reach the Land Rover. Simon tells Rory to climb into the passenger seat and strap himself in. His reasoning is simple: if Rory decides to try to run away, he will have to unstrap himself and climb out of the Land Rover before he has got anywhere, giving Simon plenty of time to take remedial action.

Rory looks perplexed as he settles into the passenger seat. He is obviously expecting Simon to join him on the driver's side. But Simon doesn't want to have to think about driving at the same time as questioning a potentially hostile target. Instead, he signals to Rory to lower the window, which he does with laborious effort on the stiff winding handle. He stares out at Simon, who is standing about five feet from the car – deliberately out of reach, but close enough for detailed revelation. Simon puts the pistol in his waistband and places his hands in his pockets.

'Okay Rory, I want you to tell me about Peter Mackenzie, Georgy Sidorov and COSTELLO. We haven't got that much time, actually, so let's get to the point, shall we?' Simon tries his best to sound business-like, reasonable. He wants to send the message that Rory just has to tell his story and then all of this can be finished, for ever.

'Er, not sure I know anything about that, actually. Who are these people?' asks Rory in a cocky voice that Simon recognises from endless broadcast interviews. Is he playing for time?

'The explanation, Rory. Back at Oxford, Mackenzie sent you for a meeting at the Russian Embassy. Why?'

'Mackenzie did what?' Rory looks confused, dismissive. For a moment Simon wonders whether the whole case is flawed. Did they get some detail wrong? Maybe Mackenzie had never 'spotted' Rory. But Simon calms himself. The evidence is overwhelming.

'Georgy Sidorov. Cultural attaché at the Russian Embassy in Kensington Palace Gardens. You had a meeting there, thanks to an introduction made for you by Mackenzie. This was in our final year at Oxford. When you were about to go to Russia.' Rory blinks. Is this recognition or remembrance?

'That is a *very* long time ago, Simon.'

'It might well be, but I think you'd remember a visit to the Russian Embassy, wouldn't you?'

'Why does it matter?' says Rory, a tone of defiance growing in his voice.

'It doesn't, really. We have found out so much about your relationship with the Russians over the years that it doesn't really matter at all if you don't tell me about your first meeting with the Russian intelligence officer Georgy Sidorov.' Simon pauses for effect. 'What about COSTELLO? Does that mean anything to you?'

'What, like Abbott and Costello? Old-time comedy? Not really my style. I prefer something a bit *edgy*.' Rory is smiling, but it doesn't feel like a confident smile. Simon shifts his weight. He'd like to sit down.

'Don't fuck with me, Rory. Be in no doubt: I am deadly fucking serious. Tell me about your little trips round Europe. Düsseldorf, Trieste, Milan. What is all that about?'

Rory clears his throat, shakes his head slightly, and smiles awkwardly. Simon feels like this might be a moment of truth.

'Er, you might find it hard to understand,' says Rory, with an apologetic laugh.

'I think I'll manage,' says Simon. 'Just fucking start explaining yourself, okay?'

'Well, in the business world, we have these things called clients. Often I travel to meet them, for things called meetings.'

'Shut UP!' Simon is furious. His raised voice might be audible at some distance so he checks his anger. 'Seriously, Rory, do *not* fuck with me. Let's try something else. Ever find yourself meeting a Russian businessman with a St Kitts passport? Kind of unusual, don't you think? The sort of thing that would stick in the memory.'

'Can't really remember. I mean, they have those passports-for-sale, don't they? In St Kitts. So you can see a Russian oligarch thinking that might be a good option for them. But you know, at a meeting you don't usually check someone's passport, do you?'

'Does Flood 19 mean anything to you?'

'Flood what?'

'Flood 19. A company with an account at Alpenbank in Lichtenstein.'

Rory says nothing, but shrugs with a dismissive pout that implies, 'what the fuck would I know about that?' Simon realises he is getting nowhere, his frustration rising.

'Okay, let's try something it would be hard to forget. February 2016. You went on a trip with Tom Harkness and Kamran Patel. To Aachen. You met a Russian contact whilst you were there.'

'Simon, in case you hadn't noticed,' he says with exaggerated, dismissive enunciation, 'I've been fairly busy in recent years. Busy people travel. We go to conferences, we fly in and out of places, we meet people, we do things. You might not know about this sort of thing. My understanding is that you haven't been very busy. I'm sorry to hear that.' The disdain is dripping off Rory's face, splashing in little puddles of scorn. Simon has had enough. He pulls out the pistol, holding it out in front of him in a classic two-handed grip, his feet in the boxer stance. His finger tightens on the trigger.

I could just do it, he thinks. *I could end him here. Nobody's going to take action on Gough. And I'm fucked anyway. Why not just do it? Probably have more impact than a lifetime of writing bloody intelligence reports.*

With the gun pointing directly at Rory's face, Simon speaks, slowly and deliberately. 'You have been part of a spy-ring recruited from Oxford, talented-spotted by Mackenzie. It's called COSTELLO and you continue to travel for meetings in Europe with your Russian case officers. It's true, isn't it? So why don't you start by talking about Aachen?'

His hand tenses on the trigger. He can see Rory's face, crumpling slightly. At last, this thing is nearly over.

'No!' Rory is wriggling in the car seat, trying to lean down under the window.

Crouch down if you want. The 9mm round would easily pass through the skin of the Land Rover.

'It was planning!' cries Rory, panic in his voice for the first time. 'We can talk about it. Aachen. A planning meeting about political stuff. Different movements in Europe with common interests. That sort of thing.' Simon lowers the gun, relieved. He wasn't sure if he could do it. 'Fuck you,' adds Rory. 'You are in so much shit.'

'Whatever. Tell me about Aachen. Planning meeting. Who with? Why did you need to get out of the UK to talk about our politics?'

Rory is flustered, constantly looking across the Land Rover to the driver's side door, obviously wondering if he can make a run for it. He speaks softly, furious that he has been forced into it. 'We were meeting international contacts, people who would help with the campaign, financial backers, that sort of thing. And *you* know why we did it out of the UK. Twats like you, deep state, everywhere, reporting on us.'

'Who did you meet?'

'Told you: international supporters, people with common interests. People who see the bigger picture.'

'Who? WHO? Names, Rory. You need to start giving me names.'

'It's years ago. You expect me to remember?'

'Yes, I fucking do. We can do the thing with the gun again if you want. Let me help you. Sazanovich. Sergey Sazanovich. Ring any bells?'

'Never heard of him.'

Simon sighs, infuriated. 'Okay, how about "Steve Carpenter"? Funny name for a Russian.'

Rory says nothing. Simon can feel an opening.

'You don't deny meeting Carpenter?'

'Name rings a bell.'

Simon continues: 'So, let's talk about who pays for these trips.'

'Business travel, you know how that is. You get your assistant to book it. Company credit card, that sort of thing.' Rory is still trying to sound normal, boring. But there is a quavering to his voice which makes it clear he is anything but bored.

'Yes, but which company? This wasn't paid for by your fund, was it? This isn't *regular* business travel, is it?' Again, Rory doesn't answer. Simon decides to expand. 'Flood 19. Credit card issued by Alpenbank of Lichtenstein. Flood 19 paid for these trips, and the rooms were booked under the name of the Costello Trust. Explain how that happens. We know *what*, Rory, you just need to tell me *how*. So, you might as well start at the beginning: Mackenzie, Sidorov. The whole story.'

Rory takes a deep breath and starts to talk: 'Okay. Back in the day, Mackenzie got me an appointment at the Russian Embassy when I decided to go to Moscow. After finals.'

'Appointment with whom?'

'I really can't remember. Seriously, Simon. It was ages ago.'

'Yeah, right. I bet you can remember what happened at the meeting. At the embassy.'

'Well, some guy talked to me about Russia. Why I was interested in it. It was mostly a conversation about culture, history, literature. I was an Oxford undergraduate in my early twenties

– pretentious stuff. But he said it had been interesting and perhaps we could keep in touch.'

'And you agreed?'

'Course I did: I wanted a visa, didn't I?'

'And, after that, you go to Russia and you keep in touch with Mackenzie while you're there, don't you? But do you have more meetings with Russian officials? Security officials?'

'Simon, I thought you people were supposed to actually know something about how Russia works? I was a foreigner living in Russia in the nineties. Of course I had meetings with security officials! What do you fucking expect? But no, I was not recruited by the fucking KGB, if that's what you're asking.'

'But, after you came back, you've carried on going to meetings with Russians, all paid for by Flood 19. So, again, what is Flood 19? It's something to do with Mackenzie, isn't it?'

'Flood 19 was a company set up by Mackenzie. He had political projects he believed in, and I have been involved with that work.' Rory sounds pious.

'Why is it called Flood 19?'

Rory gives an embarrassed laugh. 'That's a Mackenzie thing. You know how he worshipped Thatcher. It was her address in London before she became PM. Nineteen Flood Street in Chelsea. Bloody ridiculous, if you ask me.'

There's a silence. Simon is recalling the many hours spent trying to figure out the meaning of Flood 19, which has proven to be utterly trivial.

'But Flood 19 had money flowing into it for years, up until the month of Mackenzie's death. And there's some connection with the Costello Trust, isn't there? So, what's going on there?'

Rory is sounding dismissive, peevish. 'Like I said, it's a company for political projects. Basically, a consultancy. We had revenues. That's kind of normal for a company, wouldn't you say? Maybe not any company that you run, but in general this is how it works.' Once again, the sarcasm has entered Rory's voice, as if he's forgotten that Simon has a gun, and might be prepared to use it.

'You say you had "revenues". Where from? Who were the clients?'

Rory looks exquisitely uncomfortable. He rubs his mouth, stretching his lips awkwardly. 'Banks. We had financial-sector clients.'

'Which banks?'

Another long pause. It looks as though he's wondering if he can avoid saying anything. But Simon and his gun are looking purposeful. 'Russian banks,' he says, in a strangulated voice that is all misery. 'Just normal consultancy work. Plenty of it about.'

'Rory, given that you are a successful fund manager, making millions apparently, the existence of Flood 19, a company registered in Malta which received payments from MMB, which we both know is a Russian bank linked to Russian intelligence, is not in any way "normal"...' Simon stops talking, expecting some sort of response from Rory. None comes. But he sees him gulp, blinking uncomfortably. 'This is getting boring, isn't it?' says Simon. 'I can go through all of this from the start, or you can just explain it.'

Gough lets out a huge sigh, and then starts to talk. His tone is more confident, sounding more like the Gough you would hear on the news, talking dismissively to reporters. 'Okay, Simon, if you want to do this, you might as well try to actually understand why it's happening. People like you are so obsessed with your own narratives. But it's actually just noise. You aren't actually thinking about what *I'm* doing; it's all about your pathetic little world of spies and agents. Just like the endless bureaucracy inside government. No discipline. No focus. Nobody knows why they're doing anything, they're stuck inside their narrative.' He pauses, prologue over. 'You know very well that I have been interested in Russia for decades.'

'What does that mean in practice? 'Cause it looks as though you, who likes to think of himself as a big strategist, have been completely played by the Russians.' Simon is trying to goad him into confessing, and it is working.

'That is complete fucking bollocks,' Gough answers angrily.

'Is it? Then explain what the Costello Trust is. It's not complicated, is it? Unless, of course, you have something to be ashamed
of.'

'Listen. Your people, the Whitehall crowd, Will Butler with
his obsessive Kremlinology. Idiots. You're all playing a little game.
Left, Right, Labour, Conservatives. You're all playing it. It's part
of the systems failure in Whitehall. You try to interpret what I
do as a move in your crappy little game. But I'm not playing
this game. I'm operating at a completely different level.' Rory is
animated now, his energy rising and with it his sense of awesome
superiority.

'We are living in a world,' Rory continues, 'where people of
high intelligence, people who have *real* expertise, need sovereignty. We need to be able to operate with *extreme freedom*.
There's this bureaucracy everywhere which builds in failure to
most systems. Progress can only happen if people are willing to
be bold, ignore bureaucrats' and hacks' games, and make things
happen. Take Russia. There's plenty about that country that I
don't like. A lot of Russia's state is basically non-functional: huge
parts of its population have no future to look forward to. Kind
of pointless even thinking about them. But the bits that matter
– Russia's presidency, its strategic forces, its weapons experts, its
special services – they have the ability to shape the world in ways
that suit Russia's interests. For example: Georgia wants to join
NATO? Russia carries out the first real cyber offensive in history,
followed up with a lightning ground war, and Georgia is finished.
End of. Ukraine fucks around with being too close to the EU?
Russia takes the Crimea before anyone has realised what they're
up to. Hostile candidate running for the White House? They
hack and leak her emails, destroying her campaign. These people
actually know what their goal is, and how to achieve that goal.
And then they just fucking do it.'

'Yeah and their army has really showed its worth in Ukraine,
hasn't it?' says Simon, the sarcasm dripping from his voice as he
thinks of that country's heroic resistance.

'The Russian regular army has always been the bottom of the pile. What you're failing to look at is strategic depth. Nuclear forces. Oil and gas. Minerals for batteries. Control of global grain markets. You wait – Western economies are collapsing.'

For the first time, Simon is starting to hear the zeal of a convert. But in a good interrogation, you need patience. Let the subject get comfortable with talking. Let them fill the silences. But Simon doesn't have time, and he is getting impatient. 'Yeah Rory. You have to believe, even when your side is losing. I get that.'

Rory blinks several times. 'Losing? Who the fuck are you to talk about *losing*? Your people, the civil service, the Remainer deep state, the fucking *blob* have run Britain into the ground. Whitehall is basically a bomb site. It can't make decisions, effect change, do anything. You are completely parochial. Like, your lot are obsessed with NATO – and everyone knows that's finished. *Brain dead*. You're banking the entire defence of this country on the mysterious idea that the Italian navy and the Portuguese parachute regiment are going to come to our rescue in the event of a major conflict? I mean, we already know most Americans aren't interested. It's all fucking bullshit. And you talk to *me* about losers?' Simon doesn't respond, so Rory picks up his thread again. 'Listen, one thing *you* probably understand is the concept that sometimes, smart people have to do things that the masses *don't* understand. That is sort of how the intelligence services work, right? You give the people what they think they want, so that the ones who can actually *do stuff* can get on with it. Which, if you can get off your moral high-ground for more than thirty seconds, is the whole point. The political stuff, the prime minister, all that, is just what's on the surface. But it allows me to get to remake Britain in the way I want. *We* want, I suppose.'

'But who's *we*, here, Rory? "We" is Russia, isn't it?'

Rory lets out a frustrated groan of the sort schoolboys make when they want to accuse someone of being mentally deficient. 'You really *are* stupid, aren't you? Do you still actually not get it? Yes, some of these people are Russian. But I am not working with them because I want Russia to "defeat" the West.' He resorts to air quotes to make his point. 'Russia is just one geopolitical space. I believe in maximum freedom. Radical deregulation. Hyper-mobile finance. The sovereignty of the individual. Shrink the state. And of course, there's culture. Just like that first meeting back in the Russian Embassy all those years ago. Faced with the choice, do we choose Russia's European, Christian culture, or Western Europe's post-Christian culture, allowing itself to be replaced by a Muslim demographic timebomb? We have to take back control, actually make a choice. Leaving NATO is one of the ways we do it – regain *our* sovereignty over *our* armed forces. We shouldn't be called on to defend the fucking Ukrainian border just because they mistreat their Russian minority. NATO's finished anyway. Then, we slim down the British state and focus on becoming the world's leading hub for financial innovation. If that happens to overlap with the goals of a bunch of Russians, I don't care, really. *By any means necessary*, as the saying goes. You see, you need to remember that history changes through conflict. That was something Mackenzie taught us. Incremental change never works. Your lot will just stumble into a nuclear war. So, for us, this thing with Moscow is win–win.'

'For *us*, or for *you*? Who's the beneficiary here?'

Once again, Rory sounds infuriated that his simple concept is apparently unclear. 'There are a few of us, yes. But we only need a few. This is where your Russia derangement syndrome is so pointless. We are not trying to do something for Russia. We're getting Britain ready for the post-liberal world. There are people around the world who can help with that. Some of them are Russian and we work with them. Where we have shared interests, we share outcomes.'

Ultimately, Rory had been right: Simon was thinking inside a box. A box containing espionage, double agents and other counters spread across the spying board-game. He had believed that Rory had decided to work for Russia. But he hadn't expected that Rory saw Russia, Britain and everywhere else as working for him.

'So what does this mean in practice, Rory? Who is it you go to meet at all these Costello Trust sessions?'

'Seems like you already know, Simon. There's Harkness, me, Camondo, Patel. We meet the St Kitts guys—'

'You mean the Russian intelligence officers using St Kitts alias passports,' interjects Simon.

'Well, you might say that, Simon,' says Rory, smiling. 'All I know is that I have met businessmen, international types, who have made use of citizenship by investment programmes. I mean, I should have thought a metro-liberal like you wouldn't obsess over nationality, right?' He says this final point with a teasing sneer that Simon finds infuriating.

'Anyway, one thing I know for a fact,' says Rory, now clearly enjoying himself, 'is that none of those people work for the SVR or GRU.'

Of course they don't. That's the whole COSTELLO model: an off-books organisation, not connected to the existing intelligence agencies.

'But do they have some connection with the Russian state?' asks Simon. 'Former intelligence officers? Advisers to the intelligence services?'

Rory gives his smug, sneering grin again. 'How would I know about that? Possible, of course. But, like I said, this is about my agenda, not theirs.'

'But your initial introduction was through Sidorov, Russian Embassy, all those years ago, wasn't it? Last time I checked he didn't have anything to do with St Kitts.'

'I guess, probably.' Rory sounds unsure, as if he can't work out whether it matters.

'So there's a link, isn't there? A link between a serving Russian official and your little Costello Group.'

Rory snorts impatiently. 'Yeah, whatever, Simon. A link. Sure. Everything in Russia links back to the government. Like I said, it's my show, not theirs.'

'Yes but have they – the St Kitts guys – have they ever asked you to do something for them? Support a project, get some business over the line with a whisper in the right ear in Downing Street? Get someone fired? That sort of thing.'

Rory looks mildly confused, as if this isn't very important. 'They might have. Not often and nothing compared to the *endless* requests I get from the Whitehall blob. "Oh, Rory, can we present to you our new ideas for tech development?" I mean, that stuff seems to take up most of my life. So, yeah, now and then, I'll put my thumb on the scale if I see an alignment of interests.'

'Care to give me an example?' Their tone is now more like two undergraduates debating the merits of the Corn Laws. 'I mean, what about Will Butler? Your idea? Their idea?'

'Not a bad example, actually. Will's bloody useless. Archetypal product of the blob. Incapable of innovative thinking. Locked into the bureaucracy. Totally doesn't *get* Brexit. As far as I'm concerned, firing him is long overdue, country's interest. And the St Kitts crowd think he's an escalation risk. So obsessed with punishing Russia that he might just start World War Three over some shithole town in Eastern Ukraine where everyone speaks Russian anyway. They know I can have a word with the PM and so we just get on with it. Job done. You got a problem with that?'

'Well, you call yourself a "senior adviser" to the prime minister. He might be interested to understand there's a bunch of Russians with St Kitts passports egging you on.'

At this, Rory laughs. A genuine outburst of ribald ridicule. 'The prime minister?' he pauses and looks at Simon. 'D'you actually think we don't have leverage?'

Simon sighs at the thought of the overweight prime minister, floundering in debt, sexual compromise and policy incoherence.

Rory has started speaking again. The sneer has returned to his tone, perhaps because he realises he has given away just a little too much? 'Since I can tell you're too chickenshit to shoot me, are you gonna let me go now? 'Cause my parents will be back anytime now and the dog doesn't like to be on her own in the house. Oh, and you probably need to get a bit of a head-start because I am going to get the entire fucking Cumbria police special branch onto you. I mean, they'll get you anyway. But you probably want to think you've got a chance.'

There was something about this last statement that was too much. Simon had heard enough. He pulls out the gun, shoves the barrel against Rory's temple and rests his finger on the trigger.

For a moment, Simon is remembering an interrogation. It happened in a dusty cell in the Middle East. He had only been an observer. But he had learned a lot. The pistol thrust against the temple. The theatrical sound of cocking, making ready. The shout, you have to fucking start talking to me, RIGHT NOW! And then a pause. Does the prisoner answer? Give him time. But if he doesn't answer, tilt the gun slightly, so it's pointing just away from the curve of the skull. Then, fire the fucking thing. There's a moment, when the prisoner has been deafened by the shot right next to his ear, felt the rush of air, and can't work out if he's already dead. And when they realise they're not, they start to talk.

But Simon doesn't need to fire the gun. Rory's swagger has deserted him. His voice sounds panicky, if defiant. There's a soft patch of skin in his temple where the barrel of the Glock makes a little dimple.

'You're making a really big mistake,' he says, in a strangulated tone.

For most of his adult life, Simon has done what he's told. He's avoided big mistakes. He's served other masters. And it hasn't got him anywhere.

'I'm not actually,' replies Simon, leaning most of his body weight into the barrel of the gun, the muzzle digging into Rory's head, his finger playing on the trigger. 'As you've said, time is running out. So you need to give me the lowdown: what's the role of the others? Harkness, Patel, Camondo? Anybody else?'

Rory is talking quickly. Almost a panicky gabble. 'I can't read their minds. But I have my agenda and I don't mind when their, er, *suggestions*, overlap with my interests. Gonna be the same for the others: Harkness – it's obvious. He's spent his life on Brexit. It's literally the only thing he cares about. Russians helped him along with that because they saw some value in it. Patel: it's a worldview thing. He gets the civilisational aspect of this. Camondo I know the least about. But you know the story of his bank, don't you?'

Simon doesn't have time to listen to Rory tell him what he already knows. 'Anyone else?'

Rory pauses. Simon nudges with the gun barrel. Rory is breathing heavily, almost hyperventilating. 'Wittenberg. You know where he's at now, don't you?'

'Yes, but what is he doing for the Russians?'

'Well in his context it's more fundamental. If you are in Germany you have a choice to make, don't you? It's energy security, export markets, strategic questions. Geography. But, the details of his relations with them? No idea.'

'What do you mean "no idea"?'

'I mean I don't have the bandwidth to be dealing with German politics. Big topic. I stopped following it around the time of Bismarck. You know how this stuff works. I don't know anything about what Heinrich does when he meets the COSTELLO guys. I just know that he's part of the group.'

'And Berezina?' As Simon says this, insistently, he hears the distant sound of a car's tyres crunching on gravel. This can only mean that Rory's parents have returned from their shopping trip. He has seconds left.

'Last chance, Rory.'

He speaks, urgently and in terror. 'Berezina. It's a fucking filename. You know, the French use it to mean a hopeless defeat. At the hands of the Russians, originally. Means nothing more than that.'

Simon can hear a car door slamming. There's no time. 'It's more than a filename, Rory. It's the holding company that owns Powerstream, isn't it? We've figured it out.'

Rory screws his eyes shut, then opens them again. He's going to say something. But he stops himself, reconsiders. 'You've left it too late.'

Simon knows he has to go, that Rory's parents are now back in the house, wondering where he's got to.

'It's all done,' Rory adds, gnomically.

'What do you mean?'

'Today. It's all done. Powerstream. They're finishing the engineering right now.'

'Okay. Yeah, right. "It's all done." So there's no way of stopping it. How convenient,' replies Simon, sarcastically.

'You can imagine how little of a fuck I could give about whether or not you believe me. But just so you know, if you hadn't fucking kidnapped me, I'd be on my way there. Big meeting with the key people at the site happening today. Job done… But it's fine – I'm not really needed. You see, we all know that if there's facts on the ground, the government will never stop it. Like I said, you're too late.'

Too late. Running out of time. He can hear Rory's parents talking. They must be wondering where he's gone, without the dog. There isn't time to ask any more. 'Okay, Rory, you just need to do one last thing for me for me. Shut the fuck up and sit still. I'm going to drive a little, then let you out and this little episode will be over. But first, we're going to need you to cover your face. You know how it is.'

Simon reaches down into the large poacher's pocket of the borrowed shooting jacket. It has a smooth, satin-like lining. With a sharp tug he rips this out. It proves about the right size to pull over Rory's face, if a little tight, a sinister hood-like mask. Probably involuntarily, Rory puts his hand up to the mask. Simon pushes the gun into the back of his head.

'You're going to keep very quiet, aren't you? Until I tell you it's time to get out.'

'Yeah, fuck off,' was Rory's confirmation.

He walks round to the driver's seat and hauls himself up. Rory can probably see a fair amount through the thin fabric of his improvised hood. Simon worries that he might try to grab him while he's making a gear change. So he decides to lay out the rules very clearly. 'Listen, Rory. I'm going to drive for about half an hour. Not too far. This is your area. You'll be fine. Nice day for a walk. So, don't panic. Shut the fuck up and I'll let you out pretty soon.'

'You are so fucked, matey.' Rory sounds furious. He folds his arms and thrusts his chin, concealed under the shiny hood, down towards his chest.

Simon reckons Rory won't try anything really stupid. So he turns the ignition key. Momentarily he has a feeling of panic as the Land Rover's starter motor retches spasmodically on the dying battery, before firing into life with a triumphant roar. Simon drives as quickly as the ancient vehicle will let him, away from the little settlement which had Rory's family farm at its heart. After only a couple of minutes they are out of the woodlands and on a high moor, clumps of reeds whizzing past the windows. He is thinking about stopping when Rory speaks from under his silky mask. With the layer of fabric and the noise of the vehicle, he has to talk at an exaggerated volume.

'You know that there could be an upside for you.'

'Rory, there's no reason you should know any of this, but I can assure you there have been no upsides whatsoever.'

'Yeah I get that. Up till now. I'm saying there could be.'

'Oh yes? Seems to me that, with Ukraine and all the sanctions, your little business model is no longer sustainable.'

Rory pauses before replying. 'I'm taking off this stupid mask. I'm not going to attack you or whatever. But I'm getting car sick.' He swipes off the hood. 'Pull over up here somewhere.' Reluctantly, Simon does as he is told: this was more or less where he was planning to let Rory out, in any case. As a precaution, Simon puts one hand on the gun, ready to draw if necessary.

They pull into a stony passing place. There are little mounds of horseshit and Simon can see wild ponies grazing the moorland. An occasional car shoots past, but otherwise there is no sign of human life. Simon is struck by the speed of the transition from village to wilderness.

'Okay. This is kind of your last-chance saloon,' says Rory.

Simon feels this is admirable chutzpah from a man who's about to be thrown out onto a deserted moor.

'I can see you've gone quite a long way with this. And actually, I admire what you've done. In some ways, we might not be so different, you and me, if you'll forgive the cliché. You've worked outside the system, got away from the horrific bureaucracy, made stuff happen. That's what I do. But in this particular situation, you have created a problem for me, and now I am going to create a much bigger problem for you.'

'Yeah, remind me: you've just admitted to regular contact with high-level Russians, including their involvement in a part of the critical national infrastructure. That feels like it's a problem for you, not me.' Simon is sure he has the upper hand.

'Russia, Russia, *Russia.*' Rory's tone is a sneer. 'For the last time, this isn't about Russia. You still think there's something called the *government*, don't you? And you think this *government* thing doesn't like "Russia",' he emphasises the word, making little air quotes. 'And now because of Ukraine we're changing all the rules. Do you actually think it's that simple? Do you not understand that the prime minister is hopeless on this stuff? I *am* the government! *I am* the person who tells him how far to go with the sanctions. There's loopholes so fucking wide I can drive my dad's tractor right through. A little bit of restructuring, remove some outstanding risk factors, and we're good to go. On the other hand, you've got *nowhere* to go.' A pause, definitely for effect. 'So, last chance. Berezina is going to generate a lot of revenues. And yes, some of the investors are Russian. We will have incredible power over the energy price, just as the markets are going crazy. There's probably something for you in there. Going to take it?'

They sit in silence. He confronted Rory because he'd realised that the system wasn't going to take any action. But now he realises that Rory is right: he *is* the system. There is no sanction, no institution or authority that can touch him. On the other hand, Simon is about to be on the run, again. If he cuts a deal with Rory, he could make most of these problems disappear.

Nobody is on my side, thinks Simon. *This could change all that. A life of being on the wrong side of the fence, of not seeing fair recognition for your work. You could be inside the tent with Rory Gough. That*

would show the gainsayers at the Pole. And no more financial worries.
Go quietly, take the money.

It is so tempting. But he knows he can't do it. He doesn't really know why he is driven to defend a country that won't defend itself, but he knows he has to. That's what he does.

And now there's something else he needs to do.

'Sorry, Rory. Not sure I can really take the idea of a deal with you very seriously. Sovereign individual and all that.'

It's Rory's turn to sit in disappointed silence. 'I think you're going to regret this,' he says, proving his own need for Simon's co-operation. This strengthens Simon's resolve and he pulls back into the road, driving east. They both sit in sullen silence, more like a feuding couple than a kidnapped agent and a desperate spy.

'Okay, time you fucked off, Rory,' says Simon, after another ten miles. 'Go on, don't make me push you out.' With a theatrical sigh, Rory unclips his seatbelt and opens the door.

'Big mistake,' he says, cold fury in his voice. 'I gave you a chance.' He turns and looks around the moorland scene, perhaps trying to see whether he recognises where he needs to go to get home. Simon reaches across to pull the passenger door shut. 'Wait a minute,' calls Rory. 'My phone. You don't need it now. Come on. You can at least give that back.'

Simon can feel the large phone in his back pocket, digging into his bum. He says nothing and pulls the passenger door shut. The window is open and Simon wonders whether he should just end it now. A single head-shot. It might be hours before they find the body. But in truth he hates bloodshed and he has something else he needs to do, as quickly as he can. So he slams the Land Rover into gear and speeds off, the engine screaming. Rory's face is a snapshot of bemused rage, shrinking in the rear-view mirror.

Chapter 34

Northumberland
May 2022

Three hours. Is it enough?

He drives on small roads, heading east, wondering if there are teams already pursuing him. The ancient Land Rover is slow and thirsty, so he finds himself stopping for fuel in a quiet filling station where he pays in cash, a flat cap he'd purloined from Ereby Hall pulled low over his face. Rory would have got back home and Simon wonders whether he should be alert for police. But Simon sees that Rory also has to make a choice. If Simon were arrested, he would have nothing to lose from accusing Rory of treason. Even if Rory assumed he could control any aftershocks, he would probably prefer not to have the hassle of making the accusations go away.

After the ridges of the Pennines, the scenery has changed to a rolling, agricultural landscape. But the wind-bent trees tell a story of harsh winters. And the light has changed, with that special quality that tells Simon he is near the coast, even before he has his first glimpse of the North Sea. And then, rounding a corner, he sees it. A grey line on the horizon, much darker than the sky, distant but unmistakable. The wind has picked up and it is raining determinedly. He turns onto a small lane with a view over the coast. The sea is choppy, white horses galloping towards the shore. He can feel the gusts swaying the tinny cabin of the Land Rover. A storm seems to be on its way.

About two hundred and fifty meters inland is a football-pitch-sized area of turned-over grey soil in an otherwise green landscape. There's a chainlink fence and a bank of earth surrounding the compound, which is dotted with portacabins, shipping containers, and various bits of earth-moving machinery. A bland sign reads 'POWERSTREAM' in block letters. Encircled by mounds of rocky earth is a deep pit. Simon can make out a thick black cable snaking out of the hole in the ground into a massive junction box. There's also a collection of cars parked near the gate – including a few large, dark-coloured saloons. Not the sort of vehicles to be driven by construction workers, Simon reasons. Simon pulls the Land Rover into a small passing place. He ferrets around the car in the faint hope of finding some binoculars, but there's nothing of use. Simon decides the beat-up Land Rover fits in well enough in this agricultural landscape and stops at a walkers' car park, strolling out like a hardy rambler enjoying the buffeting of a North Sea storm, the squally rain spattering his shooting jacket.

He skirts along a coastal path, using it to approach without appearing overly curious. The perimeter has no razor wire and security seems to be limited to a few cameras. He decides to gamble that they are not well-monitored and walks obliquely towards the fence – on a CCTV monitor he will appear to be passing on the coastal path rather than heading straight for the compound. Then, checking for no signs of human attention he drops to his stomach and crawls the last twenty metres, the wet grass soaking through his jeans and making his knees cold. He is soon inching up the stony bank of newly turned earth, peeking his head over the top.

He is momentarily shocked: the two portacabins are in front of him, closer than he had expected. It's a weekend and no heavy work seems to be going on, but he can see people sitting around a table inside one of the cabins. He ducks down below the bank and crawls sideways for a few metres, popping up again directly in front of the window. He waits in silence, listening to the sound of his own breath, surprisingly heavy. Then he pulls Rory's top-of-the-range smartphone out of the coat pocket and takes several pictures on full zoom. He squirms back down below the bank to check his work. The phone is locked with a passcode but he can access the pictures he's just taken, scrolling through for the best one. He stretches his fingers across the screen to zoom in. He can make out several faces. There's Jeremy Rathbone, Rory's money man. No surprise. He slides the image sideways past other faces he doesn't immediately recognise, although they look like central-casting Russian oligarchs. And there, sitting in a corner, wearing a high-viz waistcoat over his tweed blazer, looking for all the world like a politician visiting a construction site, is Marcus Peebles.

—

Months later, he finds himself saying, 'I'd always known it was Marcus.' But he hadn't. He had talked to Sarah about it, and ruled it out.

Now he is experiencing a rush of connections, like an optical illusion suddenly becoming clear. And with it, a crushing sense of failure.

His mind begins to replay conversations, sentences he wished he could unsay. A phonecall with O'Brien: 'I need an advance for a trip I'm going on.' He hadn't said he was going to the Alps, but he'd signalled intention to travel – enough to get a surveillance team put together? A rushed conversation with Sarah: 'I'm going to need some transport from Hampshire at some point in the next twenty-four hours.' He'd told her he was at Gloucester Green. How many coaches were going to Hampshire at that time of that evening?

And, most painfully: an email to O'Brien with flight details and hotel bookings for Prague, for him and Evie. Simon, cash-strapped as ever, desperate to get his expenses paid ahead of the trip. And an image he has tried, and failed, to bury: Evie's body cartwheeling, like a ragdoll flung in the air.

As the bits of the puzzle click together he feels one thing: rage. Peebles, the impeccably connected networker. Peebles, highly regarded with his friends in Whitehall and all over the intelligence community. Peebles, with clients across the City. Peebles was not Rory Gough, a friendless oddball with too much money and no humanity. Peebles was one of *us*. A former public servant, colleague, a friend. A patriot.

And yet it made perfect sense. Peebles, with his charm, his urbanity, accessible to all. Discreet, obliging, attentive. Peebles with his office in Mayfair, where the oligarchs have their dens. Peebles, who'd said: *Our job is just to provide the intelligence, not set ourselves up as some sort of ethical oversight board.*

And now that the puzzle is completed, Simon can see that he had failed for the oldest, simplest reason. The human factor. They hadn't hacked his phone. They hadn't tracked his signal or read his messages. The operation had failed because of Simon's boring weakness: a lack of cash. They'd had a man on the inside, and Simon had given away too much, because he needed the money. And that was how they'd got Evie.

The only question remaining is whether O'Brien was with Peebles, or an unwitting, useful idiot?

Simon is distracted by a click and the creak of the portacabin door opening. The men file out into the driving rain. Rathbone first, three others Simon doesn't recognise, and then Peebles, his mane of silver hair clearly visible despite the weather. Simon snaps several images, before rolling back down below the safety of the earth parapet. He can hear talking, some in English, some Russian. Peebles making everyone laugh at his witty asides. But he doesn't have time to listen, crawling frantically along the ground until he believes he can safely stand up to rejoin the path. He walks back to the car park as quickly as he can, turning repeatedly to catch a glance of the men, chatting idly in a huddle around their cars. They are sufficiently interested in talking to each other not to notice Simon, or not to regard him as anything more than a rambler heading back to the welcome shelter of his vehicle.

As Simon climbs into the cabin of the Land Rover he can see Peebles, pulling off his high-vis tabard and splashing towards a large, dark-coloured saloon. Whatever model of car, it will be faster than the old Land Rover. Simon needs a different plan. And he needs Marcus on his own. He is holding a locked phone he can't use to make calls and he's running out of options. He realises he can scroll through the pictures he's taken, and then he has an idea. The phone is locked but it will let him send his recent pictures. And, most importantly, this is Rory Gough's phone. He finds the best image of Marcus and clicks the share button, scrolling through until he finds Peebles in Rory's contacts. He writes a message to go with the picture of Marcus: *You have a problem. Meet me on the Holy Island causeway. Come alone.*

Simon strains his eyes, trying to see. Marcus has shifted slightly and is doing something with his hand. Simon can't make out the phone, but he sees Marcus raising a hand to his ear. Moments later, Rory's phone vibrates. Simon rejects the call, responding by resending the same photo and the same text.

He sees Marcus twisting round, staring at his phone screen worriedly. And then opening his car door and climbing into the driver's seat.

Simon starts the engine of the Land Rover. He knows that the only route to Holy Island for Peebles in his car will be several miles via the winding lane. But in the Land Rover he can cut cross-country, following a farm track and an open gateway he had noticed earlier.

He is now bouncing along a muddy track by the side of a field, the steering wheel kicking crazily in his hands, the ageing engine whining under the strain. Ahead of him he can see a stretch of sea and a wide, flat island, spread out below a gunmetal grey sky. Large waves are now visible, some crashing against the shore with spectacular plumes of spray.

The Land Rover screams around the edge of a cultivated field, the back fishtailing in the mud. He has cut off a large dog-leg in the road and is now comfortably ahead. He can see the junction where the lane turns down to the causeway. If Marcus is bringing followers they'll come this way.

He waits, nervously checking the pistol and the phone. Time is running out. He has ten minutes left, after which the route across the tidal causeway to Holy Island will disappear under a rising tide.

'Come *on*!' he exclaims in frustration, willing Marcus to appear.

After a couple of minutes Simon sees him, driving cautiously down towards the causeway. Marcus is focused on the road and doesn't spot Simon in the Land Rover, nestled behind a hedge. Simon pulls slowly into the lane and confirms that no car is following, so he swings the Land Rover into pursuit, down a shallow hill to where there are large warning signs proclaiming 'DANGER' and exhorting travellers to know the tide times. Ahead of him, crossing a liminal space of saltmarsh and mudflats, the thin road snakes improbably across the water to the island on the other side. Towards the middle of the causeway, the road is no longer visible and is merely a swirling mass of seawater, waves breaking where the roadway should have been. Above all, most of what he can see is sky. Huge, with louring clouds racing towards the coast.

The storm is rougher than expected, upending Simon's careful planning for tide times. He feels a flash of fear surging through his body, like a jolt of electricity. But there's no time for plan B.

Marcus's car is rolling gingerly across the first part of the road, still largely dry but spotted with huge puddles. The BMW draws to a stop and Simon pulls in behind him. He sees the car door swing open and notices Marcus's shoes – smart, leather-soled brogues in a light brown leather, polished to an admirable shine. Almost endearingly inappropriate footwear. Simon jumps out of the Land Rover. Marcus is standing ten metres away, his back framed by the swirling sea and drowned causeway. His bouffant hair flutters in the wind and his face is a mixture of confusion and panic.

'Simon?' His voice is quavering. He's had a few minutes to worry about what's happened and is now looking seriously nervous. 'What...? Where's Rory? I was supposed to meet him here.'

Simon has to raise his voice to be sure that Marcus can hear him over the breaking waves. 'There's been a change of plan. You're going to tell *me* what *you're* doing here.'

Marcus turns to look down the causeway, as if wondering whether that offers him a way out. It doesn't, so he turns back to face Simon. He's struggling to say anything. 'I have... I have clients involved with Powerstream.' There's a hopelessness to his voice, as if he doesn't even believe what he's saying himself.

'That doesn't really explain why you were expecting to meet Rory here, does it?'

There's a silence. Momentarily he looks defeated, and then he seems to rally. He assumes an air of mock outrage. 'Powerstream is a perfectly legitimate infrastructure project. You don't seem to realise my clients are bringing valuable inward investment to the UK.'

'I don't care about Powerstream, or should I say Berezina? I care about Prague. O'Brien was reporting to you and then you passed that on to... Well, you tell me, on to who?'

There is a wobble in Marcus's composure. An awkward smile which turns to a grimace. Simon notices Marcus reaching down towards the car door handle.

'STEP AWAY FROM THE CAR!' Simon has pulled the pistol and is holding it in front of him in a two-handed grip. He has surprised himself at the ferocity of his voice. It has shocked Marcus who has stepped hurriedly away from the shining black wing of his BMW and is now standing on the edge of the causeway, his shoes part submerged in a deep puddle.

Marcus pauses and then starts to laugh. It is an unconvincing, confected bark, but a laugh nonetheless. 'Of course he was reporting back to me!' His voice has a forced bravado. 'He bloody well works for me. Poor old Ben, not the sharpest, he didn't need to know the details. But I told him there were wider interests and he needed to keep me in the loop.'

'And you made sure Rory knew everything, didn't you? That's treason, pure and simple.'

'Not sure it was, actually, Simon. Think about it: your little operation with Sarah wasn't classified. You were working in the private sector. *Ergo* –' he emphasises his Latin with a vulpine smile '– it's not a proper secret. Rory is a senior adviser to the PM. Business card, Number Ten email address, the works. He'd a legitimate interest, as far as I'm concerned.' For the first time since he'd climbed out of the car, Marcus looks pleased with himself.

Simon feels pure rage. Marcus was part of a chain of treachery that led back to COSTELLO and to the Chechens that had killed Evie. His body is hot with the urge to shoot Marcus in the chest. He looks for the sight picture on the pistol, but thinks better of it. A deep breath.

'You know what happened in Prague, don't you?'

'I do.' Even Marcus is sounding less pleased with himself now. 'And that was never the plan.' He seems to be searching for the right words. 'Evie was…' And then Simon gets the flashback again, Evie's body cartwheeling through the air, and he fights a desperate urge to kill Marcus.

The wind has dropped slightly, and the rain abated. Simon's feet are wet from crawling outside the Powerstream compound. He shakes his torso in a vain attempt to dislodge some of the water and warm himself a little. He puts the pistol back in his pocket. He's too tired and cold to think about using it. He hasn't got the energy to interrogate. He just wants it to be over.

Marcus changes tack. 'I know how you live, in a shitty flat in Kilburn. I know your business has gone nowhere. And I'm pretty sure that wasn't the plan when you started out. I mean, do you have any idea how fucking expensive life is these days? I mean, *real* life?' Marcus has thrust his hands into the pockets of his tweed jacket, and a slight movement of the hips says confidence. 'Do the sums: two kids at boarding school: sixty-a-year. House in

London. House in the country. House in France. Mortgages, lots of them. Couple of decent cars, holidays, wine cellar. Pension. Then you've gotta think about the kids' flats. In London. They don't need them yet, but they will. Probably a million each. I'm not an oligarch. No private jet or yacht. Just a middle-class chap living in Fulham. Do you have any idea what all that adds up to? Or do you think I should be living in some dive in Kilburn?'

'Prague. Tell me about Prague.'

'I'm not doing this, Simon, until you tell me what's going on with Rory.'

Simon pauses, wondering what he can say. He decides on nothing. But Marcus is smelling blood. He's figured out that Simon is improvising. 'The thing is, Simon –' he is now shouting to be heard above the rising wind and waves, his body buffeted '– you and Sarah have got obsessed with the idea of Rory the mole. But guess what? Nobody fucking cares. Spying is just a game and no one else is playing. Look – we can supply weapons to the Ukrainians on the one hand and do business with the Russians on the other. This is the future. Trade deals. Britain open for business. Foreign investment building our infrastructure. So, either you let me go back or I drive over to the island. I will happily sit in the pub over there and wait for the police to come and get you. Because, I can assure you, they are on their way. This bit is over. You're not going to shoot me. You haven't got it in you.'

He's right. Simon does nothing. He blinks hard but seems not to be able to see very well any more. The stabbing pain in his shoulder has come back and he's struggling to stay upright in the gusting wind.

Marcus turns dramatically and climbs into his car, slamming the door.

Simon has lost. Marcus doesn't fear him. Rory will have got to a phone. The police are coming. Berezina has worked. And Simon has run out of time.

Marcus has been standing with his back to the water and Simon realises he has not noticed the storm surging, buoyed by the rising tide. The centre of the causeway is now invisible under a maelstrom of white horses. But Marcus has made a gesture and needs to follow through. Gamely, his BMW speeds towards the water. Soon there is a plume of spray cascading up from the wheels on either side. Incongruously, it reminds Simon of one of those high-production car ads, showcasing the BMW's remarkable road-holding ability, or something. And it seems to be working, it's ploughing through the water even as it splashes over the front radiator.

He's going to make it.

And then the car stops. Was it a fatal moment of hesitation or mechanical failure? He sees the reversing light come on and the car seems to rotate slightly. And then a huge wave crashes against the side of the vehicle and it turns, lightly as if a piece of driftwood, rolling a couple of times. He catches a glimpse of Marcus, looking slightly confused, before the car disappears beneath the grey water.

Simon jumps into the Land Rover and fires the engine, grabbing the lever for low range. With his higher clearance, if he can time his run between the breaking waves, he thinks he can get through. He is frantically trying to keep his eyes on the spot where the car submerged, watching for any sign. But there is a swirling sea and all he sees is grey, surging water. He curses at the old engine, screaming in protest, grinding far too slowly.

Simon hasn't got a plan. He wants to stop the vehicle with the engine running and jump in to search for Marcus. But as he nears the likely spot, water is already swirling around the doors of the Land Rover. If he stops he will not be able to start, in either direction.

Then he hears it. Muffled by whistling wind and the crash of the waves, but unmistakable. A police siren. Transfixed, Simon cocks his head to get a better view in the rear mirror. He can see blue lights, screaming towards the causeway. Rapidly they become the clear shape of three police cars, skidding to a halt at the waterline.

Two minutes. He needs to make it to the island.

In a moment of clarity he slams his foot to the floor, the water now level with the bonnet. Simon is just focused on maintaining a bow wave ahead of the Land Rover and not losing traction. He hits the deepest part just as the sea has sucked away some of the water before the next crashing breaker. He is briefly mesmerised by a wall of water visible to his side, surging towards him. He is not sure if the wheels are turning on the road any more. *Brace for the impact*, feeling for the door handle, ready to swim out.

And then he notices that the sea in front of him is no longer lapping over the top of the bonnet. There is a faint rise and he can see the approaching saltmarsh. Not dry land, but an approximation of it. He has reached Holy Island.

As soon as the water is below the chassis he yanks the handbrake and jumps out, up to his shins in ice-cold water, foamy wavelets surging around his sodden trousers. He runs back along the road until the water is above his knees, straining his eyes for sight of Marcus or his car. Instead he sees an angry, swirling, wine-dark sea. A surging, freezing wave reaches his midriff and he struggles to keep his footing. He can see the police cars, now distant, but visible, blue lights flashing. Uniformed figures are milling around the vehicles, some waving in his direction.

With a mixture of regret and relief he turns and runs back to the car, hauling himself onto the driver's seat and cranking up the rudimentary heating to full blast. He drives onwards, finding himself on an exposed coastal road. The waves keep coming, some of them breaking across the carriageway, but there is no danger of losing control.

As soon as he knows the vehicle is safe, Simon pulls into a passing place on the narrow lane. He puts the gun on his lap and disassembles it in a matter of seconds, his hands working on autopilot, Cardross training kicking in. Soon he has nothing more than a pile of components. He speeds onwards with the window down and flings the gun, piece by piece, into the sea. There is no chance it will ever be reassembled or identified.

After a couple of miles the road cuts inland and Simon has little to worry about beyond the risk of being stopped for speeding through a small village. He follows the lane through a sort of high street, equipped with coffee shops and tourist pubs, but in the storm the streets are deserted and he barely slows. He is willing the sluggish Land Rover onwards, skidding round corners and slamming the stick between gears. He is sure he has missed his chance, but continues, hoping against hope.

Soon he has crossed the island, skidding round a road that skirts a slightly sheltered beach, although the fishing boats moored in the bay are tossing wildly on their buoys. Simon sees what he is looking for, a narrow harbour wall with a concrete jetty, and pulls to a halt next to a scrappy boatyard. He is cold, wet and exhausted.

He looks at his watch. Five minutes too late.

Chapter 35

The Holy Island of Lindisfarne

May 2022

It takes almost all of his willpower to open the door again and climb out into the gale, the wind slicing through his wet clothes. He's going through the motions now: he stares out across the bay. The moored boats are rocking on the waves but nothing is travelling in this foul weather. He's blown it. They've given up on him.

He leans against the car and shuts his eyes. It's over. In a few hours the tide would subside enough for the police to cross the causeway. As the wind drives squally rain, stinging onto his face, he opens his eyes again and walks to the edge of the jetty. The foaming sea, dark and mysterious, is inviting. The pain in his shoulder is stabbing and he wants it to end. He has a moment of clarity: he has cared far too much about what people'think of him. But in the end, everyone let him down. There's nothing he can do about that. He decides to stop caring about it and let go. Let the waves take him. He has done his best for his country. That is enough, even if nobody cares.

But there is one last thing to do before the end. He pulls out Rory's phone and scrolls through the pictures, until he finds the one of Marcus sitting with Rathbone and the two unknowns. He presses the share button and chooses the Twitter icon. Simon had taken little notice of Rory's presence on Twitter, but was dimly aware that his updates sometimes moved markets, or ensured that a certain underperforming government minister was moved on.

Not that Simon knew, Rory had a quarter of a million followers and took delight from his online influence.

With the photo ready to transmit in a Twitter window, Simon writes the caption 'JEREMY RATHBONE WITH MARCUS PEEBLES AND THE TWO RUSSIAN OWNERS AT THE POWERSTREAM ENERGY SITE, ONE OF MY MOST IMPORTANT INVESTMENTS. #INFRASTRUCTURE #FOREIGNOWNERSHIP' He presses Tweet, waits as a blue line passes across the screen and then shoves the phone back into his pocket. He might have failed, but he will take some others down with him.

Then he turns to face the pounding waves and walks right to the edge of the jetty, so that his toes are jutting out over the water, the spray splashing on his sodden shoes. He takes a breath, tries to relax, and focuses on the next step. Just one step.

A buzzing sound, like an especially angry wasp fighting to be heard over the crash of waves against the jetty.

Simon is trying to focus on that step but he can't because of that annoying buzzing. Is it willpower he lacks? Or is the will to stay alive too strong? The buzzing is getting louder and then he can see a shape rounding the headland. It's no more than a patch of white on a disturbed sea, but quickly it takes shape. A small Orkney fishing boat, its dark hull and white pilothouse bobbing on the angry swell.

With a grunt of relief, he steps back from the edge of the jetty.

The boat is coming slowly towards the sea wall, but the violent swell makes this a complex manoeuvre. There are two figures inside the pilothouse and it's hard to make them out in the driving rain. But then one steps out onto the heaving deck and the mane of long dark-brown hair flapping in the wind is familiar. Carefully and calmly, she waits for the swell to wash the boat within reach of a metal ladder that descends the sea wall to the waterline. With a neat step she is on the ladder, climbing upwards.

Simon blinks and reaches down to help her up the final rungs. The first thing he notices is that Sarah is looking serious, regretful even. The second thing he notices is that she is dressed with a sort of Italian country-chic elegance, as if she were on her way to a smart shooting-party, accessorised with a red self-inflating life jacket draped round her shoulders like a Hermès scarf. She has made it, as planned, and fashionably late.

Instinctively, he pulls her up onto the jetty and throws his arms around her. He is cold and wet but she feels warm with an aroma of expensive soap or a scent that he had no chance of recognising. He just wants to hold her tight. As he does so, he realises why he was unable to step off the jetty into a heaving sea.

'Ooh you're soaking!' Sarah's voice brings him back to the present. Sometimes there is a coldness in her tone that left the listener feeling like a pawn in a complex geopolitical game of chess. But this time it is pure warmth. She puts a hand gently on the back of his head. Is it a consoling gesture? He notices she's wearing brown leather gloves and expensive-looking wellies.

The wind has dropped a little, but it is now raining, hard. He clears the lump from his throat. 'I thought I was too late. I thought you'd given up on me.' He doesn't want to sound cynical, but he has been living with constant tension for so long that he is incapable of anything else. The stabbing neck pain has spread down his shoulder towards his elbow.

Sarah buries her head in Simon's neck and is saying something. He can't work out what it is. He has to make a physical effort to concentrate on the sound.

'*Simon.*' Her tone is insistent. 'It was a nightmare getting in here. Why did you pick this spot?' Simon looks straight into her eyes as she says this. He'd forgotten how much he liked just to look at her eyes. But Sarah seems to want to look away. Are they tears, or is it just the rain? He blinks and takes in his surroundings. A wild sea and there, rolling and bobbing on the water, is the small fishing boat, its captain visible inside the pilothouse, expertly keeping it in position near the jetty.

'Causeway. Because the tide would stop the police coming after me. They're on the other side, right now.'

'Christ.' Sarah looks genuinely shocked.

'And because it's near Powerstream,' he adds. He pauses, wondering how to change the subject. He's too tired though, so he just pulls out Rory's phone and opens the last picture he'd taken: 'It was Marcus,' he says, handing the phone to her.

Sarah's face freezes, and then recoils as if she has been struck, hard.

'Oh Christ. Are you sure?'

'He was *there*.' He hadn't meant to sound angry, but it comes out that way. 'I went to the Powerstream compound, and there he was, sitting in a portacabin with Rathbone and some Russians. All along, O'Brien was telling Marcus everything. And Marcus was telling Rory. But I don't think O'Brien realised,' he adds. 'Wasn't his fault. Thought he needed to keep Marcus in the loop.'

She reaches her hand out and strokes it gently against his chest, then turning her eyes upwards she kisses him, slowly and deliberately. Whispering into his ear, she says: 'I can't tell you how sorry I am. I trusted Marcus completely.'

He has passed the phone to Sarah and she is manipulating the image so that she can see Peebles's face clearly. She lets out a huge sigh.

'I could kill him. I mean it.' She has a quiet fury in her voice.

'Too late.'

'So you did it?' she asks with exaggerated calmness. 'Do the police know?'

'Wasn't me. His car was washed off the road. I tried to find him. Hopeless...' His voice tails away. But he hasn't finished. 'And you? Were you in it too? Was the whole idea to get me to find out what was out there about Rory, but then I found out too much? Was that it?' His voice is quiet. Calm. Now it really is the end there doesn't seem to be any point worrying too much. He wishes he still had the gun. That would have been the easiest way out.

'No, Simon, I promise you.' Sarah is talking, but Simon isn't taking it in very well. As quickly as ever, Sarah is working through this new information. 'Fuck. *Fuck!* When they sacked Will I knew they were ahead of us, somehow. And now I get it… And Evie. Oh Jesus I am so sorry. Evie… It's my fault… How could he? I mean, Rory's always been a freak. Nobody actually *likes* him. Even the prime minister just keeps him around because of his money. But Marcus. He was one of *us*. A proper insider.'

One of us.

'That's what I'd thought. But, d'you see, Sarah? "Us" isn't what we used to think. National security. Intelligence. Patriotism. They've all gone. "Us" might just be you and me.'

Sarah seems to be ignoring him. She is staring at the photo on Rory's phone with greater intensity, poking at a particular part of the photo.

'Oh my *God*! It's Sazanovich.' Sarah's voice is breathless with excitement.

'What?'

She responds by holding the phone in front of Simon's face. 'Look! The guy next to Marcus. That's Sazanovich, Steve Carpenter. I mean, I bet he's not here in either of those names. But I'd know that face anywhere.'

'Right.' Simon tries to inject some enthusiasm into his response, but he's lost the motivation. Sarah is fired up with energy and reaches an arm around Simon's shoulders, squeezing them excitedly.

'Don't you see? We knew that Sazanovich was part of COSTELLO. And now here he is popping up in the middle of Berezina.'

'Yeah, but nobody cares. We've failed, Sarah. I failed.'

Sarah isn't listening. Instead, she's looking quizzically at Rory's phone, as if it is suddenly an unfamiliar object.

'Something's funny about this phone. It keeps buzzing.' She passes it to Simon. It is vibrating as if a silent alarm has gone off, like an old-style pager. Simon fiddles with the screen and finds the notifications.

A little surge of triumph puts energy into his voice. 'I decided to Tweet from Rory's account that Powerstream was a

Russian-owned infrastructure project he was invested in. Seems like it's gone viral.'

'You did what?' Her incredulity seems a little forced. She reaches into her pocket and pulls out her own phone, her fingers rapidly typing, shaking her head as she does so. 'Oh, look at that. The number-three trending topic is "Russia Powerstream".' She lets out an incredulous laugh. 'There's no way this thing will be able to go ahead. It'll be tomorrow's front pages... Si, you might be a crazy loon but you're my crazy loon and that makes it all okay...' Her voice falters. She is looking down at her phone again. Frowning. She shakes her head.

And then Simon sees it. Her eyes are welling with tears, not rain. And now he feels tired and wants to sit down. His head hurts, he's cold and wet. He has a fantasy of curling up in a ball. Instead, he leans against the cold, metallic Land Rover. He can't bring himself to give a shit about Powerstream. The possibility of its failure doesn't seem enough of a compensation. He is still grappling with the realisation that Marcus betrayed the entire project. And Evie. He can feel the unwelcome but familiar sensation of freefalling.

'There's something you're not saying, isn't there?' he asks.

'O'Brien didn't turn up for a meeting yesterday with Kemi...' She stops. Gulps and then tries again. 'I had some people go round to his flat... They've just found his body.' Her voice disappears into a gulp. 'Signs of torture... Oh God.'

Remove some outstanding risk factors. Simon had felt strangely flat when he heard about Radcliffe. But with O'Brien, he feels incredibly sad. He instantly regrets thinking of him as a silly posh boy. Like his father, he had served his country well. Even if his country had never known.

The shock gives Simon focus. 'Sebastian Ereby. I stayed there last night. Perhaps he's next. We need to get someone over to him.'

The clear instruction seems to focus Sarah and she starts tapping frantically at the messaging app on her phone. And then she looks up at Simon, shaking her head.

'There's more. We didn't have any options left. I've had to move some things around.'

Simon looks up. Sarah is standing in front of him. She is tearful again.

'What?'

She takes a deep breath. 'Okay. Even before today I could see that Rory was ahead of us, somehow. They announced the successor to Butler. The new National Security Adviser.' She stops. Simon feels irritated, as if she is pausing for effect.

'And?'

'It's Patel.'

Kamran Patel. Academic, culture warrior, think-tank and COSTELLO agent. And now Britain's national security adviser.

'Patel? What the fuck? He's never even been in government before. Just some Tufton Street rent-a-quote.'

'That's the world we're in now, Si. Anyone with the right ideology can get any job, basically. I had to cut our losses, protect what we have so far. So I told the intel guys at the Pole that you had disappeared.' She pauses, looking for the right words. 'And I said… that the plan to use you to find out about possible Russian infiltration of Whitehall hadn't turned up any verifiable intel. Proved a dead end. A few threads buried in the late nineties, none of it led anywhere. I need to shield you from Patel. From COSTELLO. So you can carry on this work.'

Simon tries to speak but no words come out. There's something worse than the betrayal: it's the guys at the Pole being told he'd failed. Again. *Just another one of Sharman's dead ends. He always screws up.*

Finally the words come.

'So now I've been betrayed by literally everyone. Even you. I should have fucking shot Rory. I was this close to doing it. What would the difference be? Prison and the problem actually fixed, or being on the run for the rest of my life?'

Sarah gives a huge, sobbing sigh. 'Right now I get that you probably want to kill me. But I am trying to protect you. If they

315

knew that you knew everything, imagine how much worse that would be. Look what's going on around you!'

'Except Rory knows now. Knows that I know. And they have Patel as NSA.'

'Yeah but Rory's not going to tell anyone, is he? There aren't any witnesses to the conversation, are there? He's going to be frantically trying to explain why he has tweeted an incendiary statement about an infrastructure project he has no declared connection to... Radcliffe is dead... and Ben. And Marcus.' Simon doesn't respond. 'This way, I can stay inside the system, try to keep an eye on what's going on. Limit Patel's room for manoeuvre. And help you.'

Simon is too tired for anger. He sighs, deeply weary. 'You know, Sarah, I've been dropped in it again and I am just thinking about the next stage. Gotta get off this crazy island.' He looks over at the boat. 'I probably shouldn't keep Blondie waiting.'

'Just one other thing.' Sarah is fiddling around with the large hip pockets on her pristine Barbour jacket. She has pulled out a small notebook, bound in a purple-coloured leather. She hands it to Simon, who confusedly turns it over in his hands. He realises he is holding an Italian passport. Sarah is wiping tears away from her cheeks. 'Open it,' she says.

Nonplussed, Simon flicks through the passport until he reaches the data page. He blinks at the face in the photo. It takes him a couple of seconds to realise that it is him. His name is Simone Sartori. Simon looks up at Sarah, who nods, sadly.

'As soon as you got back from Prague I knew this might be an issue, so I got in touch with some, ah, *allies* in the Italian service. Say what you like about them, but they can sometimes deliver in a way that we never could. Can you imagine the form-filling to get an emergency alias passport out of the Pole? It's not quite genuine,' she says apologetically. 'But it's made by a genuine Italian passport office. I can still pull the odd string in my mother-country. And I thought you'd like to be a proper tailor, at last.'

Simon doesn't know what he should feel, but he is surprised to feel tears pricking in his eyes. For the first time since Prague he can begin to see a way out. He wants to say something, but words don't come.

'It might not work very well if you overuse it, but you'll definitely be able to move around Europe. Blondie will take you to one of the small ports in Holland.' She looks at her watch and seems to switch into a faster gear. 'We need to get going, *Simone*,' she says, emphasising his Italian name. Sarah strides towards the steel ladder, stands purposefully, looking down at Blondie. Simon, still slightly dazed, follows her, clutching his new passport.

Simon is still processing. But he has started to catch up. 'So,' he asks, 'you knew all along that they'd refuse to take action on Rory?'

'Not completely, but I knew all along that there was a chance you'd be hung out to dry. And I felt responsible for that. So I needed to get you a way out. It was the timing that caught me by surprise. But what did he actually say? Rory, I mean?'

'I think we've got it, not that it matters very much,' says Simon. 'He was very evasive, dismissive, all that. But in the end he was sufficiently pissed off with me that he talked about his relations with the Russians. Not a come-to-Jesus confession, but a pretty damning explanation. And he named some of the others.'

'But why? Why did he do it?'

'That's the bit we'd missed – or at least I had. He says he worked with the Russians because they could get him what he wanted, you know, help his funds make even more money. Claims he's not really into the Russians at all. Just a marriage of convenience.'

'Did you believe him?' The sharp tone of a tutorial inquisition is beginning to seep back into Sarah's voice.

'Partially. He admires them. The fuck-the-rules-while-we-do-what-we-want. That sort of thing, you can tell he loves that. But fundamentally, yes, *in his mind* he's not working *for* them. This isn't Blake or Philby. He sees them as working for *him*. Co-operation, at the very least. But here's the thing…' Simon pauses. He knows he's figured it out in his head, but this is the first time he's tried to say it out loud. 'He admitted that he sometimes does their bidding. Not in those words, of course. But, like with Butler, he says he wanted him gone, and then he admitted that was what COSTELLO wanted too.'

'But is this a Russian op, or just a collection of useful idiots?' Sarah's tone is insistent, impatient even.

'I reckon it's both. That's the genius of it: COSTELLO's been running this ring of unwitting agents at the heart of the British state for decades. Like an extra hand on the tiller, but so subtle. And until we started picking the thing apart, COSTELLO didn't need to take any risks, do anything dramatic. It was just nudging us to help Russia. But once you know it's there, lots of things, over *years*, start to make sense.'

Sarah is shaking her head, not in disagreement, but in realisation. 'And it's only when they overplayed their hand that we started to notice,' she says, with a regretful sense of understanding.

Fumbling in his soaking jacket pocket, Simon hands her Rory's phone. 'It'll all be on there. Audio file.'

–

Simon is about to step onto the steel ladder, down towards the pitching boat. But Sarah is still talking about something.

'You're Simone Sartori. You live in Umbria. Perugia. Not the city, but in a rural area on the edge. Your mother was Canadian, which is why you speak perfect English. You're a bit of a drifter. You say you're a writer but you haven't published. You look after a family property in Italy. And this is the phone number,' she adds, handing him a scrap of paper with a number and an address. 'You know someone there called Livia Esposito who'll vouch for you. It's not a particularly deep cover. Just enough to get you there.'

The professional challenge of learning a cover legend was reassuringly familiar, taking him back to places and activities he knew well. It seemed to make the thought of getting on the boat easier, too.

She passes him a phrasebook. '*So che parli un po' di italiano. Probabilmente non è sufficiente.*' Simon enjoys the iambic bounce of the language and shoves the phrasebook into his jacket pocket. 'We got the stuff from your room in college,' she continues. 'I put it in a little rucksack. Blondie has it onboard. Hope it's all here. I shoved in some Euros to keep you going.'

Simon's entire life now appears to fit into a small nylon bag.

She speaks quickly, as if she wants to get it over. 'Simon, you don't have anywhere to go in Italy. The address is my house near Perugia. You'll figure out how to get there. Nobody really uses it.' Simon nods. But he already has another plan. He won't be going to Italy.

She looks around but the entire bay is deserted in the terrible weather. He's too tired to care. 'This is it, then' she says. 'I'm sorry this hasn't worked. Maybe we just weren't ready.' Is she talking about their relationship, or the attempt to prevent Russia from infiltrating the highest echelons of the British state?

She hugs him, with an intensity that tells him she is talking about them, not the operation. He wants to tell her he loves her. But he thinks she might know that.

—

He clutches the ladder and lowers himself down, deliberately slowly. Then, watching the pitching of the boat he tries to familiarise himself with the natural rhythm of the swell. And on the next rise he takes a quick step and is pleasantly surprised to be on the gunwale, grabbing the outside of the cabin. A firm grip drags him inside the pilothouse and Blondie, a wall of a man who never lets you down, grins and says: 'Thought you were never coming mate.'

As he's talking he expertly spins the little boat around and out into the bay. They are pitching on the swell. Simon looks over his shoulder and sees Sarah standing next to the Land Rover, a dark silhouette against the lonely sea and the sky. He turns back to Blondie and hopes he won't be seasick. 'Bloody good to see you, Blondie. Been a while.'

'Yeah. Don't mind me if you need to get your head down. You've got dry clothes down there. And get some wets going while you're at it.'

He is incredibly grateful and heads below, putting the kettle on in the little galley before stripping off his sodden clothes. As he busies himself he focuses his attention on imagining his cover legend, memorising his address and telephone number, as well as his new date and place of birth.

On a small boat in a heavy sea, for the first time in weeks, Simon feels safe.

Chapter 36

Den Helder
May 2022

The crossing was rough, and Simon spent an embarrassing proportion of it clinging to the gunwale, puking. Blondie was unperturbed, grinning from inside his pilothouse as he calmly guided the little boat overnight through the surging waters.

The following morning, in a flat calm, Blondie had moored up in the small Dutch harbour at Den Helder and completed the formalities, leaving Simon hidden down below on the boat.

When he climbs ashore a couple of hours later, Simon is, once again, a ghost. Unknown to any immigration authority and carrying a clean identity. Simon walks through Den Helder, happy to be back on dry land despite the soulless, windswept town he finds himself in. He walks to a public library, a functional red-brick building by a canal. It is populated by brisk librarians only too happy to show him how to buy a token for internet access on one of the public computers. As he navigates to Twitter he has that strange sensation of walking into a house where a huge argument has been raging but the newcomer has not fully understood the dynamics.

It takes Simon a few minutes to figure out the story: in the previous twelve hours, Rory Gough's strangely incendiary Tweet about Powerstream, at the same time as the disappearance of Marcus Peebles after an investor visit to the site, had become headline news. This previously little-known project has rapidly become the subject of intense scrutiny. The existence of a strategically significant power and data cable owned by an opaque group of foreign investors with links to a prominent former intelligence officer excited huge public interest. Simon sees that Gough has deleted the original Tweet and released a statement about a stolen phone. But the existence of a photograph verifiably taken minutes before Peebles's disappearance adds to the speculation. Given the controversy and the fact that Gough has hidden his interest behind a series of shell companies, he seems unable to explain what is going on. The hashtag #Powerstreamgate is trending.

But Simon's concerns lie elsewhere. He logs on to the secure messaging site with nervous anticipation. And there it is: the answer he needs. With a renewed sense of purpose, he checks the route to the railway station and begins a long journey east.

–

Back in the UK, the #Powerstreamgate story refuses to go away. Asked about it in parliament, the prime minister finds himself boxed in to commissioning a public inquiry into the project. Backbench MPs, surprised to receive letters on the subject from worried constituents, start to lobby the government for a 'sovereignty guarantee' on the country's critical national infrastructure. Berezina has failed.

When Simon had taken Rory's phone from him, he had set a voice memo running, recording their entire encounter. Sarah had sent this audio file anonymously to a small, carefully chosen group of journalists. Most of them decided they couldn't touch it. Some had editors and political columnists that valued their relationship with Gough over any need to report the news. Other channels were concerned that there was no way of validating the recording. Eventually an internet-only news website of uncertain credibility put together some excerpts from the audio and released it as a 'bombshell exposing the Russian penetration at the heart of the British Establishment', linking it to the Powerstream story. The BBC ignored this altogether. Most of the attention came from

Gough's allies in the media who penned lengthy articles defending him and speculating darkly about 'deepfake audio'.

One of Gough's most reliable courtiers went all-in, writing a detailed hatchet job on Simon, which could only have come from an extensive briefing from Whitehall sources. Simon, changing trains in Berlin, had checked the latest and was intrigued to read of himself as 'an embittered, failed, ex-intelligence officer' – a description he agreed was not entirely inaccurate. 'Sharman's current whereabouts remain a mystery of some interest to the British police in connection with the disappearance of Marcus Peebles and his colleague Benedict O'Brien,' the article continued. Rory's history of co-operation with Russian officials was ignored in a story that focused on a 'deep state conspiracy' against one of Britain's leading entrepreneurs. Berezina had failed, but Gough had survived.

Around the same time, Kamran Patel had begun a 'review of nuclear competences'. This bureaucratic-sounding exercise gave the new national security adviser, who had spent his professional life in universities and think-tanks, an excuse to go around the key sites of the British deep state to talk to people engaged in operations. In National Security Council meetings, Patel would urge caution over supplying ever more sophisticated weapons to Ukraine, drawing on obscure Cold War documents to make his case, confident that nobody else in the room would have read them.

On a less visible level, Simon's work had a direct operational impact. Whilst the country was focused on #Powerstreamgate, an investigative website that styled itself as a 'citizens' intelligence network' posted a lengthy report on Russian intelligence's use of fake St Kitts identities for their operations. The report, read by hardly anyone outside Moscow, named Walter Pinsent, Steve Carpenter and a long list of other COSTELLO operatives, as well as drawing attention to the role of Iain Radcliffe, acting as supplier of the passports. His apparently brutal murder only added to the intrigue. There was a muted response from the British Government, but the United States ordered an immediate suspension of

St Kitts entry visas until 'urgent clarification of recent reporting on use of alias names' was provided by the St Kitts government. The same report also noted that the Costello Trust in Cayman had been wound up, according to a recent gazette.

–

Not long after Simon's departure, according to the website of Christ Church, Oxford Professor Sarah du Cane completed her *magnum opus* on the complex and varied languages of the Caucasus region.

Not listed on any website was her continued role as a strategic adviser on Russian affairs. Senior figures across government relied on her knowledge and understanding to shape their decision-making on this difficult subject. None more so than Rory Gough, who had added chair of the National Security Strategy Board to his long list of titles and responsibilities at the heart of the British state.

Chapter 37

Lviv

June 2022

The train from Przemyśl on Poland's border with Ukraine is populated with a certain sort of person. Simon knows these types from warzones all over the world, although he is used to seeing them in airports, not railway stations. Most people are lugging large bags containing their flak jackets and ballistic helmets in addition to normal luggage: the close protection crowd, all thick necks and shaved heads, tattoos on their bulging arms, resolutely monosyllabic, their military training having taught them to hurry up and wait. Diplomats and media crews, more social, chatting with a nervous jollity that was meant to signal nonchalance. And aid workers, quieter, serious, poring over their laptops. And between all of them, thinks Simon with grim amusement, a fair sprinkling of people like him, who aren't quite in any crowd, travelling alone and avoiding getting into conversations. They would be the spooks, all pretending to be something else. Simon is equipped with a press card he'd had put together in Warsaw by an old contact, proclaiming that he worked for a South African newspaper. That and his small bag of possessions are all that Simone Sartori has in this world.

He feels a frisson of nerves as the train slows for its final stop. The crowds of Ukrainian refugees have become denser at each stage of his journey. But little prepares him for Lviv. The platforms at the grand, high-roofed station are completely covered by a sea of humanity. Children sitting on cases, harassed mothers clutching children, cat baskets and bulging suitcases. Men, sombre, some tearful, bidding farewell to their families before they return to military duty. And everywhere, faces of exhaustion and sadness. But what strikes Simon most is the quiet. He'd expected a tumult, wailing, shouting, jostling to get onto a train. But there is none of this. Just numbed quiet, the rustle of people speaking in low voices, listening out for train announcements, resigned to the fact that their lives have changed for ever, that they are saying goodbye to their home country for a life of uncertainty.

Station officials in high-vis vests have kept one platform closed to give space to the arriving passengers. Simon walks out of the terminal, blinking in the summer sunlight. He wanders down a wide boulevard, past a seemingly endless line of would-be passengers and their luggage waiting patiently to be admitted to the station. After a few hundred metres he stops at a cafe and orders a coffee, a weird juxtaposition of European normality in a country at war. Slowly, almost laboriously, he pulls out a small notebook from his bag. Flicking through the pages covered in deliberately illegible scrawl, he finds what he is looking for. It is the reply from Vasya to the encrypted message he'd sent from Ereby Hall. Simon had asked Vasya, who'd always had a soft spot, 'Who killed Evie?' On arrival in Den Helder, he'd picked up Vasya's reply.

'Chovka Buchayev. He's in Ukraine now.'

Simon has nowhere to go, nobody to meet, no clear plan.

But he knows what he has to do.

Acknowledgements

Many people helped, unwittingly, in the creation of this novel. Others generously assisted me directly with their time, expertise and connections. Unfortunately I cannot name any of them here. But they know who they are, and they have my profound gratitude.